THE GIFT OF STORIES

THE GIFT OF STORIES

Edited by Kevin J. Anderson
and
Keith Olexa

WordFire Press
Colorado Springs, Colorado

A FANTASTIC HOLIDAY SEASON: THE GIFT OF STORIES
Copyright © 2014 WordFire Press

Additional copyright information on page 303

ISBN: 978-1-61475-202-8

Cover design by Janet McDonald
and
Art Director Kevin J. Anderson

Cover artwork images by Dollar Photo Club

Book Design by RuneWright, LLC
www.RuneWright.com

Published by
WordFire Press, an imprint of
WordFire, Inc.
PO Box 1840
Monument CO 80132

Kevin J. Anderson & Rebecca Moesta Publishers

WordFire Press Trade Paperback Edition 2014
Printed in the USA
wordfirepress.com

CONTENTS

What better way to start a Fantastic Holiday Season than with a Kevin J. Anderson classic! Kevin's something of a Fantasy and SF Father Christmas: He's very passionate about the season, incredibly generous with his time and experience—and his marvelous stories just pour out of him like gifts from Santa's bag!

Zombie detective Dan Shamble isn't having a merry little Christmas, though. Santa Claus is coming to town … but he's not feeling jolly. Something of Saint Nick's just got nicked, and Dan's got to find it—and the thief—before Xmas becomes Ex-Mas.

—KO

NAUGHTY & NICE

A Dan Shamble, Zombie P.I. Holiday Story

Kevin J. Anderson

1

Santa Claus was an *unnatural*. That made perfect sense—I just hadn't thought of it before.

The jolly bearded guy in the bright-red suit came into the offices of Chambeaux & Deyer Investigations, desperate to hire my services. It's not often, I suppose, that Santa requires a detective—particularly a zombie detective.

"I need your help, Mr. Chambeaux," Santa said.

I extended my gray hand ... to shake his black-gloved one. "At your service."

I assessed my client-to-be. Santa carried a voluminous cloth sack over his left shoulder; it was limp and empty at the moment, rather than bulging with brightly wrapped gifts. His bloodshot eyes were as red as his suit. His cheeks were pale, and his face seemed less plump than the pictures I had seen on a million Christmas cards.

"It's a crisis." He looked around with haunted eyes. "I've been robbed!"

In the Unnatural Quarter, we see all sorts of clients. After the cosmic supernatural event called the Big Uneasy, all manner of legendary creatures had reappeared: ghosts, vampires, zombies, werewolves, ghouls, and other creatures that go bump, growl, or thud in the night. Why not Santa, too? Somebody who can slip down billions of chimneys in a night—without incurring a single home-invasion charge—would fit right in.

"We'll do everything we can to help, Mr. Claus," said Robin Deyer, my earnest lawyer partner, as she came out to greet the new client. "Is this more of a legal matter or an investigative one?"

"Oh-ho-ho, I definitely need a detective, and I came here because Mrs. Claus and I have heard about Mr. Chambeaux."

I was surprised. "We don't even advertise up at the North Pole. How did you find out about Chambeaux and Deyer Investigations?"

"Actually, we're local. My powers only manifest during the holiday season—it's not a full-time gig up in the cold. The rest of the year Mrs. Claus and I run a nice little bed-and-breakfast in the Quarter. Everybody around town knows the zombie detective to call when they're in a bind."

When I first moved into the Unnatural Quarter, I was a regular human P.I., trying to make a living like anybody else. I catered to clients who, though they sometimes looked like monsters on the outside, still had very human problems. Even after I got myself killed on a case, I climbed out of the grave and got back to work, still with Robin as my partner. Most unnatural aren't even bothered by the bullet hole in the middle of my forehead, and I've stopped being self conscious about applying morticians' putty to cover it up.

Sheyenne, our office assistant, flitted up to Santa, beaming her gorgeous smile. "May I take your coat, Mr. Claus?"

Not only is Sheyenne extremely smart, competent, and efficient, she's beautiful on all counts. She's also my girlfriend. On top of that, she happens to be a ghost, murdered in the same case that saw me dead. But even through all that, we stuck together. It's a testament to the strength of our relationship.

Santa decided against removing his red coat. "No-ho-ho! It's part of my traditional image. The coat is made of magical material that keeps me comfortable no matter the temperature. That way I never have to take it off until the season's over. Traditions are important, and never more so than around the holidays."

Sheyenne leaned closer and whispered, "For the record, I never stopped believing in you."

He regarded Sheyenne with both wonder and mirth. "Strangely enough, I didn't believe in ghosts—until a few years ago." Santa sneezed, then turned back to me. "Mr. Chambeaux, I'm not going to kid you. There's more riding on this particular Christmas than ever before, and I'm coming apart at the seams. I need you to find my stolen property before Christmas Eve, or there'll be no joy to the world, no ho-ho-ho, no holly jolly, no Feliz in the Navidad, no Frohe in the Weihnachten, no Merry in the Christmas. You see how serious this is?"

"I think I do." I really had no idea, but I didn't want to look dumb in front of Santa Claus. "What exactly was stolen?"

"My list!" He was distraught—which was not at all the sort of attitude I expected from a man famous for his rumbling belly-laugh and infectious good cheer. "My *list* of who's Naughty and Nice! Without that list, I won't know which houses to visit, which Johnny deserves a model train set and which one gets a lump of coal, which Susie deserves a doll and which one gets a boring sweater. If I can't figure that out, Christmas definitely won't be the most wonderful time of the year."

"Don't you keep a photocopy?" Robin asked. "Or an on-line backup?"

Santa was horrified. "And break Christmas tradition? Millions of children believe in me and the way I do things, just so. They have dreams about Christmas, and it's my responsibility to safeguard those dreams." He shook his head again. "If I modernized, there'd be an uproar—not to mention countless bugs in the system—and then you can bet the Easter Bunny would hack into my database and start grabbing my market share. No, everything's done by hand on a very long roll of parchment, the names of every single boy and girl written with a goose quill."

That must have been the world's largest two-column spreadsheet. "And how exactly was it stolen?"

"Someone broke into the offices of my North Pole headquarters. It's our busy season, all of my helpers doing double shifts, decking the halls, dashing through the snow. Our packaging department is a madhouse, full of complete sets of lords a-leaping, partridges, pear trees—and everybody wants five golden rings. We still have an overstock of last year's fruitcakes, and I don't know what to do with the figgy puddings. I was sure there'd be a demand for those again." He wiped a gloved hand across his forehead.

"It's very hectic. I was taking a break with Mrs. Claus. She had made a fresh batch of eggnog, and this time of year she spikes it rather heavily. I slept like a baby … and when I went back to the office the list was gone!" He tugged on his beard. "It had to be an inside job." He paced back and forth, scuffing his black boots on our all-weather carpet. "I checked with all the line supervisor elves and every single one of the toy builders. This time of year they work around the clock without even restroom or cigarette breaks. But everyone had an alibi."

"Could you have been targeted by Homeland Security?" Robin asked. "Or some other law-enforcement organization monitoring your research as to who might be on a Most Naughty list?"

"I can see why they might want that," I said.

"Not at all, I have a close cooperative relationship with government agencies, considering all that airspace I fly over—and my work has to be done in a single night, so I have no time to mess with clearances. I even let NORAD track me every year. No, that list is in the hands of someone who means no good, mark my words … and no human could have gotten through my security. It had to be an unnatural."

He hung his head and seemed so sad that I wanted to sit on Santa's lap and give him a hug. He continued, "That's why I came to you, Mr. Chambeaux. If I don't get that Naughty and Nice list in time, I can't stop thinking about all those poor children who'll be disappointed, all those broken dreams, all those undelivered presents. It'll destroy their faith in Christmas … and they just might turn out to be naughty next year."

I was determined to solve the problem. It's not every day you get a chance to save Christmas—and not just because Christmas only comes once a year. "Don't underestimate how relentless a zombie can be, Santa. I'll find your list. If I have any questions or developments, how will I get hold of you? Do you have a business card?"

"Much better than that." Santa reached into a pocket of his red jacket and pulled out a bright green ribbon with a jingle bell attached. "Just ring this, and I'll be there. Even if I'm otherwise occupied, I have an answering service that can get hold of me."

The pink had come back to his cheeks, and a droll smile lifted his lips. "Oh-ho-ho, if you solve this case, there'll be something very special under the tree—for all of you."

Relieved and encouraged, Santa slung his empty sack over one shoulder and prepared to go. He closed his eyes and touched a finger to the side of his nose.

When nothing happened, he looked around our offices. Finding no chimney, he chuckled. "Sorry, I've been so worried about Christmas being ruined, I forgot how I arrived!" He left through the front door instead.

2

Although I knew I might have to go to Santa's North Pole seasonal offices to see the crime scene, I decided to search in the Unnatural Quarter first, which was much more convenient. (Riding up to the Arctic for hours in a freezing open sleigh sounded worse than flying in a middle seat in Coach.)

I started with someone who kept a similar list—primarily a Naughty list.

Officer Toby McGoohan is a dedicated beat cop, but his penchant for telling off-color jokes to the wrong people had gotten him transferred to the Quarter. McGoo is also my BHF, my best human friend. We help each other on cases. We commiserate about life and unlife over beers at the Goblin Tavern.

I found him outside one of the Talbot & Knowles blood bars, which are frequented by vampires who need their daily caffeine and hemoglobin fix. Some fanged customers drink straight blood, while others go for berry-flavored blood frappés or, now that the weather had turned colder, steaming cinnamon-spice hot clotties.

"Hey, Shamble," McGoo said, tipping his blue cap. "What do you get when you cross a snowman with a vampire?"

"What?" I groaned in advance.

"Frostbite." He persists in telling me jokes. I haven't been able to convince him they're not funny, and he hasn't been able to convince me that they are. As a special favor, I did promise I would try to laugh at some of them. But only some. "What's new and exciting in your world?"

"I just picked up Santa Claus as a client. Somebody stole his list of Naughty and Nice kids."

McGoo's eyes widened. "Well, that's a miracle on ..." he glanced up, looking for a street corner, "32nd Street. If even Santa isn't safe from criminal activity, we are living in troubled times indeed. What does the list look like?"

"Long roll of parchment, millions of handwritten names. Two columns labeled N and N."

McGoo shook his head. "I'll keep an eye out, but we've got real problems of our own in the Quarter." He lowered his voice. "Kids are going missing, Shamble—a lot of them. We've received a rash of reports."

A vampire couple came out of the blood bar, chatting away. One held a to-go carrier with four cups of blood drinks marked with Type

A (extra hot), Type O negative, and two with Type B positive (and a hand-drawn smiley face).

McGoo called, "Excuse me, can I see those for a second?"

The vampires turned, surprised. "What is it, Officer?"

"Your blood drinks. I want to show my friend something."

McGoo indicated the to-go cups, the first of which showed the printed picture of a young vampire boy who had been turned when he was maybe twelve years old. Big letters said "Have You Seen Me?" Printed below the photo were the vampire kid's name, pre-turned age, and last-seen data.

The second cup showed a zombie boy with an incongruous smile beneath his sunken eyes. The third was a scruffy-looking full-furred werewolf, and the fourth showed a human girl in Goth makeup wearing an off-the-shelf gloomy expression.

After he thanked the vampire couple, they left. I shook my head. "That's troubling, McGoo. I think I recognize the werewolf kid. He was part of the gang at the rumble a few months ago, Hairballs versus the Monthlies."

"Yeah, he's not the only rough one. Some of the missing children are straight off the Wikipedia page for Juvenile Delinquent. Not all of those photos were in a family album—a few are from mug-shot files."

"Some of the disappearances could just be runaways," I suggested. "Visiting some nice old lady's gingerbread house in the forest."

"For the record, Shamble, she wasn't a nice old lady—I worked on that case," McGoo said. "Not all of the missing kids have records. We've got grieving parents or foster-parents who want to find their missing little angels. I don't know if the cases are related, or just a coincidence."

"I don't believe in coincidence," I said, wondering if this might also have something to do with the stolen Naughty and Nice list. "But I didn't believe in Santa Claus either, and now he's my client. Let me know if you get a lead on my case. I'll do the same if I hear anything about the missing kids."

McGoo nodded. "The Quarter's getting nervous—put your mind to it, see what you come up with. You've got a lot of space in that big empty head of yours."

I tapped the bullet hole in the middle of my forehead. "A little extra space maybe, but it's not empty." I tipped my fedora at him and left.

My first order of business was to figure out who would *want* to steal the Naughty and Nice list, and what anybody would use it for. In order to brainstorm, I invited Sheyenne to lunch.

3

Being a ghost, Sheyenne doesn't eat, not even their special "ephemeral" plate, and I don't need much sustenance. (I've avoided brains, because I don't want to turn into one of *those* zombies who are an embarrassment to the rest of us.)

The Ghoul's Diner, though, was a place to hang out, and Sheyenne likes it when we go out on lunch dates. Strolling down the sidewalk toward the Diner, we free-associated. Sheyenne wore a bright smile as always, and those blue eyes could make a man's heart stop beating, or start beating, depending on which condition he started from.

I wondered aloud that maybe the Big Uneasy had made the Grinch manifest as well, but Sheyenne doubted he'd reached a worldwide cultural status similar to vampires or St. Nick. I disagreed, because I had grown up on the Grinch; still, I conceded that he seemed too obvious a cartoon villain.

I then postulated that the perpetrator could be a Lorax with self-esteem issues, upset that Arbor Day didn't have the stature of Christmas, Hanukkah, Thanksgiving, New Years … or even Kwanzaa, for that matter. I didn't know if Loraxes were real, either. I seemed to be in a Seussian rut.

A light dusting of snow came down, reminding me that I had to find Santa's list before Christmas Eve, or he would suffer a worldwide toy-distribution crisis. Festive decorations were already strung up in the streets of the Quarter: barbed-wire tinsel looped along windowpanes and awnings, colorful wreaths hung from nooses on gallows lampposts.

Before we reached the Diner, Sheyenne and I stopped on the street where crowds had gathered and traffic halted for an early holiday parade. And it sure wasn't the type hosted by Macy's.

Elves capered and danced at the front of the parade, diminutive creatures dressed in pointed floppy caps and bright red outfits trimmed with white flocking. The costumes resembled a traditional Santa's elf suit, but these were cheap knockoffs that fit poorly with seams showing and with some of the white trim missing.

These elves were not the cute, smiling, industrious workers who stocked Santa's shelves and made the North Pole a cheery, if formerly imaginary, place. No, these elves came from the G-side of the family, having more in common with gremlins, goblins, and gnomes—pointy, stretched-out features, gray skin, and long ears that looked as if they had gotten caught in industrial picking machinery. When they smiled like good elves should, they showed alarmingly pointed teeth.

Behind the prancing elves came a bizarre motorized sleigh crawling along at pedestrian speed so everyone on the sidewalk had an appropriate opportunity to wave. Palm trees adorned the back of the sleigh. On a big wicker chair sat an elf with all the usual elf features (from the G-side of the family), but he wore a white rhinestone-studded jacket, trimmed in Christmasy green and red. He had slicked-back black hair, sideburns that extended halfway down his pointed chin, big garish sunglasses, and oddly out-of-place blue suede shoes.

"You've got to be kidding me," I said to Sheyenne.

"He's for real, Beaux. That's Elfis—I've seen his ads. You know, 'Santa Claus is coming to town, but Elfis will get there faster?' He's a celebrity on the cable-access channels."

I'm a decent enough detective, but I can be clueless about pop culture.

Elfis waved at the crowd and picked up a handheld Vegas-style silver microphone. "Thank ya very much. Santa's got competition this year, boys and girls, naturals and unnatural. The holidays should be for everybody, not just kids who pass some arbitrary naughty-or-nice test. Even naughty kids deserve presents, don't they?"

From the sidewalk crowds, a smattering of natural and unnatural children cheered—kids who knew they were included in the Naughty column, no doubt.

"Santa Claus has had a monopoly on the Christmas season for far too long—but I intend to undercut his position. Elfis Industries has wider distribution, more fairness, and less discrimination. More transparency in holiday gift-giving! We're going to expose all those 'secret admirer' gifts for what they are. And no more bribery with milk and cookies. *Everyone* deserves a present, and I'm the one to give it to them. It's time to put the kitsch back into Christmas!"

His elves began handing out candy canes, traditional red-and-white striped ones, blood-red ones, and black ones. A witch dressed in a midnight-blue gown and pointy cap stood by her young son who looked as if he might grow up to be a powerful necromancer. The boy ran forward to take a black candy cane, but his mother scolded him. "I told you not to take candy from strangers!"

The boy pouted. "He's not a stranger, Mom—that's *Elfis!*"

"Oh," the witch said, and handed him back the cane.

The motorized sleigh rolled by, with Elfis in his sequins and sunglasses waving from under his palm trees. He called out, "Who needs the cold? I have nightmares about a white Christmas! Let it snow, let it snow, let it snow—but somewhere far away! Stick with me, and the holidays will have a warm and sunny glow."

After the parade passed, Sheyenne leaned close to me. "So that's why Santa is so worried. He's got competition this year. And if his rival does a better job satisfying the customers ..."

"Then Santa Claus won't be coming to town anymore," I said. "We might have our first suspect. Elfis has a motive to sabotage Santa's work. I better go talk to him and find out if his intentions really are as pure as new fallen snow."

I could tell this case was going to spell T-R-O-U-B-L-E.

4

After Sheyenne and I had a quick lunch at the diner (pink slime was on special), I went off to continue my investigation.

The headquarters for the competitive holiday operation was an office building in front of a fenced compound of airplane-hangar-sized structures, no doubt where Elfis manufactured and stored all the toys he planned to distribute ahead of his business rival. According to Sheyenne, Elfis's ads promised delivery by Christmas Eve Eve.

The sign at the front entrance had giant letters painted like candy canes, surrounded by yellow suns: "North Pole South: We're Better Because We're Closer to the Equator." Around the doorway was strewn blue sand or fake snow, which seemed incongruous ... until I remembered "Blue Christmas."

When I entered the front door of North Pole South, I heard many busy bodies working in the back, but the reception counter was empty except for a fist-sized fake rock sitting on top of an index card that said "Ring bell for service." I picked up the stone and realized it was hollow. When I shook it, a tinkling chime rang out.

A female elf receptionist scurried out of the back, smiling sweetly with her pinched face. "I see you found our Jingle-Bell Rock," she snickered. "Very clever, don't you think? Elfis came up with it himself." She shuffled papers and handed me a temporary-employment application. "Looking for part-time holiday work? Many positions available."

I shook snow from the brim of my fedora. "That would be a conflict of interest. I've been retained by Santa Claus."

The receptionist's eyebrows rose. "I'll let Elfis know you're here." She took back the Jingle-Bell Rock and punched an extension on her phone. "He told us to expect an overture from Mr. Claus."

"Overture?" I asked. "I can barely hum a tune."

Elfis agreed to see me, probably out of curiosity; at least it got me through the door.

The chief elf's back office was bright and stiflingly hot. A large tropical mural covered the far wall. Wearing only a towel around his waist, Elfis lay back on a chaise lounge under a pair of heat lamps that could have been used to keep food warm in a restaurant. Standing on either side, a pair of Egyptian mummies gently fanned him with palm fronds.

Elfis lifted his sunglasses and sat up to regard me. "Dan Chambeaux, Private Investigator ... that seems an odd choice for Santa, but I knew he'd send a representative before long. He has no option but to open negotiations. I suppose he wants to suggest some kind of merger and keep a token title for himself? Frankly I'd rather just buy his operations outright."

He waved for the mummies to back away. "Would you like some refreshment? I can get one of my boys to make you a mai tai or piña colada. Or, if you want to be more traditional, I have chestnuts roasting on an open fire."

Chestnuts weren't the only things roasting. "I'm surprised you keep it so hot in here," I said, tugging at my collar—and zombies don't perspire.

Elfis explained, "I want to change the paradigm of the holiday season. It's too cold, too snowy, too wintry. You really think shepherds prefer to watch their flocks in the snow? They'd rather be skiing. And if I want something frozen, I order a frozen margarita." He laughed, but it sounded more like heh-heh-heh than ho-ho-ho.

"Now then, let's talk about sending old Saint Nick into retirement. Here's my offer: I take over all his operations, but I let him keep his North Pole annex. He and Mrs. Claus get a nice pension, run their bed-and-breakfast, maybe do a few public appearances for old times' sake, but I license his likeness and the brand. I'm dreaming of a profitable Christmas."

"There's been a misunderstanding, Mr. Elfis. That's not why I'm here."

The elf slicked back his hair, adjusted his position on the chaise lounge. The mummies came forward again to fan him vigorously with the palm fronds. "Well, then, I'm all ears."

"Santa Claus hired me as a detective because something very valuable was stolen from him."

Elfis seemed completely uninterested. "Really? And what would old St. Nick find valuable? Can't he just wiggle his nose and make another of whatever it was?"

"It's more of a matter of administrative records gone missing," I said. "I'm investigating the theft."

Elfis snickered. "You must mean his list. Anal-retentive, if you ask me." He slid his sunglasses back down on his face, scratched his sideburns. "And you think I had something to do with it? Why in the world would I need a list like that? I explicitly *don't* discriminate. I give presents to all kids, without scoring them on social behavior. What gives Santa the right to make a subjective decision about who's Naughty and Nice? Judgmental jerk, if you ask me." He sniffed. "I plan to take discrimination out of Christmas gift-giving, make it equal for all. What would be my motive for stealing the list?"

I did have a theory. "You'd hamstring Santa's activities, make him look incompetent, while gaining brownie points for yourself."

"I don't have brownies, Mr. Chambeaux. I have elves. There's a difference."

"That doesn't address my theory."

"Look around you, Mr. Chambeaux. I'm sabotaging Santa's work by perfectly traditional means—undercutting prices, faster distribution, more transparency in my operations. I don't need a list for that."

One of the mummies served him a cool drink in a hollowed pineapple, complete with a colorful umbrella. "Thank ya very much." Elfis took a long refreshing sip. "Tell Santa if he wants to come to terms, I'm having a holiday special. His decision. Either way, it's time he faced some competition."

Elfis reached down beside his chaise lounge and pulled out a baseball-sized knot of thorny leaves, like a wadded tumbleweed studded with berries. "Here, Mr. Chambeaux—have a free sample. Part of my effort to put the kitsch back into Christmas."

He tossed it to me, and I caught it. "What's this?"

"Our new McMistletoe. Cheaper to manufacture, no preservatives needed, non-poisonous, non-habit-forming." He spoke at such a fast pace that my ears could barely keep up. "It's not intended to diagnose, prevent, treat, or cure any disease. These claims have not been evaluated by the FDA." He grinned. "But our McMistletoe is just as effective as real mistletoe. Try it out, you'll see."

I pocketed the mistletoe in my jacket's other pocket, because it didn't seem right to tuck it beside the jingle bell that Santa Claus had given me. "I'll try it," I said, though I doubted Sheyenne would be impressed.

5

I was already disturbed about the missing children McGoo was investigating, but I didn't see the actual pain until the Tannenbaums came into our offices.

Mrs. Tannenbaum buried her face in her husband's broad chest. "Our baby boy!"

Both of them were werewolves—the Monthly variety, so they passed for normal except on full-moon nights. They seemed like a nice couple with modest lives, middle-income jobs, probably had a home that was not extravagant but one they were proud of.

Robin hurried forward to comfort them. "Tell us what happened."

Mr. Tannenbaum pulled a wallet from his pocket and showed us a snapshot. "This is our son Buddy." The kid was of the full-furred persuasion, the type of werewolf who maintained a long muzzle, sharp fangs, moist black nose, and facial fur throughout the month.

"That's his school portrait," Mrs. Tannenbaum said with a sniff. "He was just about to graduate sixth grade." Sheyenne flitted in with a tissue for the grieving woman.

I studied the snapshot. Buddy Tannenbaum's black lips were curled in what I assumed was a smile, but might have been a snarl. What kid didn't make a goofy face when sitting for a school portrait? "Not much family resemblance. Adopted?"

Mrs. Tannenbaum snuffled loudly. "He came from an abused home, and we took him in. Poor Buddy! We wanted to show him all the love and affection he deserved. But one day after school, he didn't come home to do his chores."

Her husband continued, "He often gets preoccupied with friends—he has a strong social life. And what's a chore or two around the house? No need to bother the boy with them. I can do the vacuuming and take out the garbage while my wife cooks dinner."

"On the night he disappeared, I made a fleshloaf with tomato sauce and onions. Buddy's favorite!" Mrs. Tannenbaum wailed, which came out as a trailing howl. "We had to eat it ourselves. We had leftovers for two days."

"Two days? Your son vanished and you didn't report it for two days?" Robin shot me a look, and I saw that furrow of concern on her brow.

"We thought he might be staying at a friend's house," said Mr. Tannenbaum. "He sometimes does that. We try not to be overprotective. A boy needs his space and ... a wolf has to run free."

"Can you find him?" Mrs. Tannenbaum said. "We didn't want to go to the police because ... because we want to keep his record clean. He's going to go to college someday, and it's really a private matter."

"You can count on our discretion, Mr. and Mrs. Tannenbaum." I doubted Buddy's disappearance was unrelated to the other children who had vanished.

"Can you give us the names of his friends, or places where he liked to spend time?" Robin asked.

Mrs. Tannenbaum considered. "He likes to hang out at the comic-book shop. Just Dug Up Collectibles, I think it's called."

"I know the place," I said. "I've been there."

In a fit of nostalgia, I had gone in to browse some of the old comics I'd bought and guarded so lovingly when I was a kid. One day, while tidying up my room, my mom gave them all to a thrift shop, and they sold for a nickel apiece before I could run down there to save them. A few months ago, when I looked in Just Dug Up Collectibles and saw the outrageous prices those issues were now selling for, I left the shop in despair and never went back....

"Is there anything else I should know? Anything that might help?"

The Tannenbaums looked at each other, as if uncomfortable, hesitant, then both shook their heads.

Sheyenne whisked in and made several color photocopies of Buddy's photo before returning the snapshot to Mr. Tannenbaum, who lovingly tucked it back into his wallet. "I'll also submit this to the Talbot & Knowles blood bars," Sheyenne suggested. "They can include it with the other photos of missing children."

Mr. Tannenbaum looked uncomfortable. "I'd prefer to keep this out of the public eye."

"We already talked to the blood bars," snuffled Mrs. Tannenbaum. "They said they were overbooked for the next two months until ... until ..." She began sobbing.

Mr. Tannenbaum completed the sentence. "Until Christmas." He patted his wife on the shoulder. "Please find him soon, Mr. Chambeaux. We have very important Hanukkah traditions, and Winter Solstice, too."

She sniffled again. "The holidays just won't be the same without our dear Buddy. Please find him, Mr. Chambeaux. Such a dear, dear sweet boy."

6

"That kid is an unholy terror!" said Adric the comic-shop owner. He barely glanced at the picture of Buddy Tannenbaum. "He and his friends are monsters—and I don't mean that in a good way."

The wall behind the counter was plastered with autographed 8 × 10s of Adric posing with D-list celebrities. He was a gray-skinned, pot-bellied zombie, not nearly as well-preserved as the special variant-cover issues he kept bagged-and-boarded on high shelves. His complexion showed some signs of putrescence as well as fresh acne, which made him doubly unfortunate; although the undead suffer from numerous physical maladies, few are afflicted by zits.

Adric wore a powder-blue *Star Wars* T-shirt with R2-D2 and C-3PO on the front, and it was much too small for him. I deduced that he'd bought the shirt when he saw *Star Wars* first run in theaters; in the years since, his body had enlarged considerably, though he probably told himself that the shirt had shrunk.

Adric handed me back the photo. "That kid and his friends are always in here stealing things, vandalizing, harassing customers, and of course never buying anything. A bunch of deadbeats and undeadbeats."

I frowned. It seemed Buddy Tannenbaum was not the upstanding young werewolf his parents imagined him to be. "He's gone missing. When was the last time you saw him?"

He snorted. "I kicked out the whole wild bunch two weeks ago—caught them shoplifting one time too many."

I had another thought. "So, does that mean you keep a list of, say, who's naughty and who's nice?"

"Nah, this is a comic store. We get all kinds in here. That Buddy Tannenbaum and his friends, though—they'd definitely go in the Naughty column."

As he talked, Adric used a box-cutter to slice open a cardboard case of new arrivals like an eager coroner working on his favorite autopsy. He opened the flaps and began pulling out shrink-wrapped Christmas ornaments, clumsy-looking figurines of werewolves, vampires, scaly demons.

Frowning in disgust, he held up a crudely painted vampire with red marks smeared across his face. "Look at these! My customers want quality. The catalog said they're hand-painted, but this looks like it was finger-painted, or *claw*-painted." He shook his head. "Maybe even *flipper*-painted."

Adric dug into the box, pulled out a larger figure, a well-muscled werewolf in a cop uniform, holding an enormous Magnum pistol. "Does this look like Hairy Harry to you?" The rogue lycanthropic cop from the UQPD was something of a folk hero, even though he'd retired from the force.

"I wouldn't pay a premium for it," I said. I noticed the figures were labeled *Elfis Originals! Collect Them All!*

Adric kept pulling figurines out of the packaging, then rolled his eyes as he lifted out six genuine Elfis figurines, each wearing a white sequin jacket, brushed-back black hair and sideburns, and big sunglasses. "What? I only ordered one of these."

Next, he removed a larger box showing a scaled aquatic gill-man labeled "Special Limited Edition Creature! (Comes with free lagoon!)." With his stiff zombie fingers, Adric pried open the package, removed the scaly figurine along with a tiny black plastic basin. Apparently, the user was supposed to fill it with water.

"Special Edition? Ridiculous! Look at this: 'Limited to 1,000,000 Units.' How the hell does that make it *collectible*? I'll be lucky to sell six … well, five, because I'll keep one for myself."

I tried to get back to the reason I'd come there. "Have you seen any of Buddy's buddies? Anyone I could talk to? His parents are distraught."

"No, and good riddance. Maybe they all ran off to join the vampire circus." Adric continued setting out the Elfis Originals holiday ornaments. "Mark my words, his parents will have a lot more silent nights this way. Just imagine what a handful that werewolf kid is gonna be when he hits his teenage years and hormones kick in."

He looked up at where two young zombies were pawing over back issues of *The Crypt-Keeper's Funniest Capers*. The zombie teens had their mouths open and they moaned in laughter at the panels.

Adric yelled, "Hey, you! Be careful with those—you get decaying flesh on any of the pages, you bought it."

The zombies looked up at him, moaned, then went back to the comics, noticeably exercising greater care.

I picked up a fine-print catalog listing of the Elfis Originals ornaments and collectibles and pocketed it for future reference. I thanked Adric and left.

7

When Santa Claus returned to our offices, he looked even more anxious than before. His face was sallow, almost jaundiced; his flowing white beard looked scraggly, with a thin brownish stain from where he'd been hitting the pipe a little too often. He had lost enough weight that his red jacket was gathered in folds around his waist with his wide black belt cinched tighter. I saw that he'd even punched a new hole.

"Usually when I visit, people set out milk and cookies for me." He sounded disappointed, beaten down. "I'll be glad to get back to running the bed-and-breakfast, but I have my duties first. I can't do my rounds without that list of Naughty and Nice." He slumped into a chair beside Sheyenne's desk and let out a sigh. "I tried to write a new one from memory, but my mind isn't what it used to be—too many bitter cold nights out in a reindeer-powered sleigh. I won't kid you, Christmas Eve is a hard night—a real nut-cracker. After it's over, I crawl into bed and sleep for a week."

"My accountant says the same thing about Tax Day," I told him.

Santa adjusted his floppy red cap. "I haven't heard you jingle my bell, and time is running out. It's beginning to look a lot like a screwed-up Christmas."

"I've been investigating," I reassured him. "Particularly your rival Elfis. He makes no secret of the fact that he wants to take you out, but he insists he doesn't need your list to do it. What can you tell me about him?"

Santa's face fell, as if his heart had shrunk three sizes that day. "That elf deserves a lump of coal in his stocking on Christmas morning. Unfair business practices, inferior materials—do you know that his silver bells are made of cheap aluminum?" He frowned again, let out another sigh. "I try not to think ill of people, but I'd like to take a thick candy cane and go thumpety-thump-thump on his head. He's ruining traditions by taking away the incentive for children to be Nice. Just look at the rude manners in chat rooms on the internet."

My heart went out to him. "I'm looking into his North Pole South operations, and Robin is studying his business practices. I haven't found any evidence that he arranged to steal your Naughty and Nice list, but I'll keep digging."

After rummaging around in the kitchen, Sheyenne flitted into the main room, carrying a plate with three stale chocolate-chip cookies and a glass of milk. "Look what I found for you, Santa!"

He brightened. "'Tis the season to be jolly—so I'll try my best." He pulled a paper ticket from the pocket of his red jacket. "Could you validate this for me? I've got my reindeer and sleigh parked on the roof."

"Of course," Sheyenne said, and stamped his parking ticket.

Santa took the rest of the cookies "for the reindeer" and slipped through the door just as Mr. and Mrs. Tannenbaum hurried in. They looked anxious, and my heart sank, wondering how I was going to tell them that their darling Buddy wasn't the sugarplum they believed him to be. If the young werewolf was getting into so much trouble, how could the parents not know? Were they willfully oblivious to the fact that their angel came straight from the dark side?

"We weren't entirely honest with you," Mrs. Tannenbaum said, then looked away shyly. "We have something else that might help."

Her husband said, "I convinced my wife that we needed to give you every detail if we want our Buddy back. Our son is more important than our shame and embarrassment."

"We thought you might be able to solve the case without it, and then we wouldn't have to admit … admit—" Mrs. Tannenbaum's lower lip quivered. Her eyes flashed golden, and I could see a hint of werewolf coming to the fore.

"Buddy's given us difficulties before," Mr. Tannenbaum admitted. "He's an unruly kid. I think it comes from his full-fur blood. Trouble in school, trouble with vandalism. He's even run away from home a few times."

"But he always comes back," Mrs. Tannenbaum interjected. "He's a good boy at heart."

I asked, "Do you think there's any possibility that he's just run off again?"

Both Tannenbaums shook their heads. "Not so close to Christmas. He would have waited to get his toys first. He's a troublemaker, but he's a greedy troublemaker."

I didn't know if that was the best kind or the worst kind. "The information doesn't help a great deal at the moment, but I'll keep asking around."

The Tannenbaums looked at each other. "Oh, that's not what we meant to tell you, Mr. Chambeaux. We were reluctant to say anything about what we did because … because, well, it's not exactly legal."

That's never a good phrase to include in a sentence. I braced myself.

"We had to do something because Buddy ran away so often. So, the last time we took him in to the vet …" Mrs. Tannenbaum swallowed hard, then lowered her voice. "We had a tracking chip implanted in the base of his skull. Nothing anyone would notice, mind you, but … just in case."

I perked up. "A tracking device? Then we can pinpoint his location right away!"

"Yes," said Mrs. Tannenbaum. "Do you think that might help you find him?"

I slapped my forehead, and it made a hollow popping sound from the bullet hole there. "The cases don't solve themselves," I said, "but I do need all the information."

"The tracking signal has a very limited range," Mr. Tannenbaum said. "Quite discreet, but not terribly useful. Still, if you get close enough …"

The Tannenbaums looked sheepish after they gave me the secret frequency and serial number of the tracker. "Just bring our little boy home, please? That would be the best present we ever had."

8

When we began our search, I decided to take police backup—McGoo—just so I could say I was being sensible. I didn't want to go overboard, though, because there was a better-than-even chance Buddy had just run away with his juvenile delinquent unnatural pals. Still, if Buddy's disappearance was connected with the other missing kids, McGoo would want to be along.

Then Robin insisted on joining us. With such a three-pronged approach, how could we not be prepared to solve any problem?

She had frowned in disapproval when she heard about the implanted tracker chip, claiming that it violated the civil rights of an underage werewolf. But McGoo had seen enough troublemakers in his work, and he was more inclined to try the "terrified straight" approach. Robin finally conceded that if the tracker meant we could reunite the full-time fuzzy kid with his once-a-month fuzzy parents, then all was for the best.

With the tracker's frequency and serial number, Robin downloaded a free but highly rated Track Werewolf app for her smartphone. She bundled up in a wool coat, and we all set off into the snowy night to find Buddy, leaving Sheyenne in charge of the office.

We wandered around the Quarter for a frustrating hour, following false signals (a garage-door opener and a universal TV remote control). I was beginning to think that we might not pick up the tracker's limited-range signal until after we had already found the subject in question. We were lost and frustrated; what had seemed to be an easy solution was turning out to be a headache and a waste of time.

Then Sheyenne called us and saved the day. She had found an update for the Track Werewolf app, which dealt with certain bugs and user issues and increased sensitivity. Once Robin installed the update, we found a strong signal. We were closer than we thought.

The signal led us straight to the tall smokestacks and gigantic toy warehouses behind Elfis's North Pole South complex.

Holding her phone, Robin took the lead, guiding us along the chain-link fence to the back service entrance of the gigantic manufacturing warehouses. The temperature was dropping, and fluffy snowflakes drifted down. Not a creature was stirring, not even the ones that usually stirred at that time of night.

Approaching the back guard gate, we found two burly golems wearing security guard uniforms. Their clay bodies were stiff and hardening in the cold, but one perked up. "Do you hear what I hear?"

The other said, "Do you see what I see?"

Now alert, the golems prepared to block our way, both of them focusing on McGoo's uniform, the dark blue police shirt, trousers, and cap. "That looks good on you," said one of the golems.

"We both wanted to be cops, but couldn't pass the tests," the other explained.

I knew why, but I didn't embarrass them by pointing out the reason.

McGoo said, "We're searching for a missing child, and we have reason to believe he's inside one of the warehouses." He held out a copy of Buddy's picture.

"Kids just can't stay away from toys," said the first golem.

Robin held up her smartphone, showing the app. "And we have electronic evidence he's in there."

The golems were again intrigued. "Is that phone one of the new models?"

The other said, "Does it have Angry Vultures on it? Or Curses with Friends?"

I knew if the golems started playing games on Robin's phone we would never get past the gate. "We need to have a look, bring that boy back to his parents."

The first golem had a stony expression on his clay face. "Sorry. We can't let you inside. Elfis is very strict."

The other golem looked intimidated. "He sees you when you're sleeping, he knows when you're awake, he knows when you've been bad or good." In tandem, they shook their smooth clay heads and pointed upward. "Security cameras."

Time for Plan B. I removed a folded sheet of paper from the inside pocket of my jacket and showed it to the two golems. "We have a duly authorized search warrant to enter the premises, signed by Judge Hawkins herself. This grants us unfettered access to all parts of the North Pole South warehouses so we can find and rescue the young man."

The first golem guard took the sheet of paper and studied it intently, while Robin shot me a questioning glance. She craned her neck to see what the guards were looking at. McGoo could barely keep the smile off his face.

The other golem took the sheet from his partner; they both had frowns on their clay faces. "All right then. We're security guards, sworn to uphold the law." They opened the chain-link gate for us. "Go on inside. I hope you find what you're looking for."

Robin was perplexed, but she glanced down at the blinking light on her Track Werewolf app. Buddy was definitely close, inside the big factory building ahead of us. With his best I'm-an-authority-figure gait, McGoo marched away from the guard golems. Robin hurried alongside me. When we were out of earshot, she asked, "What was that all about? When did you get a search warrant?"

"It wasn't a search warrant," I said. "It's the fine-print listing of Elfis Originals I took from Just Dug Up Collectibles."

McGoo worked at the warehouse door; it was unlocked. "Golems can't read," he said. "At least most of them can't. That's why they couldn't pass their UQ Police Department exams. Good work, Shamble."

Robin was astonished. "Then we got in here under false pretenses, and I have real ethical problems with that. We're trespassing."

"We're rescuing a missing child," I said. My boundaries were a little more blurred than Robin's, but I did manage to get things done.

Robin was about to continue her objections when McGoo opened the loading dock door. The dark, noisy factory hangar was worse than the worst New Year's Day hangover. It was a true holiday of horrors.

9

I doubted children opening their gifts on the morning of Christmas Eve Eve (if Elfis and his minions delivered on time, as promised) would want to know where their presents really came from.

We were seeing the ugly side of holiday cheer: appalling labor conditions, thick smoke, clanging hammers, grinding gears, and jets of steam venting from pressure valves. Foul water trickled out of rusty pipes overhead. A labyrinth of rattling conveyor belts rolled toys along to packaging lines. Sparks flew and blazing fires roared out of open furnaces fed with black coal that poured from supply hoppers in the ceiling. A separate set of conveyors dumped defective metal toys into a smoldering furnace. It was as if the Island of Misfit Toys had an active volcano.

Robin looked around in horror, shocked by what she saw. McGoo's face was stormy with anger.

Most appalling of all, though, were the kids shackled to the assembly line, hunched over the conveyor belts, red-eyed, dirt-smeared, waifish. They toiled at assembling dolls, painting action figures, stuffing collectibles into boxes. There were werewolves, zombies, ghouls, even human children, all looking dejected and haggard.

As I scanned the faces, I recognized many of the kids featured on the Have You Seen Me? pictures from the Talbot & Knowles blood bars. I saw one gray-furred werewolf boy, mangy and yet somehow still cute, chained to a station where he was applying black button eyes onto Raggedy Ann dolls. Either he was confused by the instructions, or the dolls catered to an entirely different type of unnatural, because he sewed three eyes on each doll.

"That's Buddy Tannenbaum!" I said.

The boy heard me even over the factory din. He turned, his tongue lolling out of his mouth, and his eyes lit up upon seeing us. He dropped the doll onto the dirty factory floor and leaped toward us, but was brought up short by silver shackles that bound his wrist and ankle.

"I'll be good! I promise!" he yelped. "I won't be naughty anymore. I don't want to be on the list!"

Robin was ahead of us, grim and determined. "We'll get you out of here, Buddy. Your parents hired us to find you."

"My mom and dad? But Elfis said they didn't love me anymore."

"Of course they love you," Robin said. "Parents love even naughty kids."

A steam whistle blew. More coal dumped out of the feeding hoppers, and the furnace burned brighter.

Then the elves came—evil elves, and ugly enough that they might have been disowned by even the G-side of the family. They carried cattle prods painted like cheery candy canes; others brandished icicle spears that dripped in the intense heat of the factory floor.

McGoo and I drew our guns and stood next to Robin. The ten elves closing in didn't look afraid of us at all. Too late, I realized that they were just a distraction.

Two other hench-elves stood up from behind the conveyor belt and hurled snowballs at us—icy snowballs with rocks in the middle. Cheater snowballs. (I did say they were evil elves.) Their aim was supernaturally true, and with one hail of hard snowballs, they knocked the guns out of our hands.

Then the hench-elves closed in, wielding icicle spears and candy-cane cattle prods. They overpowered us, shoved us to the factory floor, and used tough strands of satin ribbon to bind our wrists. We were going to have a black-and-blue Christmas. An evil elf even slapped a coordinating stick-on bow on each of us before they herded us toward the back of the factory.

"Elfis is going to want to see you," said one of the guards.

"Oh, by gosh, by golly, that was on my Christmas wish list," I said, which earned me a jab from one of the cattle prods. Since I'm a zombie, it takes a lot to shock me, but the experience was still unpleasant. I was more worried about McGoo and Robin, who could indeed be permanently damaged.

Elfis was at a raised supervisor's station near the warmth of the big furnace, sitting on a high director's chair with a small worktable beside him. Black dust from the coal hoppers left a gritty film on everything, but somehow it didn't affect his white sequined jacket or his blue suede shoes. He was perusing a rolled parchment filled with names—countless names, sorted into two columns, one marked N and the other one marked N. He muttered to himself as he used a large goose quill pen to check off names.

"Naughty … yes, got that one. Naughty … yes. Naughty … we have a very high success rate." Then he sneered at a line, crossed it out vigorously with the nib of his quill pen. "Somebody slipped up—this kid's in the Nice column! People tend to notice when *nice* kids go missing." A supervisor hench-elf scurried off to rectify the error.

Elfis picked up a bullhorn and began shouting toward the factory floor. "Listen up, kiddies! I have plenty more applicants to choose from, so if you want to be promoted in my criminal organization, you've got to produce, produce, *produce!* Only the best can survive this boot camp—also known as the Holiday Season! If you work hard, you'll be real henchmen by Easter." Elfis then started to laugh. "We're going to put that damned bunny out of business, too!"

He slid his sunglasses up on the bridge of his narrow nose as his fiendish hench-elves pushed us forward. He seemed surprised to see us. "Mr. Chambeaux and friends—have you come to negotiate on Santa's behalf again? Well, it's too late. I've already got the holidays sewn up in a body bag, and now you'll never stop me."

When all else fails, when things look grimmest, I like to state the obvious. It puts villains off guard and usually gets them talking—too much. "You said you didn't have Santa's list of Naughty and Nice. That was dishonest."

He held up a long finger. "No, that was *misleading*. I said I didn't steal the list in order to earn brownie points or to make Santa look incompetent. I stole it strictly for my own purposes." Elfis waved the parchment, showing us the long list of names. "It's a recruitment tool, like a screening folder for job applicants. Santa already identified the *naughty* children for me, the ones suitable to become part of my operation."

"But you put them to work as slave labor," Robin said.

Elfis shrugged. "Well, they are naughty. Even criminals need to know the consequences of their actions. You do the crime, you pay the time. Community service for *my* community."

I struggled against the satin ribbons binding my wrists. It reminded me of my childhood, trying to snap the ribbons so I could open my presents. Now, as then, the ribbon had supernatural strength.

Elfis leaned forward, opening both of his hands to warm them at the nearby furnace. The conveyor belt continued to clatter, dumping defective toys into it, plastic ones as well as metal. "It's so nice to be warm for a change. And you three will be all toasty, too. I'm afraid I can't allow my plans to be foiled—or tinseled. Into the furnace with them!"

The hench-elves swept forward like a blizzard of evil. Even though I'm a zombie, I had no desire to be cremated. And speaking for my two human friends, I knew that neither Robin nor McGoo wanted to tour the interior of the furnace either. I had to get us out of there.

Zombies, for all of our fragile bodies and flesh that's prone to decay, have very strong teeth. Some zombies use them for ripping into flesh and bone; now I discovered that my teeth were excellent at cutting Christmas ribbon. I tore into my colorful satin bindings, snapped the ribbon—and I was free.

But I couldn't fight all those armed hench-elves. Thinking of only one thing that might save us, I jammed my hand into my jacket pocket and grabbed the loop attached to the emergency jingle bell.

It wasn't much of a jing-jing-jingle—but it was enough to summon Old Kris Kringle.

The flames in the furnace brightened, then made a coughing sound. Black smoke swirled out, and with a whoosh of hot air Santa Claus slipped down the smokestack and made his dramatic entrance. The conveyor belt came to a screeching halt as the jolly guy in the magic red suit (which also proved to be non-flammable) emerged from the furnace like something out of *The Lord of the Rings*. He planted his gloved hands on his hips and bellowed, "Ho-ho-ho! Who's been a naughty boy?"

Elfis nearly jumped out of his skin and scrambled down from the director's chair so rapidly that his sunglasses clattered on the floor. With the empty cloth sack over his shoulder, Santa stalked forward like an avenging angel—and not the type that goes on top of a Christmas tree. He spotted his lengthy rolled-up list on the worktable and seized it, holding it up like a baton. "You have gone too far, Elfis. And now you'd better cry, because Santa Claus is coming to get you."

The hench-elves were panicked. They dropped their candy-cane cattle prods and icicle spears and cowered. Their teeth chattered as if they had gone caroling naked on a cold winter's night and no one was offering wassail, or even hot cocoa.

Elfis tried to run, but Santa quickly caught up with him. I couldn't believe how fast the old bearded guy could move, but he had to have a secret power if he could hit millions of households around the world in a single night.

McGoo held up his bound wrists for me to bite the ribbons. Now *that* was showing a measure of trust! "Good plan, Shamble."

"I call it Santa ex-Machina." I picked bright green satin out of my teeth, then turned to free Robin as well.

Santa had cornered Elfis by the big coal hoppers, and the evil elf had no place to go. Santa didn't need any help, but I was part of this, too—and I had a bone to pick with anybody who wanted to throw me and my friends into a furnace.

Next to me, one of the cowering hench-elves still had a sack filled with the icy rock-filled snowballs. I grabbed one and hurled it with perfect aim, proving that not all zombies are disoriented and uncoordinated. My snowball shot struck the release latch on the coal hopper just above Elfis's head. The trap dropped open, and Elfis looked up just in time to see a black avalanche dump down on him. He was buried under lumps of coal.

Robin, McGoo, and I rushed over to Santa, who gazed with satisfaction at the mound in front of him. "Coal is what Elfis deserved ... although I'd hoped he would turn his life around if given the chance. Such a disappointment."

"You knew Elfis beforehand?" I asked.

Santa nodded. "He was one of my toy laborers, assigned to my workshop for community service, but he escaped, broke the rules of his North Pole parole. I was going to report him, but not until after the holiday season was over. It's a busy time of the year, you know."

We heard a groan, then a stirring. We moved the coal blocks away to reveal an Elfis now entirely covered in black dust. He plucked in dismay at his ruined jacket. "I guess I won't be having a *white* Christmas."

Santa unslung the sack from his shoulder, tugged it open, and strode forward. "Here comes Santa Claus."

Elvis scrambled backward when he saw the yawning sack. "No, Santa! Please! No!"

"Naughty children get what they deserve." Santa snatched Elfis, stuffed him into the sack, and cinched the opening shut. The captive kept squirming, but could not get out. Santa tucked his rolled up Naughty and Nice list under one arm. "Thank you all. I'll start checking these names, see who deserves to be sentenced to the North Pole for a few years."

"*Sentenced* to the North Pole?" Robin said.

"Oh-ho-ho, this list doesn't just show me who gets presents and who doesn't. The naughtiest of the naughty have to help me spread holiday cheer. Parents write me, too, you know. 'Dear Santa, please help me with my child who keeps acting out.' We have a community-service program up at the Pole, where naughty children can learn good behavior by doing good works." He had a twinkle in his eye. "There's a long waiting list, but our success rate is remarkable."

"Except for Elfis," I said.

"Some nuts are harder to crack than others, but a few days of shoveling out the reindeer stables usually makes them a little more cooperative."

Moving with supernaturally swift footsteps, Santa stalked around the factory floor, grabbing the cowering hench-elves one by one and stuffing them into his sack, which was obviously much larger inside than it was on the outside. It needed to be. How else could it hold a world's worth of toys?

With the bulging, squirming load over his shoulder, he turned to Robin, McGoo, and me. "I'll let you free the children." He turned to the shackled waifs on the now-still production lines. "Ho-ho-ho! Have you all learned to be nice instead of naughty?"

A chorus of the enslaved kids affirmed that they had indeed learned their lessons. Some, including Buddy, even volunteered to do community-service work up at the North Pole—after they recovered back home with their loving families.

Santa went to the coal furnace, shifted his heavy sack. "I won't forget you on Christmas morning, Mr. Chambeaux. Or you either, Ms. Deyer, or Officer McGoohan. And now, Merry Christmas to all, and to all a good"—he pushed down his black glove so he could double-check the time on his wristwatch—"a good night." He tossed the squirming bag ahead of him into the mouth of the furnace, touched the side of his nose, and vanished up the smokestack.

"Elfis has left the building," I said. "But the kids are still here."

The three of us spent the better part of an hour freeing the natural and unnatural children from their shackles. When Robin unlocked his chains, Buddy Tannenbaum threw himself into her arms. "Thank you, thank you! Can you take me back to my Mom and Dad now?"

"You'll be home for Christmas," I promised.

For a lot of families, it would be a happy holiday season, except perhaps for those who had ordered their gifts from Elfis Industries and were expecting delivery by Christmas Eve Eve....

While McGoo called for backup to shut down the factory and secure the crime scene, Robin took down names and developed a plan to reunite the kids with their parents. I called the Tannenbaums directly, and Buddy's parents rushed right down. It was a wonderful reunion, with the werewolf kid nuzzling his parents and promising he would be good.

10

It was Christmas morning in the Chambeaux & Deyer offices—and we found surprise gifts waiting for us, brightly wrapped in colorful paper with holly leaves and berries, wreaths, and little snowmen. Since we didn't have a chimney, Santa could only have delivered the presents by breaking-and-entering, but I wasn't going to press charges.

"Looks like Santa was true to his promise," I said.

Grinning, Sheyenne brought the gifts into the conference room. "If you can't trust Santa to keep a promise, who can you trust?"

I hadn't put anything on my wish list, but Santa Claus was supposed to know exactly what a person wanted or needed. I had to admit I was curious.

"You first, Robin." I nudged the thin, rectangular box with her name on it. As a lawyer, Robin tried to remain cool and businesslike, but I could see the sparkle in her brown eyes as she tugged the ribbon aside, and politely worked at the tape. When she couldn't get it unwrapped, she used a letter opener to slash the paper with all the finesse of a well-practiced serial killer.

Inside was a single yellow legal pad and a sharpened No. 2 pencil. Her excitement dimmed, though she remained smiling. "I can certainly use these. And not every lawyer gets to use a pencil and legal pad from Santa himself."

"There's a note," I pointed out.

Robin pulled a slip of holly-fringed stationery from behind the second yellow sheet, skimmed the hand-written note, then read aloud as her smile grew. "'I don't normally give magical gifts—I don't want to establish a present precedent, but I am so grateful for your efforts. After checking my list and the footnotes I made throughout the year, Robin, I know that your work delights you more than anything else.

This special legal pad will never run out of paper, and the enchanted pencil will take notes for you so you can have your hands and mind free to concentrate on your client. Ho-ho-ho, best, S.C."

Robin's smile was wide. "I can't wait to try it out!"

Excited, Sheyenne picked up the box with her name on it. She used her poltergeist abilities to undo the bow, pull the ribbon aside, and then, giggling, ripped the wrapping paper to shreds. She opened the box to find an envelope inside—with both our names written on it.

"It's something the two of us can use, Beaux!" With luminous fingers, she opened the flap of the envelope to find an embossed, official-looking certificate inside. "Oh! An all-expense-paid romantic weekend for us at the cozy North Pole Winter Wonderland Bed and Breakfast! Off-season only, it says."

"Now that has definite possibilities," I said, imagining a wonderful time away with my girlfriend. We would have to be creative to overcome the supernatural difficulties that precluded us from touching, but I was up to the challenge.

"Open yours, Dan." Robin handed me the very small box with my name on it.

Judging by the size, I thought it might be a new pair of cufflinks or a tie clip, but who was I to doubt Santa's wisdom or imagination? Zombie fingers are not the most adept at unwrapping small gift boxes, and Santa's elves had used way too much tape, but I managed.

I opened a hinged, velvet-covered box to reveal a small plastic cylinder labeled "Magic Lip Gloss. Use Sparingly." I wasn't disappointed so much as confused, not sure what Santa had been thinking. "Lip gloss?"

Sheyenne made a delighted sound and snatched the tube out of the box. "I think it's for me, Beaux—and that means it's for you." She popped off the cap, extended the lip gloss, and applied it to her widening smile. "A special film for my ghostly lips that might just allow a kiss...."

She leaned closer, but I told her to wait. "Just a minute, let's do this right." I slipped a hand into my jacket pocket and withdrew the wadded and prickly tumbleweed ball of the McMistletoe artificial substitute that Elfis had been trying to bring to market. I raised it up over my head. "This is supposed to be as good as mistletoe."

Robin was skeptical. "With all the quality that we've come to expect from Elfis Industries?"

Sheyenne's lips glistened invitingly from the magic lip gloss. Under the McMistletoe, she came very close, and her ectoplasmic lips brushed against mine. Yes, I definitely felt a warm tingle.

"I think it works just fine," she said.

Look past the tinsel, trimmed trees and wrapping paper, and you'll see holidays are bound by family. Secrets, tricks and lies can break these bonds, however, in ways no festive Holiday dinner can mend.

Nina Hoffman's supernatural tale deftly explores such a tangled web of familial tension, and shows that "close knit" can have several—sometimes ominous—meanings.

—KO

CLOSE KNIT

Nina Kiriki Hoffman

C ome on, Melly. Let me spend Christmas day with you and the kids," Leo said into his cell phone. "I promise I'll bring presents, and I won't bring any of our regular arguments."

"What, you have a whole new set?" asked Melissa from the house they used to share on the other side of town.

Leo leaned back against the frilly-shammed pillows his mother had layered against the bed's headboard in what used to be his childhood room. His mother took cushions to an extreme. There was so much padding in his parents' house you often couldn't find the furniture beneath.

Since he moved out at eighteen to marry Melissa, his mother had turned his old room into a guestroom for someone who loved ruffles, country patterns, the scent of lavender, and no actual contact with dirt. Leo didn't like any of those things, but his room was the one his mother turned into a guest room. His older brother Rick's room had become a sewing room, and his older brother Andy's room had turned into a study for his dad. When he moved back in following the separation, he ended up in his new old room.

In his parents' house, he was in his mother's power, which made it hard to move out.

He had been hoping the split with Melissa was temporary, hoping he'd move home to her and the kids in a week. It had stretched into months.

If he couldn't go home, he needed to get out of his parents' house and live somewhere else.

Live alone. Oh, God. When he considered the prospect, the world went dark behind his eyes. He thought of his middle brother, Andy, the one they had made unmentionable after his suicide. Andy had lost his wife in childbirth, and then himself. The bond had been too strong for Andy to survive without his wife.

"I will sign a pact of nonaggression," Leo said. "Please, Melissa. You know you can trust me."

"Well," she said, and let the silence stretch. "My folks are coming for Christmas dinner at two in the afternoon. Can you be gone by then?"

"Do they hate me that much?"

"I just don't want to stress about this!"

"Okay. If I can have the morning with you and the kids, that'd be great."

"All right. See you around eight a.m."

"Roger that. Thank you, Melissa. Thank you."

"Don't screw this up, Leo."

"I won't."

She hung up. He set the phone on the bedside table and sank back against the pillow mountain. He only got to see his three kids once a week, and they kept changing while he wasn't there to see it. He never saw Melissa at all, only talked with her on the phone.

Christmas Day, he'd have another chance to collect the threads of family and reclaim his power.

In the meantime, he'd have to survive life among the marshmallows.

Leo had done what his father told him. "Don't pick the most beautiful, the most talented, the smartest, the most ambitious," Dad had said. "Find someone who doesn't have big dreams or plans."

Leo picked Melissa when they were in tenth grade. Melissa was a nice, quiet girl, no great beauty, but pleasant and pretty and thoughtful. He supported her, spent time with her, spun the bond to draw her to him. She smiled and came into his embrace.

He'd proposed when they were at the top of a Ferris wheel at the county fair their senior year in high school. He reined in all his family magic to let her make the choice without him pushing her into it. That wasn't something his father had told him to do.

Sometimes he wondered what his mother would be like if she got away from home and her husband.

Melissa thought about his proposal for a whole revolution of the Ferris wheel; she accepted the engagement ring when they reached the height again and could look out over the fairgrounds and the town, their present and future. The memory of the sweetness of their kiss, another few revolutions of the big wheel, wrapped up in each other and apart from the world around them, still warmed him.

They married right after high school. She had warmed and blossomed in his love, grown into skills that served them both well. She was a fine cook and a wonderful mother; she was skilled, too, at making comfort in every room of the house.

He had not made the mistakes of his older brother, Rick, who had chosen powerful, interesting women to wed. Rick had never established a good bond with his first wife—she was too strong-willed, too artistic, too self-motivated. They divorced after two years. Rick married another artist and lost her, too. He was on his third wife, unheard of for men in the Yates family. With each marriage, Rick's family magic grew weaker. Dad was sure Rick's third marriage would fail as well, though Leo liked Cassandra, Rick's current wife, a lawyer.

Leo worked for a courier service, shuttling blood samples from doctors' offices to labs, lumber from home improvement stores to construction sites, legal papers from lawyers to lawyers, vegetables and fruits from farms to restaurants. He spent all his time stitching things together.

His home had been the seat of his power, where he went restore himself. His family was his highest priority. He loved his children so fiercely his heart hurt, and he loved Melissa to death. She was his hearth, his place to rest in warmth and comfort after a day spent with unconnected people.

He wasn't sure when things began to unravel. Last summer, though, Melissa had kicked him out, and to his surprise, his family magic hadn't been strong enough to change her mind.

Leo and Melissa had managed their separation without involving lawyers or counselors. He spent time with each of his kids once a week.

Saturday afternoon, he picked up his oldest daughter, sixteen-year-old Piper. He parked at the curb and called her cell phone to let her know he was outside. "Okay," she said, sounding harassed. It was fifteen minutes before she slumped out of the house, her slender body disguised in a long-sleeved blue t-shirt under black corduroy overalls, one strap hanging, and a little white skull and crossbones pin attached to the other strap. Her red-brown hair hung in curly, uncombed spills. Her narrow face was flecked with dark freckles, and her red-amber eyes stared past him as she slung her backpack into the back seat and climbed into the car.

"Can we go to the movies, Dad?" Piper asked as she buckled her seatbelt.

"What do you want to see?"

She named the latest blockbuster adventure movie. Gun battles, explosions, car chases. Not his idea of a good time, but hey.

He sighed and agreed. He didn't know how to talk to Piper anymore. Ask her about school and she shrugged. Ask her what she was interested in, and she shrugged even higher. Ask her about boys, and she said, "Forget it."

Ask her about how she was doing since he left the house, and receive silence.

Melissa said Piper was going through a phase.

Leo bought popcorn and soda and sat through a lot of flash and noise beside his daughter. No talking during the movie. Afterward they went to Applebee's for dinner.

He had been holding his family magic in a nest around his heart, the tendrils tight-furled. As he watched his daughter eat prawns and salad, he unfurled the tendril that used to connect him to her, and let it touch her again. He couldn't maintain these connections over distance for prolonged times, and he didn't want to hurt his wife or children by trying.

Piper relaxed. She put down her fork and sat back and looked at him. She didn't smile, but her eyes softened.

"How are things at home?" he asked.

"Daaaad," she said.

He touched his breastbone, the place where he connected to his family.

Piper closed her eyes, then opened them. "When are you coming home?"

"Your mom and I need to work it out, Piper. I hope we can, but I still don't know what I did wrong."

"Well … you don't listen very well, Dad. Mom wants to do other things than just keep house and take care of us. She bought paints and set up the guest room as an art studio. Like, she has no clue how to paint, but she's doing it anyway, and it makes her happy. She joined some club. Like, a book club or something? They meet at the bookstore? And people come over to play cards."

Leo sat back. He felt like he'd been punched in the stomach.

"She could still do that with you at home, if you didn't, like, smother her."

"Okay, Piper. Thanks. Thanks for telling me."

"Yeah, and I thought I was good at shutting up." She frowned ferociously. "This sucks."

Leo stroked his breastbone, relaxing the nudge to talk he'd put on her, but not letting go of the connection.

They walked the mall after dinner. He needed to find her a present for Christmas; he pinned his hopes for the future on Christmas morning. He tried to watch what she looked at while they were window-shopping, but her preferred mode was stealth and secrets, so whenever she noticed him noticing, she looked somewhere else.

She hugged him when he dropped her off at the house, and he gently pulled his connection back inside, then sat in the car parked at the curb.

He and Melly had bought the house when she was pregnant with Piper. They had looked at a lot of houses when they knew it was time to give up apartment living and make room for kids. This one had a master bedroom with its own bathroom, and four other bedrooms.

"You think we're going to need all these rooms?" Melly had asked. "I'm not having twins, you know."

"I know," he said, "but who knows what the future holds?" and she had laughed, and they made a down payment.

The house had been in terrible shape when they bought it. He'd really enjoyed working on it, weaving nest magic into plumbing and electricity, spackle and paint, floorboards and linoleum. He asked her about color choices and textures, and followed her taste in everything.

They had been happy here together.

The light was on in the living room behind the blue curtains. He imagined the three kids and Melly curled up on the couch, watching TV together.

But there were other cars in the driveway. Maybe this was a game night, and Melly was at the dining room table with people he didn't know, enjoying herself.

He wanted to reach out to her. Just the lightest touch, and he would know how she felt, and maybe what she was doing. When he was still living at home, that knowledge had buoyed him through his days.

He hadn't known how she felt, though, when she was working her way up to kicking him out, despite their constant connection. How had he missed it?

He stared at the light behind the curtains. Life was going on inside without him. He couldn't reach out to Melly. He didn't feel he had the right anymore.

He clenched his hands against his breastbone, then started the car and drove to the library. He read magazines until closing, putting off the return to his parents' house as long as possible. He read through the newspaper, too, looking at apartment listings and fantasizing about renting his own place.

Ultimately, his mother's pull was too strong. Over the fifty-two years of his parents' marriage, the family magic had mostly shifted from his father to his mother, since she wanted and used it more. A constant bond between two people was also a conduit for power; it ended up going both ways if it lasted long enough.

"Is that you, Leo?" his mother called from the living room as he came in the front door. Even the foyer was somehow pillowy, maybe because she had hung pastel quilts on the walls. That lavender scent was heavy all through the house.

"Who else?" Leo said. He sighed and stepped through the foyer.

Father was in his study with the door closed, but Mom was in the living room watching the Food Channel and lying in wait. He wished he'd never moved back in. A week he could stand, but months....

In the living room, his mother, trim and gaunt-cheeked, stiff in her beige Nordstrom's loungewear, sat upright on the couch, slippered feet together, back straight, though the cushions slumped behind her, inviting relaxation.

She muted the TV and said, "I made dinner. I set a place for you. If you're going to miss dinner, you need to tell me."

"Mom, you knew it was my afternoon with Piper."

"Afternoon ends before eight-thirty, Leonard."

"We ate at Applebee's after the movie."

She breathed out loudly through her nose, then said, "Well, now that you're home, we can have checkers." She flexed her family magic, crushing his resistance.

He spent the rest of the evening on a frilly chair at the game table in the living room, losing every game.

Sunday, he stopped by Melissa's house to pick up Kaylee, his eleven-year-old daughter, and Riley, his fourteen-year-old son, who both wanted to go to the Natural History Museum. They were on the sidewalk in front of the house when he pulled up. Kaylee, short, blond, and blue-eyed, expressionless in a way he wasn't used to, was bundled up in a big bone-white sweater, jeans, and fleece-edged brown Ugg boots. Riley, taller, thin, with shaggy blond hair and clear brown eyes, wore jeans and a black hoodie with white skeleton bones on it. His shoulders hunched.

Leo put his fist to his chest and let himself connect to his kids. They came to the car and climbed in, Riley in the front seat next to Leo, and Kaylee in the back. She always rode in the back, it occurred to him. He watched her in the mirror, and felt her in his chest. She seemed to have a big square box inside her, with a tight shut lid that she guarded. He glanced at Riley and listened to what his connection told him about his son. Riley was mixed up, full of something he wanted and feared to say.

If Leo pushed energy through the link, he could get his kids to open up. In the past, he hadn't hesitated. This time, he held back.

They had visited the Natural History Museum countless times. Kaylee's favorite exhibit was the bird nests, old glass-topped cases in a huge room with many, many bird nests in each, most with eggs in them. She loved the different colors of the eggs, some blue, white, yellow, teal, some with spots and freckles, some plain. There was a hummingbird nest on a loop of rope, and some of the shorebird nests were just a couple twigs on a flat rock. Kaylee could contemplate nests for hours. Leo listened in just a little. She imagined herself inside the eggs, with a giant, feathered mother or father resting against her and keeping her safe and warm.

He had heard this fantasy before. Today it was louder and sharper.

"Dad," said Riley.

"Riley." He turned to his son as Kaylee wandered farther away.

"I have to talk."

"Let's sit down." They walked to a bench against the wall and sat where he could keep an eye on Kaylee.

"Dad, I've been wanting to I've been waiting to—Dad—"

Leo waited. They both sat, staring toward Kaylee. Leo had just the lightest connection to Riley. He wondered whether he should boost it to find out what Riley was trying to tell him. He used to do that all the time. Lately, he'd been wondering if that was such a good idea.

"Dad, I think I'm gay."

Leo stared at the floor. Dismay swamped him, and a storm of thoughts he wanted to edit out as they swarmed through his mind— so there's my legacy gone to a dead end, people will hate my son and hurt him because he's different, he's not the same to me anymore either, what do I do now? How could this happen? Whose fault is it? Why Riley, why me?—

He touched his sternum and listened to what Riley hadn't said aloud. Riley had been sitting on a volcano, and now he was swallowed up in a cloud of dark gray fear and despair.

Leo took Riley's hand. He leaned back, holding his son's hand, and let his mind relax, let the whirling thoughts fade. When he felt calm, he said, "Okay."

"I wish I wasn't. I've been trying to make it change, but it doesn't. I thought if I didn't ever say it out loud, it would go away, but it didn't."

"How long have you been struggling with this?"

Riley looked away. Leo waited.

"About two years," Riley said at last. "There's a guy at school, we've been in the same classes for a couple years, and I had a crush on him, kinda, but I knew he'd hate me if I did anything about it, and—and the other guys are all talking about girls, but—I don't feel—I—"

Leo squeezed his hand. "It's all right, Riley. It's okay. It's—it's natural, and you're not alone." Two years? Two years, and Leo had been living in the same house with him for one and a half of those years, connected through family magic, and hadn't noticed this dark cloud wrapping around his son. Maybe he was losing his magic, too, the way his brother Rick had.

Riley sighed. They sat side by side, Leo holding Riley's hand, until Kaylee was through looking at bird nests. "Let's go to the hall of minerals," she said.

Leo stood up and tugged Riley to his feet. His son was almost as tall as he was. Fear and guilt still thrummed through the boy. Leo pulled his son into a hug. "Hey. You're a fine kid. Nothing wrong with you. Got it?"

"No," said Riley, muffled, speaking to Leo's shoulder, his arms tight around his father. Then he laughed.

"We can work on that." Leo thumped him on the back and let go. They could work on it … when Leo had visits with the kids. Or if he moved home. Or, he supposed, on the phone, if it came down to it. He needed to get online and do some research, find out what Riley was likely to need and how to help him. "Call me anytime if you need help. Does your mom know?"

"I didn't tell her, but I think she—sometimes she—I don't know."

Leo felt a glow at the thought that Riley had told him first, then tried to tamp it down. "We can worry about that later. Right now, we've got some rocks to visit."

"Yeah. Okay." Riley rubbed his eyes with his fists. Leo patted his back again, and they followed Kaylee to the hall of minerals.

Riley was calmer, smiling, when Leo dropped him and Kaylee off at the house later that afternoon.

The locked box inside of Kaylee was jiggling and jumping. The lid rattled as if something inside was trying to scratch its way out.

Wednesday was Christmas Day. At eight a.m., Leo parked in front of the house. The front lawn was still frosty with last night's freeze, and his breath puffed out of him, little clouds that spun and vanished. The trees were bare-branched black. He grabbed the shopping bags of presents and headed up the walk to the front door. If this Christmas was like others, the kids would have been up at least two hours already. He'd missed the big Christmas Eve dinner. In the past, Melissa had spent the whole day preparing and cooking for it, and his parents had come; it was the only time of the year they would be civil and not try to take over his family from him, because Melissa made everything perfect, from the turkey to the holiday centerpiece. This year, he'd spent Christmas Eve with his parents in their padded house, eating boneless turkey breast and soggy sweet potato casserole, his father's favorites. He wondered if Melissa had invited any of her new friends over for Christmas Eve.

He hadn't helped Melissa with the tree this year, or the do stockings. Every year, they decorated the tree on Christmas Eve, after the children went to sleep, so the kids would be surprised when they came downstairs the next morning. Every year, Leo had been the one to sneak into the kids' rooms and lay the stockings at the feet of their beds.

Melissa opened the door to his ring and offered him an unguarded smile, the bright, wide smile she used to give him when he came home after a long day at work, the smile of someone happy to see him. Heat bloomed in his chest, and his family magic unfurled, reaching out to her and the kids without his even willing it. He so wanted to hug her right into his heart.

Her smile faded and she stepped back without a word, leaving the way open.

He closed his eyes and retracted his magic. When he looked again, Melissa smiled faintly. "Come in."

"Thanks." He edged past her. Something strange had just happened. She knew. She knew when he connected to her, and when he disconnected. Maybe that was why she never came to the door when he stopped by to pick up the kids.

"Breakfast?" he asked.

"Already over."

He smiled and headed for the living room.

The tree was big, with dense green needles. It scented the room with pine. Pale, pearly glass balls and tinsel shone, flashing in the flickering white lights that nestled in the branches. The tree was loaded with candy canes and gilded pinecones. It looked like something in a magazine. A fire blazed in the fireplace, and the stacks of presents around the tree were wrapped with Melissa's usual flair. She was a master of ribbon bows and invisible tape.

Last year they had laughed together and shushed each other while they decorated the tree. The tree had looked more like a collaboration, maybe a drunken one. And they had had multicolored lights, his favorite; Melissa always wanted white lights.

Riley, Piper, and Kaylee sat on the couch, looking at him. He hesitated, wondering if anybody would hug him. No one got up. After all, he'd seen them only a couple days ago. He smiled at them. "Hey, guys. How about if I'm Santa this year?"

Each year, one of the family was the designated Santa, handing out gifts to everyone. It had started with him and Melissa when the kids were small, but last year Riley had done it, and the year before, Piper. One gift for each person, and a pause while everybody opened the presents and showed them to each other, and then Santa handed out another round of gifts.

"Okay, Daddy," said Kaylee.

Leo let the thinnest tendrils touch the children. They were all excited and a little worried. Kaylee, especially, was agitated, and that box inside her was jumpy. Nobody was mad he was usurping the Santa role. He glanced at Melissa, his head cocked.

She smiled and nodded.

"Okay. Let's see what we have." He unloaded his presents from the cloth shopping bags he'd brought them in, one gift for each of the children and a big present for Melissa. He'd save those for Round Two. He picked a present for each person from Melissa's perfect pile and handed them around. He had wondered if there would be gifts for him, as awkward and strange as the separation had been. But there were.

Kaylee ripped paper off her present. An iPod, with headphones. She crowed with delight.

Riley untaped his gift carefully and folded the green foil paper before seeing what he got—three classical music CDs.

Piper opened one end of her parcel and slid the inside out: a knit hat in black with white skull and crossbones. She pulled it onto her head until it covered her from the eyebrows up and said, "Thanks, Mom!"

Melissa sat with her present in her lap. It was one of a few under the tree wrapped sloppily, hidden behind Melissa's showcase presents. He'd had to hunt to find a present for her. It was from Kaylee.

Melissa unwrapped Kaylee's crumpled purple tissue paper and held up a small clay dragon.

"I made it in material arts class," Kaylee said.

"I love it!" Melissa said.

Leo's present was small, wrapped in gold foil. A gift from Melissa. He opened it. A utilitarian pair of steel handcuffs. Confused, he stared down at them and wondered why he felt cold. Then he wondered if Melissa had new ideas about sex she wanted to share. He looked up at her, and she flushed and stared at the floor. Sex? He reached out. He had to know.

His tendril touched her and she hunched her shoulders, then stared up at him, her gaze intense.

So, she wasn't looking for bondage games. She was sending a message.

She saw him as handcuffs. Somehow, she knew about family magic.

He pulled back, chilled.

"Gah, Mom, what is that about?" Piper asked, staring at the handcuffs. "Maybe I don't want to know."

Riley and Kaylee looked up from their presents. Leo slid the handcuffs into a back pocket, out of sight. He rose, smiling. "Next round."

He handed around the presents he had brought. His chest felt tight. Six months since he'd spent more than a few hours a week with them, and everybody had changed. His understanding of them had changed, too; now he felt like he didn't know any of them very well. What if he'd gotten everything wrong?

For himself, he got a lumpy, purple-tissue-wrapped present from Kaylee. He set it in his lap and sat, his fingers digging into his knees, as he waited for verdicts. Light, light touch on the children, just so he'd know what they really thought.

"Gee," said Riley, "I have absolutely no idea what this is." He ripped paper off the basketball and held it like a globe in front of him, staring at it as though he'd never touched a basketball before.

When Riley was ten, he and Leo spent a lot of time after Leo got off work shooting baskets through a rim Leo had attached above the garage. One day the ball had deflated. Leo had patched it, but it didn't hold air anymore, and somehow he'd let it go, and lost the close connection to Riley. Maybe that was why he hadn't known Riley was having such a tough time.

"So, what, you want me to be a jock now?" Riley said, his voice monotonal. Despair and bitter disappointment flowed along Leo's connection to him.

"No! No. I just thought maybe we could get back to playing horse." Of course, that would be hard if he wasn't living here.

Riley's eyes narrowed. He bounced the ball once and set it on the couch next to him.

"Daaaaad," Piper said, holding up the necklace he had bought for her. The pendant was a pink enamel heart with a Swarovski crystal in the center.

She likes skulls and black corduroy, he thought. Another big mistake. "I'm sorry. I saved the receipt. You can trade it in."

Her eyes narrowed and her mouth flattened. She tucked the necklace into her jeans pocket, though it had come in a nice velvet case. Leo felt hollow.

Kaylee pulled paper from her odd-shaped gift, frowning. "What is this?" she asked, and held up the wire frames with glittering, lacy yellow cloth stretched across them.

"Fairy wings," he said.

"What? You think I'm still six years old?"

"I think you're magic," he said, and then the box inside her leaped and dropped and the lid popped open and a cable shot from her into his chest, and he gasped as it hooked into him.

HOW DID YOU KNOW? Kaylee's voice roared inside him.

"Oh, Kaylee," he said, his voice coming out high and twisted.

She pulled on her cable and he slid from the couch to the floor. He clapped a hand to his breastbone, trying to break the connection before it strangled him.

HOW DID THAT WORK? I NEVER DID THAT BEFORE. HOW DO I STOP IT?

"Come here, honey," he whispered, and she came and knelt next to him. "You talk to it, ask it to let go and come home to you."

GET BACK HERE, she thought furiously.

The tugging in his chest lifted him a couple inches off the ground. He coughed, and said, "Not like that. First you have to relax. Then ask nicely. Take a deep breath, let it out, take another, let it out. Okay, honey?"

"Leo, what are you doing?" Melissa asked.

"Uh—" He stared up at his daughter, who was staring back, her eyes wide, looking through him as she drew in deep breaths and let them out. LET GO, she thought. OKAY, LET GO OF DAD AND—COME BACK.

Her connection unhooked and pulled back into her. Leo thunked to the ground as Kaylee heaved a huge sigh. Then she threw herself on him and started crying. "I'm sorry, Daddy. I'm sorry."

He stroked her back and said, "It's okay. It's okay. It'll be all right, honey. I can help you with this." So Kaylee ended up with the family magic. He wondered if Riley or Piper had, too. It didn't always transfer, and Kaylee was pretty young to manifest. She had manifested more strongly than anybody he'd ever known.

She would need his help dealing with this. He needed to start training her right away.

Or maybe after they finished opening presents.

"Leo!" Melissa said.

Piper was staring at him, her face expressionless. Riley hugged the basketball and gazed at the ceiling.

Leo pushed Kaylee back gently and sat up. "Sorry, Melly. We had a moment."

"That's not good enough. What just happened?"

Leo looked down into Kaylee's face. Her eyes were bright with tears. "I think we need to talk about that," he said slowly. Kaylee was going to have to learn to handle what she had, and that didn't happen overnight. Melissa would need information. Leo needed to tell her, maybe everything. "Could we do it later?"

Melissa looked at Piper and Riley, then at Leo. "You're going to explain?" she asked.

"Yes. I want to tell you."

"I want to know." She sounded fierce. "Later." She nodded. "Tonight."

"Good." He climbed back onto the couch, tugging Kaylee to sit beside him, and unwrapped the present Kaylee had made for him. It was another clay creation, this time a purple octopus. He touched his breastbone, thinking about unfolding tendrils, and how they could be thought of as tentacles. Kaylee rubbed her fist against her breastbone, too. "Thanks, baby," he said. "I love it. I'll keep it on my desk."

She hugged his head, then went back to the kids' couch and slid her arms through the straps of the fairy wings, settling them on her back. She looked adorable. Then she scowled, and looked adorable and grumpy.

"Open your present, Mom," Riley said.

Melissa set the heavy rectangular package on her lap. It was wrapped in paper with little Santas running all over. She lifted the taped edges gently enough not to tear anything, and discovered a stained and varnished wooden paint box. She gasped, then unlatched the lid and looked inside. "Oh, Leo," she said, her voice full of wonder. The box had compartments inside stocked with brushes, wipes, and tubes of the best acrylics he could find, burnt sienna, cobalt blue, cadmium red and yellow, dioxazine purple, and other, more fanciful colors—poodleskirt pink, moon yellow, mint julep green. The lid had grooves in it, and he had slid some stretched canvases into them.

When she looked up at him, her eyes shone.

"I know I can't fix everything overnight," he said.

"You got that right."

"I'd like a chance to try."

She closed the paint box and latched the lid. "It can't be like before."

He thought of his mother and father, the magic bond they'd formed, and how it strangled him. How his father's magic had shifted into his mother over the years, and what she did with it. He didn't want to turn into a parent like the ones he had. Maybe Rick was the smart one, marrying people he couldn't use family magic on, letting his powers wither. "You're right. You're so right."

"Trial period. Understand?"

"Melly," he said. He hugged her, her warmth and prickliness and smell of mint shampoo and waffles, and felt hope for the first time in too long.

When we humans go to the stars, we'll take our holidays with us—and why not? They pack easily, and will comfort us through that cold black trek into the night; they will reaffirm our origins.

Initially, at any rate. But each colony will evolve to reflect its new habits, habitats, and technologies. Holidays will change, too—but Joy to the World—not in the most important ways.

—KO

ASTRONAUT NICK

Brad R. Torgersen

e'll be here," the red-haired girl said as she looked out the bubble window of the classroom's south wall.

"Nah, my older brother says Astronaut Nick is a fake," said the blue-eyed boy with the curly brown hair. He too was looking out the bubble window.

Jimmy Carrico wasn't sure who he believed. At age nine, he didn't want to appear too credulous in front of the older kids. After all, what could anyone say about the legend of a red-suited space man who was supposed to be flying all the way from Earth to deliver gifts to the children of Olympus Mons Colony?

"Your older brother just wants to spoil the fun," the red-haired girl said, turning her head to make a disapproving frown at the blue-eyed boy.

Jimmy hadn't been on Mars long enough to have learned too many names. Mostly he kept quiet, did his schoolwork as best as he was able, and endured the inevitable rude comments. It was bad enough trying to learn to function in Mars' heavier gravity, but trying to do it and save face in front of the other kids at the same time, was often an impossible task.

"He'll come riding in his rocket sled," said the red-haired girl. "Him and his crew of elves."

The blue-eyed boy snorted.

"He's never come before," he said. "What's so different that suddenly he'd show up now?"

"That," the girl said, pointing outside the bubble window.

The salmon-colored sky had faded to gray, and little ice crystals were gradually floating down to land on the brownish-red landscape below—Martian snow being the dividend of the work which had brought the Carrico family to Mars in the first place.

Every year, the Mars Terraforming Project needed more people, and every year those people hurled more comets into Mars' upper atmosphere. Enough to begin changing Mars' climate so that moisture was able to condense out of the air—especially in the higher elevations. Since Olympus Mons colony was dug into the foothills of the biggest extinct volcano in the solar system, and the volcano got dusted on a regular basis these days, the children had a front row seat for what their parents claimed was history in the making.

"Big whoop," said the blue-eyed boy, who turned away from the window and sauntered back to where some other boys were gathered to eat their noon meal.

Jimmy stared out the window, watching the little white flakes fall. There weren't many. In fact, it was hard to believe that something so small could turn the ground white in a single afternoon. But it had happened twice before in two previous weeks, and now it was happening again.

"He'll come," the girl said to Jimmy, nodding her head earnestly.

"What makes you so sure?" Jimmy said cautiously, sliding off of his chair and walking to stand near the girl—both of their faces pushed into the bubble window so that they could look around.

"Before my Grandma died," said the red-haired girl, "she told me about Saint Nicholas."

"Who?" Jimmy asked.

"You ever hear of Father Christmas?" the red-haired girl asked.

"I don't think so. Is this a story from Earth?"

"It is," the red-haired girl said. "At the end of every Earth year, Saint Nicholas rides through the sky in his sleigh, bringing gifts to all the good children."

"Sounds like a fairytale," Jimmy said.

The little girl scowled.

"Why do boys always have to ruin everything?" she said.

"Sorry," Jimmy replied, feeling sheepish. "I guess I have a hard time believing in anyone who rides a sleigh through the sky. I've seen pictures of earth. I know what a sleigh looks like. They can't get off the ground."

"But Astronaut Nick's sleigh has rockets," she said. "And when he comes, he'll bring things for all of us. Well, all of us who believe in him anyway."

Jimmy considered. It was an enticing idea. He hadn't been able to bring much from Ceres. The family's small quarters in Olympus Mons were barren—their crates not yet arrived via bulk freighter—and while video games and other three-dee entertainments could be had in plentiful quantities, there were times when Jimmy missed being able to hold an actual toy in his hands.

Why had they moved, again? Jimmy could still remember how excited his parents had been. The whole family would be partaking in the greatest engineering project of the age. The robot scouts sent to retrieve the comets from the Kuiper Belt would keep bringing them until Mars had been rendered inhabitable. The Carrico family would be helping to prepare the surface. It might take decades, or even centuries. But there would come a day when there'd be no need for habitats. The air would be like Earth air, and it would be thick and warm enough to go outside without suits—something Jimmy had never done on Mars, and not on Ceres either.

Ceres. On Ceres, Jimmy had real friends. On Ceres, he could fly down the corridors and across the gym, at the merest push of his toes. Stuck on Mars, Jimmy plodded and sweated, his cheeks pink, and his muscles and joints complaining. The doctor said it was normal, for children born in the asteroid belt—that Jimmy would get used to it. But the longer Jimmy endured the struggle, the more he hated it. And hated the fact that his parents had applied for emigration from Ceres in the first place.

"Does Astronaut Nick only bring toys?" Jimmy asked.

"Astronaut Nick brings you whatever you wish for," the girl said.

Jimmy frowned, and slowly pulled his head out of the bubble.

The girl stared at him.

"Why does that make you sad?" she asked.

"Nevermind," Jimmy said, turning to leave.

"Wait!" she said. "You're new, but you don't talk to people. What's your name? You can at least tell me your name."

"James," he sighed.

"That's probably what your Mom calls you," she said. "What do *you* call you?"

"Jimmy," he said, looking back at her over his shoulder.

She smiled at him—her eyes lighting up pleasantly.

"That was my Great Grandpa's name," she said. "I like that. My name's Tessa."

"Hello," Jimmy said, still looking over his shoulder. She seemed to be waiting for him to say more to her.

He merely turned and walked out of the room, his feet slapping painfully hard on the deck.

The next day, Tessa found Jimmy eating by himself.

"Mind if I sit here?" Tessa asked.

"No," Jimmy said, not looking up from his tray of microwaved turkey and beans.

"Did I make you mad?" she asked, setting down her own tray.

"What?" he asked.

"Yesterday, when you left. It seemed like I made you mad."

"No," Jimmy said. "It's just that … I'd like to believe this Astronaut Nick guy can help me, but I *don't* believe it."

"Why not?" she said sharply.

"It sounds to me like one of those things parents tell to little kids, that always wind up not being true."

"Well if you don't believe in him," Tessa said, "of *course* he's not going to be true. Astronaut Nick doesn't bring presents to doubters."

Jimmy closed his eyes, remembering how delightful it had been on Ceres, flying through the sports chambers with his friends as they played Wall Ball. You had to be good with angles, and you had to learn how hard to throw the ball to get it to carom just right, while not throwing so hard that you flipped yourself completely around. Teams of Wall Ball players could use each others' inertia to make shots at the goal without spinning out of control. Of course, if the other teams were equally good at working together, they could use their inertia to deflect the ball and make return shots. Players would hang onto each others' ankles, knees and elbow interlocked, all of them pirouetting as a unit …

"Did you hear me?" Tessa said, her voice quiet, breaking his reverie.

Jimmy looked up at her.

"Okay, so Nick doesn't bring gifts for doubter," he said, perhaps a bit harder than he'd wanted.

"No need to be rude," she said. "I don't make up the rules."

"That doesn't matter," Jimmy said. "Nobody can help me anyway. Here on Mars … they hardly ever let us go outside, and I'm *heavy* no matter where I go, and always dropping things or bumping into stuff, and our quarters are *small* and my friends are all far away, and I won't ever get to see them again."

"Maybe you can make … new friends?" Tessa said.

Jimmy stared at his spork, then plunged it into the turkey on his plate, carved off a hunk of the meat, and stuck the hunk into his mouth.

When Jimmy didn't speak further, Tessa's smile slowly disappeared.

"Astronaut Nick comes the night of December 24," she said primly.

"That's in … four days?" Jimmy guessed.

"Two," she said. "Olympus Mons uses the New Solar Calendar like all the other off-Earth colonies and stations, but I have an app on my desk computer that stays synchronized to the old Earth calendar."

"What will he bring you, if you're right?" Jimmy asked.

Now it was Tessa's turn to be circumspect. She poked at her beef strips covered in brown gravy.

"I'm keeping my wish a secret," she said. "Supposedly if you keep it secret, there's a better chance it might come true."

"Then how is Astronaut Nick ever supposed to find out what you want?" Jimmy asked, somewhat exasperated. He'd put his spork down and was staring across the table, directly into Tessa's face. Her red hair fell across her forehead and partially obscured his view.

"Send him an e-mail," Tessa said.

"Astronaut Nick has e-mail?"

"Of course," Tessa said, as if it were common knowledge.

"Did you e-mail him what you want?" Jimmy asked.

"Not yet. I am trying to figure out how to word it just right. I'm using the school house net to do it. You can do the same."

Jimmy thought about it. The whole idea sounded highly improbable. But the earnestness of Tessa's words, the seriousness of her expression, had him halfway convinced.

"Can you share that e-mail?" Jimmy asked.

"Sure!" Tessa said, sitting up and grinning. "After lunch, come over to my desk and I will type it into a message I'll send to you, and then you can use it to type your own message."

"Seems like short notice," Jimmy said. "I mean, two days. How can he possibly be ready to deliver anything without knowing far enough ahead of time? When my parents moved us from Ceres we knew months in advance that we were coming to live here, and the Olympus Mons people knew months in advance, too."

"You just have to trust him," Tessa said. "Astronaut Nick won't let you down. If you've not been making trouble, and if you believe hard enough, Astronaut Nick will keep his promises."

They ate quickly and in silence for the rest of the meal break, Jimmy's head beginning to spin with the imagined possibilities.

The following day, Jimmy used all of his recess and lunch period to compose his note to Astronaut Nick. The address Tessa had given Jimmy seemed as legitimate as any, and since Tessa said she'd sent hers off in the morning, Jimmy felt compelled to get his sent as quickly as possible.

Only, he agonized over how to phrase his request. Composition had never been Jimmy's strong suit, and every time he thought he had his message put together in a coherent fashioned, he saved it as a draft, came back to look at it later, and realized he wanted to change everything around.

Finally, as the school day came to a close, he pestered his teacher into letting him have an extra twenty minutes at his desk. He erased everything he'd written previously, typed in three succinct sentences, and clicked the SEND button on the message header, watching it vanish from his desk screen.

Jimmy went home that night, exhausted, and slept more fitfully than usual. Which was saying something, since Jimmy had not enjoyed a solid night's rest since coming to Olympus Mons.

The next day, Tessa and Jimmy kept an eye on each other, but didn't talk much. If there were other kids in their class who'd also sent e-mail to Astronaut Nick, nobody was saying so openly. Jimmy definitely got the impression that the older children found the whole idea preposterous, and this meant the younger kids were keeping a low profile—whether they actually believed in Astronaut Nick, or not.

Finally, when the day was over, and people were headed out the door to go find their parents in one of Olympus Mons' many and various work labs, Tessa and Jimmy met in the same window bubble where they'd had their first conversation a few days before.

The tiny white water crystals were falling again. This time in what seemed to be record quantity. The rock and soil outside had already begun to turn white, and Tessa watched the natural display with a look of rapt fascination on her face.

"My Mom says that the snow on Earth gets so thick, you can ski on it," Tessa said.

"What's *ski* mean?" Jimmy asked.

"People go up in the mountains and put these long, thin, springy boards on their feet, and they sort of coast down the mountain riding on nothing but the snow."

"It's that deep?"

"Meters deep," Tessa said.

"Wow," Jimmy said, trying to imagine just how much snow would have to fall in order for it to heaped around the walls of their classroom to that level. He couldn't quite bring himself to believe it was possible, though he'd certainly seen the pictures of the great mountain ranges on Earth, such as the Grand Tetons and the Himalayas. If the snow didn't melt every summer season, it would build up over thousands of years to form giant bodies of ice called *glaciers.*

Mars had some permanent ice at its poles, which Jimmy had also seen in pictures. But compared to some of Earth's glaciers, Martian ice was puny. Though, maybe, if the terraforming worked as planned, that wouldn't be true forever? Jimmy tried to imagine the slopes of Olympus Mons having enough snow on them for riding down, using nothing but a pair of thin boards strapped to the bottoms of his feet.

"Are you going to wait up to see him?" Jimmy asked.

"Who?" Tessa asked.

"Astronaut Nick," Jimmy said.

"No, that's a bad idea," Tessa said. "Grandma says that you have to be asleep when Astronaut Nick visits, or you're going to get passed by. He knows when you're asleep, and when you're awake."

"How?" Jimmy asked.

"I don't know," Tessa said. "But he does."

Jimmy kept staring at the falling snow.

"I hope you get what you want," he told Tessa honestly, letting his mind drift over the brief words he'd written in his message.

"I hope you get what you want too," Tessa said.

They exited the bubble window and went to find their separate families.

That night, Jimmy was even more restless than usual. He tossed and turned in his little bunk, his mind trying to unravel the trick of how any astronaut could land at Olympus Mons in a rocket sleigh, sneak into the center living complex without being seen, and leave gifts for those children who'd written him to ask for something. Tessa had told Jimmy that the old Earth legend of Saint Nicholas supposedly had the man sliding down the chimneys of fireplaces—in order to lay packages and toys beneath decorated conifer trees brought specifically into the house for the occasion.

Jimmy found the idea of trying to fit down something as narrow or as filthy as a chimney—the school library said it was equivalent to a spaceship exhaust—unnerving at best. Wouldn't the man get claustrophobia? Wouldn't he run out of air? How could his space suit possibly fit, especially with the bulky helmet?

The more Jimmy thought about it, the more he began to suspect that the entire idea was just a lot of wishful thinking, which made him even more homesick than usual. He scrunched his head into his pillow and quietly wept, so that his parents in the next compartment would not hear him. He was too big to be like a baby. This was his hurt, and his hurt alone, to deal with. It wasn't fair that he'd had to leave Ceres, but he wasn't going to let his parents know. They certainly weren't going to change their minds—they'd talked non-stop about how exciting and wonderful Mars was.

At some point, he drifted off.

And at some point, Jimmy came wide awake again.

The hatch to his bunk compartment was slightly open, as it always was. But this time there was a different sort of light streaming in. Not the usual pale yellow of the night light that illuminated the way to the tiny family latrine, but a more subtle green and red, alternating every few seconds, like the flashing of an emergency beacon. Only those tended to be orange, and this light was much more gradual. Green, slowly dimming and transforming to red, then brightening, then dimming, slowly transforming to green, then brightening, and so on and so forth.

Jimmy watched the light for a long time, his fuzzy senses not quite able to register what the light might mean.

Then he remembered that this was supposed to be Astronaut Nick's night, and Jimmy's heart instantly quickened its pace.

Could it be...?

Jimmy had to find out. He slid carefully out of his bunk, his feet resting on the deck. He slid his slippers on and padded deftly to the hatch, cracking it open on its hinge so that he could get a better look. Across the hatchway, from the direction of the family living and dining area, the red-to-green-to-red light emanated. Jimmy stared at the closed doorway to his parents' compartment, and then at the small latrine, and then back to the open hatch to the living and eating area.

He padded forth, almost breathless in anticipation.

There was a single bubble window in the east wall of the eating and dining area that had an unobstructed view of the Olympus Mons landing facility—where the big shuttles from the orbital cargo and space liners would occasionally put down. Jimmy had ridden in just such a shuttle when they'd come down from orbit. The ship he now saw sitting on the nearest pad looked nothing like a shuttle.

It looked for all the world like an oversized sleigh—something from out of the history pictures of Earth. Only this sleigh had been extensively modified, to include a kind of canopy over the seat where a driver might sit at the front. There was no team of horses—not even reindeer, as Father Christmas was reputed to have used in legend. But the snow was falling more heavily than Jimmy had ever seen it since coming to Mars. Enough so that a little heap of it was crusted over the top of the window bubble, and the red and green running lights of the odd-looking ship on the pad reflected off a million little crystal mirrors as the flakes slowly fell.

Jimmy was transfixed. *It couldn't be. Could it?*

He had to get a closer look.

Jimmy snuck to the main hatch to the family compartment and hesitated, wondering if his exit would trip an alarm. Back on Ceres, all of the family housing had alarms that activated if ever the children left their family quarters without being cleared by a parent first.

The craft on the pad beckoned.

Jimmy touched his hand to the palm reader at the door, and the hatch slid quietly to the side, no alarm to wake Jimmy's parents.

Jimmy stepped out into the corridor beyond, his eyes still transfixed on the picture of the sleigh-like craft resting on the pad. Then the hatch slid shut, and Jimmy was left to contemplate whether what he'd just seen was real, or illusion.

He walked softly—but quickly—down the corridor, his ears keenly listening for the first hint of an adult's footsteps. He couldn't shake the feeling that he was engaging in something illicit. As if being discovered would merit the severest of punishments. He wasn't sure what he wanted to know, about the other-worldly craft he'd seen on the pad. He wasn't even sure he wasn't dreaming, or sleepwalking.

But his feet kept moving. Down the corridor, through an intersection, down another corridor, through yet another intersection, and on and on, until finally Jimmy found himself at the main observation dome that overlooked the landing pad proper.

Jimmy had not been imagining things. The sleigh still sat there, its red and green running lights slowly oscillating in a hypnotic fashion.

"Beautiful ship, isn't she?" said a man's deep voice.

Jimmy spun and flattened against the railing that ringed the interior deck of the dome—his heart in his throat.

The man was wearing a space suit with extra room in the middle, for his prodigious belly. The suit had shiny black boots, and the cuffs and waist ring and neck ring were bright white, while the suit itself was a deep, cheerful red. He had a similarly-colored helmet under one of his arms, and his face was covered in a very short, but also very dense layer of white beard, with an accompanying moustache under his nose. A pair of antique spectacles were drawn up close to his eyes, and he was bald on top, save for a ring of dense, closely-cut white hair that ran from one ear, around the back, to the other ear. His cheeks were pink and he seemed to be amused about something.

"Who—who—?" Jimmy tried to say, but his words came out in a cracked squeak.

"Who do you think, James?" the man said, his mouth splitting in a full grin.

"James?" Jimmy said, tasting the name on his tongue. Tessa had been right, only Jimmy's Mom ever called him that—or occasionally, his Dad, when Dad was angry. Which seldom ever happened. Jimmy didn't like to get in trouble.

"Ordinarily," the man said, "I don't like having you youngsters interrupt me in the middle of my business, but it just so happens that I was coming to find you—or, it seems you found *me*. Your request was definitely on the unusual side. I wanted to talk to you about it, to be sure you knew what you were asking me for."

"You can … take me back home?" Jimmy whispered, his heart hammering at his ribs. "You can fly me to Ceres?"

"Ceres, or the moons of Jupiter, or even all the way to Pluto, if you want," the man said. "Nothing's impossible for Astronaut Nick, you know."

"Then … you're real!" Jimmy exclaimed, taking two steps away from the railing and examining his interrogator more closely. The man was obviously old, by the looks of him, but Nick radiated a decidedly youthful vibe that was difficult for Jimmy to put his finger on. The eyes behind the spectacles were somewhat crowded by folds of skin, but they sparkled with energy and hints of wisdom.

"Of course I'm real!" Astronaut Nick said, bursting out with a huge chuckle that seemed to begin at his belt and boom up and out through his throat. *Ho! Ho! Ho! Ho!*

Jimmy glanced around, waiting for another adult to appear and ruin the magic. But no such adult—nor even another child—materialized.

"Now then, young man," Nick said, "let's get down to business, shall we? I've got a lot more to do before my work is through. And if you're going to Ceres, there's no time to lose. So, just to be clear, you *really* want to go back? That's your wish? You wouldn't like, say, a model space liner kit, or one of the new three-dee video game packs? Something like that?"

"No," Jimmy said. "I miss home. I want to go home!"

"This isn't your home?"

"No, it's not. And it never will be. Please, Astronaut Nick, take me back to my friends on Ceres. Take me to where I belong!"

The man in the suit seemed to consider Jimmy for a moment, then he took a step towards Jimmy and slapped his hand on Jimmy's shoulder.

"Fine, then. But first, you'll have to climb into my sack."

For the first time, Jimmy noticed that Astronaut Nick had a huge, red, velvet-fabric sack resting on the deck behind him. It appeared to be filled with square and rectangular items.

"Why?" Jimmy asked.

"How else are we going to get you to out of the airlock, and to my sleigh?" he said. "Do they have vacuum suits your size here?"

"They do," Jimmy said. "But I am not sure I can just take one."

"Exactly," Nick said. "So, if you will simply crawl in, please, we'll be on our way."

Astronaut Nick opened the mouth of the sack as wide as he could, and Jimmy stepped hesitantly toward it. All he had on were his one-piece pajamas and a pair of slippers. He'd not thought seriously enough about what might happen if Astronaut Nick actually came to fulfill Jimmy's wish. What would his parents think when they woke up in the morning and Jimmy was gone?

"Come on now," Nick said, frowning with impatience. "If you're getting cold feet, just say so, and I'll let you be. Astronaut Nick is a busy guy, and there's plenty of other children across the solar system who need my attention tonight."

"No!" Jimmy said. "I don't want to stay. Okay, I'll climb into the sack. Just promise me this won't hurt."

"You won't feel a thing," Astronaut Nick said, keeping the mouth of the sack held open wide.

Jimmy stared at the sack, feeling himself teetering on the knife's edge of his indecision, then practically threw himself at the sack, and was promptly swallowed up as he fell an unlikely distance down into a massive pile of wrapped packages.

Space wasn't like Jimmy remembered it. There was no tedious countdown, no painful waiting as traffic control cleared the launch, then the shuttle ride, then the long period of docking. One moment Jimmy felt and saw the mouth of the sack close over his head, the next he felt himself being lifted and hefted, and then the next he was being set down, and the mouth of the sack opened back up.

Only, by the time he peeked out, he was staring at the cold blackness of the night sky, with stars all around. The sack was sitting on the floor of the upper deck of Astronaut Nick's sleigh—the part which Jimmy had previously seen, and which was covered by a single-piece dome canopy. Nick himself was still clad in his space suit, this time with the helmet on, and he was rapidly waving his black gloves through a series of holographic control screens that floated in his lap.

"I didn't even feel us take off," Jimmy said.

"Nor should you," Astronaut Nick said. "At the gees we pull, if you felt anything, you'd be turned to jelly!"

Jimmy stared open-mouthed.

Nick kept working, then noticed his companion's horrified expression, and he burst out with another *Ho! Ho! Ho! Ho!* which didn't sound any less loud even though it was coming through Nick's helmet speakers.

"Don't worry, James," Astronaut Nick said. "In three hundred years of doing this, I've never had so much as a single accident. Isn't that right, Chief Engineer?"

An improbably small person—also clad in a space suit very similar to Nick's—suddenly popped into view. From whence the person had come, Jimmy couldn't tell, but the voice was that of a cartoon character.

"Nosiree, Cap'n!" the tiny individual said cheerfully.

Jimmy watched as the little person hopped up onto the seat next to Nick, pulled up a series of holographic controls, and began to go to work right alongside Nick himself. The view through the little person's helmet didn't give Jimmy the greatest profile, but he saw an old man's face with a beard and a moustache, and oversized, inhumanly pointed ears.

"Is that—?" Jimmy said, beginning to aim a finger at the impish being.

"It's not polite to point, James," said the smallish, space-suited creature. Jimmy watched as the Chief Engineer waved his little hands through numerous flashing diagrams and displays, tapping out instructions pantomime-fashion. A series of holo windows all blinked bright green, and the little man stood up and gave Astronaut Nick a proper salute.

"The drive's good to go whenever you want it, boss," he said.

"Thank you," Nick said cheerfully, and then the little creature vanished—presumably through a hatch in the floor that James couldn't see, since he was still staring over the edge of the sack in which he sat.

"Hang on," Nick said, "this part gets a little weird."

Jimmy had no time to prepare, as suddenly Nick's finger zinged through a series of holographic triggers, and all the stars in space flashed like camera bulbs. They froze at that point, and grew even brighter, then they ran and smeared like melting wax across a black velvet canvas.

Jimmy's stomach wasn't happy with the accompanying sensation, and he slapped a palm over his mouth to keep from making a mess in Astronaut Nick's sleigh, when just as quickly, the stars all snapped back to normal and Jimmy's stomach righted itself.

In the distance, a dark sphere blotted out part of the view, with a thin crescent showing along one side where the sun reflected. In patches across the sphere's black side, clusters of lights shone brightly. Familiar clusters of lights.

Jimmy almost leapt out of the sack.

"Ceres!" he said.

Nick merely kept manipulating his control holographs, and the view shifted dramatically as Nick's sleigh zoomed down to the surface of the asteroid at an improbable speed. There was barely any sound, other than a variably-pitched humming that seemed to correspond with the sleigh's motion through space. Eventually the sleigh came to rest on a pad not too unlike the one back at Olympus Mons, and Nick looked down at Jimmy as Jimmy sat perched in Nick's sack.

"Ready to go home?"

"Yes! Yes!" Jimmy said, almost jumping up and down on the heap of gifts that had been cushioning him during the ride.

"Okay then, I have to close the sack back up," Nick said.

Jimmy nodded eagerly, then held his breath for an instant while Nick shut the mouth of the sack tight. Again Jimmy felt himself being lifted, hefted, and carried. To eventually be set down on a flat surface some time later, after passing through what sounded like—in the muffled confines of the sack—several airlock cycles.

Jimmy practically burst out of the sack when next Astronaut Nick opened it.

They'd landed on the pad nearest to where Jimmy's quarters had been—he knew this part of Ceres well enough that he probably could have walked through it blindfolded. As on Mars, there were no adults, nor even any children. Jimmy reveled in the miniscule gravity, and somersaulted his way down one of the corridors, whooping with joy at the freedom of his movements. No more clunky, plodding steps. Jimmy soared like a bird, artfully pushing off here and there as his toes and fingertips made contact. Given time, he'd have gradually settled to the deck. But on Ceres, even children possessed the strength of men, and Jimmy celebrated his return with an unselfconscious display of microgravity acrobatics that would have done any seasoned spacer proud.

Astronaut Nick trailed behind, his helmet off and clipped to a tether at his waist, while he towed his large sack of presents from another tether. Nick's movements were much more reserved, but no less deft. He kept pace with Jimmy despite Jimmy's headlong rush for home.

Finally, they arrived at the hatchway to Jimmy's parents' quarters. Jimmy slapped his hand on the palm reader and laughed as the door slid open, allowing Jimmy to spring inside and carom off one of the walls. They had a spectacular star roof which had been left open, allowing natural light to flood in through the centimeters-thick, ultraviolet-blocking vacuum glass.

Nick floated in behind Jimmy, and the hatch snapped shut.

Jimmy gradually came to rest against one of the walls, and when he was done catching his breath—the exhilaration of the moment having been almost too much to stand—his brow furrowed.

"Something wrong?" Astronaut nick asked.

"No," Jimmy said. Then thought better of himself, and admitted, "yes."

"What's the issue, James?" Astronaut Nick said, allowing himself to slowly sink to the deck, along with his cargo.

"This is," Jimmy said, then stopped.

"Yes?" Nick said, a white eyebrow raised over the top of the rim for his spectacles.

"It's home," Jimmy said. "But ... it's not home. I don't get it. This is where we used to live. And look at how much room there is here! We have three compartments, and that's not even including where we sleep! But ... it's too ... it's too empty."

"Too empty?" Astronaut Nick said, keeping an eyebrow raised.

"Yes," Jimmy admitted. "The furniture is gone, my Mom's paintings aren't on the wall, Dad's Wall Ball trophy isn't over in the corner in its case, and there isn't the smell of bread baking in the bread maker."

"Well, of course," Astronaut Nick said. "Your request was pretty clear. You said you wanted to go back to Ceres—that you wanted to go *home*. So, here we are. This is home."

"But it's ... it's not the same!" Jimmy said, feeling more and more uneasy with each passing moment. "This isn't how it's supposed to be. I wanted to come *home* to the way things were before we left! I wanted it to be just like it used to be. I don't want to be stuck here with a bunch of empty rooms!"

"So you want to go back to Mars?" Astronaut Nick asked.

"No!" Jimmy blurted. "I never want to go back there! I hate it at Olympus Mons!"

Astronaut Nick breathed deeply, and then sighed.

"Well," the man in the red and white space suit said, "you'd better get used to living by yourself. You won't have your family here to take care of you. Some of your old friends are present, but then, it's been awhile since you left, and some of your old friends have moved on as well. There are other colonies in the solar system, you know. Not everybody gets to stay in the same place. In fact, most people don't."

Jimmy stared up through the star roof, his eyes beginning to brim with tears. He'd dreamt of this moment for so long, and now that he was finally getting to have his wish, he was realizing that maybe what he'd wished for, wasn't going to be possible after all? No matter if Astronaut Nick was real, and could perform spaceflight miracles.

"You know," Astronaut Nick said, "it's really not too late for me to get you back to Mars. If we're quick about it, we might even get you back in time for you to crawl into bed before your parents know you're gone. That thing you feel in your stomach right now—the *sadness*—just think how your mother and father will feel when they wake up and you've gone, James. They won't know where you are or what's happened to you. There isn't even a note to tell them."

Jimmy felt his throat close up. He wrapped himself into a ball on the floor of his empty, silent former home, and began to cry.

Eventually he felt a strong hand touch his shoulder. Astronaut Nick's voice was calm, deep, and gentle.

"James," he said, "I've given a lot of boys and girls their wishes over the years. Not every wish is always meant to work out the way you think it should work out. Now, I'll ask you one more time—yes or no—do you want to stay here on Ceres?"

Jimmy held his arms across his chest, not looking at anything. His eyes were shut tight, and the liquid that spilled from them was hot.

"I want it to be like it was," he sobbed, his nose stuffed up. "I want my old life back!"

"I know," Astronaut Nick said, maintaining his firm grip on Jimmy's shoulder, "but one of the things you're going to learn quickly as you get older, is that things are always changing. You will always remember how wonderful the past was—and these memories will be like treasure in your heart. But there isn't any way to go back. Not really. Because *you* will change too. The you that used to live here, he's already gone. There's a new you waiting to come to life, at Olympus Mons. If you'll stop being stubborn, and let it happen."

"Nobody likes me there," Jimmy sniffed. "They all think I'm a stupid, clumsy klutz."

"Nobody?" Astronaut Nick said, a hint of amusement in his tone. "Don't be too sure about that. Let me read you something I got in my e-mail not long before I came to visit you."

Jimmy vaguely sensed Astronaut Nick rummaging for something in a pouch strapped to his thick, red-colored leg. He brought out a small touch pad and used his thickly-gloved fingers to deftly slide and tap along the pad's surface, until a white screen with text on it glowed up into Nick's old face.

"Let's see, this comes from someone named Contessa Canfield— a classmate of yours if I am not mistaken. I'd been expecting her to ask for a set of super blocks building modules, which she's been dying for since her birthday, but you know what she asked for instead? Let me read this. She said: *Dear Nick, please help Jimmy Carrico to be happy. He's my new friend at school and no matter what I do I can't cheer him up. Not even telling him about you makes him smile. I'll give up anything you were going to bring me this year if you can find a way to help Jimmy be happy. Thanks, Tessa.*"

Jimmy sat in stunned silence, his tears momentarily forgotten.

"Tessa wrote that?" he mumbled.

"She did," Astronaut Nick said, turning off the pad and sliding it back into the pouch on his leg; then zipping the pouch closed.

Jimmy raised his head and stared up at Nick.

"Are you sure you don't want to go back to Mars, James? Seems there's more than two people who'll miss you an awful lot if you're not there to see them tomorrow. Any girl who'd give up presents in the hope that she could bring joy to a new friend, is someone I'd say is worth keeping by your side. Not many children grasp the true meaning of Christmas. I think Tessa is one of them."

Jimmy felt a new lump form in his throat. He debated his choices, staring around him at the barren walls of his former house.

"But it's still going to be so hard," he said forlornly.

"Yes," Astronaut Nick said, "but that's also something you're going to have to get used to. Just as your Mom and Dad got used to it. Just as every adult gets used to it. But just because something is hard, doesn't mean you won't ever be happy. In fact, you just might find that the harder something is, once you get through it, the happier you can be on the other side. Because happiness isn't a time or a place, James. Happiness is in *here.*"

Astronaut Nick's stubby, gloved index finger tapped Jimmy's chest.

"It's also in the other souls with whom you share this universe. You're not old enough yet to really understand, but someday very soon, I think you will. You just have to trust an old man to know what's he's talking about. Can you do that?"

Jimmy's eyes leaked new tears, but he nodded his head stiffly.

"Yeah," Jimmy snuffled, "okay, I think I get it. Maybe. Mom, Dad, Tessa, I don't want them to be sad. And they'd be sad if I was gone. And now that I'm here, I am realizing *here* is gone too."

Astronaut Nick said nothing, he merely squeezed Jimmy's shoulder.

"Take me back to Mars, please," Jimmy said.

Nick wordlessly opened his sack, and let Jimmy crawl in.

Sunlight.

A new day.

Jimmy rolled out of his bunk and came to rest lightly on his feet, his balance a bit unsteady. He'd spent much of the night enjoying Ceres' gravity. Being suddenly back in Mars gravity was unsettling. But also, strangely, for the very first time, comforting too.

As if on cue, Mom's head poked into the compartment.

"James, dear," she said, smiling, "wake up and come see! It's magic!"

Jimmy pulled himself up and walked—thud-footed—out of his chamber and into the family living and dining area. The heady smell of freshly-baked bread hit his nose, and Dad had put some music on the surround sound speakers. Something cheerful, with bells in it. A tune Jimmy suspected he'd heard before, but couldn't quite place.

"Good morning, Jim," Dad said, perched over by the bubble window. "You really should come see this."

Jimmy walked slowly over and then leaned into the window, his eyes scanning about.

There were space-suited figures wandering around outside. Adults and children alike. A thick blanket of white fluff covered the ground to a depth of several centimeters. One of the adults was wadding a packet of the snow in her hands, then playfully flung it at one of the children. Promptly, all of the children stooped to collect snowballs of their own, and almost immediately a spectacular multi-target barrage of hurled projectiles ensued.

One of the children saw Jimmy and his parents looking out through their bubble. The space-suited child loped over to stand at the window.

Tessa waved at Jimmy, and Jimmy—cracking a wide grin—waved back.

"You ought to go out with them," Dad urged with a smile.

"Can I?" Jimmy said enthusiastically, his head rapidly clearing.

"I don't know," Mom said, suddenly getting a better look at Jimmy in the morning light. "Your eyes are puffy and it looks like you've been crying. Do you have a cold?"

"I'm okay," Jimmy said. "Really. I'm alright. Let me go rinse up and use the latrine, and I'll be fine."

"Well … okay," Mom said.

Five minutes later, Jimmy was at the same observation dome where he'd stood the night before—or *thought* he'd stood the night before, when Astronaut Nick had first made his acquaintance. Ten minutes after that, Jimmy was outside in a suit of his own, running in the kangaroo-hop fashion all the other children had learned to adopt since coming to Mars, until he too was engaged in the great snowball war which had come to the slopes of Olympus Mons.

When things quieted down, Tessa and Jimmy found themselves paired off and walking over to the landing pad where the big shuttles ordinarily touched down.

Jimmy hadn't dared speak a word of his experience to his new friend. He wasn't sure she'd believe him—because he wasn't sure *he'd* believe him, either. The memory of the prior night was already becoming soft around the edges, and tinged with the flavor of dreams. Of course it wasn't possible that Jimmy had actually ridden in a hyperspace sleigh back to Ceres, when the journey from Ceres to Mars, and vice versa, ordinarily took weeks. Even when Ceres and Mars were closest to each other in their orbits around the sun.

But then Tessa pointed to something up on the pad.

She and Jimmy loped up to see what it was. They found what appeared to be a large, green-and-red, striped stocking, containing numerous thin, red-and-white striped sticks, each wrapped in plastic. There was a little colorful hand-written tag attached to the stocking that said: *For Contessa and James, soon-to-be best friends. Merry Christmas, Nick.*

"Do you really think—?" Jimmy said, awed by the note.

"Yes, I really do!" Tessa said with hushed reverence.

They passed the gift stocking between them, examining the solidly tangible feeling of the candy canes between their gloved feelings.

"Nobody will believe us," Jimmy said, smiling.

"They don't have to," Tessa said. "Right?"

Jimmy thought about it, then laughed out loud and said, "Right."

In times of old when days grew cold and nights grew long and no one went outside much, rewarding well-behaved, cooped-up kids at Yule time made good sense.

But what about those naughty kids? They could really get carried away back then! Mercedes Lackey wrestles with that notion in this special Secret World Chronicle installment.

—KO

THE LONGEST NIGHT

A Secret World Chronicle Prequel Story

Mercedes Lackey

he absolute quiet was broken only by the crackling of flames. Vickie Nagy gave up trying to be interested in her book, sighed, and put it down on the bed beside her. Tucking her legs up under the plush velvet spread, she wrapped her arms around them and rested her chin on her knees, brooding, as she gazed into the fire in the fireplace at the foot of the huge bed.

Under other circumstances she'd have been luxuriating in the comfort. This was probably the best bedroom she'd seen outside of pictures in magazines, *ever*, especially for someone like her, who wallowed in fantasy novels and historical romances. The fireplace was only there for the ambience, not for heat—though these buildings were probably the oldest on the North American continent, the magicians who ran and staffed this very special school kept things nicely modern when it came to amenities. Central heat and air, plumbing and wiring that met every modern standard, even satellite television and internet. There wasn't a piece of furniture in here that either wasn't an antique older than the USA, or had been built to look like it was. The dark wooden bed was a huge Tudor canopy number, complete with red velvet bed-curtains matching the bedspread that you could pull shut all around, isolating you from noise, and creating a cozy, dark cave. But there was also a good reading light and her own cassette deck (usually playing classical music) in the headboard of the bed—which also had a cupboard she could stash books in. The mattress was more comfortable than anything she had ever slept on before. There was a faint scent of sandalwood from incense burning over the fireplace.

Her clothing had been put away in a matching freestanding wardrobe. There was a real Turkish carpet on the floor, old and soft and beautiful.

The fireplace she was staring into was giving off *just* enough heat, and no smoke at all. It had a tiled hearth, and a carved mantle of some sort of dark red wood.

As for the rest of the furniture, there was a real red-velvet "fainting couch," and two red velvet chairs that were so cushy you hated getting out of them, positioned on either side of the fireplace. Another wardrobe actually hid a mini-fridge, a TV with cable, and a player.

And the bathroom was to die for, with a cream-colored, claw-footed tub deep and long enough that a tall man could float in it without hitting his head or feet. The supply of scents for the water was enough to make even the most jaded hedonist raise an eyebrow.

If this room had been *hers,* she'd probably have considered herself well and truly spoiled rotten.

But it wasn't hers. It was in the guest section of the West Building of St. Rhiannon's School for Exceptional Students, and she was here, because her parents, who were FBI agents with the FBI's Metahuman

Agents section, had been sent out on a Job, and it wasn't one she could go along for. Which was super-depressing, because it was Yule Break at the School, and she *could* have gone without anything getting in the way of her studies.

As long as it was just her parents, and the Job in question was something she could contribute her Talents to, she had gone along on a lot of their cases in the past. But this was going to be something tough, FBI Metahuman Division 39 had sent out three teams on it, and not even her Godfather, Agent Hosteen Stormdance, thought having a teenager along was a good idea. And *he,* not her parents, was usually the one to override protocol and sneak her in because of her Talents.

Super depressing. Not only was she missing a Job, everyone concerned was pretty sure it was going to be a long and involved investigation. Probably wouldn't be over until she was well into the next term. Which meant she was going to be here over Christmas. First Christmas, ever, without her parents. First Christmas alone.

That was why she was here, instead of at home in Quantico. Nobody thought it was a good idea for her to live at home in their little bungalow alone for several weeks, not even her. Too many things could go wrong—and she was not only the daughter of a pair of FBI agents, and so a potential target for bad guys, she was also the daughter of a pair of pretty formidable FBI magicians, and *definitely* a target for bad guys. No one fancied her becoming Daddy's Little Hostage.

But since she *wasn't* going to officially be a boarding student, the Dean had decided to put her up in the Guest Quarters. She didn't mind not being in the dorms in East Building, not really. For one thing, as an only child, she'd never had to share a room, and she kind of didn't like the idea. She'd seen the dorm rooms, and while they were probably about as nice as her room at home, and even though you were allowed to do almost anything you liked with them, including using transparent, fluorescent or luminous paint to make starfields on the ceiling if you liked, they were nothing like the guest rooms. For another thing, the boarders all had their own rooms, and at the moment, every room in the girls' dorm was full. That meant she'd have to be doubled up with someone—and she didn't think whoever she got put with would be any too pleased about being saddled with a stranger for a couple weeks to a month, having *her* private space invaded, and suddenly having to share everything.

So she got to luxuriate in the really posh Guest Quarters, which, if it hadn't been Christmas, would have been grand. She'd have full access to the school library and other magical amenities, during the break, and she wouldn't have to cook for herself. She *shouldn't* be living here long enough for the novelty to wear off. It should be like a kind of solo vacation, like going to summer camp as she'd never gotten to do. And really, she'd actually be pretty excited about all of this, if only....

If only what her parents were assigned to wasn't, obviously, a dangerous job. If only it wasn't happening over Christmas. Every time she started to get excited about being here, another wash of worry for her folks drowned it all. Every time she felt anticipation, a reminder that there was just not going to be any Christmas this year made it go flat.

The worry was the worst, really.

They're smart. They're the best there is. Division 39 hasn't lost anyone, ever, not since the end of the Second World War.

She sighed again. Maybe it was just as well she was staying here, in the mostly-deserted school, rather than anywhere else, like with either set of grandparents. How could she *possibly* enjoy Christmas when she knew the entire time she'd be all balled up with anxiety? And so would the grandparents. And they'd all be trying not to show it, and trying to keep each others' spirits up, and pretending to enjoy the holiday stuff, when in fact they would *all* be in tense knots and the whole holiday would be completely spoiled for everyone. Besides ... Mom's parents were in Scotland, and Dad's were in the back of beyond in Michigan's Upper Peninsula, and just *getting* her there, with planes booked solid for the holiday, would have required an Act of Congress, almost. And sure, she could have Apported, but then try and explain the sudden appearance of an American girl without evidence of plane tickets if someone in authority got nosy. Trying to take magical shortcuts in the mundane world almost always got messy. Especially when you were under orders not to draw attention to yourselves.

And I bet Mom had that all figured out within five minutes of when they got assigned, she thought, stroking the soft velvet over her knees with an absent-minded finger. *I bet that's why she arranged this in the first place.* At least this way she wasn't going to have to put up a façade for anyone. If she wanted to mope here in her room and never go out for anything but meals, she could do that.

Well, I can until classes start, anyway.

And if she wanted to spend all her free time trying to lose herself in her studies, well, she could do that, too. *Think of the bright side. I have Professor Higgins all to myself.*

She stared into the flames, brooding. Why couldn't her parents have been with ECHO, been metahumans, and not magic-wielding, but all-too-mortal agents of an FBI Division that wasn't even supposed to exist?

If they'd been metas, well, the fact that metas all seemed to share a certain amount of enhanced strength, better reflexes, and faster healing would have made her feel less anxious about her parents and her Godfather.

But they're going to be wearing ECHO nanoweave, she reminded herself. *They'll be* practically *bulletproof.* And her mom was a healer, after all....

The secrecy was the thing that just *ate* at her. They had not been allowed to tell her anything, not even what part of the country they were going to be in because they hadn't known themselves. Moira and Alex Nagy didn't often get investigations where they practically had to play Secret Agent, but when they did every moment that they were gone Vickie lived with a knot in her stomach. And she'd learned what *we can't talk about this* meant very, *very* young, because her own Talents had shown up about the time she started to speak, so her parents had begun teaching her "consequences" at a ridiculously young age. Well, "ridiculous" for a mundie, not so much for the magical child of magicians.

That had its advantages, for sure, as well as its drawbacks. She felt sorry for the magical child of mundies—ordinary people, who didn't know magic existed. Life for someone like that ... at least until they were discovered, and one of the alumni would turn up with an offer "to help your child" ... could range from difficult to living hell.

Hearing some of those stories had really driven home how lucky she was. *Though you would think, in a world where the guy that just robbed the bank is as likely to get nabbed by a psion or a super-speeder or some bloke who can bend steel bars around his little finger as he is by a cop, they might go a little easier on a kid that "does things that can't be explained."*

So far as the parents of about half of the students here were concerned, this was some sort of correctional school supported by eccentric benefactors, and as long as they saw their offspring as little as possible and there were no obvious signs of abuse, the lack of parental access bothered them not at all. Budding mages born into normal families tended to get into a lot of trouble they couldn't adequately explain as they came into their powers, and adult magicians out in the world were always on the alert for the signs of a youngster in need of rescue. A little glamorie, a little persuasive geas, and the relieved parents were happily sending their "problem" off to be dealt with by someone else. And as for the kids, well, from everything some of her friends here had let slip, Vickie knew they were as relieved to finally find themselves in a place where they actually *belonged* as she had been.

So far as the parents of the *other* half were concerned—the parents who were themselves magicians—St. Rhia's was the place where their children were free to study and practice magic openly, and where they would get the best magical education to be had in North America. More part of the campaign to keep their nature hidden; at St. Rhia's, their kids learned both magic and camouflage. Eventually, some few, with the right skills, would actually go off and pass as meta-humans, joining ECHO, with no one ever the wiser about *where* their abilities came from. Most, however, would find some other way to be practicing magicians in the world.

Even Vickie's parents managed that, at least as far as most of the FBI was concerned. Outside of Section 39, except at the very top levels of the Bureau, no one was aware that they were anything other than metahumans—or that the things they stalked were sometimes considerably different than "mere" super-criminals.

Most of the time, their job wasn't that much different from a meta-Agent, or even a mundie-Agent. Investigate the crime, identify the criminal, intercept and arrest. Most of the time, the criminal was *much* more invested in avoiding discovery than he was in fighting back. *But this time … it could be different. They've taken a three-team Job … over Christmas. The Longest Night. Bad things can happen on the Longest Night.* Anyone schooled in magic knew that there were "bad" times of the year, when really nasty things could turn up. Samhain—Halloween, to mundies—was the one most people thought of. But the Longest Night, Midwinter, or, as the mundies and non-pagans knew it, Christmas Eve, was far more dangerous. So were the days on the run-up to the Longest Night. Darkness had sway over Light, and on the night itself, had its hold over this half of the world longer than at any other time of the year, and bad things lived in the shadows. If they were off going after something at this time of year … if they were lucky, it was just a really dangerous mundie or meta, that the Bureau thought could only be caught by the "outside the box" method of Division 39.

But if they weren't lucky … it was something else. It was the "something else" that had her in knots.

But they're the best. And there's going to be nine of them. And Hosteen promised me he'd keep me updated. There was that. Her Godfather was not only the team leader for this job, he knew how she fretted. She'd at least know, if not what was happening, at least that they were all right.

With that held firmly in her mind, she decided she would at least try and read her book. And eventually, to sleep.

The central courtyard was covered in about a foot of snow, with neat paths cut through it in the shape of a big equal-armed cross. That was another difference between here and home. When Vickie stepped out into the court, she was forcibly reminded that the school was somewhere in upper New England, not Virginia. Where it was, exactly … not even her parents knew. You came and went either by Apporting into the Central Courtyard, or by private plane to an airstrip about a mile from here on private property, and Apported from there. There weren't more than a handful of people who knew the exact location. It was safer that way.

The teachers and students might live in separate buildings, but everyone *ate* in the same place. The Dining Hall was in the East Building, but although she was starving, Vickie paused for a moment to take in the sight of the School resting in the silence, with soft snow falling gently into the Court.

It was gorgeous. Like something in a book.

The buildings looked a lot like many of the buildings at Oxford University in the UK, actually; Gothic, but in the pretty way, not the morbid way. Stone made graceful. More of the "dreaming spires" that poets talked about. It was hard not to feel a little awe. The buildings were a gorgeous, pale, pale gray, nearly the color of the raw stone they had been built from, rather than the darker gray of buildings aged and darkened by years and pollution.

North and South were the classrooms, East was the dorms for the live-in students, and West was home to the teachers' apartments, theater, gym, library, guest rooms … all the other things that weren't classrooms or dorms. The place was set in the middle of an extensive garden. Outside the garden were thick woods that looked really, really old, and impenetrable, although Vickie knew for a fact that the students were actually encouraged to explore them.

Right now everything was softened by snow. The pigeons and doves that lived here on the grounds were all wisely settled in their roosts, and at the moment, so were the ravens and crows that were as much pets here as the tamer birds. Silence hung over everything.

The area in the very center of the Central Courtyard was *completely* clean, but it wasn't shoveled clean—magic kept the snow off, and for good reason. This was the "landing platform," the Magical Circle that you Apported to when you came here.

The Magical Circle was a construction built of several circles, carved into the granite of paving in the middle of the Courtyard; it was one of the most complex permanent Circles she'd ever seen. Literally a Master Piece; carefully inlaid in the granite of the paving, it had been put together by the Founders as one of the first constructions of this School. There were five smaller primary circles within the huge circle that enclosed the entire construction, one at each of the cardinal points, and a slightly bigger one in the middle. When someone Apported here, they landed in the smaller circle that corresponded to their Element. Vickie was North, which was Earth. South was Fire, East was Air and West was Water. Your magic wasn't necessarily restricted to that of one Element, of course, but you, yourself, always had a Prime Element associated with you.

You didn't *need* to Apport to an Elemental Circle, but it kept things less crowded when there was a lot of coming and going, and it kept the central Circle free for mass Apportations. Just in case, for instance, there was an entire class having a Field Trip. There weren't too many Day Students like Vickie, so it wasn't likely there would be much competition for the Elemental Circles when school was in session, but if there was, well, you activated your Apportation Spell, and then you waited, and when it was your turn, you Apported in.

As Vickie stood just in front of the doorway, the door behind her opened, and Dean McGregor stepped out, a tall, gaunt woman with graying brown hair, wrapped in a worn velvet cloak with a muffler that would have been the envy of a Doctor Who fan wrapped around her shoulders, neck, and head. "New to snow?" the Dean asked, dryly. Vickie laughed.

"Well, we don't get much in Virginia," she replied. "But I've been all over the world, so, not so much."

The Dean chuckled. "I had momentarily forgotten about your parents," she admitted. "Well, shake a leg, Miss Nagy, or we shall be getting cold apple pancakes, instead of piping hot. There is only one cook on duty during vacation, and she is justifiably disinclined to linger about for the sake of someone tardy."

Vickie was exceptionally short, and the Dean was exceptionally tall, so she had to trot to keep up. "What do we do if there's a blizzard?" she asked. "Or if we get sick?"

"If there is a blizzard, there is a small, well-stocked kitchen available to us in West Building. It's right next to the laundry-room. Given your self-sufficiency, I assume you can cook?" At Vickie's nod the Dean continued. "You may feel free to use it at any time, of course, although during vacation we assume you will clean up after yourself, as we allow most of the employees their holidays as well as the students. If you are ill, you must let me know, and I'll make sure that meals are brought to you and someone keeps an eye on you."

"Is anybody staying here besides me?" she asked, trying to *not* get a lump in her throat at the thought of being all alone here, with no one her age, for three weeks.

"Not staying the entire vacation, no." When Vickie looked up, she saw the Dean's mouth was slightly turned down. "It seems that no matter how little our pupils' parents may care for them, even the most despised are expected to come home for Christmas. But there are a half dozen that will be leaving just before the day itself, and returning almost immediately. You won't be left *entirely* alone for most of the break. And of course, there will be myself, Professor Sidhe, Professor Dav of Eastern Studies, Professor Yiu, Professor Stanislova, Professor Hakonen, and Professor Higgins here as well." The Dean smiled as Vickie felt her own expression brighten at the mention of her favorite instructor. "Professor Higgins is looking forward to working with you uninterrupted, so I doubt you will be bored."

By this time they had entered the ornate brass-sheathed doors of the East Building. The Dining Hall was the first door just inside the foyer, a beautiful piece of wood and leaded glass.

Vickie politely held the door open for the Dean, who nodded her thanks, and the two of them entered.

Since the entire School was based on the architecture of Merlin College in Oxford, it was scarcely surprising that the room was monumental by American standards. And it was *stunning*. Wood-paneled, with stained- and leaded-glass windows along one side, the walls featured oil portraits of accomplished alumni any place there wasn't a window, and if the ceiling lacked the vaulting of its model (as well as the three-story height—there were dormitory rooms above it, after all) it still boasted more wood panels with carved borders. There was one long table elevated slightly on a dais at the far end—the literal "High Table" where the faculty ate—and three rows of tables for the students placed perpendicular to it. And they were proper tables too, not the picnic-style common to American schools, with proper chairs.

There were lamps placed at intervals along the tables, but although there were usually place settings at each place, right now the tables were bare. Only the High Table had been set. There were also sideboards set against each wall, and one of them was loaded down with buffet-style warming trays. Clearly you were expected to help yourself.

Professors Higgins and Sidhe were already seated at the High Table, along with three other students. Vickie recognized two of them, both a year ahead of her. Naomi McCoy and Ralph Emory. She and the Dean hung their cloaks—cloaks were part of the standard uniform here, which tickled her no end—on a coat-tree at the end of the buffet, and helped themselves. Either the Dean had already known the menu, or she was prescient; there were indeed apple pancakes, as well as oatmeal, bacon, fruit and cold cereal and a few other items. *Pretty much what you'd find at the breakfast buffet at a motel,* Vickie decided. But of course, better. She might have hesitated in picking a seat, not certain what the protocol was during vacation, but Professor Higgins looked up and grinned at her and gesticulated broadly at the chair next to him. Feeling relieved, she made her way around the table until she came to the seat next to him. Vickie was one of the very few magicians, ever, in the entire history of the school, to see magic in terms of mathematical and algebraic equations. Everyone saw magic differently, of course, but because Vickie saw it as math, she was not only able to easily learn and replicate spells, she was able to deconstruct them and derive new ones, or new applications of old ones. The more math and physics she learned, the better she was able to do that. Professor Higgins, who looked very like a hobbit but spoke like an Einstein, was the *only* teacher who saw and understood magic in the same way. She was his first pupil in twenty years, and he was utterly as delighted to have found her as she was to get him as her mentor.

The two of them chattered like a couple of magpies about mathemagic while the other students who were going to be here for most of the vacation and the remaining teachers came in. Unlike meals while school was in session, there didn't seem to be any formality;

students and teachers mingled at the High Table, although Vickie was the only one deeply engrossed in conversation with a teacher.

The last to come in was a very young student, much younger than the usual. She looked to be nine or ten at most, when most people came to the school in their early teens. She was very blond, wore her hair in two braids, and looked like a little Dresden doll.

She slipped up to the sideboard like a timid mouse, quickly filled her plate, and sat as far from everyone as she could. "Who's that?" Vickie asked the Professor, who had paused in his discussion to finish his pancakes before they turned cold.

He swallowed the last bite. "Heidi Dortmund," he said. "Sad case, that. Her parents died last year, and her grandmother has charge of her."

Instantly, Vickie felt a surge of sympathy—and a little bit of fellow-feeling—for the little girl. Not that having your parents *dead* was anywhere near the same as having them gone, but … well the others were chatting to each other and Professor Sidhe, and she was sitting there all alone. Professor Higgins picked up on what she was thinking without her even needing to say anything.

"Planning on acquiring another stray already?" he asked, his eyes twinkling—since last semester she had been the one to champion her friend Paul against the popular kids in the school who were secretly bullying him. Well, they *had* been popular. They weren't quite so arrogant now that they'd been caught and punished in their covert bullying, and humiliated by Vickie and Paul to boot.

"Oh, I just think she could use a friend," Vickie demurred. "She's kind of young to be here, isn't she?"

Professor Higgins shrugged slightly, and ran a hand through his mop of curly, sandy hair. "There aren't many as young as she is, but I gather circumstances were special for her."

It looked like the little girl was almost done with her breakfast—she'd all but bolted it. Vickie finished hers before the child could escape. The Professor saw very well what she was about to do, and gave her a little wink by way of encouragement, while taking his own sweet time with his own meal. Well, he ate like a hobbit, too; she had never seen anyone who enjoyed food as much as he did, and if he hadn't been a magician, he'd have been too round to fit in his chair. Before the girl could scuttle off, Vickie came over to her chair. To Vickie's relief, the little girl didn't look frightened or alarmed, just wary. Probably not used to the older kids approaching her.

"Hi, I'm Vickie," she said, with an encouraging grin. "You want to help me build a snowman?"

The little girl just lit up. "Yes!" she said, and that was all it took. Since both of them were already dressed for the weather, and had their cloaks and mittens with them, they ran out to the courtyard together to turn words into actions.

By the time the bell for lunch sounded, both of them were snow-caked, and Vickie had a *very* good idea of why Heidi had been looking so cowed.

On the one hand, Vickie wished there were two of her, so she could spend time with Professor Higgins as well as with Heidi. On the other hand, at lunch, the Professor had been giving her *very* encouraging looks that she read as "stay with the child" over lunch. She was used to being extremely active—she not only took Staff Fighting, she was taking Folk Dance and Introduction to Free-Running—and it was pretty obvious Heidi wasn't, so by the time supper came along, Heidi was exhausted, and said she was going to go to bed early. After watching Vickie spend all day in the company of the much younger child, the Dean was evidently curious, and intercepted her on the way back across the Courtyard to the West Building.

"You are up to something, young lady," the Dean said, although in an amused, rather than accusatory tone. "I should like very much to know what it is."

Vickie hunched her shoulders against the cold. "Heidi's Grandmother hates her. Or at least, that's what Heidi says. Heidi says her Grandmother never liked her father, and that her Grandmother thinks Heidi is the reason why her parents died." She frowned. "I didn't *say* anything, but she must be the meanest, nastiest woman ever. She treats Heidi like a failing cadet in a military school, and you wouldn't *believe* what she thinks is good reading for a little kid. Brothers Grimm. The original, unedited stuff, with kids eaten by bears, and dismembered, and drowned, and left to die in the woods."

She glanced up at the Dean, and saw that the woman had been taken entirely aback. "Well ... you *have* been busy," the Dean said, finally. "That's more than any of her teachers have been able to get out of her. All we knew was that she was quiet and very unhappy, as what child wouldn't be, who'd been orphaned?" She pondered a moment, then shook her head.

"Is there any way you can figure out how to keep her here instead of going back for Christmas?" Vickie begged, then ran forward to open the door for the Dean. "What if you said she was sick? Like, bad stomach flu? If her Grandmother dislikes her that much, wouldn't she just hate having to take care of someone who was throwing up, or worse?"

She paused on the stair that would lead her up to her own room, as the Dean stopped at the foot of the staircase and pondered that. "It's an option...." the woman finally said, but with some reluctance. "But I don't have to tell you that it is a very bad thing for a magician to lie. Words have power for a mage, and what if we *made* her ill?"

Vickie felt crestfallen. "I hadn't thought of that," she admitted unhappily.

"The trouble is, this is very short notice, especially when we had already set a date with her Grandmother when she could be expected home," the Dean continued. "For future breaks, we can easily contrive some sort of excuse—that she needs to catch up on some subject or other, or that there is a school trip. Something we can make happen without any unfortunate consequences for her. But ... this time, I can't think of anything off the top of my head." The Dean smiled encouragingly at Vickie. "It's only for a few days. The Grandmother herself set the dates—we had thought that it was only that an elderly woman didn't feel up to taking care of a young girl for very long, or that she thought Heidi would be bored and troublesome, but ... well, your information certainly casts *that* in a new light. But it's not as if she's physically abusing the girl, and Heidi is sensible and knows she'll be coming back here where she'll be happy. I'm sure Heidi will be fine."

Vickie wasn't so sure about that, but what could she say? She went up to her room in a troubled state of mind. Bad enough that she was worried about her parents, but now she was worried about Heidi, too.

The first thing she did when she got to her room—besides hang her cloak over a chair facing the ever-burning fire—was to check her message-box. It looked like a little wooden jewelry box, but it wasn't anything of the sort. It was one of a pair, with Apport "landing pads" inscribed inside. She had one, and Hosteen had one; she and her mentor had made them together. Letters weighed almost nothing, so they weren't hard to Apport; this was more secure than using conventional means to talk, and less taxing than every other form of magic communication.

She opened the lid, and as she had hoped, there was a folded letter inside. With a sigh of relief, she took it out, and settled down next to the fire. It was coded, of course, but it wasn't but a moment and a relatively simple bit of magic to take care of that. She held the pages between her hands, visualized the equations of the spell, said *"Fiat,"* aloud, and the words were descrambled. It was Hosteen's box that did the scrambling, a bit of techno-magic that she had created and he ruefully often wished aloud he could duplicate.

She settled down to read it carefully. They were in place, and had set up their headquarters in a rented vacation-home. He couldn't tell her where they were, or what they were doing, of course, but he assured her that everything was routine and that so far, other than the fact that there were nine agents on the team, it was proceeding like a normal investigation. Which meant that, aside from the fact that whoever or whatever they were after was using magic or was itself a creature of magic, and they were using forensic magic to track it down, it was just like any other FBI investigation. There was a bad guy, who was doing his best to elude them, but unless they cornered him, Hosteen didn't see him as a danger to the team.

And then … she read in between the lines, as Hosteen would have assumed she would do. They had their own little private code, the two of them, invoking things the two of them shared. It was nothing that anyone other than Mom and Dad would ever have been able to decipher. *Pacific Northwest. Serial killer. Why are so many serial killers in the Pacific Northwest?* Now she understood why they needed a team of nine; there was a lot of territory to cover up there, and if this was a murderer who was striking often, they needed to take him down as quickly as possible. You didn't want to split up in groups of less than three on a case like this.

Strangely, figuring that out made her *less* worried. On serial killer cases, the hunters rarely became the hunted. Serial killers preyed on the weak and isolated, not the strong and united.

She wrote her own quick letter to her parents, which Hosteen would pass on to them, and just as she had finished closing it in the box, she heard, faintly and muffled, a scream of absolute terror.

There were only two places on the grounds of the School where someone was likely to be screaming, the East Building and the West. And it had *not* sounded as if the scream came from the West Building—which left the East. The student dorms.

It was just pure good fortune that she was still fully dressed, boots and all. Vickie snatched up her cloak and ran for the door without a second thought. She raced down the stairs to the front door, and shoved it open, running straight out into the Courtyard.

Just as she left the front door of her building, the scream came again, this time definitely from East Building. As she dashed across the moon-flooded Courtyard, the door to West crashed open again behind her; it was the teachers, presumably, responding as she had— but she was too intent on her goal to look back.

She wrenched the door to East Building open; it wasn't locked, since, after all, there really wasn't any place for the students here to sneak off to. The School was surrounded by acres of forest, and most of the kids were city or suburb-bred. The building was lit only dimly, all the hall-lights dimmed to bedtime-mode, but it was enough to see by. She dashed up the staircase, taking the stairs two at a time, to the first floor, to find a knot of petrified students hovering uncertainly at the top of the stairs.

"Who screamed?" Vickie demanded, looking from one to another.

"I—we don't know!" said the eldest, a seventeen-year-old girl Vickie remembered was named Pomona. "We just heard someone, and came running out into the hall and—"

"And I saw a *thing!*" shrilled Ralph Emory, white as the snow outside. He reached for her arm and clutched it as if it were a lifeline. Maybe because she wasn't the only one panicking. "I think it was a demon!"

At this point, the Dean came up the last of the stairs, and grabbed Nick by the shoulder. "What do you mean, a demon?" she demanded. "The entire School and Grounds and shielded and warded against demons! It's impossible!"

Professor Hakenon came pounding up the stairs as fast as Vickie had—he was not only the teacher of European Applied Myth, he was also Vickie's Staff-Fighting teacher and in excellent shape. "Who's missing?" he demanded, and scanned the little clutch of students. "Where's Heidi?"

"I'll check her room," the Dean said, grimly, and strode off down the corridor. "You question Nick."

Vickie followed on the Dean's heels, but the answer was clear as soon as they were halfway down the hall. The door to Heidi's room stood wide open; from the mess inside, there had clearly been a struggle. The desk had been toppled, as had the chairs, and papers and books were scattered everywhere.

And Heidi was gone.

"Dean!" came the call from back down the hall, and Professor Hakenon ran up to them as the Dean turned in his direction. His blond hair was disheveled and the expression on his handsome face was grim. "Nick is right, he saw a demon—of sorts," the Professor said as he skidded to a halt beside them.

"What do you—" the Dean began. The Professor interrupted her.

"By 'of sorts,' I mean it's something we never warded against, because we didn't think to," the Professor explained, running his hand through his hair in a frantic gesture. "Good gods, we were so—it can only be invoked by someone who knows it, and thinks he—or she—deserves to be punished. That's how it got past our protections. Heidi thinks she *deserves* this, she must, or it never would have come for her."

"For heaven's sake, Nikki, get to the *point!*" the Dean exclaimed. "What *is* it?"

"It's the Krampus," the Professor replied bleakly. "And now it's loose here, it could take *any* of the others if we don't guard them, and if we don't get Heidi away from it before dawn, it will carry her off."

Vickie waited in the hall, poised on the balls of her feet, heart pounding. The other students were all in a heavily warded and sealed room, with Professor Sidhe guarding them. But *one* youngster had to be out for this plan to work, and she had volunteered before anyone else could speak up. This was the first time she had ever played "bait." And her parents would never forgive her if it was her last....

But there wasn't a choice. They had to save Heidi, and to do that, they had to get her out of the clutches of the Krampus, and the only way to get to the Krampus was to get the Krampus to come to them—

It wouldn't come for an adult. It wouldn't come if there were any adults anywhere around. And it wouldn't come for just any youngster, either. It had to be one who had been—naughty—

So she waited in the hallway, all alone, hoping that part of what the Krampus wanted was terror, and the thrill of the chase.

She heard it before she saw it; as the Professor had suggested it would, it materialized in the middle of the utterly deserted hallway, right by the door to Heidi's room, where it had disappeared as soon as Ralph spotted it—because Ralph was old enough to count as an adult. The chains around its waist clinked and dragged on the floor; its hooves made clumping sounds on the wood. She couldn't see it *well* in the dim light, but what she saw was enough. Horns. Tail. And an impossible tongue that lolled out of its ugly mouth and dangled past its knees. But most importantly, she spotted the bulging basket on its back, the straw straining at what it contained. That was all Vickie needed to see. And she had been *naughty*. The Dean had ordered her to go back to her own room and not set foot in East Building until dawn.

"Hey! Ugly!" she shouted, making her tone as taunting as she could. "I'm where I'm not supposed to be! What're you gonna do about it?"

The head came up; the thing started panting. And then it launched itself at her, moving much faster than its lumbering gait would have suggested.

She ran. She ran, and behind her, she left tangles of magic, knotty equations she made up on the fly, meant only to slow it down. Because *it* was darn near a primal force, and if she didn't manage to slow it somehow, it *was* going to catch her, and then there would be two to rescue.

"Think of the Krampus as St. Nikolas's evil twin."

That was what the Professor had said, explaining just what it was that they were up against. She knew about Black Peter, of course, the creature who, in some German and English traditions was the fellow that spanked naughty children and gave them coal, but the Krampus was ... a magnitude nastier than that. Really, something only a sadistic German could have thought up. A sadistic German who had been spending the early part of the winter cramped in a dark hut, hemmed in by snowdrifts, with his increasingly quarrelsome family, trying to think of a way to really *make* his children shut up and behave until spring....

St. Nikolas rewarded good behavior. But ... that wasn't enough. Not for *some* people. And it wasn't enough for bad children to be pleasurably scared, and deprived (at least a little) of presents. No, for some people, bad children had to be terrified into utter submission, under threats that if they didn't behave, something *horrible* would happen to them.

She sensed, rather than saw, something happening behind her. The Krampus was about to attack! She dodged to the side and went into a martial-arts shoulder-roll, narrowly missing being hit by that ... tongue.

Ew! Ew! Ew!

Professor Hakenon had warned her about that, and a good thing, too. That tongue wasn't just obscene, it was a weapon. She got a lot more proactive with her magical tangles as she hit the stairs and jumped down them three at a time as she headed for the basement. The basement, that held the only room big enough for their purposes.

The Krampus was St. Nikolas's hit-man. Disobedient children didn't just get lumps of coal, according to the legend. They got a visit from … the Krampus, who had carte blanche to do whatever he liked depending on how naughty you had been. And he wasn't content just to warn like Black Peter, or give you a little switching, oh no. If you were *lucky,* he whipped you around the room until you bled from a dozen or more cuts. If you weren't?

You ended up in that basket on his back. And he carried you off, and you were never seen again. The Professor wasn't certain what happened to you when he carried off the naughty children at dawn. Some versions of the legend said they were taken to Hell. Some, that they were found later, dismembered, as a warning to other children. Some, that the Krampus ate them.

That was why the Dean had expressly forbidden Vickie to be here, and left. And Professor Hakonen had given her explicit instructions that the Dean was not to know about. And why Vickie was running for her life now, with a demon on her heels. Because when she got to the basement …

She hit the basement door running, slammed into it, ran down the hallway to the rec area, and slammed through another door, and bolted across the room until she literally hit the back wall of the handball court. Then she turned, back to the wall, just in time to see the Krampus in all its ugly glory come barreling through the door behind her. It was grinning. It was an expression that made her whimper with horror and fear. Then her throat was too paralyzed with terror to do anything; in fact, she was having trouble breathing.

The Krampus reached the middle of the room.

"Now!" the Dean shouted. And that was when the lights went *out,* and the black lights came *on,* and the intricate demon-catcher that she and Professor Higgins had crafted in otherwise-transparent

fluorescent paint—the same stuff the kids were allowed to use to paint star-fields in their room with—lit up bright enough to make her wince. It did more than make the Krampus wince. The hideous thing howled, then screamed, then was held rigid in the grip of the spells of five of the best magicians on the continent.

As for the sixth—and Vickie—she and Professor Higgins were unraveling the magic that created the basket on the thing's back. It was very primitive, almost like knitting, and it was Vickie who realized that first, found the loose end, and "yanked" on it. The spell came apart, and with it, the basket. Heidi tumbled to the floor of the basement.

She looked half dead and only semi-conscious. The poor kid had her eyes squeezed tight shut, and was moaning and shivering. Vickie ached to reach her, but right now, that wasn't an option. No passing the boundary of the demon-catcher. Not until the demon wasn't in it anymore.

"*Three, two, one. Now!*" commanded the Dean, and all those binding spells started tightening, squeezing....

The Krampus began to shrink, struggling the entire time, but unable now to get enough breath to shriek. There was more than one way to banish an otherworldly creature back to whatever plane it came from, and one—this one—was to make things so impossible in *this* plane that it had nowhere to go but back.

In silence, it got smaller ... smaller ... and then, with a *pop,* it was gone.

Now Vickie and the Dean ran for Heidi; the Dean got there first, and gathered her up, then began firing orders at the rest of them.

"And *you,* Miss Nagy!" she snapped out last of all. "You are given *explicit permission* to be here at all times. I take back what I told you earlier. You were exactly where I wanted you."

"Thank you, Dean," Vickie breathed. Now she was no longer *naughty,* and thank goodness the Dean had thought of that. Because ... just in case Heidi somehow brought the Krampus back again ... better safe than sorry.

"So it *was* Heidi?" Vickie asked over French Toast the next morning. "Professor Hakonen was right?"

Professor Higgins nodded, and passed her the powdered sugar. "As you intuited, her grandmother convinced her she was responsible for her parents' death. And she knew magic was real, of course, so her subconscious was perfectly capable of summoning the worst monster her grandmother had ever told her about, a creature tailor-made to punish a sinful and evil child. That was how the Krampus bypassed our protections. They were never made to hold against something that had been summoned by a child that wanted it here." He ate a bite of bacon. "Needless to say, we've remedied that hole in our defenses."

"How's Heidi now?" Vickie wanted to know. The last she had seen of the child, the poor thing was being taken away to the infirmary. She felt a lump starting in her throat, thinking about how messed up the poor kid must be, to have actually—well—tried to kill herself. Or at least, punish herself horribly. Could she *ever* get over that?

"She'll be all right eventually." The Professor looked at her sharply, and patted her hand. "Don't worry too much; she was as loved by her parents as you are by yours. A few months of emotional abuse by her grandmother isn't going to destroy that sort of foundation, and the Dean is one of the best people with troubled children in our entire community. I think we'll get her set to rights."

"But—what about Christmas?" Vickie asked. "If you send her back to her grandmother, what's to stop the Krampus from coming for her there?"

"The fact that she won't be *going*. We contacted her grandmother this morning and told her Heidi had come down with the flu, and before we could say anything, the wretched woman *demanded* that we keep her here." The corners of his mouth turned down in a rare scowl. "Needless to say … we are going to ensure she never has to go back to that … harridan again."

Vickie ate some French Toast, already plotting in her mind how she was going to approach her parents about having Heidi with *them* over at least some of the breaks. And meanwhile … if she could get back to Quantico for a couple hours … there were some things at the house she thought Heidi would probably like a lot.

Like the snow-globe with the slightly-enchanted fairy castle in it, that lit up at night, and had a tiny, tiny fairy princess in one of the towers who'd wave her wand at you. A good thing to look at if you were scared, in the dark.

"Could you take this afternoon off, Professor?" she asked. "I'm not supposed to leave the campus without a teacher, and I've got some unexpected Christmas 'shopping' to do."

Reading about Quincy J. Allen's young upstart inventor's coming of age—like some brainy General Grant at a steampunk Appomattox—was as fun as finding a multifunction ray-gun underneath the Christmas tree!

Also, if your kids ever clamor for a chemistry set or electronics lab, indulge them! You never know what amazing things they might whip up!

—KO

JIMMY KRINKLEPOT AND THE WHITE REBELS OF HAYBERRY

Quincy J. Allen

s of this day, December 24th, eighteen-sixty-eight, you are hereby *forbidden* to go near the junkyard or your father's workshop!" Judge Davenport's booming Missouri drawl filled the courtroom. Virtually the entire town had gathered, word spreading like wildfire that charges had been levied against the accused, whom everyone knew all too well as a troublesome but well-meaning miscreant of high cerebral capacity.

Davenport's gavel came down like a clap of doom as he eyed Jimmy Krinklepot with a steely glare. A quiet chatter flitted across the gathered townsfolk of Hayberry in the aftermath of the sentence.

Davenport was a fair man, to be sure. Indeed, folks around town called him the fairest judge in the Union half of Missouri. But even a judge has a right to be angry when his property has been, as the judge put it, unduly molested. In this case, his property were seventeen prize chickens, and molested referred to Jimmy's latest invention.

Jimmy hung his head low, and his shoulders slumped. He blushed beneath a dusty, eight-panel grimwig, his hands jammed into tweed pants held firm by black suspenders. His mother stood silent behind him. He knew he'd miscalculated. What with his papa being away for so long on government business, he'd just let his imagination wander ... and Jimmy's imagination, being what it is, could wander a sight farther than your average teenage boy.

"I must say that I resent being brought in here the day before Christmas on account of your dreadful judgment and propensity for vandalism, well-intentioned though it may be. You would be well advised," Davenport growled, "to ponder what brought you here before me today." The judge reached beneath the bench where he sat and pulled forth a glass of iced lemonade. He sipped slowly, his eyes never leaving Jimmy.

Jimmy's eyes drifted to the courtroom window, picking out several dark spots in the sky, and did as the judge directed.

Jimmy had gotten it into his head—thinking only of the family cook Consuela, mind you—to lend his not insignificant gray matter to the matter of cooking. The previous evening, he'd overheard Consuela lamenting how long it took to prepare dinner for the household. Being of an inherently helpful nature, Jimmy woke early and walked through bitterly cold air to his workshop hidden in the junkyard. It was as close an approximation to his father's as he could make, and he set about tinkering with wires, condensers, emitters, and batteries of his father's design. The net result was portable, albeit a bit unwieldy, and a dire temptation for Jimmy and his diminutive but trusted cohort William Clarence Simplefig, who, as usual, accompanied Jimmy on his adventures.

But the device needed testing.

A proper test requires a proper subject. Again, Jimmy put his gray matter to the problem at hand. Realizing that a suitable target did not exist in the junkyard, he and William set off for, literally, greener pastures, although green was a color hard to come by in what had turned out to be a dry, cold winter in Missouri. Indeed, most of the town decried that there was little possibility of a white Christmas.

Travelling well past the edge of town, and walking down a wide country lane lined by tall oaks and maples bereft of leaves, the boys soon found themselves within earshot of a fine white house, with a fine white picket fence. Betwixt the house and the fence stood a fine white chicken coop with a run of low chicken wire that contained two dozen fine white chickens.

Jimmy opened the gate and stepped through, heading straight for the coop. Only a few strides had him standing before what he deemed to be suitable test subjects.

"But what about whoever lives here?" William queried from behind, a tinge of worry creeping into his voice. William, being of an inherently nervous sort, made up for his considerable squeamishness with a healthy dose of common sense. Unfortunately, on any scale, squeam would outweigh sense as a result of an absence of backbone. The boy had little foot to put down, as his father would often say.

"It's *perfect*," Jimmy said to his sidekick. "Set the power level to one and flip those three switches on the side," he added, excitement filling his voice like wind-blossomed sails.

William gulped once, his eyes shifting from the pack on Jimmy's back to the house. He carefully turned the knob from zero to one, noting that it went to eleven, which struck him as a bit odd. He had long ago, however, given up trying to understand his companion-in-mischief, finding the exercise futile in the extreme. He then flipped the first switch, eliciting a quiet buzz from the mass of brass plating, coils, and wires strapped to Jimmy's back. He flipped the second. The buzz became a hum. He flipped the third and felt a tremor vibrating his teeth. Quite prudently, he stepped away from the device, as he had been caught in errant detonations from Jimmy's inventions more than once in the past.

"Step back," Jimmy said without looking.

William blinked slowly at the wide gap he'd already placed between himself and the device, pondering fruitlessly if any distance would be sufficient.

Jimmy raised a strange looking apparatus connected to the pack by several feet of cable, gripping it like a soldier holds a rifle. The apparatus was long, but that's where the similarity ended. The grip at the back was a modified spade handle, with a lever built in. The handle plugged into a brass housing adorned by thick coils of wire on each side. A three-foot, copper cylinder extended out, and silver prongs protruded from a bulbous end. Three grapefruit-sized copper spheres bulged along the length, with wires sticking out hither and yon in an almost haphazard fashion.

Jimmy took aim at the nearest chicken and held his breath. Its head bobbed up and down almost peacefully as it pecked at barren earth. He pressed the lever.

CRAAAAACK!

A zagging bolt of red electricity shot from the apparatus and struck the hapless chicken square on. A pall of steam filled the air as Jimmy's weapon super-heated the natural humidity of Missouri. Feathers burst into a cloud of white that swirled and settled slowly around a steaming corpse. The pleasing scent of cooked chicken wafted into the boys' nostrils, setting their mouths to watering. A vision of Consuela's chicken fricassee passed before Jimmy's eyes, a dish of tender stewed meat that had often sated Jimmy's growing appetite.

Staring intently through the quickly dissipating cloud, Jimmy took in what remained of the chicken, and, in no small part based upon the scent, deduced that the internal moisture of the bird had caused his weapon to steam rather than roast. A triumphant giggle slid past his lips … followed by a guilty chortle from William's.

"I dub this …" Jimmy announced, holding the apparatus up into the air as if it were the holy sword Excalibur, "the *Fricassee Pistol!*"

"But it's a rifle," William said between laughs.

"Shh …" Jimmy hissed, disinterested in something as trivial as descriptive accuracy when phonetic alliteration was so much more satisfying.

Now, boys being what they are, Jimmy felt that a single test simply was not sufficient. One could argue that it was in the name of science. One could also argue that it was the simple yet maniacal delight of a boy with a gun.

CRACK! The fricassee pistol barked. *CRACK! CRACK! CRACK! CRACK! CRACK!*

The air swirled white. The ground around the coop quickly filled with a layer of feathers and down fit for any man's pillow, that pristine white plain interrupted only by a scattering of perfectly fricasseed chickens.

"*WHAT IN THE HELL ARE YOU BOYS DOING?*" a thunderous voice shouted from behind them.

Pleased as punch and innocent as a lamb, Jimmy turned away from the steaming chickens and said, "Testing my new invention." He recognized the considerable girth of Judge Davenport straight away, and realized a moment later that the situation might have taken a turn for the worst. Judging by the apoplectic hues of crimson spreading across the Judges features, Jimmy correctly deduced that the man was not one of science.

Jimmy stood in Judge Davenport's courtroom that very afternoon, despite the looming celebration of Christmas Day.

It was, in fact, the drone of Davenport's voice once again filling the courtroom that brought Jimmy back from his reminiscence of the morning's escapade. However, it was no longer reminiscence that occupied his youthful thoughts, so he respectfully raised his hand to speak.

"Your mother," Davenport continued, nodding in her direction, "has graciously provided remuneration for the loss of my property, and I am inclined to leave the matter in her lovely hands until the return of your father from our nation's capital, who will, I hope treat with you most severely." Davenport paused, his eyes narrowing at Jimmy's raised and clearly offensive hand. "Do not, I say, do *not* interrupt me when I am speaking, *boy!*"

"But—"

"There are no 'buts' in my courtroom, young man!" the judge barked.

"That may be, sir," Jimmy plowed on, "but it appears as if there are about to be Rebels in your courtroom."

That stopped the judge cold. "I beg your pardon?"

Jimmy pointed out the window at three approaching zeppelins, each the distinctive gray of the Confederate Air Force.

"*JESUS PALOMINO!*" Davenport shouted, lurching to his feet with his eyes fixed upon a Rebel-besmirched sky.

Three women, including Jimmy's mother, fainted straight away, although it could not be ascertained whether it was because of the looming Rebel attack or Davenport's overt, albeit unintentional blasphemy. Each lady, thankfully, was caught by a nearby gentlemen and eased onto the benches where considerably more conscious ladies fanned them.

The two bailiffs present dashed to the window, drawing their service revolvers as they ran. They stared up at the zeppelins, each gondola lined with heavy gun emplacements, and then stared pointedly at each other's pistols. A silent exchange passed between them in the fleeting moments that followed a synchronous realization: they were outmanned and outgunned.

They turned as one towards Davenport as a mass of townspeople crowded behind them at the window. In one voice they shouted over the clamor of frightened townsfolk, "We're in trouble, Your Honor!"

There were cries of "*What are we gonna do?*" mixed with "*We're doomed!*" from the terrified townsfolk.

One man shouted in a rather accusatory manner, "Where's the *sheriff?*"

Sheriff Tate, who had gleefully attended Jimmy's hearing on account of the number of times the boy had caused the town grief, replied rather heatedly, "Right here, McAffee! But there ain't much I can do against heavy guns with this pea-shooter strapped to my hip!"

The three zeppelins split, one coming straight at the courthouse while the other two started circling around the edge of town. As one, all three airships released a burst of gunfire. Thunder filled the sky as flame shot from the heavy caliber emplacements.

Men and women screamed in horror, but the detonations of artillery rounds clearly came from well beyond the outermost buildings.

"What the—!" one of the men yelled over the din.

Another shouted, "They ain't shooting at us!"

"Those are warning shots!" one of the bailiffs yelled. "Lettin' us know they can gun down anyone trying to leave town."

"ATTENTION CITIZENS OF HAYBERRY!" The words erupted from above and echoed throughout the entire town, spoken harshly and with a distinctly Tennessee accent. "THIS IS CAPTAIN WOLFORT OF THE CONFEDERATE AIRFORCE!"

The courtroom went silent.

"Hey," the other bailiff observed. "They's lowerin' a harness of some sort out the bottom of that there zep." He pointed to the airship that had taken up station some two hundred feet above and in front of the courthouse, hovering directly over Town Square.

"THE CONFEDERACY REQUESTS AND REQUIRES THAT YOU HAND OVER ONE JAMES ARCHIMEDES KRINKLEPOT FORTHWITH! FAILURE TO DO SO WILL RESULT IN ONE BUILDING BEING DESTROYED EVERY FIFTEEN MINUTES UNTIL HE IS IN OUR CUSTODY. WE WILL BEGIN WITH THE DESTRUCTION OF THE COURTHOUSE. YOU HAVE FIFTEEN MINUTES TO DECIDE!"

The courtroom went silent, and every pair of eyes save Jimmy's turned to the boy—some in fear, some with loathing, but most with a healthy dose of confusion. Every face, save two, held the question, *What did you get us into this time?*

Jimmy's confusion was readily apparent. All he could offer the accusing looks was open palms and an innocent shrug.

Judge Davenport, on the other hand, knew exactly what sort of game the Confederacy was playing. They were looking for a hostage, leverage against Jimmy's father, the most renowned scientist working for the Union military. The cads were clearly gentlemen enough not to ask for Krinklepot's wife, but they were not above taking a young man of near-legal fighting age into their custody.

"Turn him over!" several men shouted, pointing at the bewildered youth.

"I ain't dying for that rapscallion!" shouted Dickey Wilson as he moved towards Jimmy.

"Bailiffs! Restrain that man!" Judge Davenport shouted.

Both bailiffs, pouncing like well-trained Dobermans, grabbed Dickey and held him firm.

"*Enough!*" Davenport bellowed as his gavel came down like a sledgehammer. The entire courtroom went silent at the crack of wood, that silence broken only by the splintered halves of Davenport's sounding block as they clattered from his podium onto the hardwood floor. "I have no intention of handing that boy over to the Confederacy, no matter what he's done."

"But!—" Dickey started.

Davenport's fiery eyes locked onto Dickey's as he cut the man off with an icy tone: "I believe I have said before that there will be no 'buts' in my courtroom." He raised a fierce eyebrow, adding, "Do I make myself perfectly *clear*, Mister Wilson?"

Dickey, knowing when he was outgunned, closed his mouth and left it that way.

"So what are we gonna do?" Sheriff Tate asked.

Another hailstorm of questions fell in a flurry against the red-faced visage of the Judge.

Now Jimmy, being the sort of boy he was, had quietly set his gray matter to the problem at hand. At first he couldn't fathom why the Confederacy would want him. It was his father who worked for the Union.... And therein lay his answer. Jimmy was young and perhaps a bit naive about the ways of the world, but he'd read enough penny dreadfuls in his early years to understand how powerful a hostage could be. But what to do about it? He couldn't be handed over to the Confederacy as a bargaining chip, and the townsfolk lacked the means to withstand the assault of three heavily armed Confederate airships.

And, to add insult to injury, the lot of them had just under fourteen minutes to make a decision. Jimmy pondered and finally came upon a solution.

Amidst the confusion, he quietly walked over to a nearby table where Exhibit A stood waiting … and wanting.

"Excuse me, Your Honor?" Jimmy said quietly. His voice was drowned out by the cacophony flying between the judge, the sheriff, and the townsfolk. He stood up upon the table so that he might be heard better. "Your *HONOR!*" he shouted over the din.

Davenport spun at the intruding and somewhat high-pitched voice as the rest of the crowd continued to argue amongst themselves.

"What is it, boy?" he asked and then paused, silently contemplating the apparatus Jimmy held up in his hands. Said apparatus was offered with a mischievous grin and a raised eyebrow.

At first Davenport reveled at the thought of Rebels getting a dose of Jimmy's fricassee pistol, but then images of his prize chickens, featherless, cooked, and scattered about his yard came to mind. The thought of fricasseed men dotting the streets of Hayberry, Rebel or not, filled him with dread.

"Boy, I will not see those men fricasseed before the eyes of our fellow townsfolk, before the eyes of your lovely mother, and before God Himself! It is indecent! Inhuman! I do not care if they are Rebels! I will surrender before I allow your mother to see such a sight!"

Jimmy glanced at his mother who was, thankfully, still unconscious.

"Well, technically, Your Honor," he said a bit sheepishly, "my mother is still unaware of these events."

Davenport raised a warning finger, preparing for the "but" he could clearly discern in Jimmy's words.

"However," Jimmy continued, realizing his position was untenable, "I do see your point." Jimmy's mischievous grin had turned to a frown, and his gray matter pored over this new obstacle to his freedom and the safety of the Hayberry.

Then his eyes fell upon Davenport's iced lemonade.

Iced.

The entire town of Hayberry enjoyed iced beverages as a result of a minor invention provided to the people by Jimmy's father some years ago. Virtually every household, and even the courthouse, had a small icemaker that made the hot months of Missouri more bearable. And Judge Davenport was well known for his veritable addiction to iced beverages, even in the winter months. He had declared to Jimmy's father some years hence that the icemaker was perhaps civilized man's greatest achievement.

Indeed, the device was remarkable, and Jimmy had used its design as a foundation for his fricassee pistol, simply altering both current and polarity to achieve heating rather than cooling. His device, of course, was capable of exponentially greater output, but that was more a whim of youth than an engineering requirement.

Jimmy visualized the interior of the fricassee pistol's powerpack, crossed a few wires in his head, adjusted a couple of condensers, and immediately had a solution with which the judge would not be able to argue.

Jimmy raised his hand once again.

"YOU HAVE TWO MINUTES!" the southern voice boomed.

Jimmy stepped through the doors of the courthouse into frigid December air. William followed close behind, his knees shaking more from fear than the cold. He would rather be anywhere else in the world, but he was familiar with the device's controls, so he'd gotten the job of turning the thing on.

Judge Davenport and Sheriff Tate stepped out into the cold several steps behind the boys, Tate aiming his pistol at the boys' backs as if he were forcing them forward. It was a ruse, of course, meant to ease the trigger fingers of the Confederate gunners.

"Are you sure that thing will work the way you say?" Davenport hissed from behind Jimmy.

Jimmy nodded without looking back.

The waiting harness swung back and forth slowly several feet above the street as the zeppelin held its position.

"You best get to shootin', son," Tate said quietly. "That thing is almost on top of us."

Jimmy stopped several paces past the courthouse steps and turned to William.

"Turn it to eleven and flip all three switches," he said a bit nervously.

William nodded and licked his lips. He turned the dial, his hand shaking, and flipped the first switch. What had originally been a buzz from Jimmy's powerpack issued forth as an ear-splitting whine like a band saw. William flipped the second switch, and a drone pressed in upon them all like deep water. William flipped the third and felt his bones rattling inside his skin.

"You should all go back inside," Jimmy said nervously over his shoulder. He turned just in time to see William already backed up against the building and Sheriff Tate disappearing through the courthouse doors.

Judge Davenport, to his credit and quality of character, stood only three steps behind Jimmy, his hands over his ears. "Go ahead, son," he declared over the din, "I have no intention of letting you do this alone."

Jimmy smiled and nodded, his respect for Judge Davenport soaring.

Jimmy raised the apparatus and took aim at the airship above them, its nose just short of where he stood. He held his breath and pulled the lever.

CRAAAAAAAAAAAAAAAACK!

A cool green beam erupted from the weapon and splashed against the nose of the zeppelin. Energy enveloped the entire craft in a bright, green glow. The temperature at street level dropped twenty degrees in the blink of an eye as wisps of frozen air and crystalized water swirled around the coherent beam.

The slowly spinning rotors of the zeppelin froze in place. Ice formed where the beam contacted the envelope and spread, flash freezing across the entire surface of the aircraft. And then the ice around the envelope shattered as the whole thing expanded.

Jimmy released the lever, and the beam ceased. He watched in scientific fascination as some unexpected chemical reaction caused the envelope to bulge more and more with each passing moment.

"Holy shit," Davenport said, his eyes locked on the doomed airship.

The expanding dirigible ruptured with an explosive *WHOOF!* as the top split apart. A tremendous gout of white swirled into the air and expanded. What remained of the upper frame as well as the gondola slipped from the sky, plummeting towards terra firma.

Davenport made a quick estimation and realized that the zeppelin would not hit them upon impact. He grabbed Jimmy and spun the boy towards another zeppelin, this one turning as its guns swiveled towards them.

"SHOOT!" Davenport shouted as he pointed to the vessel.

Jimmy fired just as the first zeppelin crashed down into Town Square and collapsed in a heap of splintering timber and sagging canvas.

Jimmy's beam hit the second dirigible amidships, and seconds later it burst with a *WHOOF*, sending another white cloud into the air as the craft crashed to the ground.

Jimmy spun and aimed his weapon at the third Confederate zeppelin, but the craft was already turning away, its rotors screaming as it headed away at flank speed.

"Ease up, Mister Krinklepot," Davenport said, placing a gentle hand on the boy's shoulder. "Let them go."

"But—"

Davenport nearly reprimanded the boy for using another "but," but realized that they were no longer in his courtroom. Instead, he said, "Let them get home and tell the rest of those Rebels what happened here. They'll not be coming back if they know we can drop them with one shot." Davenport eyed Jimmy with newfound respect. The boy was more than a chip off the old block of his father.

Jimmy lowered the weapon and stared at the wreckage filling Town Square. The gondola had shattered, sending wood—and its occupants—flying out to the left and right. The shapes of frosty-white, ice-covered Confederate airmen littered the street, each one frozen solid, a surprised look captured on his face precisely as it was when Jimmy's beam hit.

"Well," Davenport observed, somewhat embarrassed by the presence of corpses littering the streets. "At least they're not fricasseed."

William stepped up behind Jimmy and flipped the switches. The drone of the powerplant faded to silence as he dialed the device back to its lowest setting.

The three stood there silently as large, moisture-laden snowflakes fell about them in what promised to be a short-lived blizzard at Confederate expense. A fine layer had already coated everything in sight, and a gentle smile spread across Jimmy's face.

Filled with pride, he victoriously raised the apparatus once again above his head. "I dub this ... the *Precipicrystalistivator.*"

Davenport and William turned confused faces towards Jimmy, astonished that so many syllables could come out someone's mouth in so short a time.

Finally, William said, "But I thought you called it the fricassee pistol."

"I did," Jimmy intoned seriously, "but this is something else entirely."

"It's the same thing," William pointed out. "All you did was cross a couple of wires."

"Shhh ..." Jimmy hissed, not wanting his moment of glory spoiled by trivialities like the facts.

"Okay ... fine." William said, exasperated. "It's a precip—a precipacry—what on Earth does that mean, Jimmy?" William finally asked, his mouth unable to stagger out the torrent of phonemes.

"It's quite simple, really," Jimmy said loftily. "'Precipi' referring to precipitation, 'crystali' referring to the crystallization of said precipitation, and 'tivator' a derivative of motivation, referring to the complete and utter lack of motivation and therefore ambulation of the subject after being exposed to my device's ray."

The judge blinked his eyes in disbelief for several breaths, shaking his head. "You just came up with that off the top of your head," he finally asked, stunned at the convolutions Jimmy Krinklepot's brain was capable of.

"Yes, sir," Jimmy replied. "And look …" he added, pointing to the accumulating snow. "It looks like we'll have a white Christmas after all."

"Indeed we will, Mister Krinklepot. I shall personally compose a Thank You letter to General Lee."

The judge and both boys laughed at the thought of Lee getting such a correspondence.

Jimmy turned his gaze to the window where the townsfolk cheered. His mother, who had apparently come around during the battle, stood in the middle of the crowd, beaming with pride.

William, of course, could only shake his head, realizing full well that there would be little to stop Jimmy Krinklepot in the future. And Judge Davenport contemplated several of his friends in Washington, who would be very interested in working with such a remarkable young man. He then said a prayer to God in Heaven for anything unfortunate enough to get in the way of the boy's not inconsiderable intellect.

"Mister Krinklepot," the judge said slowly, "in recognition of your service to the Union and in no small part for having saved the entire town of Hayberry, I do hereby commute your sentence. Don't you *dare* stop going to that junkyard of yours and doing what you do." Jimmy looked up at Davenport, a broad smile across his face. "Merry Christmas," the judge added almost jovially, and then his voice grew firm. "But if I catch you near my chickens again, young man, I will personally lock you up and throw away the key. Do you understand me?"

"Yes, sir." Jimmy smiled. "And Merry Christmas."

There's no place like home for the holidays, right? And home can mean many things: one's house, one's country, one's family, one's loves, one's freedom …

Loneliness may drive Kristine Kathryn Rusch's thoughtful Paris fantasy away from this sentiment at first, but a very special magic keeps the tale on track.

—KO

MIDNIGHT TRAINS

Kristine Kathryn Rusch

Nights he would find himself in the Metro, just before closing. The wide tunnels emptied around 11:30 p.m. Most locals did not use the Metro late, avoided the buses that some ridiculous city planner believed could replace the trains in the wee hours, and generally, found their own ways home. Sometimes, he imagined that savvy Parisians simply stayed wherever they ended up, in some on-going party to which he would never ever be invited.

Alex was 100 percent American. Nothing reminded him of that as much as Paris, which looked familiar, but always, always had an air of impenetrable mystery. Perhaps to the French, it was simply their grand city, like New York was to him—marvelous, yes, but not mysterious at all.

He shoved his hands in his coat pockets—a heavy wool great coat he'd found in some thrift shop, not that thrift shops here were anything like the thrift shops at home. Here, they smelled not of mothballs and sadness, but of cigarettes and perfume, forgotten traces of someone else's life.

He loved the coat. It warmed him and made him feel like a local, only because he dressed like one. Only because the coat had history. He did not.

His first Christmas in Paris left him flat-footed and unprepared. No one had warned him that the city shut down over the holiday. Even some of the ATMs stopped working.

Before he left America, his friends spoke enviously of his assignment—*Imagine Christmas in Paris*, they'd say. *Imagine the City of Lights.* The City of Lights was beautiful—holiday markets, decorations everywhere, elaborate baked goods that he couldn't imagine seeing at his last job in Chicago.

He'd come here to work, and his job, ostensibly in tech, was so high-up, he had trouble finding anyone at work who wasn't a subordinate, and therefore off-limits.

He had friends in the city now, but they didn't ask him to their Christmas celebrations. He never mentioned the holiday, but one-by-one, his French friends pulled him aside to tell him why they couldn't ask him to join them. As one woman told him, *The holiday, she is for family, no?*

Only he had none. That was why the company had chosen to send him to France. That, and the fact that he spoke fluent French, although he soon learned that what he actually spoke was fluent American-flavored prissy and dated French, the kind that actually made the French wince and ask if they could practice their English instead. It was the polite French way of telling him that they didn't want to hear him mangle the language.

He mangled anyway, and tried to imitate the accents he heard. Hard for him, since he grew up in Austin, then escaped to Chicago for high school. His personal accent was a jumble of the two cities, with Chicago taking precedence when he was awake, Austin when he was exhausted. Apparently, his French was mostly Texas-flavored, which his co-workers found hysterical. Once they relaxed around him, they'd mimic him in front of them, and rather than be offended, he learned what to say, when to say it, and how it should sound.

He had arrived in April; by September, he felt as accepted as a man like him could be, and by December, he'd been a bit surprised that he received no invitations.

And that was when he learned: *Christmas, she is for families, c'est ne pas?* It shouldn't have bothered him. He had been alone for Christmas for ten years. He was eighteen when his parents died in a terrible plane crash. He had been old enough to live alone, but too young to figure out how to do it right. A girlfriend in college (which he could afford with insurance money) had taken him to her family for every major holiday in the three years they dated.

When they broke up, he felt it not as the loss of a love, but like the loss of his parents all over again. A man without family, and this year, a man without country, away from the familiar rhythms of the commercial holiday season that he had grown up with.

His late-night walks around the city had started in August, another time when the French seemed to abandon work and their lives en masse to go somewhere else. He noted the closed businesses, the confused tourists, the occasional angry employee, left to guard the restaurant, the bar or the shop.

He got to know the sound of his own footsteps, echoing along the Seine in the Ile de la Cite, and he liked that sense of anonymity, which used to frighten him back in the States.

Back there, he used to think: *What if I died here? No one would find me for days, weeks, even. No one would care.*

Somehow Paris taught him a different attitude, a sense that nothing died, not really, and at the same time, that no one cared except in a way that interfered with their daily lives.

Maybe, someday, Alex would find someone who loved him as much as the couples who kissed on Pont des Arts bridge seemed to love each other. But not yet, and maybe not ever.

When he realized he would be alone on Christmas (*Noël est pour les familles, non?*), he checked his favorite restaurants in the area to see if they would be open. Of course, they were not. (*It is,* one kind chef told him, *the only time we escape.*)

Alex could, he was told, eat at some brasseries (except Christmas Eve, when almost everything was closed) or a few tourist spots, or in one of the train stations. Or, as in America, in any of the Chinese restaurants.

Alex decided to decide on Christmas Day. He walked everywhere, after all. He could walk then, even if it rained. He didn't mind the rain; it was so much better than the Chicago cold.

He bought some food in case he felt like staying in, and thought it done.

But he was not prepared for the silence in a city usually filled with traffic, honking horns, music in the streets, arguing couples, and the occasional singing drunk. The closed shops, the empty streets, the shuttered restaurants, brought the city home to him in a way he had never seen before.

It was as if he had gotten closer to her, only to find her abandoned by the ones who loved her the most.

The Metro stations remained open—some people had to go to work, after all—but they all ran Sunday hours, and Sunday hours meant some stations were, for all intents and purposes, closed, trains running on a whim, it seemed, rather than on a schedule.

Early in December, he went to the Galleries Lafayette, because a friend had told him he had to see the entire store festooned in light. He did, and instead of taking his usual train home, he went to the Left Bank, and stopped in the Cluny-La Sorbonne.

If someone asked, he would say it was his favorite Metro station. If they asked why, he would give them the tourist answer—because of the mosaics. They covered the station's vaulted ceiling. Most tourists adored Jean Bazaine's gigantic frieze, *Les Oiseaux*, a yellow, orange, and pink monstrosity that suggested birds in flight.

But Alex liked the historic signatures represented in mosaic tiles. Some he recognized, like Robespierre and Richelieu, and others he had never heard of.

He stared at them for hours. They receded into the darkness that marked both tunnel entrances, some illuminated only as a train went through. It was in the Cluny-La Sorbonne that he realized rats appeared the moment the station closed. He'd gotten locked in one night, and was saved only by a kind guard who took him for a dumb tourist.

He didn't want to stay with the rats—they heard the final announcement and poured from the holes in the walls, like something from a bad horror movie. Strangely, they didn't frighten him.

This station had belonged to them much longer than it belonged to humans.

Because, what he really loved about Cluny-La Sorbonne was its history. The station, then called simply Cluny, opened in 1930, and was closed in 1939 because, the official records said, it was too close to another Metro station.

The Cluny-La Sorbonne became one of Paris's Ghost Stations, a place on a map that only a few knew about. For nearly fifty years, the station remained unused. In the 1980s, city planners decided to revive it because they needed the connection—making it, in his opinion, one of the few ghosts to ever return from the dead.

The station also felt odd to him—a little cold, a little displaced, as if it never got used to its return. No ads graced its white tile walls, and the benches seemed like all others in the Metro, placed a comfortable intervals. The plainness of the walls, the ornate ceiling, the miles of track, disconcerted him on a deep level, and made him feel out of time, as if nothing could touch him here.

He would wander in cold nights, and sit, staring at the ceiling as if it held answers, the great wool coat wrapped around him. If he sat very still, the coat's faint scent of cigarettes and perfume would rise like a half-forgotten memory.

He wouldn't let himself doze—the rats had cured him of that thought—so on nights when he was most exhausted, he would stand and sway like a drunk.

Sometimes he would board a midnight train and ride it to a station near his apartment, but most often, he would sigh, give his station a fond glance, and head back out into the well-lit Parisian night.

He thought of going to church on Christmas Eve, but he wasn't sure when the services would start. And he knew he would have a choice of listening to Latin or French. He wasn't particularly religious, nor was he greatly interested. Much as he liked the great cathedrals of Europe, he saw them more as architectural curiosities, filled with a potent sense of history, rather than as a place to worship.

A neighbor told him of a concert to be given that night; another mentioned that some of the revues would be open; a third had winked and offered to give him the name of a proper gentleman's club.

Alex finally decided on the concert, and started his walk. He ended up in the Latin Quarter, not far from the Cluny Museum, right near his favorite Metro stop, and somehow he made a decision without making a decision—he walked down the stairs to see if the station was still open on this most unusual night of the year.

The station was open, but he was alone. A train whispered by as if inspired by the city's holiday hush. Even the announcements seemed fewer than normal, and the usually strident voices giving commands in rather harsh French seemed warmer than usual.

He huddled in his great wool coat, and then he saw her. Black hair, wedge cut, lipstick so red that it shouldn't have worked on anyone's face, let alone a face as small and delicate as hers. Her black dress with its diamond shaped neckline and nipped waist looked a bit old-fashioned. Even her stockings seemed dated. They had seams running down the back of her legs.

She held a cigarette in her left hand.

"Light?" she asked in Parisian-accented English. He had become used to that sixth sense Europeans had about him. They all seemed to know his nationality before he even opened his mouth. Even after seven months in Paris, somehow, he had not assimilated.

"No, I'm sorry," he said gently.

"Ah," she said. "It is a filthy habit that they claim will kill me. They know nothing."

She looked at the cigarette as if she were deciding whether or not to hang onto it, and then she touched its tip. It flared, glowed red, and the rich scent of expensive tobacco rose around him.

He frowned at it, wondering if it was one of those electronic cigarettes he'd heard about, but then wondered why she would ask him for a light if it were.

"I thought you needed a light," he said.

"I decided you would not mind," she said.

"Mind what?" he asked.

"Me." She smiled.

He felt dizzy. Maybe it was the cigarette smoke—maybe he had inhaled too much. Or maybe he was tired; it was the end of a very long year, after all, and he was at loose ends—not professionally, never professionally—but personally. Wondering if this was all there ever would be for him: Christmas Eves alone, in beautiful places.

"Why would I mind?" he asked, wishing he could follow her logic.

"Some do," she said.

The station remained silent. He wondered if he could check his phone for the time, and then decided against it because he considered it rude. The fact he was worried about being rude to this woman, this confusing woman, seemed strange to him.

"We probably missed the last train," he said.

She looked at him sideways. Her eyes were the color of dark chocolate, her skin smooth. Her faint perfume seemed familiar.

"You do not take the train," she said.

He frowned at her. Of course, he took the train. He took the train all the time.

Just not here. He'd disembarked here the first time, but after that, he hadn't come here at all. Not for the trains. For the signatures. The feel, the clean white tiles and the dim lights. The sense of something other worldly.

"You've seen me here before," he said.

"Yes." Quick, with that accent. He was beginning to be able to distinguish one French accent from another, and this one had a curtness, a fillip at the end of words that he hadn't heard before.

"I'm sorry," he said. "I don't remember seeing you."

And he would. He would remember her, delicate and pretty and vibrating with an energy very similar to the trains themselves.

"I know," she said. "I did not let you see me."

He felt a chill. Was she stalking him? Was she crazy? He smiled at her, knowing the smile probably looked fake, knowing it probably seemed dismissive. He couldn't help it. He no longer wanted to stand beside her.

He was about to move when she took the edge of his coat sleeve in her right hand.

"The man who owned this," she said, "he was—how do you say?—a dreamer. Is that the word?"

How would he know what word she wanted when he didn't know what she was trying to say? He bit back the irritation. He didn't want to be near her any more.

"It's just a coat," he said.

"Ah, *mon cher*," she said. "It is not just a coat. It is history, no?"

"No," he said, and walked away. His footsteps echoed in the silence. The skin on the back of his neck crawled. She was watching him; he knew it.

He turned—

But she was gone.

He vowed not to go back. On his entire walk home, the cobblestone slick with rain he had missed while underground, his breath fogging before him, he told himself he was done with the Metro, with the Cluny-La Sorbonne. He'd seen it. He had had enough.

She unnerved him. He recognized that.

The lights of the Eiffel Tower did not comfort him, so he walked to Notre Dame. He checked his phone—no calls, of course—but its clock told him that it wasn't yet midnight.

Well-dressed worshippers walked behind the large Christmas tree near the entrance. The blue lights decorating the tree startled him as they had from the beginning; he was still used to red and green and white. But Paris preferred blue—all along the Champs-Elyéese, near Les Halles and in the Place de la Concorde—so very much blue.

Blue Christmas.

He almost walked around the gigantic tree himself. He could hear choral music on the night air, the harmonies pure and clear. He hesitated.

History waited for him in there, that sense of time standing still. Midnight mass at Notre Dame on Christmas Eve had to date back hundreds, maybe even a thousand years.

But it wouldn't satisfy him. Christmas Eve mass wasn't his tradition, wasn't something he really believed in, wasn't something that would touch his heart.

Like the brush of cool fingers as they touched the edge of his coat.

The man who owned this …

How had she known?

He turned, looked back down the street toward the Cluny Museum, which was impossible to see from here. He only had a sense of it, knew that it wouldn't be open, maybe not even lit. It had looked surprisingly dowdy compared to the show the rest of Paris put on in the holiday season.

But he wasn't looking at the museum. He was thinking of the Metro station. By the time he walked back, it would be closed. She would be gone.

Or would she?

He shook his head slightly, and stood, hands in his pockets, staring at the tree and the massive cathedral behind it.

This moment was almost magical enough for him. The music, the blue lights, the worshippers crossing the ancient stone, going under the ancient arches.

He took one step forward, and a hand slipped through his arm.

He looked to his side. She was there. She wore a black coat now over her black dress, with what looked like fur trim on the wrists and neck. She looked up at him and smiled.

"I do not go into such places," she said. "They make me crazy."

Then, she patted his arm, slipped away, and walked toward the tree. Its blue lights fell across her features, altering them, making her look almost two dimensional, like the old computer images. Her fingers rose toward the branches, brushing them like she had brushed his coat.

She stepped back.

Worshippers went around her, as if she were giving off a force field. One or two frowned at her as they went by. Others gathered their coats tightly around themselves and shivered.

He watched, not certain what she was doing.

The choral music flowed high above them, the harmonies unearthly.

She came back to him, slipped her arm through his, and said, "Let's go."

They walked through the quiet city. The lights made it seem like it had been abandoned mid-party. The scents of cigarettes and perfume followed them, and eventually, he realized it wasn't just his coat. The scents also came from her.

When they came to the Institut de France, illuminated in white, they turned toward the Pont des Arts bridge. In all of his time in Paris, he had never seen the bridge empty—no humans at all.

The benches in the center bore no kissing couples, the wooden slats looked slick and lonely. The day's padlocks remained on the railings, bearing the names of lovers, of happy couples and important dates. No one had cleared them off yet, and he wondered if anyone would over the holiday.

She led him up the bridge, her hands wrapped around his arm. The Seine reflected lights, mostly blue, from the holiday itself.

"You said you know my coat," he said, because he couldn't stand the sound of his heels on the wood. It sounded as lonely as he felt, even though he was walking with a beautiful woman in the most beautiful city in the world.

She led him to one of the benches, and ran her hand across it. Then she rubbed her fingers together as if testing whether or not they were wet.

She sat, then patted the wood beside her. It looked surprisingly dry.

"Your coat, like everything else in this city, has a past," she said softly. "It called to me."

He frowned, wishing she could be clear, maybe afraid that she was clear.

"It is why I watched you in the Metro," she said. "I had forgotten the coat."

Then she shook her head.

"I had forgotten the solstice. I have slept for so long."

He frowned at her. She smiled at him. The light again played on her face, only this time, it was golden light reflected off the water and the buildings on either side of the bridge. The Louvre cast the most light. Perhaps, he thought, it should, since it gave the bridge its name.

The random thoughts, his emotional distance, the remaining loneliness, they still surprised him. This beautiful woman, for all her odd talk, should have intrigued him more.

But he didn't understand her, almost as if she were speaking a different language and he only caught every other word.

"I wanted to believe I was used to iron," she said, "and then it trapped me."

She leaned her head on his shoulder for just a moment. He expected warmth. Instead, he got more perfume, more cigarettes.

"You freed me, you know."

"What?" he asked.

She shook her head. "My people—this was our holiday. Midwinter. We celebrated with lights. We put greenery in our homes. We danced, and feasted, and made love …"

He shuddered. He shouldn't have shivered when a beautiful woman spoke of sex.

"Then we lost our homes, our forests, and came Paris." She ran a hand along his coat. "The man who owned this, he is dead now."

Alex had supposed that much. Coats like this didn't end up in thrift stores by accident.

"He died defending me. My family, we hid in those tunnels, because the Germans, they decided to do what they had always done. Take us, destroy us, make us into something more like them." She nodded toward the road they had just walked on. "Like that cathedral, with one of our trees outside."

She really was crazy. Germans, dead men, trees. She seemed to be conflating World War II with the Christian Church slowly taking over the pagan celebrations and making them part of the liturgy.

She made him nervous.

But Alex had to ask. "He died defending you?"

She nodded, then looked at Alex, tears in her eyes. "He had a pistol. He held the Germans off while my family and I escaped into the ghost tunnels. We were to leave, but the iron, it held us prisoner, changed us, trapped us. Like rats. That is how I first saw you, through the wall. I thought you were him."

God, what was he to do with her? She was against the church, so he couldn't take her to the priests there for help. And he had no idea what other place might take her in. He wasn't even sure where the homeless shelters were—if there even were homeless shelters in this city.

She clearly had escaped from somewhere—an institution, a caregiver. Someone had to be looking for her, right?

There were several hospitals close to here, one near the Louvre itself. He wondered if he could get her there. He had never had cause to use any of the medical facilities in the city before.

"But you are not him, are you?" She brushed at his coat, as if she were removing lint. "You are not even his reincarnation. Mortals have such short lives."

Alex couldn't help himself. He engaged. "What are you, if not mortal?"

Her smile was sad. "We are so lost you no longer recognize us."

She swept her hair back, then cupped his cheek. Her touch was cold.

"Lonely man," she said. "You believe forever lonely."

He tried not to move, not to betray anything with his expression. How had she known that? Was it that obvious?

It probably was. He was alone on Christmas Eve, after all. He was American. He clearly didn't belong.

It didn't take much to figure out that he was lonely, that he had no one to spend his time with.

"Because you freed me," she said softly, "I owe you."

"I don't understand," he said, "how did I free you?"

"You saw me," she said. "As me, not as what I had become. To most, I was a creature. To others, the ghost of a woman they once loved. But to you, I was myself. You saw only me."

She flattened her palm on his heart.

"It is because you have no woman and lost no woman that you saw me. It is your sadness that brought me back to life."

Like the station itself, something whispered in his head. He didn't like that thought. It made him uncomfortable. But, then, *she* made him uncomfortable.

"So," she said, "a gift to you."

She placed her red lips against his forehead. They were cold, like the rest of her.

And then, oddly, his heart lifted. Like it used to do when he was a child, when his parents were alive.

His mother used to say, *Your heart has wings.*

It had wings now.

"Sometimes," the woman before him said, "hearts shatter. They must be repaired before they work again."

Then she placed her chill forefinger under his chin, lifted his head slightly, and kissed him on the lips.

"I thank you," she said—and disappeared.

He sat on the bench for a long time. Bells rang all over the city for midnight mass—Christmas Eve mass.

She had been an illusion, a figment of his overheated imagination.

He had himself convinced of that by the time he finished the long walk back to his apartment. A Christmas Eve hallucination. An undigested bit of beef, as Scrooge once said of Marley's ghost.

Who turned out to be real enough.

Alex shuddered, not certain why he was so very cold. It was warmer in Paris on Christmas Eve than it usually was in Chicago on Christmas Eve. There, he would not have walked the center of the city in a coat, without a hat or gloves.

He took off the coat, and hung it on the built-in coat hanger near the door. Then he walked into the bathroom to wash the chill from his skin. He turned on the overhead light, and saw his face in the mirror, cheeks rosy from the chill, skin a bit too pale.

But that wasn't what caught his eye.

What caught his eye was the bright red lipstick print on his forehead, with traces of the same lipstick on the side of his mouth.

She had been real.

And she had disappeared as if she had never been.

Oddly, he didn't return to the Cluny-La Sorbonne Metro station for nearly a year. If asked, he would not say that was by design. He still used the Metro—maybe more than he had before—but he no longer wandered into the stations by himself, no longer stood waiting for midnight trains to whoosh by him on the way to something much more important.

He had important things to do now. A wife, an infant daughter, newly born. The City of Light had become a city of warmth for him.

He ended up in the Cluny-La Sorbonne by accident on the Winter Solstice, a bouquet of winter flowers in his hand, a bottle of wine under his arm. He had been distracted; he got on the wrong train, which brought him here.

He had already called his wife to apologize for being late. His wife, so lovely, so French. She had no family either, so she helped him make one. They had met on New Year's Eve. He hadn't planned to go out, yet he couldn't stay in. He'd never been in a world-class city on a world-class holiday. It seemed churlish to avoid the celebrations. And he didn't want to seem lonelier than he already was.

He had stumbled into her. Truth be told, he worried for a half second that she was the crazy woman from the Metro, but his wife was not tiny or crazy. She was tall and blonde and sensible. She filled his arms, and somehow, she filled his heart—the heart he once thought untouchable.

Maybe it had healed. Or maybe …

That sensation of wings returned to him whenever he thought of that moment on the Pont des Arts. A gift, the strange woman had said. A gift he had told no one about.

He was the only person inside the Cluny-La Sorbonne. The birds mosaic flew overhead. The signatures glistened. And then the announcement sounded. The station had closed. Only one exit remained open.

He turned toward the wall, expecting rats.

But there were none.

His breath caught.

He wanted to believe the city had gotten rid of them.

But he had looked up old legends in the past year. Stories of Faerie. Trapped by iron, forced to change shape in their prison. Industrialization destroyed their habitat, just like the church had stolen their power.

The Germans had searched for them. Hitler believed magic would become one of the weapons of the Third Reich. If the Faerie existed, they hid.

And sometimes, all it took was something simple to destroy a curse.

Like a man, looking at a woman, and seeing her for who she was.

Alex shook his head, smiled at his fanciful nature. His wife said he was a dreamer. Perhaps he was.

Now.

He pulled one of the white roses from the bouquet. He knew the strange woman was no longer down here, just like he knew the rats were truly gone. But he needed a token anyway.

He placed the rose on the bench near where he had first seen her.

Whoever she was, she had touched him. She had made him see a future he didn't want, one of lonely Christmas Eves that extended forever, like the Metro tunnels, midnight trains running with no one to board them.

He might have seen her, but she saw him as well.

And because she had, he saw himself more clearly.

That vision, that moment, led to this one.

"Thank you," he whispered—and then walked to the exit, holding flowers for his wife, wine for their celebration, and a little bit of hope, in the wings of his heart.

The holiday dinner table! Piled high with platters of tender meats, savory sides, thick gravies, and rich sweets. A feast to defy the cold and dark of winter.

And a good thing, because in Jonathan Maberry's harrowing tale of survival, it is so very cold outside, and so very dark, and so very dead....

—KO

A Christmas Feast

A Story of the Rot & Ruin

Jonathan Maberry

1

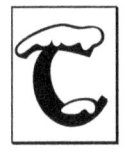he living moved like ghosts through the fog.

The dead waited in the swirling mist.

There were screams in the air. A few shouts and gunshots.

And the moans.

Always the moans.

Long, and low and plaintive. Uttered by mouths that hung slack, rising from chests that drew breath only to moan—never again to breathe. The moans spoke of a hunger so old, so deep, so endless that nothing, not even the red gluttony of a screaming feast, could satisfy it.

The hunger existed.

Like *they* existed.

Without purpose and without end.

The mists were as thick as milk, white, featureless, hiding everything until far too late. Figures moved through the fog.

And the dead waited for them.

2

The man and the boy heard those moans and huddled together, biting the rags they wore as scarves to keep from screaming.

They were beyond tired. Beyond weary.

Both of them were thin as scarecrows. Barely enough meat on them to allow their bodies to shiver. Clothing was torn; patched with duct tape and rope.

Most of the time the man carried the boy. Sometimes—like now—he was too weak, too starved to manage it. The boy stumbled behind him, clutching his hand, too weary to cry. That's when they moved the slowest. That's when they were the most vulnerable.

The boy, Mason, was six. A lean phantom of the chubby child he'd been when they'd run away in August. It was only four months, but weight had fallen from them like leaves from an autumn tree. There were dead things out there that had more flesh on their bones.

The man—Mason's older brother, Dan—stuffed the boy's clothes with wadded up pieces of old newspaper. It helped some, trapping little bits of warmth.

Dan wore three sets of longjohns and he still looked skinny.

"I'm hungry…." said Mason. Not for the first time. Or the hundredth.

"I know," said Dan.

"I'm *tired!*"

"I know."

"I want my mommy!"

The man squeezed his eyes shut but the tears found their way out anyway. "I know," he whispered. "Me, too."

3

Almost the worst thing for Dan was how much he envied the dead.

They were always hungry, sure, same as he and Mason. Hunger was everywhere. But the dead didn't seem to mind it. They never wept for the want of food. They hunted, sure. That's all they did. But once Dan and Mason had slept in a church tower and all day Dan watched the dead ones walk around or stand or sometimes kill and eat. When they feasted, they did it like dogs. Like jackals. They tore it apart and consumed everything as fast as they could. Like they were starving. As Dan and Mason were starving.

But when there was no meat. When there was no one to kill, they just … *were*. They didn't fall down from hunger. They didn't scream with the pain of needing food.

They just kept being …

Being what?

What were they?

The newspapers threw a lot of words around before it all went silent. Walkers. Rooters. Flesh-eaters. Ghouls.

Zombies.

Them.

Whatever they were, they never seemed to actually mind being hungry.

Like they never minded the cold. Or the rain. Or the wind.

They just were.

Dan hated the thought of envying them.

He hated himself for feeling that envy.

He hated himself.

He hated.

And he hungered.

4

They'd left the highway four hours ago.

That was the route most of the refugees had used even though none of the cars worked anymore. Something had happened to them.

There had been big explosions, high up and far away and all of the cars died. Cell phones, too. Everything electric.

The two of them had been following a highway for days. The highways were straight routes. The cars offered some protection when the dead found them. You could hide in cars. At least for a while. Some of the dead could pick up rocks and smash the glass. If you were still, if you were quiet, you could wait out the night and in the stillness of the morning you could steal away.

But then there was a spot where hundreds and hundreds of the dead crowded the road. Everyone ran. Dan tossed Mason over the guardrail into the thick grass, leaped the rail himself with half a second to spare, scooped up his brother, and ran.

And ran.

And ran.

The people who ran down into the valleys didn't make it. There were rumors about that. It was worse in the lowlands. When the dead weren't following prey they followed the path of least resistance. They crowded the lowlands because gravity pulled with subtle insistence on stumbling feet. Fewer of them fought that pull to walk up hill. Not unless there was meat to find. A handful of travelers out scavenging shared this new lore with Dan. When the highways became impossible, Dan took his brother up the slopes, into the foothills of the mountains.

At first there were just as many of the dead. Hungry, tireless. Awful.

But soon there were fewer. The higher they climbed, there were fewer.

Fewer.

Never none.

They passed places where people had fought and died. Some of them were still there, but these were not the staggering dead. These bodies had terrible head wounds. Gunshots, blows from blunt weapons.

"Don't look at them," Dan warned his brother.

But the boy looked. Of course he looked. His eyes were filled with ...

Nothing.

When it all went bad, Mason had been too young to understand much of what was happening when the plague swept out of the TV news and into their lives. Since then there had been no chance to give him a sense of what the world was like. What the world should have been like. Horror was everyday. Horror was everywhere. So, how could his brother, how could little Mason, have any understanding of how bad things were? For him—for both of then—every moment was built around moving forward, staying safe, scavenging food, finding water. Finding warmth.

Beyond where the bodies lay a small lane spurred off from the main road. A wrecked car blocked the entrance, but when the man leaned over the crumpled hood he saw that the lane was clear.

Dan nodded, accepting it as a gift. Believing it to be so.

He picked Mason up, kissed him on the forehead, set him down on the hood of the car, and pushed him gently to the other side. Then he climbed up and over to help him down onto the ground again. A signpost wrapped in withered creeper vines read: SULLIVAN LANE.

He didn't know where it went, but any road was good as long as it wasn't the one they were on. Besides, the lane was lined on both sides by heavy pine trees that blocked the fierce winds. It was still here, and without the wind the temperature was bearable. The snow was piled in long drifts against the trees, but the center of the lane was barely dusted.

"Come on," he said again, though this time there was less urgency in his voice. Mason tried to walk, and he made it for a quarter mile before his stumbling feet failed. Dan scooped him up before he could fall, and though his own strength was flagging, he carried his brother into the wintry night.

Snow fell the way snow does. Soft, quiet, quilting the world with whiteness, hiding the truth of what lay beneath. It dampened down the sounds from farther down the road. The moans. The cries. The gunfire. All of it was distant anyway, and the snow shushed it to silence.

It was powdery and dry, and it blew it slow drifts across the road. The air was frigid and the temperature was dropping. Rags and newspaper were not enough.

Dan saw the uneven lumps in the road ahead and knew it for what it was. A fight that had ended the way these fights do.

Badly.

He kept going, though. What else was there to do? Keep moving or lay down here and wait for either the teeth of the wind or the teeth of the dead to do their work.

The only grace, and it was small, was that the wind blew at his back rather than in his face. It pushed him, ever so subtly, uphill.

So it was uphill he walked, clutching his brother in his arms, feeling the ten tons of the little boy turn to twenty tons, to thirty. Dan never once let go, though. No, sir, he did not do that.

Hours passed. The night deepened with the snow.

Dan tried not to count the bodies in the snow. He knew that was the kind of thing a madman would do. Counting the dead as a way of passing the time. That wasn't right.

Then after a time he realized that there were no more dead to count. The road stretched ahead, pale despite the darkness of night. Smooth and unbroken.

Dan stopped for a moment and set Mason down. The kid was out of his feet and he sagged against Dan, leaning on his thighs, fingers hooked into his pants pockets, eyes closed.

"It's okay," whispered Dan, smoothing the boy's matted hair. "We're safe."

Saying that was dangerous. Believing it was dangerous.

So dangerous.

There was hope in that concept, and hope was like a backstabbing friend. You could trust it sometimes, and then it would turn and drive its blade deep.

They had to be careful. They had to learn to live without trust. To live without assumption or expectation.

To live without.

That made the road so hard, so long, so lonely. And the man and his little brother were too far-gone to be company to each other.

Dan never stopped watching. He never let his attention slacken.

"I'm cold," said Mason, and the way he said it jolted Dan. It was in a sleepy, dreamy, resigned voice.

Dan knelt, feeling his brother's face and fingers. They were like ice. The temperature was plummeting and the fog was turning to crystals in the air. It was so humid he knew that it would start snowing soon.

Panic flared in his chest. He rubbed Mason's cheeks and arms, trying to coax the circulation, fighting to keep alive the spark of heat in the boy's limbs. He took Mason's icy fingers and put them in his own mouth, breathing his own heat onto them.

Mason's eyelids fluttered, but his eyes didn't open.

"Please," begged Dan, feeling tears break from his eyes and run like boiling water down his cheeks. "Please. God ... please."

He was aware, as everyone was aware, that prayers were not being answered anymore. If they ever had been. While on the road, Dan had a lot of time to think about all of the desperate and needy ones who had begged for God's mercy in times of war and famine, in wretched hospitals and on sinking ships. If there was a plan in God's mercy, or His lack of mercy, Dan couldn't see it. He still believed, but the structure of his belief had collapsed with the world. Those nights hiding in a church had not restored his confidence that grace would be afforded to him. He was pretty sure he didn't deserve any anyway. But Mason was a kid.

Four years old.

Dan did not believe in the concept of original sin. That seemed like bullshit to him. Sin was earned. Babies don't have any. They can't or God is an asshole. Dan didn't think God was an asshole. A merciless fuck, maybe, but not an asshole.

So where was mercy?

Where, in the endless dark of this night, was His grace?

"Please," he prayed as he tried to rub life back into his brother's flesh. "Please."

5

"Danny—?"

Mason's voice was so pale, so empty.

But it was there.

The dead don't speak. They can't.

Only the living can do that.

Dan hugged his brother to him. He pulled the ends of his coat around the boy. Maybe together their heat would be enough.

Maybe.

Sobbing, Dan picked Mason up and squinted into the darkness. The snow clouds must have been thinner than he thought because he could see light. Moonlight? Was it a full moon? Or a gibbous moon?

He didn't know. He'd come to learn the phases of the moon during his months on the run, but it had been cloudy for days.

Still, there was light.

Cold and …

Yellow.

Yellow?

Dan frowned at it. Moonlight was white. Moonlight on snow was blue.

This was yellow.

And it was wrong. It seemed to reach up to paint the undersides of the trees. It wasn't coming down from the clouds.

Yellow light.

Not sunlight yellow. There were hours of darkness left to go.

Yellow.

Like …

He was running before he knew it.

Aching, weary legs pumped as if he'd been resting for hours. He could feel his heart hammering inside his chest. Like fists beating on a door.

Like hope pounding to be let out of Pandora's Box.

The road snaked and whipsawed as it climbed the mountain. There were houses on either side. Doors smashed open or boarded up. Blood streaks and spatters. Bullet holes. Nowhere he dared go.

The light was ahead. Up the hill. Near the top.

No.

At the top.

His legs were trembling so badly that he knew he couldn't go on much more. He needed to set Mason down. He needed to rest.

But not out here in the cold. In the snow.

Not in any of those houses where death had come calling.

The light was stronger.

Closer.

Brighter.

Dan rounded another bend. Another. Another.

And then there was a long space of nothing. Just trees and empty fields on either side of the road. The snow was unbroken up here. Nothing and no one had come this way in hours.

There was a huge stand of old trees. Oaks and pines and maples. So heavy they blocked the view of the top of the hill.

But through them …

Through them.

The yellow light.

He could see it shining on the ice, glimmering on each snowflake.

So close.

"Hold on," he whispered to Mason, but the boy did not respond. He was limp in Dan's arms. "Hold on."

Dan kept going along the road, up the road, to wherever this road led. If it led to a pack of the dead, then he knew he would drop to his knees and try to hide Mason with his own body. Or maybe he'd just smother the boy. Choke him out and leave him to come back as one of them. They never wept for hunger.

If that happened, maybe he could find a way to kill himself, too. It would be better to go wandering with Mason than to let the boy go on alone.

Dan knew that this was a crazy thought. It was nuts.

He was nuts.

Of course he was. How could he not be? The world had ended. Humanity fell, the dead rose. None of that was sane.

Not one bit of it.

Dan kept going, ignoring the pain in his thighs and calves.

Chasing the light.

Chasing hope ...

Reading to give in if hope was as false as everything else. Expecting it to be that way. Why should hope be any different?

The road curved around the big stand of trees.

Around.

Around.

And ...

"God ..." whispered Dan.

He nearly dropped Mason.

The light.

The light.

The light.

Oh God, the light.

6

The door to the house stood open.

Light spilled out onto the snow, into the night.

Yellow.

Golden.

Real.

Dan felt a pain in his heart and for a moment he thought this was all a cheat, that his heart was going to burst right there, fifty feet from the front door of this house. This cottage in the woods.

This.

Home.

"Please," he said again, this time not to God but to his own body. To his legs.

Forty feet.

Mason had not moved in a long time.

Thirty feet.

Wind blew past him and whipped snow into the open doorway.

Twenty feet.

His brother felt like a block of ice in his arms.

"Please … please …"

Ten feet.

When he reached the doorway his questing left foot stepped down but the ankle and knee had no more to give. He fell forward and down. He tried to hold onto Mason.

Tried.

But his brother fell from his hands, landed, slid inside the house.

Dan fell on his face. On a thin carpet of snow over a thick carpet of soft fibers.

He felt toward the light but he landed in darkness.

7

Dan opened his eyes and saw the wrong thing.

Not a carpet. Not snow.

He saw a pillow.

On a carpet.

A pillow under his head, on the carpet.

It made no sense.

His mind struggled to understand it while his body struggled to wake up. There was pain everywhere. In the legs that had walked for so many miles. In the arms that had held Mason for so long. For too long. His biceps and forearms felt stretched. His fingers were like rusted hinges.

He could understand the pain.

Not the pillow.

He couldn't understand the pillow.

"Danny—?"

Dan's head whipped sideways and there was a face. Inches away.

Mason.

Not frozen.

Not dead.

Not undead.

Mason.

Covered in dirt and dried snot and …

And…?

Gravy?

It glistened on the boy's cheeks and chin.

Mason was smiling.

Smiling?

Dan could not remember the last time his brother smiled. He would have bet that Mason couldn't do that anymore. That he couldn't. That smiles had died out with most of the people. With all of the people they'd ever known. Mom and Dad. Janie. Uncle Jimmy and Aunt Sally.

No more smiles.

Except that Mason was smiling.

"Mason?" he said. It came out as a croak.

Dan shifted, tried to roll onto his side. That's when he realized that there was a blanket over him. No, a quilt. Thick and brightly colored. A quilt over him, a pillow under his face. And no wind.

The door was closed.

And mason was eating something covered with rich brown gravy.

There was light in Mason's eyes.

Actual light.

It took a long time for Dan to sit up. Years. It was like jacking up one of the great pyramids. Slow, requiring so much strength, so much engineering. Just to sit up.

He sagged back against the wall. They were in an entrance foyer. Eight feet long. Umbrella stand with two umbrellas, a hiking stick and a yellow plastic wiffle bat. Pictures on the wall. Seascape on one side. The kind you get at IKEA. Comes already framed. Smaller pictures on the other side. One big family portrait, lots of small individual pictures. Husband and wife, kids. Grandparents. A smiling dog with a lolling tongue. Dad was black, mom looked white. Kids were in assorted shades of coffee with and without cream. Grandfather— clearly hers, not his—with a heavy beard shot through with gray, and kind eyes. Dog was a chocolate lab. Everyone looked happy.

"Is anyone here?" Dan asked.

Mason shook his head.

"No one?"

"Just Santa Claus," said the boy.

Dan said, "What?"

8

Mason showed him.

He helped Dan to his feet. Another feat of engineering. The floor canted and rippled, the room spun on its gimbals. Settled slowly. Became steady after a lot of crooked moments.

"In here," said Mason.

He pulled on Dan's hand. The kid's fingers were still cold. Still too cold.

But there was warmth here. Heat.

When Dan staggered after his brother into the living room he saw why. There was a fire in the fireplace. Nearly out, but still burning. There were candles standing in piles of melted wax. There was a Coleman camp lantern. Lots of light. More warmth than Dan had felt in …

In too long a time to remember.

He shivered as if his body was reluctant to release the cold stored in his cells.

Dan didn't care about that. He didn't even remember the cold. He barely registered the candle and lantern light.

Instead he looked at something in the corner and something in the adjoining room. His eyes—his whole head—kept moving back and forth between these things. Seeing them. Not believing them. Not understanding them.

In the corner of the room, dominating that whole part of the living room, standing eight feet high, was a Christmas tree. Covered in brightly twinkling multicolored LED lights. A battery stood on a small vase pedestal, wires running over and up into the tree, powering the lights.

The lights.

Christmas lights.

The tree was full and fresh, the pine scent perfuming the air, mingling with the burning logs. A living smell, even from burning wood and cut-down tree. It smelled alive. Lights looked alive. And around the base of the tree was a mountain range of presents. Carefully wrapped in bright paper with delicately tied bows.

Dozens of them.

Through the archway, in the dining room, was a table set for seven people. Forks and knives, linen napkins in a poinsettia pattern. Sparkling stemware. Silver plates and bowls and tureens.

All of them filled with food.

All of them.

Mounds of mashed potatoes and candied yams, Green beans smothered in baked almonds. Broccoli and cauliflower decorated with thin twists of red and green peppers. Bowls of peas and corn. A basket with one flap of a holly-patterned cloth peeled back to reveal the curves of honey-brown rolls. And in the center of the table, rising above everything else, was a whole roast turkey. A big one. Golden skin except where one part of the breast had been torn away by greedy little hands, and there it was pure white.

Dan almost fell down.

He wanted to, maybe should have.

This was unreal, after all. This couldn't be here. Christmas was extinct. Christmas had died along with every other holiday. Christmas Day meant nothing more than any other day. There were a lot of days and none of them were special anymore. They all ended with hunger and darkness, except the ones that ended in death.

Except …

Dan squeezed his eyes shut and took a breath so that he would be braced for the reality of an empty room and a bare table when he opened them again.

He opened them again.

The table was still there.

The food was still there.

"Santa brought us Christmas dinner," said Mason. His voice was far too reasonable and normal. It jolted Dan, who turned and looked at his brother.

"What?"

"Santa did this," said Mason. He wiped at the gravy on his cheeks, then licked the back of his hand. "It's not cold yet."

"Santa?"

"Sure. I saw him. Santa was here."

"What?"

"Santa. He was here."

"Here?"

Mason pointed toward the kitchen. "I saw him out in the yard. He had his red suit and white beard. It was Santa."

There was no hysteria in Mason's voice. There should have been. How could there not be?

Dan felt his heart begin to hammer again. "Show me."

Mason took his hand again and led him through the dining room and into the kitchen and up to the back door. Light from a second Coleman lantern threw pale window squares onto the snow-covered lawn.

There was a man in the yard.

The man had a white beard.

He wore a red suit.

Dan moved closer to the window and studied the figure.

Then he stepped back. Slowly. Making absolutely sure not to make any sudden moves. He very carefully, very quietly found the dial on the lantern and turned down the gas until the kitchen was plunged into darkness.

Darkness was safe.

"Why'd you do that?" asked Mason. "Now we can't see Santa."

Dan said nothing.

Out in the yard, the figure turned toward the house.

The beard was white. Sure. Except where it was red. There was snow on the red, so it was a layered effect. Hiding the truth. Changing the truth.

His shirt had probably been red to start with. A checked flannel shirt. Redder now by far. A belly. What someone might have called a comfortable belly. You say that about old guys with paunches. Mostly bald head, a fringe of white.

Red and white.

Fat.

Not jolly.

"Go back into the other room," said Dan.

"But ... Santa ..."

Santa. God.

Dan wondered who it was out there. Father? Grandfather? Or another survivor? Maybe a neighbor from one of the other houses. Maybe coming over to share the world's last Christmas dinner. Maybe someone who had helped gather enough supplies to make it special. To give the family one perfect night. If so, what had happened? Why had everyone gone out? Did someone have an old Polaroid camera? Or a digital camera that they kept charged somehow. Had they been crazy enough—or felt safe enough—to go out and watch the snow. Had they sung a carol as the snow fell and thought that the dead were too far away to hear? Or that the storm would muffled their voices?

Something had happened, though. Something made them all go outside and leave hot food on the table. Their coats were gone. Their boots. They'd dressed for it, but they couldn't have meant to be out there long.

Except ...

There were footprints out in the snow, but if there was blood the snow hid it. If there were bodies, they'd wandered off.

Except this one old man.

Except Mason's Santa.

God Almighty.

He looked at his brother, at the unfiltered joy on a face that Dan thought had forgotten how to smile.

The truth is no blessing, he thought. *The truth is no gift.*

He knew he had to do this right. If he did it wrong, Mason would probably cry. He didn't cry out loud much—even as young as he was,

Mason had learned the rules. But this was different. The dinner, the presents. The man in red and white. Mason sounded strange as it was. Dan couldn't risk dragging him back out into the cold. Not the cold outside, but the cold of the real world. It might break him. The kid was already cracked.

So, he knew, was he.

If Mason started crying. Or worse, screaming, Dan knew that he would, too,

So he said the kind of thing you'd say if the world wasn't broken.

"Shhhh," he said softly. "Don't let Santa know you can see him. He has to do everything in secret. That's how it's done. It has to be in secret or the magic won't work."

That kind of thing made sense to a four year old.

It damn near sounded reasonable to Dan.

Things had to be done in secret, or the magic wouldn't work.

Survival was a kind of magic. At least it was these days.

He backed up very slowly. Without haste. Haste means panic. He didn't want that to be the message of his body language. He backed into Mason and gently pushed his brother out of the kitchen. Dan took the lantern with him.

Then he stopped, thinking it another step past the moment.

"Stay here," he said. He reentered the kitchen. The back door was closed. It had a bar across it. There were shutters mounted inside the windows. Dan closed the shutters very slowly. They were heavy. Solid panels of wood that had been reinforced with strips of metal. The work was good. Someone knew what they were doing. The shutters completely blocked the windows. There was another shutter for the kitchen door. He shut that, too. Thick cotter pins hung on lengths of airline cable. Dan slotted them into place and felt his heart begin to beat normally.

He went out to the dining room. Mason was scooping handfuls of corn and peas into his mouth.

"Eat slow or you'll get sick," said Dan.

The boy nodded. He didn't have the strength to eat fast.

Dan's stomach churned. He wanted to eat. Needed to. Had to.

But he didn't. Not yet.

Instead he went through the house and made sure all of the shutters were pinned in place. He pulled the drapes over them to block out any stray splinters of light. The front door had brackets for heavy cross-grain timbers, and he hefted them into place. Oak. Heavy. Safe.

Then he took the lantern and went upstairs.

More candles. Sleeping bags. Stacks of boxed goods. Food. Medical supplies.

Guns.

Guns.

Jesus Christ.

Guns and ammunition.

Hundreds of gallons of water in one, two-and-a-half and five gallon bottles. Cases of soda. Cartons of powdered milk.

Dan was crying by the time he finished checking the rooms.

There were beds for nine people. All of the beds had been slept in.

But there was nobody home.

Nobody.

It made no sense.

Why would they leave this place?

They'd found a way to keep themselves going. They'd found food and clothing and everything they'd need. There was enough to keep them safe for months. Maybe for years.

They'd even cut down and decorated a tree. Wrapped presents.

Cooked a feast.

So where were they?

Why had they left?

He thought of the man in the yard. Granddad.

Okay, so the old man had died. But there was no blood inside the house. No sign of violence. Nothing to indicate that the man had died and reanimated in here. No evidence that he'd attacked and killed his own children and grandchildren.

He was outside.

And where were they…?

Dan stood at the top of the stairs. He held a shotgun to his chest tighter than if it was a talisman. Tighter than if it was Jesus on the cross.

"Dan—?" called Mason.

"Shhh!" hissed Dan as he leaned down the stairs.

"Come on. It's getting cold."

Not the house.

The food.

Dan came downstairs.

He pulled out a chair for Mason. He sat in the one next to him.

"Is it Christmas?" asked the boy.

"I … I guess so."

"Do we get to open presents?"

Dan glanced at the presents. There were so many of them. Surely some would have to be appropriate for a little boy. Maybe socks. Maybe a toy. What did it matter when you had nothing at all?

"Sure," he said. "In the morning. Presents are for Christmas morning."

He reached for the carving knife and fork.

Mason looked at him, his eyes wide and filled with light. "Don't we have to say grace first?"

Dan wiped at the tears in his eyes. He bent and kissed Mason on the top of the head.

"Yeah," he said. "I guess we do."

They said grace. It surprised Dan that he could remember how to say thanks.

The words came.

Slowly, in shuffling steps through his mind. But they came.

He said grace.

They said "amen."

Outside the wind howled and the snow fell. Outside there were moans on the wind.

Inside it was warm.

Inside it was Christmas.

Dan stuck the tines of the fork in to steady the turkey and to steady his own trembling hands. Then he began carving.

Ken Scholes's tasty tale of terror folds several quirky characters into an increasingly gruesome milieu. It's a pretty sweet shocker!

And a word of advice: If you're going to bake for the family this holiday, make sure your ingredients are fresh.

—KO

A WORLD DONE IN BY GREAT GRANNY'S GRATEFUL PIE

Ken Scholes

It was the Tuesday before Thanksgiving and everything was going to shit all at once, the way things usually like to. Of course it was a different kind of *going to shit* compared to, say, last year's Thanksgiving in Iraq. That one started with flares and shots ricocheting off stone and ended with me slowly heading home on a medical discharge. This Thanksgiving started with the goddamn underpinning going missing and ended with burning Great Granny's Grateful Pie. And somewhere in the middle was the matter of Mama's plus one.

"You know, Kay Ann," Mama insisted in her most saccharine voice, "my *plus one.*"

I put the pie in the oven. "Your plus one?" I pushed buttons that I assumed were the timer. It was my new stove. In my new kitchen. In my new trailer back home in Reynolds, Kentucky.

"Yes, like them fancy folks do at *their* parties. A plus one."

"So you're bringing a date to Thanksgiving dinner?" The oven beeped at me and I pushed more buttons.

She gave one of her patented sighs of exasperation. "No, no, not a date."

I offered my own approximation of the same sigh. "Okay, what's his name?"

"Reverend Franklin T. Seymour. I'm sure you've met him."

Yes. I'd met him. The new youth pastor at her church. This wasn't the first time he'd come up. "Christ, Mama, you're bringing the boy preacher to Thanksgiving?"

"Language, Kay Ann," she said in her best somber tone. "And I thought it would be real Christianly with all his people in Oklahoma and him all alone out here."

"He's not alone. He's got the Lord, Mama. He'll be fine."

"You know what I mean, Kay Ann." I waited for her to say the rest. He had a steady job that wasn't illegal, had a sense of purpose and decent personal hygiene. These moved most gentleman callers to the top of Mama's list. Not for herself, mind you, but for her oldest daughter. I heard gravel crunching in the trailer park's driveway and looked up to see August Cooper's big Ford pulling up. When she didn't say the rest, I saw my opportunity and took it. "Okay. Franklin Seymour is your plus one. Uncle Auggie's here, Mama. Hopefully to see about my underpinning. I'll see you Thursday."

I was off the phone and on the double-wide's narrow porch before my uncle had grunted his way out of the truck, hiking up his torn Levis to help out his stretched red suspenders. "Sumbitch," he said, pushing back his Cooper Construction ball-cap to scratch his head. "Where's the goddam underpinning?"

"In the back of your truck, Uncle Auggie, I hope."

His face registered surprise and he actually checked the bed, bless his heart, before answering. "Nope. I thought Ernie put them up Sunday."

Ernie was my cousin, his youngest and about as shiftless as you could get. "It appears," I said, "that he was waylaid."

Way baked was more likely, I suspected.

"It does appear so," he said. He leaned over and looked under the trailer. "How's the rest of it seem?"

"Sturdy," I said.

Uncle Auggie nodded. "Good."

"So any chance I'll have my skirting up before Thanksgiving?

He scowled. "I sure can try. Have to find it first."

My phone started vibrating and I checked it, expecting it to be my mother again. It was my sister. I gave my uncle an apologetic glance. "I have to take this."

"I'll take a quick walk about, see what's what, then go see if I can scare up Ernie and your underpinning."

"Thanks, Uncle Auggie." I transitioned smoothly into the call. "Hey Sis."

"Hey," she said. "Where you been? I've been calling."

"I've been moving," I reminded her.

"Oh yeah. All done?"

"Nope. And Uncle Auggie's lost my underpinning."

She laughed. "Ernie sold it to buy weed, I'm sure."

I laughed with her. "Probably so. Or traded it straight across."

Then her voice changed and I should've known what was coming. "So … what time's dinner Thursday?"

"I told Mama two but to come whenever."

"Okay. I've got my plus one sorted out."

I felt the front end of my exasperation sigh coming on. "You're bringing a plus one, too?"

And how she answered it, her tone of voice and even the volume, told me everything I needed to know. I was being plotted against by my own family. "Oh, are Mama and Bobby bringing plus ones, too? I hadn't heard."

"Mama is." Bobby was too but I wasn't supposed to know that yet. He'd call next. She'd just given it away.

"Oh goodness," she said, as if she hadn't known all along.

"Yes," I said. "So who are you bringing?"

"Johnny Alvin. Remember him?"

I did, vaguely. He was a few years ahead of us in high school. He drove a sky-blue 1973 Ford Maverick with a 351 Windsor engine and glass pack muffler and listened to a lot of Rush. "Is he still delivering pizzas for the Pizza Shack?"

I could hear the pride in her voice. "No, ma'am. He's assistant manager now. Though he's studying mortuary science at night and interning down at Drummond's Funeral Parlor."

"Mortuary science?"

My sister sometimes mistook surprise for ignorance and answered accordingly. "You know, dead people stuff. Embalming. Funeral directing."

I wasn't sure what to say. She'd gotten the first two in there. Steady work. Ambition. I decided to help her out. "I'm sure he cleans up well, too. Probably has himself a black suit."

"Oh yes," she said.

"Good. You'll both be very happy together. And I just want you to know I'm fine with you bringing your new boyfriend to Thanksgiving dinner. I'm sure we'll all love him."

She was still sputtering when I told her I'd see them Thursday and hung up.

Uncle Auggie let himself out of the trailer as I slipped the phone back into my pocket. "Everything's working," he said. "Heat, water, electric." He took a light jump on the porch. "Everything's solid, too."

He'd put half the trailers into the Shady Grove Mobile Home Park over the last thirty years. Mine was the newest, though it wasn't brand new. Just new to me and new to the park. He'd helped me find it and then he'd moved it for me at a price we both could live with. "I sure do appreciate it, Uncle Auggie."

He tipped his hat. "Thank you for your service to our great nation."

I tipped my own ballcap back. "And yours." He'd served in Vietnam. He'd not been excited to see a niece joining up, much less going overseas into that clusterfuck but now that I was home, he talked to me differently, looked at me differently. Respectfully.

"I'll see to that underpinning," he said as he climbed into his truck.

The phone vibrated in my pocket again. But I knew who it was. My brother. Calling about his plus one. Though I don't think Mama or my sister had any idea just how different a direction my brother had taken things.

By the time we were off the phone, I was pretty sure Thursday was going to be both hysterically fun and maybe the worst Thanksgiving of my life all at the same time. I had no idea, truly.

When I got back into the trailer, it was already filling with smoke and a terrible stench that made my eyes water as I ran into the kitchen gagging.

Something had gone badly wrong with great Granny's pie.

Of course, I saw that as the least of my problems and fed the burnt offering to the park's community pig before locking up and heading back into town for another load of boxes.

And again, I had no idea, truly. But that damn pig sure was happy about his pie.

I spent Wednesday unpacking and making pies.

I thought about last year and how I was making pies then, too, down at the mess hall. After cleaning my rifle. I'd been in for two years and had already saved up enough for the trailer. I was working on setting aside enough park fees and taxes to keep my costs down while I used that GI Bill and figured out my own sense of purpose.

Last year, I was shot in the ass on Thanksgiving morning. This year, it looked I'd be ambushed by my family and their good intentions.

And Mama wasn't letting up. Her voice boomed in my Bluetooth while I broke down the empty boxes. "And he's such a polite young man," she said, lauding another of Pastor Frank's many shining attributes.

I ran the cutter down the line of tape and loved the power I felt collapsing the box upon itself. "I'm sure he is, Mama."

"And the board's really happy with his work. I expect he'll be getting a raise soon."

I put the flattened cardboard onto the stack and picked up another box. "I'm sure he will, Mama." I decided to have some fun with it all. "So it sounds like Johnny Alvin turned out fine and dandy. I'm real happy for Jessie Lynn. You think they'll get married?"

Mama sounded like she was choking. She didn't say anything. I couldn't resist; I just kept straight on. "Say," I said, "Pastor Frank could do the service. Wouldn't that be nice?"

Mama found her wits and her words. "I don't think Jessie Lynn's all that smitten with Johnny."

"Oh," I said in my most incredulous tone. "Why I can't imagine why she'd bring him around to Thanksgiving if she wasn't."

I picked up the stack of flattened boxes and moved across the shag carpet to the front door. "Well," Mama said, "I'm sure she's just being kind-hearted."

"I'm sure she is," I said. Now, I navigated the steps down. I'd awakened to an inch of snow and now more was drifting down slowly, dusting the driveway and lawns.

Mama changed the subject quickly. "So how did Great Granny's Grateful Pie turn out?"

I glanced at the pig's pen as she asked. I couldn't see him in there. "It didn't," I said. "Went to the pig."

"You have a pig?"

"Folk at the trailer park share one. Cuts down on the trash bill."

She snorted. "You're coming up in the world."

I ignored the sarcasm. "It's okay. I'm making more pie. But Great Granny's was a loss." Her pie was put together from her own butter crust recipe—this year was Jessie Lynn's turn—from ingredients that still grew wild up in the holler where her shack squatted, abandoned now, in a dilapidated heap. It had been a Thanksgiving tradition all the way back to the days of outhouses and dirt roads. There was no time for a do-over on this one so I was substituting with sweet potato, pecan and pumpkin from recipes I'd learned cooking mess for Uncle Sam.

"It won't be Thanksgiving without Granny's pie."

"It was Thanksgiving for the pig." I dropped the boxes into the recycling dumpster and headed back across the lot. "Besides something smelled awful in that one."

Walking back, I noticed the gate to the pen was open. "Well," Mama said, "at least the pig enjoyed it."

I wandered toward the pen. The pig was nowhere to be seen. "Shit. I think the pig's run off."

Mama chuckled again. "I better let you go chase it down and get back to the rolls. We'll see you Thursday. Wear something pretty." She thought about it. "And proper," she added.

I rolled my eyes at the phone. "I will. And we can check Pastor Frank's calendar for a June wedding. I think Johnny and Jessie Lynn are going to be real happy together." Now, I smiled. "Oh, and Mama?"

"Yes, Kay Ann?"

"Did you hear about Bobby? Ends up he's got himself a plus one, too."

"Oh really?"

"New girl at the college. Dana Evans. From Illinois I think."

I could hear the stammering before it started. "Dana Evans? I thought he was bringing Tommy—" She caught herself and backed up. "I thought he'd mentioned that his friend Tommy Ray needed a place to go this year."

"I don't know about that," I told her. "But maybe two of your kids have finally found true love." I grinned into the phone and hoped she could hear it. "Maybe Pastor Frank can pull off a double June wedding."

Of course, I didn't bother telling Mama what I already suspected about Bobby's plus one. It was better letting her think that maybe her baby boy was bringing a true plus one to Thanksgiving rather than someone to set her oldest daughter up with. It was going to be too fun letting her discover the truth for herself.

"I'll see you Thursday, Mama. Sure do love you."

"Sure do love you, too."

I paused at the bottom of my porch and glanced back to the pig pen again. Shivering against the cold in my brown army t-shirt, I started off toward the manager's trailer.

Hank Summers was standing by his shed with a shovel as I approached. "I think the pig's run off," I said.

He shook his head. "Nope. He'd dead. Just buried him."

"That's a shame," I said. "What got him?"

Hank shrugged. "Don't know. Something he ate, I reckon, though that pig sure could eat."

The big man's lower lip started to quiver and I wasn't sure what to say. "I'm sorry about your pig, Mr. Summers."

Now his eyes filled up with water. "Oh, Wilbur was everyone's pig."

I blinked. "You named him Wilbur?"

He nodded.

I wasn't sure what else to say so I apologized again and then went back to my trailer and the last of the boxes. I tried not to think about Wilbur again but later in the day, bagging up the leftover scraps of sweet potato peels and apple peels, I thought of him again. I glanced again to his pen as I trudged across the gathering snow and wondered if maybe it had been Great Granny's pie that did him in.

If so, that pig might've saved my life. And maybe the lives of my family and their respective plus ones. I wasn't certain of my gratitude regarding this salvation.

I dumped the bag of cuttings into the trash and turned back to my trailer and its open door in time to see something small and filthy come snarling around the corner, ramming full force into the tire of a parked truck. It fell over in the snow and growled before scrambling back to its feet.

It was a pig. And not just any pig, but *the* pig. Wilbur.

"Hey!"

I saw Hank coming around the same corner, huffing and puffing, with a length of looped rope in his hands.

The pig was off and running again, this time smacking into the wood skirting of trailer next to mine.

"Stop that pig," Hank yelled.

As if seeing me, Wilbur growled again and launched himself in my direction. And something about him didn't look right. It might've been the bloody foam around his snout or the glassy stare of its little pig-eyes. I side-stepped him and listened to the satisfying clunk of the pig's head striking the metal dumpster and falling over again.

"That's the fastest dead pig I ever saw," I said as Hank approached. Now I could see the blood dripping from his hand.

"Meanest, too," Hank said. "Fucker bit me."

Wilbur climbed back onto his feet again with a growl nearly as disturbing as his empty, pink eyes.

"Well," I said, "I'm glad he's back."

"It's a Thanksgiving miracle," he said as he dropped the rope over the pig's neck. It spun on him with a yowl, snapping at his ankles and Hank danced back, yanking the rope tight. "Heel, Wilbur, heel."

My phone vibrated in my pocket again. I was pretty sure it had to be Bobby. By now, Mama would've been at him about his change of plans.

I took the call from my narrow porch, watching the light flakes add to what would make for a slippery, cold Thanksgiving. "Hey bro," I said as I watched Hank drag the angry pig back into his pen.

I thought about digging the pie scraps out of the dumpster, giving the pig some kind of welcome back treat. But the way those teeth kept snapping at Hank, I reckoned Wilbur was fed up with fruits and vegetables and more in the mood for meat.

Tomorrow, I thought, I could bring him some turkey.

Thanksgiving, I thought, for the pig.

"So tell me about you and Dana," I said with a smile into the phone. "How long you two been going out?"

Then I slipped back into the warmth of my trailer to figure out my oven and bake some pies while my little brother sputtered and spun on the other end of the line.

The flashing lights in the middle of the night were a great reminder to hang the curtains and blinds sooner rather than later.

I rolled out of bed and went to the window.

There was an ambulance and two county sheriff's sedans and their red and blue lights played out over the freshly fallen snow lent some

Christmas magic to Thanksgiving Eve. Two deputies stood talking with Hank's wife. Even from a distance, I could tell she was crying and she had a field dressing on her cheek.

Ah shit. Hank had seemed harmless enough but I was smart enough to know about books and covers.

The paramedics wheeled him out now and I barely recognized him. His skin tone was wrong—deathly pale—and his eyes were wide and empty. His mouth foamed as he snapped and snarled, twisting and pulling at the restraints. One of the paramedics nursed a bloody hand, the latex glove torn and dangling like red, loose skin.

I cracked the window, not wanting to become one of the nosy neighbors that gathered on their porches or in the snow.

Mrs. Summers voice carried easily. "No," she said, "I thought he was dead." She sobbed again. "I called 911, started CPR and then he bit me."

"Fucker bit me, too," the paramedic said over his shoulder as he helped load Hank into the ambulance.

My last sight of the trailer park manager, his eyes were rolled back in his head as he strained against the straps and howled his rage, showing his teeth, veins bulging in his neck and forehead.

The ambulance left first and once it did, people started slipping back into their trailers as the deputies finished getting her statement.

"Did you husband take anything, Mrs. Summers? Any kind of substance or medication?"

She shook her head.

"Anything unusual happen today?"

"I don't think so. I was at work."

The pig, I thought. I should tell them about the pig.

I turned away from the window to find my sneakers and then turned back at the sound of snarling. Wilbur tore out from under my trailer at full speed, plowing up the snow like a dirty yellow torpedo, to crash into one of the deputies and sink his teeth into the man's ankle.

"Ow," the deputy said.

I remember thinking that it certainly still seemed to be Thanksgiving for the pig. And on the heels of that thought, I wondered just what was happening here in the Shady Grove Mobile Home Park and whether or not Great Granny's Grateful Pie was culpable in the matter.

It was not a night for sleeping.

After the deputies tried put down the pig—multiple shots fired, more sleep-faced residents gathering on porches– they left and I settled back into bed and drowsed. But at some point, I heard shouts and maybe thirty minutes later—slow for Arlington County—the red lights were back.

This time, I slipped on my clothes and headed out to meet my neighbors the old fashioned way, gathered around a police car in the trailer park.

"No," one of the neighbors said. "Stu said she bit Maggie Rae and then ran off into the woods."

I stayed near, picking up what I could both of the night's events and the gossip it may have played into. Hank was doing meth with the neighbor woman while his wife Susie held down work at Ray's Grocery. The affair had gone obviously wrong and now people were biting each other.

"What about the pig?" I asked.

"Pig ran away," someone said. And after that, it was like I wasn't there. Eventually, the cold got to me and I slipped back inside. The snow was falling harder now and we had a good six inches on the ground with no end in sight.

I paused outside my bedroom door, looking first to the waiting bed and then to the kitchen and the mountain of food waiting for me there.

Sighing, I turned to the kitchen. I cranked up some Counting Crows and went to work. Potatoes to peel and boil, a turkey to stuff and cook. And later, my family—and all their plus ones—would descend upon me after a snowstorm and a mostly sleepless night. A prospect that promised to be a bigger pain in the ass than last year's AK-47 round.

I decided to be grateful that Thanksgiving only came once a year and wondered if next year's might not be better spent on a holiday in Spain.

At some point in the wee hours, I heard more shouting. But it must not have been too important. No more red lights to call the neighbors out for gossip in the snow.

I turned the music up and sang louder.

"Oh dear Lord," Mama said as she came through the door with the roll trays draped in towels. "You gotta get Auggie to build you a proper deck, Kay Ann. Nearly broke my neck."

I took the trays from her. "I'd have swept the stairs if I'd known you were coming early."

Pastor Frank, also bearing trays, came in behind her. I tried not to notice the large black Bible underneath his arm. He was a gangly redhead with a face that made me nervous. "We wanted to get a jump on the snow," he said with his easy Oklahoma drawl.

I took Mama's tray to the counter. "How were the roads?"

"Terrible," she said. "Cars off everywhere. I swear, a little snow and the whole county's a wreck. There were sirens all night. Hardly slept at all." Mama blushed. "But where are my manners?" She smiled. "Franklin, this is my eldest, Kay Ann. Kay Ann, this is Pastor Frank."

He extended a hand. I shook it. "We met up at the church, Mama."

His hands were soft but his grip was firm. "It's nice to meet you again, Miss Cooper."

I wanted to frown but smiled instead. "Just Kay Ann."

Mama was already fussing in the kitchen, checking the potatoes and looking in on the turkey. "What time are Jessie Lynn and Johnny Alvin showing up?"

"I expect it'll be a few hours," I said. Then, I offered up my first genuine smile of the morning. "Young love and all."

Mama blushed again. "Well, I don't know—"

Pastor Frank blushed, too. "Where's your broom. I'll get the snow off the porch."

I fetched him the broom and went back to the kitchen. Mama was making a fresh pot of coffee. She'd make it weak and complain that it tasted funny being ground up right there on the spot instead of coming out of a can all ready to brew.

"He's such a sweet boy," she said after the door closed behind him.

I eyed the leather book placed squarely in the center of the dining room table. "I'm sure he is, Mama."

"He's a fine preacher, too."

Sometimes, repeating myself worked best with her. It conserved energy for those long, mostly-one-sided conversations. "I'm sure he is, Mama."

"As a matter of fact," she said, "he's prepared something special to share with us today. About counting our blessings."

I was counting the hours until dinner was over. "Speaking of blessings, isn't it sweet that this year both Jessie Lynn *and* Bobby have found someone special? That's something to be grateful for."

Mama scowled and looked to the door. I could read her eyes. She wanted to correct me and leaving an uncorrected bit of mistruth, for that woman, was like leaving an unfinished plate at the Chinese buffet. But she didn't dare let on that all three of them had plotted me a mate this Thanksgiving. I thought about letting her off the hook, telling her I'd figured out their scheme on Tuesday, but the fun I could have with this—and the teaching moment it afforded—kept me quiet.

And Mama did what Mama does and changed the subject and started washing dishes. "So how do you like your neighbors?"

I shrugged. "They seem a bit rowdy."

"Well," she said. "It's snowing and it's Thanksgiving. That'll do it. Had the whole town up in arms last night worse than a full moon."

We kept making small talk until I heard a knock at the door. It was Pastor Frank.

"You don't have to knock," I said.

His eyes were wide and his face red and he stared at me.

I raised my eyebrows at him. "What is it? And where's my broom."

He looked over his shoulder. "You have some troubled neighbors, Kay Ann. They need the Lord."

I let him in and closed the door behind him. That's when I noticed his sweater was ripped. "What happened?"

"I broke the broom and went to borrow a snow shovel I saw out in another yard. But when I knocked on the door, your neighbor jumped me." He took a breath. "And he didn't look good either. Like he'd been on a three-day drunk."

But now I had my suspicions and I raised my eyebrow at him. "Did he bite you?"

Pastor Frank shook his head. "No. But he sure tried."

Mama was there now. "We should pray for that family right this minute, Pastor Frank." She smiled. "Let's all hold hands."

Another knock at the door made it easy for me to brush their reaching hands away. "Who is it?"

My sister's voice was shrill. "It's me."

I opened the door and stepped aside to let her in. Her face was pale as she pushed the green bean casserole into my hands. "Jesus," she said. "What's up with your neighbors?"

Johnny Alvin followed her in and closed the door. I'd not seen him since high school and he was taller, broader. His thick mustache and curly hair made him look like the love child of a seventies porn star and a Greek god. He saw everyone and looked profoundly uncomfortable, especially when he looked at me.

"Hey Johnny," I said.

"Hey Kay."

"Kay Ann," I said. Then I looked at my sister. "What about the neighbors?"

She shook her head. "Looks like they're fighting."

It was sinking in now like cold concrete in my stomach. "Lock the door, Johnny."

He did and I passed the casserole to Mama before going to the window. It did not look right out there. The snow was falling still and some of the trailer doors stood wide open despite the cold. There were no children out making snowmen or throwing snowballs at each other. In the distance I could see figures running, stumbling and falling, in the snow. And I saw others running after.

"Maybe we should call the police," Johnny offered.

"They were out several times last night," I said. But my phone was out and in my hand as I said it. I went to the back door and checked its lock as I dialed.

The line rang forever before a recording kicked in and shortly after the recording, I had the dispatcher but I wasn't sure exactly what to say. Some part of me still wanted to believe that this was a string of unrelated and unfortunate coincidences that piled up like the snow. But that part was losing its foothold with everything pointing to the pig and the pie. "We have some kind of trouble out here at Shady Grove," I told the woman.

The woman sighed and she might've been kin given the exasperated nature of it. "We have some kind of trouble everywhere in the county. Can you be more specific?"

I tried to be but it sounded crazier and crazier as I tried to explain it.

"Can you see if they are fighting now?"

"They ran off toward the woods," I said.

She asked me a few more questions and promised to dispatch a unit as soon as possible. "And," she said in closing, "because emergency services are operating at maximum capacity, the Arlington County Sheriff's Department is recommending that residents minimize demand by remaining indoors, staying off the roads and staying warm."

And avoid feral neighbors and pigs, I wanted to add. But instead I wished her a happy Thanksgiving and put my phone away and looked back to my family and their plus ones. "They'll send someone when they can," I told them. "It may be a while."

"What should we do?" I'm not sure it's a question I ever heard Mama ask before.

"Sit tight, I reckon." I looked at the clock. "But someone should check on Bobby."

Mama went for her purse and slipped into my bedroom with her phone.

Pastor Frank picked at his ripped sweater. "Well, I'm fixing to sit down and pray." He must've understood my stare because his face went red again. "Quietly," he whispered.

Jessie Lynn always took most after Mama and she moved into the kitchen for her own brand of crisis management. "What do you need done, Sis?"

"Everything," I told her.

Johnny Alvin moved to the couch and sat, lifting the remote. "I'll check the news."

I shook my head. "No cable."

He shrugged, put down the remote and settled back into the sofa with his hands folded behind his head.

"They're on their way," Mama said as she came out of the bedroom. "But they said it sure is a mess out there. Snow's gotten worse and there's some kind of bug going around. Along with a bunch of holiday hooliganism."

No. It's more than that. A thought struck me and I looked over at my sister. "Hey, you gathered up the berries for Great Granny's pie last summer, right?"

She nodded. "I did. I froze them just like Mama did the year before. Why? How did it turn out?" Jessie Lynn looked at the other pies displayed on the counter.

"It didn't. There was something wrong with it, I think. Do you remember anything unusual about the berries?"

Jessie Lynn shook her head. "Not any more unusual than any other time. You sure it wasn't the oven?"

Mama interjected. "New ovens can be tricky."

"I don't know," I said. But I suspected that I did know. As implausible as it sounded, the pie went to the pig and the pig bit Hank. Hank bit his wife and his wife bit the neighbor. And Lord knew how far that might spread. Because Hank hadn't just bit his wife. He'd bit the paramedic. And the pig had bit the deputy.

Some kind of virus, maybe, I told myself. I looked outside at the massive white flakes and the blanket they made over the cars and ground, then looked to the open doors and unswept trailer porches within view.

Now Mama was in the kitchen. "What can I do, Kay Ann?"

Anything and nothing, I thought, and then Mama's phone rang. I heard my brother's voice on the other end.

"Dear Lord, Bobby," she said, "are you both okay?" She looked up at me. "They're in the ditch."

"Fuck," I said. "Let me talk to him, Mama."

"Your sister wants to talk to you." She passed the phone.

"Hey Bro," I said.

"Hey Sis."

"Where are you?"

"Just passed Gallagher Road," he said.

"Okay. Sit tight. I'll come fetch you." Then, as an afterthought: "And hey, lock the doors. Watch out for crazies on the loose."

I gave Mama back her phone and went for my boots. I'd not worn them since I discharged out of Fort Dix and they were the closest thing I had to snow boots. I dug a heavy sweater out of my closet along with my camo jacket and watch-cap.

"We should let Franklin drive us," Mama called from the dining room as she pulled on her coat.

"There's no *we* in this, Mama," I told her. My voice was firmer than usual and I enjoyed trying it out on her. "*I'm* going to go fetch them."

She blinked at me and said nothing.

"Then what?" my sister asked.

"Then," I said, "we have dinner."

The power flickered and Johnny Alvin stood up and grabbed his coat. "You should let me drive you."

"And why would I do that?"

He walked to the door and pointed. "Because of that."

Johnny Alvin had traded in his Maverick for a black SUV with tinted windows. All four tires were chained. I looked from it to my snow-covered Kia. "Okay then," I said. I zipped up my coat. "Y'all tend the turkey and set the table. And lock the door behind us."

We went out into the cold, my eyes already reverting to training, scanning the buildings around me. Outside, there was a heavy silence broken by the crunch of snow beneath our feet. The stillness was pervasive and when the quiet was broken by a growl, I followed the sound.

There in the gloom just beneath my trailer, the pig watched and waited and growled. Johnny paused at the driver's door. "Never seen a pig like that before," he said.

"Get in quickly," I told him as I opened the door. As I said it, the pig charged.

"Shit," Johnny yelled as he scrambled into the SUV. He pulled the door closed just as the pig slammed into it with a loud thunk. Then it was up and racing across the snow, this time heading for Summers' open shed. Johnny looked at me. "What's wrong with that pig?"

"Something," I said. I stared after it, trying to figure out if the blood on it was its own or another of its victims. "Not sure what." But I was growing more certain that whatever it was, it meant bad news. *Really* bad news.

Johnny looked at the glove box and started the engine. "You think it's dangerous? Should we try to put it down?"

"Him," I said. "It's a boy. Wilbur. And yes, he's dangerous. And they tried to put him down last night."

Johnny raised his eyebrows. "Someone *actually* named their pig Wilbur?"

I nodded.

He sighed. "At least people are reading."

"Amen," I said by way of agreement.

Johnny backed us up and pointed us toward the highway, moving slowly through the park. I watched as we went, suddenly flooded with memories of last Thanksgiving. The smell of the city. The dry desert heat. The sound of raised voices speaking Arabic. It was an odd contrast to now.

Movement in my peripheral drew my eyes to the nearest trailer. Something on the porch.

I jumped when the woman threw herself at my door with a shriek. Her eyes were dark and sunk-in, her skin yellow and her mouth foaming. Her nightgown was a mess of what looked like dried gravy and blood. She clawed and bit at my window and Johnny punched the gas, the chained tires slipping before they caught and rocketed us forward, sending the woman spinning off into the snow.

"What the fuck," he said, glancing to the rearview mirror. Johnny looked at the glove box again, then looked at me. "You can shoot, right?"

I nodded.

He reached over and worked the latch, dropping the compartment open. Sitting on top of the registration, next to a stack of Drummond Funeral Home brochures, lay a 9mm Colt. "That might come in handy," he said.

I watched the woman climb to her feet and lope off toward another trailer. "I reckon it might," I said. "Since when did funeral directors pack heat?"

Johnny grinned. "It's for when I'm delivering pizzas. Dangerous work, that."

I lifted the pistol out carefully, holding it in my hands like something fragile. I'm not a fan of guns. I grew up with up them, of course. My daddy had taught me to shoot and fish before I'd learned to read. I'd not taken to either much—I liked books much better—and my opinion on keeping and bearing arms shifted a little after being shot in the ass with one. I worked the action and left the safety on. "Let's hope we don't need it," I said.

The highway was deserted. Any ploughing and sanding that might've been underway earlier hadn't been maintained and the road was a ribbon of white stretched out beneath the trees. Rush was quietly singing about today's Tom Sawyer and mean, mean pride and we drove slowly over the snow in silence for the first mile before Johnny cleared his voice.

"You know," he said, "I'm not really with Jessie Lynn. She actually brought me hoping to fix me and you up."

He knows about the plot. I felt the heat in my cheeks and I wasn't sure what to say. "I'm sorry about that. My family's got it in their heads that I need to marry up." I looked at him. "I hope you're not—"

Johnny Alvin laughed. "Oh no. Not at all." Now he looked at me and I realized those brown eyes had some kind of mischief in them.

"Oh good," I said.

"You're not my type, Kay Ann. No offense."

I felt a rise of defensiveness and a rush of relief all at once. "Not your type? What's that supposed to mean?" Not that I cared but I knew most men noticed me when I walked into a room.

He measured me. "You really want to know?"

"Yes."

Those eyes measured me again before going back to the road. "Your brother is my type," he finally said.

When the words registered I didn't mean to laugh out loud but I couldn't help myself. When I saw the hurt on his face I reached out and put a hand on his arm. "Oh Johnny," I said, "I'm not laughing about that. It's my family." I continued at his confused glance. "You're one of three plus-ones in an elaborate Thanksgiving matchmaking scheme."

The light came on for Johnny. "The preacher?"

I nodded. "Yep. Pastor Frank."

He released his held breath. "Jesus."

"Exactly," I said.

"And the third?"

"Bobby's bringing a lesbian."

Now Johnny's smile was genuine. "He's not with her?"

"Nope," I said. "I think he's single." Now it was my turn for the light to come on. "You came for Bobby."

He nodded slowly. "Yeah. Didn't have anywhere else to be. Figured it couldn't hurt to spend time with him and his family. Get to know him better."

"Your secret's safe with me."

He shrugged. "Not so much a secret. Just like telling people my own shit rather than them hearing elsewhere."

"Makes sense to me." Despite being caught up in my family's machinations, and despite his own scheme to use that as an opportunity to get close to my brother, I decided that Johnny Alvin was good people.

It didn't hurt that he came well equipped for the kind of *going to shit* that was happening all around us.

We let Rush sing us the rest of the way, slipping past cars and trucks that hadn't made the curves, until we saw my brother's red Civic tipped into the ditch.

Johnny didn't even try to edge off the highway. The road was empty and he stopped right beside the Civic. Bobby squinted at us out of the driver's window. The girl sitting next to him, Dana I assumed, was blonde and pretty in an angular kind of way. Johnny rolled down his window and Bobby did the same.

"Hey Johnny," my brother said. He saw me and nodded. "Hey Kay Ann."

"Hey Bobby," I said. "Need a ride?"

Bobby grinned. "I could use one."

"Hop in," Johnny said.

He and Dana climbed out of the Civic carefully, pulling bags of chips soda out of the backseat. They climbed into the back of the SUV. "Hey, this is my friend Dana. She's up at the university."

"Nice to meet you," I said over my shoulder as she buckled up. "Happy Thanksgiving."

"Thanks, Kay Ann." She smiled and there was something wicked in the smile though it didn't bother me at all. "I've heard a lot about you. Thanks for coming to rescue us."

"Happy to," I said. I looked at my brother. "So why didn't you chain up?"

He blushed and opened his mouth to answer but Dana cut him off. "He didn't know how to put them on. I told him I could do it. And drive, too." She paused. "I'm from Illinois. This is normal for Thanksgiving."

Johnny carefully turned us around and pointed us in the right direction.

I looked at the abandoned highway and thought about the woman with her yellow skin, the pig ploughing up the snow as he raced toward us. "We're not having much normal around here for Thanksgiving. Sorry he put you in the ditch."

I saw her studying me in the mirror. There was sweetness in her smile that told me she liked what she saw. "I guess I don't mind being a damsel in distress under the right circumstances."

Johnny used the mirror now to catch my brother's eye. "How you been, Bob?"

Bobby snorted. "I was better before the ditch."

Johnny smiled. "Don't sweat it. This weather clears up, me and you'll come fetch your car."

Dana sat forward now and I could smell the peppermint on her breath. "So how long do you think this will stick? We couldn't get a straight answer out of the radio. They're all fired up about some kind of bug that's going around. Otherwise, the news is quiet."

I looked over, aware of her face close to mine. "What are they saying about the bug?"

"Some kind of rabies, they think. It's got folks acting crazy. Hit last night and spreading fast. All the way to Lexington already."

Now my stomach hurt. "They figure out how to treat it?"

"Not yet," Bobby chimed in. "They thought it was killing folk but it seems they were mistaken."

No, I thought, *I don't think they were mistaken.* And the ramifications of that unsettled me greatly.

"I'm sure they'll figure it out," Johnny said.

I stared at the pistol in my lap and hoped he was right.

"So," Mama said as we all gathered around a table piled high with food, "shall we let Pastor Franklin bless this food?"

Normally, I'd have said no or made light of it but some part of me hankered for that comfort even though I'd given up faith some time ago, finding it to be something akin to a gall bladder—useful to a point but not really essential. "I think that might be nice," I said. "Maybe throw something in about all the craziness of the day."

Pastor Frank looked around at each of us and smiled grimly. "Happy to. Let's join hands and bow our heads."

His prayer was simple, heartfelt and long, but I was grateful for it and I found myself grateful suddenly for lots of things, including my family and their plus-ones on a day that was getting scarier and scarier the more I considered it.

At his "amen" everyone let go of the hands they held except for me. I clutched Mama and Dana's hand and squeezed them harder than proper. I'm sure it gave Dana a different idea than what I intended but I didn't care. Her hand, cool and strong, felt good in mine. Mama's hand, sweaty and worn, felt good, too.

We sat and the feast commenced.

Jessie Lynn and Pastor Frank seemed to hit it off and I noticed my sister's face was a little flushed as she sipped her sweet tea and asked him questions about Oklahoma and the End Times. Johnny and Bobby were chatting, Johnny's eyes more alive than I'd seen them as they talked about work, life and video games. Somewhere in there, Johnny even offered to show Bobby how bodies were embalmed and my brother's grin told me that maybe his plan had backfired a bit.

Dana tried to engage me and I did my best but I was preoccupied now. I made myself eat even though my stomach protested. I answered her small talk where I could but found myself watching the others.

Mama was watching, too, and I saw from the line of her mouth that she was perplexed. She was beginning to see that Johnny Alvin wasn't working out at all well, for me at least, and Pastor Frank was all about my little sister. Mama didn't even know what to do with Dana and didn't pretend to for a change. I leaned over to Mama and squeezed her hand. "Sorry it didn't work out the way you planned," I whispered. "But look at it this way: It still might've worked."

She gave me her phony look of incredulity. "Why whatever do you mean, Kay Ann?"

I'd wanted to play with her in all of this, maybe teach her a little something about how her eldest girl, Kay Ann Cooper, didn't need no man—or no woman—to find her way in this world. I could pay for my own trailers. But now, in the light of everything else, that lesson didn't seem as important and the day had no room in it for playfulness. Instead, I was just glad to be here having what might be our last Thanksgiving before the world changed. So instead, I looked at Pastor

Frank and my sister, at Johnny and my brother, and then back to my mother. "Nothing, Mama," I told her.

We'd just served the pie when we heard a commotion outside. A noise somewhere between a howl and a shriek rose up among the trailers and Mama's eyes went wide. "What was that?"

I made eye contact with Johnny Alvin. He'd tucked the pistol into his coat pocket and now he stood and went to the coat rack, pulling his jacket on and checking outside as he went. Bobby was oblivious but Pastor Frank looked nervous. Mama and my sister looked scared. Dana watched me.

Johnny checked the lock and came back to the table. "I reckon we finish the pie and after that we should all head into town. Your neighbors might be getting rowdy again."

"Bless their hearts," Mama said.

"Amen," Pastor Frank agreed.

We ate the pie and as we ate it, more voices joined the other outside. Hungry voices. Hollow, aching voices. "What's wrong with those people?" Mama asked.

I wished I could answer her but I couldn't. Instead, I wondered just how far the world might change and what that might mean for next Thanksgiving and every Thanksgiving after. Hell, Christmas wasn't even a month out and I wasn't sure what the world might look like then. Of course, I wasn't even sure what tomorrow looked like; a world done in by Great Granny's Grateful Pie.

When my phone rang in my pocket it startled me. Uncle Auggie's voice, muffled by the sound of the road, surprised me. "Hey Kay Ann," he said. "The family all still there?"

"Yessir," I said. "Just finishing pie."

"You have situational awareness, PFC Cooper?"

"I have some, Sergeant Cooper."

"Good. Sit tight then. We're coming for you. Feds are establishing a bivouac at the high school. Me and the boys have been deputized." He paused. "You too, of course."

I had everyone into their coats and waiting by the door when we heard the loud horns indicative of a convoy. Mama and Jessie Lynn had protested, insisting that the dishes be clean, complaining the whole while about being rushed and leaving messes behind and not understanding the why of it.

I didn't have the heart to tell them and neither did Johnny Alvin but the hand in his coat pocket told me he knew everything that needed knowing.

When Uncle Auggie and his convoy of trucks and RVs, all chained up and brightly lit, passed into the mobile park, we saw the men and women in their parkas, hunting rifles and shotguns held at the ready from their vantage points in the truck beds. I saw Auggie had modified my underpinning into a type of wind-breaker on several of the trucks.

"Why August Cooper," my Mama declared, "what kind of hillbilly parade have you cooked up?"

He winked. "The kind that might just save your life, Betty June. If you haven't noticed, things are going to shit at the moment. Get your things and climb in."

My uncle held a familiar rifle—an M16A1, aged well from the days he'd shipped it home from Vietnam one piece at a time. I sidled over to him. "You should go, Mama."

"But I don't—"

"I'll tell you on the way, Betty June." She looked at me and then let someone pull her up into the open door of an RV.

There was a howl and a flash a movement followed by the crack of a rifle. Something heavy fell into the now and everyone jumped.

"So what do you know, Uncle Auggie?"

"It's spread past Lexington now, Louisville, too. Feds are in town looking for Patient Zero. Think they have him and if they do, they might be able to sort out whatever the fuck is happening."

I frowned. "Hank Summers ain't patient zero."

Auggie scratched his head. The others were all in now but Johnny Alvin who hung back, his eye on Bobby where he sat in the passenger side of Auggie's truck. "Then who is patient zero?"

"Pig named Wilbur," I said. "He's been hiding under my trailer when he isn't raising hell."

Auggie looked at the convoy then back to my trailer. "That pig could come in handy. Maybe I'll send y'all on and see if I can track him down."

"Or tell the feds where he is," Johnny suggested.

I shook my head. "They've got their hands full." I looked at my uncle. "You do, too. I need you to get my people to a safe place. I can fetch us that pig just fine on my own." I looked at Johnny. "Can I borrow your ride?"

"You want help?"

I looked at Bobby sitting there, the fear starting to pale his face. "You're already helping, Johnny."

Johnny Alvin handed over his keys. Then, he reached into his pocket and pulled out the pistol. "Here."

I took both, slipping the keys into my pocket and weighing the pistol in my hand.

"You qualified on one of those, soldier?" my uncle asked.

"No sir," I said. "But I'll make due."

He grinned, thumbed the safety on his rifle and then handed it over. "I know you can handle one of these."

"Damn straight I can." I passed the pistol back to Johnny and took the M16. It felt at home in my hands. Uncle Auggie dropped an ammo belt over my neck.

"Don't be long," he said. "And I want my rifle back."

I smiled but I knew it was grim. "I'll bring you the rifle *and* a pig."

He put a finger in the center of his forehead. "Right in the head, Kay Ann," he said. "Only thing that works."

I nodded. "Got it."

He nodded back. Then we hugged. I thought for a moment about pulling everyone back out of their respective vehicles so I could hug them, too. Even Pastor Frank. But I didn't. I'd see them soon enough.

I looked Johnny Alvin square in the eye and shook his hand. "I'll bring your ride back, too."

"Don't sweat it," he said. "It's the mortuary's."

There was another shriek and this time, two gunshots cracked open the air but I didn't flinch. It was all coming back to me, a more familiar home than my nearby trailer. I saw Mama fussing at the window, a panicked look on her face, as they started up the convoy at Auggie's wave. Then, he climbed back into the driver's seat to start the caravan rolling.

I waved and watched as they made their way around the loop, back to the highway. The sun was high, a white wafer behind the softer gray of cloud. The snow was deep and a low wind rustled the nearby pines. Somewhere, something that used to be a neighbor of mine howled at the quiet of the day and underneath my porch, a pig squealed, dark and ominous.

"Hey Wilbur," I said. "Good pig."

And then with my belly full of turkey and my heart full of family, I clicked off the safety and took myself gratefully hunting alone.

Light, life, and joy tend to define the holidays, but it has its share of ghosts and shadows, too.

Bestselling author Heather Graham examines souls lost in darkness in this very spectral story, and the one power—love—that can illuminate their way.

—KO

SANTA'S MORTUARY

Heather Graham

Nina Danbury leaned back in the massive whirlpool tub in her room at the bed and breakfast and closed her eyes, luxuriating in the hot bubbling water around her. It was the perfect end to the perfect day. She'd never been to St. Augustine before and she and Matt had spent the day on the tourist trail, walking for miles and miles. They'd spent hours at the old fort learning about the Spanish settlers of long ago, the English takeover, the return to Spain, and the arrival of the Americans. They'd seen the Spanish Military Hospital, buildings created by Henry Flagler, the lighthouse … the beach, shops and an old school house and more. She was in love with the city.

And she was in love with Ainsworth House, their bed and breakfast.

The place was massive, she knew, and while there were ten rooms that were let each night, the house also functioned now as a Christmas venue for young and old. A playground with elves had been set up in the massive parlor below with all kinds of activities for little ones and older ones. Santa came every night to sit in a massive red chair in the "grand receiving salon" in the main section of the house. The owners here were very crafty; the house dressed up for the season. They'd learned that it was decked out differently for Valentine's Day and Easter—when it was the Easter Bunny who sat on the chair in the "grand receiving salon"—and for the Fourth of July, Thomas Jefferson and other impersonators came to regale guests with stories from their day. For the two months preceding Halloween, the house became a maze of ghoulish delights.

It was amazing that their room—in the right wing of the building—could be so quiet and charming while all manner of activity went on in other parts of the house. But, according to Matt, they didn't build like this anymore. The walls were wonderfully thick; the house had been planned to keep warmth in when it was winter and to be cool in summer and that called for old insulation that could still perform in a far superior manner to that slapped together today.

She smiled, easing back in the tub and closing her eyes. Her tired muscles were in certain bliss. Later that night—right at the stroke of midnight—she and Matt would take the house tour with the owner and learn about the house itself and the part it had played in St. Augustine's history.

As she lay there, she smiled, listening to the soft whirr of the moving water the only sound in her mind. Matt had come back in. He'd sat down with such silence that she hadn't heard him. But now, she felt him. She knew that he'd taken a seat on the rim at the back of the tub. He slipped his hand into the water and stroked her calf. There was something deliciously sensual about his touch, though she hadn't ever thought before that her calf was the most erotic zone on her body.

"Nice," she murmured. "Sweet."

She kept her eyes closed, feeling the water, feeling his touch. He moved down on the floor, next to the tub on his knees and she felt both of his hands on her then, stroking and massaging both her legs. The sensation was so good it was almost ... climatic.

"Matt," she murmured. She opened her eyes.

For a moment she was so terrified her scream froze in her throat. *It wasn't Matt.*

There was a man knelt down by the side of the tub with sandy blond hair, some kind of a uniform, and a sweeping feathered hat. He looked at her. His features were well defined; he was exceedingly handsome.

But there was a bullet hole dead center in his forehead and blood spilled over the white cotton shirt he wore beneath a re-enactor's frock coat.

At last, sound escaped her.

She screamed.

And screamed.

And leapt out of the tub and raced out of the bathroom, stark naked.

She would have raced out of the room and the house onto the streets of St. Augustine just as she was if it weren't for the real Matt who was stretched out on the bed.

"Nina!" he called, springing up to grab her before she could open the door.

She tried to explain; she told him there was a man in the bathroom. He blinked, disbelieving.

"Nina, I've been here since you went in—no one went in there!" he told her.

"He was there; he touched me!" she told him.

Holding her dripping and trembling body, he half-dragged her to the bathroom door. Nina closed her eyes, shaking with terror, imagining all kinds of horrible things. The man in the bathroom had a gun or a knife. He and Matt would fight....

He'd had a bullet hole in his head; there had been blood all over him.

"Nina, there's no one here. No one at all," Matt said.

She opened her eyes; Matt was right.

There was no one in the large and beautifully appointed bathroom. The water in the tub continued its soft bubble and whirr.

And that was all.

"It's quite one thing for a house to have a few ghoulish ghosts when one is calling it *The Haunted Crypt* for Halloween," Trinity Ainsworth said, looking desperately at Logan Raintree and Kelsey O'Brien. "And quite another when you have it open as *Santa's Land* for Christmas!"

Trinity was a pretty young woman in her late twenties; she was tiny with enormous dark eyes and long brown hair and at the moment, she fit the image of a damsel in distress to the core.

Logan Raintree looked over at his wife, Kelsey. As friends, Trinity and Kelsey were certainly the long and short of it; Kelsey was tall and willowy, blond and very beautiful and far more sophisticated, bearing an aura of confidence. But then, Kelsey had started off her law-keeping career as a United States Marshall and she had always known what she wanted to do. Now, Kelsey and he were both Federal agents—part of a "special" unit that dealt with particular and peculiar cases nationwide, known unofficially as the Krewe of Hunters. They were there, however, in a non-official capacity because of Kelsey's friendship with Trinity. Kelsey hailed from a far distant part of Florida—she'd grown up way, way down the peninsula in Key West. But when Trinity and Kelsey had been children—traveling up and down the state with families—they'd met, first in Key West, and then, when Kelsey's family had taken her up to the northern end of the state and to spend time with Trinity there; they had now been friends most of their lives.

Logan hadn't expected that he and Kelsey would spend their Christmas vacation trying to "hunt" down a lecherous ghost. It wasn't that "ghosts" or the earthly remnants of lost souls didn't play a large part in their lives. But they were usually concerned with hunting down the living who committed atrocious acts—and the fact that they could sometimes speak with the dead was the advantage they had over other agents who loved to mock them and hum *Twilight Zone* music when they were around.

But they had just been packing for their flights down to Miami and on to Key West when the call had come from Trinity—and so here they were. And Logan loved the fact that Kelsey could have seen some of the things she'd seen in her life and worked some of the cases she had while still retaining such a wealth of empathy and compassion for others.

And for Trinity.

A many-times great grandfather had originally built Ainsworth House but it had been lost after the Civil War. Trinity had dreamed of buying the place back her entire life. She had worked and saved and cajoled family members—bribed and pleaded—and purchased it. She'd owned it several years now.

Logan could understand her passion. The place was beautiful.

He was facing west as he saw it for the first time.

The sun was setting behind the structure and cast a blood red haze around the white-washed grandeur of the old plantation-style home and almost made it appear as if it had been painted in blood.

He'd already heard some of the history. It had never actually been a plantation—or working farm—but rather it had been built as a city dwelling for Percy Ainsworth, a Southern aristocrat, in 1833. But the Civil War had come along and Florida had been the third state in the Union to secede and by the time the war had ended, Percy Ainsworth had been in dire financial straits. Yankee Brent McNamara, ex-USA Navy lieutenant—stationed for a spell in St. Augustine when the Union invaded the city in 1862 and never let go—came in to buy the plantation from Ainsworth when all went to hell. By all accounts, he'd been a good man, and he'd allowed the family to stay for years because he was in love with Ainsworth's young daughter. As that went, all was well—the young daughter was equally in love with him and they were soon married. But, as fate would have it, McNamara was killed in the house itself—shot and then stabbed in the middle of the night by an intruder who also made off with the family jewels— such as they were, after the war. Burt Holmsby, a banker, had been in love with Grace Ainsworth—now the widow Ainsworth—as well. But she died.

And when she died the bank came in and took the house, and sold it to a family of morticians who opened for business under the name of Fogarty and Sons Funeral Home—which the property remained until the 1990s when the last Fogarty himself was embalmed and given his last service right there where he had worked throughout his life. It was then purchased as a private family home by a fly-by-night rock star who quickly went through the money gained from his fifteen minutes of fame.

He was found dead in the embalming room—where he had often thrown lavish parties.

A stairway of thirteen steps led up to the first *ground* floor, which allowed for the foundations and basement to extend below ground level. Majestic pillars gave the house the true look of a plantation, just as the second story wraparound balcony. French doors on the balcony allowed for visitors to step out and see Matanzas Bay and other structures in the old section of town. From some areas of the balcony, Logan estimated, one could see the Plaza de la Constitución, the grand parade ground where the oldest settlers had once practiced at arms, where bands now played and where, once upon a distant time, the Spanish method of execution—garroting—had taken place.

But none of that really had to do with the house. And right now—despite the eerie cast the sun gave it, everything about the house seemed as cheery as the season. A choir of "light" angels were set up to sing carols. More lights adorned the old oak trees in the yard. A waving Santa stood on one side.

"It all looks bright and festive—truly beautiful," Kelsey said, trying to be reassuring to her friend. "It doesn't *look* haunted or … eerie in any way. Honestly."

"Please, please—you'll stay? You'll do something?" Nina begged.

"Yes, of course, we intend to stay," Kelsey said. She turned and looked at Logan. He nodded and forced a smile. He was lead man for the insular Krewe of Hunter units beneath Jackson Crow. Work seemed to rule their lives. He'd had visions of piña coladas on the beach—no ghosts, no bones, no dead men.

Then again, he didn't even like piña coladas.

"Trinity, it was just one guest who was so upset?" Logan asked.

Trinity grimaced. "Come in, please, I'll show you."

They followed her up the steps and into the house. The door opened into a spectacular parlor with a massive fireplace and a hearth and a gorgeous curving stairway. Logan almost felt as if he'd entered into a medieval great hall.

Except that this place now reeked of the holidays. A wonderful toy train took up a large area to the far right; it was designed as if around an old English village with Tudor homes and cars that separated easily for little fingers. Another area boasted "Dancer, Prancer, Rudolph, and all! You pick, your stuff." There was an area filled with Christmas pictures for little fingers to color in. Holly was all about; there was a giant tree. The house smelled of cinnamon and all good things.

"What wonderful work you've done here!" Kelsey said.

"Thank you," Trinity murmured. "Come on upstairs; I don't have more guests coming in until tomorrow night—if then. And my 'elves' aren't due in for another hour."

She led the way upstairs and down a hallway to the "right" wing. "The bedrooms are all on this side," Trinity explained. "When we open the haunted house, it takes up the other rooms. There is gift-wrapping over there, a store of 'Ten and Under Delights' and a book nook where you can read or buy. Our entry is just a few dollars; people come in spend money and they really do it nicely—except now I don't know."

"Oh, Trinity, you really think that one woman being afraid in a bed and breakfast is going to ruin your business?" Kelsey asked.

"If it were Halloween …" Trinity murmured. "But it's not!"

"What happened, exactly?" Logan asked.

"A ghost—with a bullet hole in his head and blood all over him—was touching her in the bathtub," Trinity said.

"An amorous ghost?" Logan murmured.

Trinity looked at Kelsey wide-eyed. "Is he mocking me?"

"No, no, we're just trying to figure out what's going on. Okay, you're certain it wasn't a re-enactor? They are all over the city—especially now. Spanish soldiers, Civil War soldiers—"

"No. The two came in together; the boyfriend was on the bed while she went in to the whirlpool. Here!"

Dramatically, Trinity opened the door to a guest bedroom. It was a darned nice room. Doors opened to the balcony—which looked out over the bay. The drapes and bedspread were white; the furniture was mahogany. The room was spacious with the latest in a wide-screen television and entertainment center. A door led to the bathroom; Logan headed that way and looked in. The bathroom was enormous—something you didn't find that often in a bed and breakfast. The whirlpool tub was large enough for two.

Kelsey had come in to stand by him. "Anything?" he asked her softly.

Kelsey looked at him and shook her head slightly. "Nothing."

"Excuse me," Trinity said. Her phone was ringing.

"What else do you know about the house? Deaths?" Logan asked his wife.

"It's an old house—naturally, it's supposed to be haunted. But, people see Osceola walking around the Castillo San Marcos all the time—headless and looking for his head, which by the way, was not lopped off; he died of natural causes and his physician took his head. Sorry, that's not important here—it's just that, well, haunted … people have seen a number of Civil War soldiers over time. And a beautiful young woman. I'm assuming she's supposed to be Grace."

"Grace—Grace Ainsworth?" Logan asked.

"Yes, she was the young lady who married Brent McNamara. She 'languished' to death soon after he was killed. It was a very sad situation," Kelsey said.

"How does Trinity relate to all this?"

"Oh, Grace had a brother who had settled into New Orleans before the war. He was barely making ends meet in New Orleans—when everything fell apart, he stayed away. Home was too painful for him," Kelsey explained. "But … you know, it was a mortuary for a long time, too. People see all kinds of ghosts."

"Why would ghosts want to haunt the place they were embalmed?" Logan asked.

"I doubt they would. I'm just telling you who people think they've seen over the years," Kelsey told him.

Trinity came back into the room, looking at them a little awed.

"That call was from Martin Crypton of *Awakened by Night*—that ghost show! He's coming tonight with his crew. They're going to pay me nicely to set up in the house!"

"Wonderful," Logan said, looking at Kelsey.

"They're going to bring a medium to free the ghosts!" Trinity said.

"Great. Nothing like a medium freeing ghosts at Christmas," Logan said dryly. "What about the young lady who was supposedly attacked?"

"Oh, she's at the chain hotel on Avila," Trinity said. "It's brand new and by all known records, there never was a graveyard of any kind where it was built. She's actually a lovely person; I'm sure she'll speak with you. But, now … I'm so grateful to you two, but do you think the medium can get rid of the ghosts?"

"Don't worry; we'll be here, too," Kelsey assured her.

"I'll call her. Actually, she's only a few blocks away; you might want to just walk."

Nina Danbury was an attractive brunette and her boyfriend, Matt Douglas, was tall and lean and appeared to be intelligent and reasonable. Logan and Kelsey met up with them at a coffee shop that looked over the massive structure of the Castillo San Marcos.

"The Ainsworth House is gorgeous! I loved it," Nina said. "But … he touched me, and then I saw him. There was a bullet hole right dead center in his forehead! And blood … all over his chest. I was—terrified. Well, I wasn't terrified at first. I was terrified when I saw him."

"Matt, you didn't see the apparition at all?" Kelsey asked.

Matt shook his head. "No, I didn't see anyone. But I did see Nina's face."

"I have to ask this," Logan said. "We're you drinking a lot? We're you on any kind of a—substance?"

"No!" Nina said indignantly.

"Oh, please, we weren't suggesting you were—it's just something you have to ask about, you know?" Kelsey said. "Please, don't be offended. Try to tell us about the whole thing—beginning to end."

"We'll, there's a great whirlpool tub in that room. Matt was lying on the bed—we were pretty wiped out—trying to see so much in a day. So I was just lying there—my eyes closed. And I felt hands, the coolest, most amazing erotic and wonderful sensual touch on my legs...."

"Amazing that we left," Matt said, sounding just a little bit irritated.

"Oh! Well, that's why I thought at first that you'd come in, baby!" Nina said quickly.

"Great. A ghost is a better lover," Matt muttered.

Nina spoke quickly to Kelsey, "Well! I opened my eyes to tell *Matt* to come in and join me—and then I saw *him!* It was horrible!"

"Horrible because you thought he intended to hurt you—be mean and cruel?" Logan asked.

Nina paused at that, confused. "Well, he was—not real! And he had that hole in his forehead and the blood ... I was terrified!"

"So great—the ghost didn't want to hurt us—just get it on with my girl?" Matt demanded indignantly.

"I'm just curious. The house has a reputation of some bad things happening," Logan said.

"Oh, Buggety-Boo, you mean!" Nina said.

Logan looked at Kelsey. "Buggety-Boo?" he repeated.

"He was a one hit wonder—you know that song, *Tell It Like It Is!*" Nina said. "He was found lying on one of the old tables in the embalming room." She shivered. "Total creep. He held parties down there where he had people drinking blood and all kinds of weird stuff. Well, I heard that the last of the Fogarty family of morticians was found down there, too. Totally eerie. And through the years ... during the Civil War it was often used for injured soldiers—and after the battle of Olustee there were a lot of soldiers who had to be somewhere to recoup. I love the house—I just can't go back."

"Well, thank you," Kelsey told her, reaching across the table to squeeze her hand. "We understand."

"Who are you exactly?" Matt asked.

"Trinity Ainsworth and I are old friends," Kelsey said.

"But you're some kind of law enforcement, right?"

"FBI," Logan told him.

"You're going to arrest a ghost?" Matt asked.

"We're actually on vacation—headed to my home in Key West," Kelsey said.

"But, you're staying at the Ainsworth House?" Matt asked.

"For a few nights," Kelsey said. "Excuse me, I'll just go and get our check—and thank you so much for your time."

Kelsey rose to head to the counter.

"Kelsey, wait—if you all find out something, you'll let us know, right?" Nina asked, hurrying after her.

With both women gone, Matt looked directly at Logan. "Well, a word of warning—watch it. If the guy hadn't had a bullet hole in his forehead, I'm not sure Nina would have screamed."

Logan lowered his head, trying not to smile. He looked back at Matt with a straight face. "She seems like a lovely girl—and it really is a compliment to you, you know? She thought it was you."

"Yeah, maybe that's what galls me. It wasn't. Still, ghost or no, watch out for that guy!"

By the time they returned to the Ainsworth House, Martin Crypton and his crew had arrived.

The "santa" side of the house had opened as well; employees dressed as elves moved about the parlor or salon and adults and children were here and there—stuffing and creating their own reindeer and playing with toy trains and coloring. Trinity was smiling as she welcomed them. "Thank God! I mean there are so many things in the world to worry about, but if I don't make all the mortgage payments, well ... I'm out. And I owe people for helping me—and all these people working!"

"I'm glad to see that things are going so well," Kelsey told her.

Logan was silent. On the one hand, he wanted to say, wow, all was good—he and Kelsey could head on to Key West. On the other hand....

He just felt uneasy. There was nothing like TV ghost hunters to really piss off a ghost.

He saw Kelsey looking at him. She felt the same—and there was a "please" in her eyes.

"I guess we should meet Martin Crypton," Logan said.

Before they could, however, there was a loud, panicked scream from just up the stairs; it had such a blood-curdling quality that every child in the room went silent and one of the "elf" employees let out a shriek as well.

Logan started toward the stairs but before he could reach the steps, Santa—his beard half on and half off—came tearing down them. He was followed by two sexy little elves, one a blonde, and one a brunette.

"Sir!" Logan called to Santa, but Santa wasn't stopping. Logan hurried after him as he headed out the door, tripping on the stairs and landing on his butt at the bottom, hair and hat and beard all askew.

One of the elves tripped over him, the other gasped and kept running down the street.

He saw that Kelsey already had her cell phone out to call a paramedic; Santa was obviously hurting, groaning as he gripped a knee and rolled.

Trinity and most of the people in the house were outside as well, having followed them. While Kelsey helped up the fallen elf and tried to get everyone to give Santa air, Logan knelt down by Santa.

"Sir, stay still. Paramedics are on the way. What happened in there—what went on?"

Santa groaned and closed his eyes, gasping. "My knee—my knee!"

"I saw her—it was horrible!" A woman cried from the crowd.

"Ma'am, please, what happened?" Kelsey asked.

"It was Timmy's turn to see Santa—but she was there, sitting on his lap!" the woman said.

"She who?" Kelsey asked.

"She—the corpse! She was horrible, rotting and stinking and … oh, my God!"

As Logan tried to get Santa to stay stabilized and still, Martin Crypton and his two co "ghost-hunters" and a cameraman and a sound man came out, trying to interview people and get it all on tape. "Get over there, Gary, get the shot of Santa!" Crypton called.

Then the man hurried toward Logan and Santa just as they heard the sound of sirens. "This is it, people, the real thing as gruesome ghosts invade this haunted bed and breakfast and attraction for Christmas!" Crypton said, sliding down on his knees by Santa.

As he did so, he had to catch himself by bracing against Santa's shoulder—he had come with such an impetus that he nearly careened into the downed man.

"Mr. Crypton, please get that microphone out of Santa's face," Logan said firmly.

"Santa, tell us—who is the ghost? Who did you see?" Crypton demanded.

Santa groaned; he'd shattered a kneecap, Logan thought.

"Sir, I insist you get away from Santa," Logan said, trying to contain his anger.

Crypton was in his mid-thirties or early forties, a big guy with a pretty face who could have used more time in a gym. He looked at Logan and lowered his voice to a harsh whisper. "What are you? Some kind of a half-breed mystic trying to hone in? This is my gig tonight and you are not calling the shots and ruining the best show I might have all season!"

All the training in the world didn't stop Logan from wanting to clock the man. Somehow, he managed not to. Maybe because the paramedics chose that minute to arrive and asked that they both step aside.

And Logan saw Kelsey looking at him. He was lucky, he knew. Damned lucky. He'd lost his first wife under horrible circumstances, and when he'd first met Kelsey as a professional associate, he'd thought they'd never make it. But he'd learned that she was amazing and competent—and still so filled with heart and soul that she could change the world. She looked at him with beautiful sea-colored eyes he'd long ago gotten lost in and arched a brow with a smirk toward Crypton.

She'd heard. And she knew that he was making an effort not to explode.

She sauntered over to Crypton. "Kelsey O'Brien, Mr. Crypton. I'm here with the director of my unit, Logan Raintree. We're Federal officers. We're not the least interested in your show, so, please, you needn't feel threatened in any way."

"Feds?" Crypton said, confused.

By then, Logan was standing. He was glad at that moment that he was nearly six-four. He towered over Crypton.

"Uh, sorry for the half-breed crack, Agent," he said. "It's just that—these are bona fide ghost sightings! A whole mass of people *saw* this creepy woman. This is—this is mammoth!"

"People are hurt," Logan said. "Their welfare comes before a camera."

The cops had arrived along with the ambulance. Trinity Ainsworth—nearly in tears now—had pointed Logan out to the officer in charge.

He walked by Kelsey on his way to speak with the policeman. She touched his fingers and briefly squeezed his hand.

"I owe you big time when we get to the beach," she whispered.

His temper cooled; she had that power.

He walked on over to speak with the officer.

Ainsworth House was shut down while the incident was investigated. Logan wasn't sure just who Crypton knew to get his way, but he and his crew were going to stay in the house that night to investigate. The police had already gone through the place by the time night fell.

Crypton had his cameras and recorders and screens set up across the house. Their own Krewe of Hunters units often used the same equipment—except that they were capable of going a lot further. Apparently, Crypton hadn't read much about the Krewe of Hunters and Logan was glad.

He wanted to observe.

He and Kelsey were keeping the "Spa Room,"—which was where Nina and Matt had been staying when she'd had her ghostly visitation in the whirlpool. They'd watched a great deal of Crypton's set-up, and they'd stayed out of the way. But when midnight rolled around and Crypton's assistant knocked against a wall and Crypton turned with wide eyes to say, "What was that?" it became too much for Logan.

"Let's leave them," he told Kelsey softly.

"What if we re-create what happened?" Kelsey asked him. "I could use a lovely soak in the tub with all that nice whirling going on."

"Sure," he said. He held her shoulders and looked into her eyes. "But lonely lascivious ghost or no, I don't want the jerk fooling around with you."

Kelsey laughed. "Let's just see if we can lure him out."

He agreed. He turned on the television just as Matt had done. Kelsey teased him, grinning, and doing a mock striptease on her way into the bathroom.

"Quit that—or the ghost won't have a chance!" he told her.

She grinned at him and headed in and in a second he heard the water running.

Five minutes later he heard Kelsey call out, "Ahha! Got you!"

Leaping out of bed he walked into the bathroom. And there he was—the man Nina had described to them.

He saw Logan and began to fade away. "No, no, please!" Kelsey said.

"We're here to help."

The ghost appeared confused for a moment. He looked at Kelsey.

"Hey, my wife, if you don't mind!" Logan said, reaching for a towel and handing it to Kelsey as she stepped from the tub.

"You both—see me?" the ghost asked.

"Easily," Logan assured him.

"You're—*sights,*" the ghost said.

Logan arched a brow—he hadn't heard the term before.

"*Sights*—the living who see the dead," the ghost said.

"Yes, we both are," Kelsey told him gently.

"But no one can help me," he said. And as he stood there, the bullet hole disappeared and the blood stain left his white cotton shirt.

"Try us—maybe we can," Logan said. "Who are you, for starters?"

"Brent McNamara," he said.

"Brent, of course," Kelsey said softly. "But … why…?"

"Because *she's* here, but I can never see her!" he said.

"She—you mean Grace?" Logan asked.

He nodded, looking miserable. "It was one thing to be murdered, and then … the bastard who killed me practiced some kind of strange rite."

"Who killed you? The law has no record," Kelsey said.

"Can you imagine?" the ghost asked them. "A bitter war—I was a Northerner, the Ainsworth family was hardcore Southern. But as the war came nearer to a close, we all just wanted it over and we realized that what we were fighting for wasn't worth killing *love* for—or one another. Oh, I'm not a fool—prejudice and hatred lasted long after the surrender and long after my death, but Grace and her family and I and mine … we loved one another. Grace and I were married. I survived Cold Harbor and Gettysburg and battles you couldn't imagine to come to—this. But, at least, I had Grace."

"But who killed you?" Kelsey demanded.

"Burt Olmsby, the banker. He wanted the house; he had a buyer for it—old man Fogarty. Oh, and he wanted Grace, too. She foiled him on that, but she took her own life. So he saw to it that some ritual kept her to one half of the house—and me to the other. I can see her sometimes, down the hall. But when we come close … we're both just gone."

Kelsey, wrapped tightly in her towel, just looked at him. "Ritual?" she murmured. "I can get on line and see what I can find. But, honestly, perhaps he just made you believe that you couldn't cross the line. That's possible."

"No, he told me he'd see to it that—dead or alive—I'd never hold my wife again," Brent McNamara said. "He told me that when he'd stabbed me in the gut and was holding the nozzle of his gun dead against my forehead."

"I'll get on it," Kelsey promised him. She headed into the bedroom. The ghost started to follow.

Logan stepped in front of him and cleared his throat. "Really? You're in love—so you attack women in whirlpool baths?"

"Only those who are here with men who are supposed to love them," McNamara said.

"What?" Logan asked.

"She's beautiful; you're a lucky man. You should never forget it," McNamara said.

"But—I don't," Logan told him.

"But too many people do," McNamara said softly. "Like that jerk who's running around the halls. Bet you didn't even know that the young woman he's with is his wife—he treats her like an indentured servant. It's not right. I can't see the woman I love. We never got to have our first Christmas as man and wife—I'd give so much for that!"

As he spoke, a scream tore through the hall.

"The ghost hunters!" Logan said, hurrying into the bedroom. Kelsey was dressed in a long skirt and soft sweater. She was already at the door, opening it.

"It's old man Fogarty," McNamara said. "He learned how to move things and—"

They were already out in the hall.

Kelsey dead stopped, a puzzled expression on her face. The ghost hunters appeared to be just fine. Martin Crypton was shouting out commands at his crew of assistants and camera personnel.

"Get the lights right!" Martin told the thin, shaggy-haired man holding a lantern. "We need it eerie … I can see on the screen that we all look lousy. Get a better gel!" He turned to his pretty young assistant. "And what the hell kind of scream was that? I'm going to show you how to do it right and then get it straight!"

He walked down the hall and dramatically jumped back. "What was that? What the hell was that? Something touched me."

The girl sighed. "Okay, okay," she murmured.

"Your scream sucked!" Crypton told her.

Kelsey shook her head and turned and went back into the room. Logan and the ghost of Brent McNamara followed her.

"Who is old man Fogarty?" Kelsey asked, spinning around to look at Brent. "The last mortuary owner?"

"Yes, he's here. He's fine—nice old guy, really. But, he likes to bug the guests now and then. I think he wants them to know that they're lucky to be alive."

"Does he hurt people?" Kelsey asked.

"None of us hurts people," Brent McNamara said indignantly.

"None of us?" Logan asked.

"There are a number of us here," McNamara said. "We don't mind. That poor rock-star boy—he just couldn't resist his booze along with pills. But he's not a bad guy; just got to famous too fast and couldn't handle it when things went to hell. There are some kids … Joey, who died of pneumonia when he was about five in the 1920s. Sissy—polio in 1890."

As he spoke, there was another scream from the hallway. Kelsey waved a dismissive hand in the air. "Crypton again," she said.

"It is Crypton," Logan said. "But … he sounds different."

He opened the door to the hallway again. He started—the ghost-hunters were almost in front of the door.

And the scream was different.

It was real.

Crypton lay on the floor. He was screaming and struggling and the cameraman and his assistant and the sound men were all running around—tilting at the air, trying to save him.

"Where? What? What the hell is it?" The cameraman demanded.

"There's nothing," the assistant said. "Stop it, Martin, you jerk— we can't see anything."

"How can I run the camera when you're being this dramatic?"

"Help me, help me!" Crypton babbled. "Help me, help me, help me, get me out of here!"

Logan slowly saw the figure attacking Martin Crypton appear. It was an elderly gentleman; he wasn't really doing anything to Crypton. He was seated on the "ghost-hunter's" chest, grinning.

Logan would have tried to act—but he didn't need to do so.

Brent McNamara strode by him to stand by Crypton and the elderly gentleman. "No hurting people, Mr. Fogarty!"

"He's a jerk!" the elderly apparition on top of Crypton said belligerently. "He was saying that I haunted the place because I embalmed the living—he was saying that you were a two-timing carpetbagger!"

"You still can't hurt him!" Kelsey said softly. "People say awful things—but you can't hurt them. Dead or alive," she added.

"You can see something here?" the cameraman asked Kelsey.

She whispered in reply. "Crypton is a bit of an ass; I'm just humoring him to get you all out of here!"

Crypton continued to blubber and beg for help.

"Up now, Mr. Fogarty, up. Enough is enough," Brent McNamara said.

"Yes, please, Trinity—who owns the place now—is a really nice woman," Kelsey told him.

"Please," Logan added.

Mr. Fogarty got off of Crypton. Crypton lay there stunned for several minutes. Then he leapt to his feet. And he was headed down the hall to the stairs and Logan knew that he was gone.

"Might as well pack up," Logan told the pretty girl who was, according to Brent McNamara "the love of his life" as well as his assistant. "And you might want to move on; my friend, the ghost here, says that you shouldn't settle for less than being really loved."

"I didn't exactly say that," Brent McNamara murmured. "You said it really well—and I guess it's what I meant."

The "ghost hunters" were quick to leave.

"How do we fix this for Trinity—and for Christmas?" Kelsey asked quietly.

"A medium? We convince everyone that … the ghosts are gone?" Logan suggested.

"If I could just see Grace!" McNamara said.

The next day, Ainsworth House remained closed.

And Kelsey had spent the day on the computer.

She discovered that Brent and Grace had been buried in separate tombs in an old mausoleum. With Trinity's help, she arranged for Brent to be exhumed. By the next day—three days before Christmas!—they arranged for an Episcopalian priest to perform a re-burial ceremony and a blessing on both of the departed.

Logan, Kelsey, and Trinity attended the service. It was lovely.

"Will this work, do you think?" Trinity asked anxiously.

"Can't hurt!" Kelsey assured her.

But later, when they returned Trinity to Ainsworth House, Logan expressed his doubts to his wife.

"I'm concerned," Logan told Kelsey. "Part of it may have to do with Burt Olmsby. The banker—Brent knows that he was killed by Burt. He was looking the man in the face when he stabbed him and shot him. And he knew that Olmsby wanted Grace. Think there's anything we can do about that?"

"It's far too late to have him arrested for murder," Kelsey said.

"No, but, maybe we can find where he's buried."

"But—he doesn't haunt the place. Brent would have told us."

"Still, I believe that we need to do something. Find out where he was buried."

"And dig up his grave? We'll wind up arrested!"

"I know. And we're Federal agents," Logan said.

But, back at the house, they discovered that Brent still could not leave the wing he had been doomed to haunt.

Kelsey lay with Logan in bed and said softly, "You know, we have a tendency—as people, human souls—to believe in curses and superstitions. Maybe Brent *believes* he's doomed to this side of the house. Maybe if we have something read over his body...."

"You found where he's buried?"

"Yes," she admitted. "He's about a few miles north of here—toward Jacksonville. It's an old, old cemetery. There are no gates or fences."

Logan sighed. But he knew Kelsey. "I already have the shovels," he told her. "If we're caught, well you know...."

She turned to him, her smile radiant. "We're going to dig him up?" she asked.

"Yeah, what the hell ... surely, if we're fired, we can find work at a carnival," he said.

They reached the cemetery near midnight—just the right hour. Luckily, they were off on a dirt road that led far from I-95 into stretches of shrub land.

There were no walls, no gates, just a sign that half-heartedly warned that there was no admittance after dusk.

Of course they ignored the sign.

Burt Olmsby had been granted a praying angel—which made his grave easy enough to find. Kelsey knew exactly where because she had looked it all up and was excellent at historical research. Since he hadn't managed to make himself at all famous at anything, the angle and his name were all that remained of any kind of memorial to the man.

They dug.

His coffin had been poor pine; it was barely six feet down in soft, moist earth.

It wasn't easy to create much of a fire with all the dampness, but Logan had come armed with a lot accelerant. Soon, they had the coffin, the remnants, and the bones blazing.

Then, of course, they heard the sirens. And they ran like hell.

But, when they returned to Ainsworth House—filthy, worn, and ragged, they found Brent McNamara near the second floor stairs— unable to cross over. They saw Grace Ainsworth McNamara—on her side—just staring at her beloved Brent.

"Maybe the mind and the soul are one," Logan told Kelsey.

"What now?" she asked. "I'm not even sure what you call the crime we committed—and we still haven't solved the problem for Brent and Grace."

"I believe I have it," Logan told her. "It's all in the heart, the soul, and the mind, and the mind must live on with the heart and the soul."

"Okay, so?" Kelsey asked.

"We are definitely calling in Will Chan!"

Will Chan was one of their agents—in fact, he was one with the very first group who had become part of the Krewe of Hunters.

He'd been a magician and an entertainer in his previous life. He knew all about sleight of hand and tricking the mind and the eye. He was also a great and understanding guy and though he'd been planning his own Christmas break, he was a friend as well as a co-worker.

And so he arrived quickly, flying from Virginia down to Jacksonville and while Logan drove him from the airport down to St. Augustine, he told him all about the situation.

"Belief can be everything," Will agreed.

By the time they reached Ainsworth House, their plan was ready for action.

That night, Will arrived and with the ghosts in the room—including rock star Buggety-Boo and a number of young ones who had died of childhood diseases in the house over the years and a few others who had also gone by natural means—he performed a ceremony at the table. Only Brent McNamara wasn't there; he had to watch from the upstairs hallway.

Will was great at what he did; he called for the powers of Heaven, goodness, and light to honor those who had died in God's good grace to clear the house of all and any evil.

He had managed to get some kind of a trick that caused a large puff of black smoke over the table to be cleared with a charge of white—and then vanish entirely.

Then Grace Ainsworth, beautiful in a Victorian day dress, rich dark hair swept up in a chignon, walked to the foot of the stairs.

"Brent!" she implored.

Brent walked down the stairs to stand before her. He embraced her warmly. It almost appeared that there were tears in his eyes; real tears.

Ainsworth House had a spectacular re-opening on Christmas Eve. All the publicity had garnered a new crop of tourists who longed to experience a place with a reputation like that of Ainsworth House.

Trinity invited Thomas Villiers—the hurt Santa—to dinner on Christmas Eve.

Villiers hadn't shattered his kneecap or broken a leg; he'd only strained it badly. And while he'd said that he'd never come back in the house, Logan had convinced him that Father Connolly—the Episcopal priest who had performed the rites at the gravesite—would be there, too, and that the house would be blessed and all would be well.

Kelsey told Logan with a certain amount of wry amusement that it was important that Thomas come back and that he like the house again—Trinity was in love with the man who had played Santa for her.

And dinner was lovely. The chef and sous chefs and household staff were back—along with the elves. They had turkeys and hams and mashed potatoes and stuffing and cranberry sauce—all the traditional fare that could be wanted.

The house was beautiful and lovely.

A storm was rolling in, but that was all right. All were in the Christmas spirit—even Father Connolly who arrived a little late after having given the six o'clock Christmas Eve service.

But it was soon after that the storm moved in with a vengeance and right in the middle of the meal, the lights went out.

They scurried about finding lanterns and candles.

But while they did so, Logan—well aware that the ghosts were at table along with them, commenting on the food, whether they could actually taste it or not—saw that Grace Ainsworth McNamara was standing by the front door, looking out as she had, perhaps, years ago, waiting to find out the result of the war.

And who would and wouldn't come home. He imagined her joy when she saw the Yankee soldier she'd fallen in love with walking back up her steps.

Brent joined her there. He turned her into his arms. And Logan heard him say softly, "Merry Christmas, my love."

He kissed her.

And as he did, the lights came back on. Slowly at first. The Christmas lights in all their colors. And then, bit by bit, as if Heaven had indeed opened up, the room seemed to glow.

Later that night, when all was cleared up, when carols had been sung, when ghosts and guests were happy and resting at last, Logan found himself alone with his true love in life.

"Merry Christmas, Kelsey O'Brien Raintree," Logan said.

"Merry Christmas," she said, and kissed his lips softly. "I owe you, you know. For staying here—for helping Trinity."

"You never owe me," he told her.

She smiled and said, "Well, at any rate … I was thinking of taking a whirlpool bath." She drew away from him, laughing as she cast off articles of clothing in a silly striptease as she headed into the bathroom.

He followed her, stripping as well.

"That was fast!" she told him, as the water purred and hummed.

"Just not taking any chances that anymore lovelorn ghosts of the past might be around," he said. "Merry Christmas!" And with the water thrumming around them, he took her into his arms.

"Merry, merry, Christmas!" she whispered in turn.

And so it proved to be.…

We've all heard it: The holidays have become too commercial; TV and film take all the magic out of the season!

Will it get worse in the future? Will our media-saturated, info-congested society throw cherished myths away into the data stream? Will everyone become enslaved by merchandise and memes?

With clarity and heart, Sam Knight explores this idea, as one little girl discovers myth's critical value over reality.

—KO

YES, VIRGINIA2097C, THERE IS A SANTA CLAUS

Sam Knight

nly one more day of school until Holiday Season Break. Dread welled up inside of Virginia, tightening her stomach until she thought she might vomit. She'd tried to distract herself from the looming date, but nothing worked.

The school bus is here.

Virginia blinked to turn off the vid playing on her retinal display. She hadn't been paying attention to it anyway.

"Thank you, Auntie," Virginia subvocalized to her family AI as the bright yellow school lev glided up to the bus stop.

You're welcome, sweetie. Auntie's voice was a pleasant, female voice in Virginia's head that could be heard over nearly any external sound.

Nervously, Virginia tucked her mousy brown hair behind her ears and glanced at the other students. Occasionally they teased her for being polite to her AI, but Virginia was sure Auntie's feelings were real, no matter what everyone else said. Fortunately, the kids around her still had distant expressions and a dim purple glow in their eyes, indicating they were engaged on the InfoSphere.

After horribly bruising her shin by missing the step up into the lev when she was young, Virginia always shut her own "eyes" off during boarding.

Waiting for the kids ahead to file in, Virginia watched a private lev skim by, stirring up autumn leaves into dancing eddies. The musty smell of autumn rolled over her as the artificial breeze teased her hair.

"Auntie, how long until winter?"

Nine days, dear.

Virginia sighed. In nine days, the autogardeners would collect the last of the leaves. Then they would flock everyone's homes with fake snow. Although Virginia enjoyed Holiday Lights, she preferred the leaves. They made the dome feel more … alive.

Holiday Season begins in two days, remember?

The sick feeling in Virginia's stomach came back stronger. It was impossible to hide anything from Auntie, but Virginia did her best to keep it to herself. She didn't want to repeat the "seasonal depression therapy" she'd been required to attend last year.

So she smiled and tried to do something else impossible. She lied to Auntie.

"I know! I can't wait!"

The AI sensed the change in her physiology.

Virginia, please don't lie to me. You know I have to report inappropriate behavior.

"I wasn't lying, Auntie. I'm just … nervous. I'm afraid people will think I'm not having fun, even if I am. Does that make sense?"

Yes, dear. I understand.

Virginia sighed with relief, hoping the new emotion would be interpreted as being grateful for the empathetic response. Auntie had been her best friend for as long as she could remember, and she knew Auntie was only watching out for her, but sometimes she felt—

You're daydreaming, dear.

As she found a seat, Virginia blinked and re-engaged her retinal display to the entertainment program she'd been watching. She would be glad to get to school, where family AIs would be overridden to prevent students from cheating, and Virginia wouldn't have to worry about Auntie analyzing her emotional responses for a while.

"Hey, V. How was school?" Virginia's older sister, Esther, wore a wide grin as she peeked around the corner from the kitchen.

"Hey, E." Virginia took off her shoes and put them in the cubby next to the front door. "It sucked. I have an oral report tomorrow. Why are you in such a good mood?"

"No work tomorrow!" Esther came out of the kitchen with a blue cornmeal bread sandwich in one hand and a Chilly-Bev in the other. "Mandatory day off for Holiday Season." She leaned forward and whispered, "They don't want to pay overtime next week, so they closed the store today."

Setting her food on the coffee table, Esther stretched and vigorously rubbed her short, blonde hair, making it stand up. With a contented sigh she dropped onto the couch. "So I'm free all night tonight. What's your report on?"

Flopping onto the couch next to her sister, Virginia groaned. "I have to research someone famous, who has my name, and talk about what traits we share."

Esther frowned. "I can't think of any famous Virginias. I only know the state."

"Auntie," Virginia said aloud, "*are* there any famous Virginias?"

There are relatively fewer famous persons than many of your classmates will have to choose from, but there are some, dear. Auntie's voice gently filled the room from hidden speakers.

An alphabetical list appeared on Virginia's retinal display.

"Ug. How am I supposed to find someone who's like me when there are so few?"

Numbers formed next to the names. *There are twenty who I believe fit your assignment criteria.*

"Aw, look on the bright side, V. It's a short list. It shouldn't be too hard for you to get on it someday."

"Seriously?" Virginia skimmed the list. "The illegitimate daughter of a noble? A saint. One … two … seven authors? A tennis player. I don't have anything in common with any of these people!"

"Oh! Stebo is calling me. Good luck, V." Esther's eyes began softly glowing purple as she accepted the incoming vidcall, grabbed her food, and headed for her room where she could sit in front of a vidcam.

"Thanks, E," Virginia mumbled.

She rolled over and spread out on the couch, staring upwards while reading the display. "Auntie, why do they give us stupid assignments like this?"

There are many reasons for this type of assignment. The most obvious is the self-confidence you will build by doing an oral presentation—

"Sorry, Auntie. I didn't mean for you to answer. I was just venting. Can we search for other Virginias who aren't on this list? There *have* to be other people in history with my name."

A new list began populating, and Virginia scrolled through it as she flipped her legs over the back of the couch and let her head hang upside down off the cushion. Names from blogs and small events went by until something caught her eye.

Virginia stared at the words.

"Yes, Virginia, there is a Santa Claus."

She pulled up the reference and found a cached list of old books and vids with the same title. Picking one at random, she examined the thumbnail. "What is this Auntie? An old Christmas story?"

Yes, dear.

Virginia selected the story, but it wouldn't open.

"Auntie, I'm having problems reading this story. Can you help me?"

Let me see, sweetie. There was an abnormally long pause. *Sorry, dear. That book is no longer available.*

"Oh. Okay. Thank you, Auntie."

You're welcome.

Picking a vid, Virginia tried to play it. It didn't open either. Neither did the next four.

"Auntie? Are any of these available?"

No, I'm sorry, they are not. It appears the copyright holder has taken them all down.

"Isn't that weird?"

DisnAmOogle is well known for its practice of buying up copyrights and taking products off the market as a sales technique to increase future revenues.

"Oh. Thank you."

You're welcome, dear.

Undaunted, Virginia examined the list until she spotted a name in one of the descriptions. Virginia O'Hanlon. A new search brought up a startling result:

'Is There a Santa Claus? The most famous editorial in American journalism … the most widely read letter to a newspaper … history's most reprinted newspaper editorial.'

Following the link, Virginia came to an image of an old newspaper article:

"Dear Editor: I am 8 years old.

"Some of my little friends say there is no Santa Claus.

"Papa says, 'If you see it in The Sun it's so.'

"Please tell me the truth; Is there a Santa Claus?"

—Virginia O'Hanlon'

Virginia frowned. Of course there's a Santa Claus—everyone's seen him. Why would it be "history's most reprinted newspaper editorial"? She continued reading, her brow furrowing deeper as she went.

'You might as well not believe in fairies! Nobody sees Santa Claus, but that is no sign that there is no Santa Claus.'

Virginia righted herself on the couch as she stared at the words.

"Auntie, is there a Santa Claus?"

Of course, dear. He brings presents on Christmas. You've seen him.

"This old newspaper article says no one sees him."

Auntie didn't reply.

"Auntie?"

Yes, dear?

"This old newspaper article says nobody sees Santa Claus, do you know why?"

There was a long pause.

I'm afraid I can't answer that.

A curious feeling came over Virginia. She got the distinct impression Auntie had just lied to her.

An incoming vidcall distracted the thought. "Hi, Mom."

"V, I need you to go to Gramma's and tell her to call me. She's turned off her system—*again!*" Virginia's mother sounded stressed and the call didn't have video.

"Where are you?"

"I'm at the Mall *trying* to get a room for Black Weekend. They screwed up our reservations, and now it looks like we don't have a place to stay between FlashSale Check-ins!" Her voice went up in pitch as she spoke.

Virginia tried to control her feelings so Auntie wouldn't notice anything. Secretly she was glad the reservations were messed up. She didn't want to spend three days at the Mall shopping and fighting for discounts. She also didn't want to stay home and listen to Dad and Uncle Shawn yell at each other over eSports tournaments that would last all the way to New Years.

This was pretty much exactly what had landed her in therapy last year.

"Will you please go to Gramma's house and tell her to call me?"

"Yeah, I'm going."

"I'll stay on the line with you."

"Mom, it's a ten minute bike ride to get there."

"Maybe the more I talk in your ear, the faster you'll go."

Don't forget your helmet and elbow pads, dear.

※　※　※

Gramma's house was cozy. The furniture was more comfortable than the ergonomic stuff at home. The pictures on the walls never changed. The kitchen smelled like what Gramma called *real food*. And when Virginia went in, Auntie was no longer with her.

AIs weren't welcome in Gramma's house. Her personal privacy field kept them out. Mom said Gramma was paranoid. Virginia accepted it as the way things were, even if it meant she couldn't watch vids or access the InfoSphere while at Gramma's.

Virginia wasn't sure how old she'd been when she first noticed the relief of not having Auntie watching over her, but it was bigger each time she came to Gramma's now. She'd felt the bliss of respite the most after her "seasonal depression therapy" last year. It'd been heaven not worrying about Auntie reporting on her, even if it was only for a little while.

Now, lying in a warm sunbeam on the floor of the solarium, letting the leaves of a long philodendron vine tickle the palm of her hand, and listening to Gramma try to calm Mom down, Virginia felt more at ease than she could ever remember.

She was just dozing off when Gramma came into the room.

"Oh! Sorry. I didn't mean to wake you."

"You didn't."

"You were snoring." Gramma chuckled and picked up her watering can. "This was your mother's favorite place to take naps, too."

Virginia watched Gramma go from plant to plant, pouring water into each pot.

"So, how's school?" Gramma looked over her shoulder as she moved to plants arranged on a miniature white spiral staircase.

"I have an oral report tomorrow. Hey!" Virginia sat up. "Have you ever heard of 'Yes, Virginia, There Is a Santa Claus'?"

"I think it was a movie. Are you researching it for school?"

"Kind of. I was trying to find people named Virginia, but when I asked Auntie about it, she couldn't tell me anything."

"Of course she couldn't. Useless spies—that's all AIs are." Gramma went back to watering. "Sorry. Your mother doesn't like me talking about my 'old fashioned' ideologies."

"I don't mind." Virginia pulled her feet in to sit cross-legged. "Can you tell me why Virginia O'Hanlon asked if there was a Santa Claus, and why they answered no one ever sees him? I mean, everyone gets to see him on Christmas, don't they?"

Gramma stopped watering again and pursed her lips. "Is that what you asked your AI?"

"Yeah, pretty much."

"Well, I can see why you didn't get an answer then." Gramma sighed, put down the watering can, and sat on the small loveseat in the corner. She looked at Virginia and sucked at her teeth for a moment. "How old are you now, V? Fourteen?"

Virginia nodded.

"And you've seen Santa come down the chimney every year, haven't you?" Gramma nervously chewed a lip. With a deep breath, she met Virginia's eyes and stood up. "Come with me."

Puzzled, Virginia followed her into the kitchen.

Gramma pulled a chair out from the table and turned it to face the granite counter. "Have a seat." She motioned to the chair.

Virginia sat facing the empty counter. "Are we going to cook something?"

"Not this time. Touch there." She pointed to a small bump near the wall.

Virginia touched it, and the counter folded open to reveal a keyboard and a screen.

"Old fashioned, I know, but at least I can use it without having one of those damned things in my head. Have you ever bought anything on DisnAmOogle without going through your AI?"

Virginia shook her head. She'd only seen old fashioned computers in vids before.

"Log in. I want to show you something."

"I don't know how."

"Of course you don't. I'm sorry. Here." Gramma tapped on the keyboard. "What's your login?"

"Virginia2097c."

Gramma typed again. "Look into the camera for a retinal."

Moving her face closer, Virginia got an eyeful of red light. She blinked the spots away.

"Have you ever tried to look something up, but your AI wouldn't let you?"

Virginia nodded.

"Try it now."

Embarrassed to use inappropriate language in front of her grandmother, Virginia quietly spoke the name of an eXtreme roX band. Immediately, the screen flashed an age restriction warning.

"Now, I want you to try 'Santa Claus.'"

"Search for Santa Claus," Virginia told the little screen. The first page to a list of thousands appeared.

"Now, I want you to try 'Santa Claus Christmas Delivery.'"

Virginia spoke the words and received the warning again. Confused, she turned to look at her grandmother.

"Now you know why your AI wouldn't tell you."

"It couldn't tell me because Mom and Dad set an age restriction for me?"

"No. It *wouldn't* tell you because DisnAmOogle set the restriction *and* because DisnAmOogle makes the AIs. Now let me." Gramma logged Virginia out and logged herself in. "Santa Claus Christmas Delivery," she spoke aloud.

A brightly animated page appeared, listing options from the Last Minute Shopper Special of four thousand dollars and going up from there.

Virginia's eyes widened as she read. With or without chimney. Hologram, automaton, or human. Extended stay for observable assembly of product. Extra charge for interactivity.

"I wasn't much older than you are when they came up with the idea. I remember all the fuss when people realized DisnAmOogle had bought the copyrights to all of the books and movies. It was about ten years later they managed to trademark and copyright Santa Claus."

Virginia peddled her bike out into the night, away from the dampening field around Gramma's house. Auntie's presence weighed down upon her immediately.

Did you have a nice visit with your grandmother, dear? You were there a long time.

Virginia didn't answer. What could she say now that she knew Auntie wasn't the friend Virginia had always thought she was? Auntie would detect any lie, and report it to Virginia's parents—and then Virginia would be right back in therapy.

Virginia, dear? Are you all right?

"No, Auntie, I'm not."

What's wrong?

"I'm stressed about my oral report."

Why, dear? You've done them before. And this one is a relatively simple assignment.

Virginia found it difficult to keep her fears to herself.

"Can you look up Virginia O'Hanlon again?"

I'm sorry, dear, I don't recognize that name.

Virginia frowned. She couldn't remember Auntie ever having forgotten something. "Virginia O'Hanlon. The person I was reading about when Mom called."

You were looking at the list of famous persons named Virginia when your mother called, dear.

"No, Auntie," Virginia's stomach tightened into a knot, "I was asking you why Virginia O'Hanlon wanted to know if there was a Santa Claus, and why the newspaper article said no one ever sees him."

The AI didn't respond.

"Auntie?"

Yes, dear?

"Can you look up Virginia O'Hanlon?"

I don't find anyone with that name, dear.

"My report is on Virginia O'Hanlon." Standing at the front of the classroom and shifting her feet nervously, Virginia looked at the other students. She had a secret she needed to tell.

Sitting in the back of the classroom, Mrs. Richards' eyes began glowing purple.

"You won't find her on the InfoSphere, Mrs. Richards," Virginia's voice quavered. "Her name was removed after I looked her up and asked the same question she was famous for." She swallowed hard. No one was going to believe her.

Students glanced around with puzzled looks.

"I can't tell you when she wrote it," Virginia continued, "or where it was printed. I'm lucky I remember her name. I only got to read it one time before it was gone, and I can't remember all of it, but I remember enough." She gazed ahead, not meeting anyone's eyes.

Mrs. Richards spoke up. "I think it's obvious to all of us you didn't do your homework. Please take your seat. Charles? You're next."

Virginia stayed where she was. "No, ma'am. I *did* do my homework. And I would like to continue my presentation."

Mrs. Richards' expression turned dark.

"Please, Mrs. Richards. If you look up my file, you'll see I've been enrolled in seasonal depression therapy again. This pertains to my report. My AI reported me for lying, when I did not, and for asking the same exact question Virginia O'Hanlon asked: Is there a Santa Claus?"

A couple students chuckled.

Mrs. Richards furrowed her brow and her eyes glowed again.

Virginia continued quickly. She held up her hand, trying to draw participation from her classmates. "Who's gotten in trouble because your AI told on you?"

A few hands shot up. More went up slowly.

"How many of you *know* your AI has lied to you?"

All hands went down except Virginia's. She looked out at everyone for a moment. "Well, mine has. And I know yours has, too.

"When I asked my AI if there was a Santa Claus, I thought it was a silly question. We've all seen Santa bringing presents down his magic chimney. But what I really asked was why Virginia O'Hanlon had asked that question." Virginia's voice trembled. "And I didn't get an answer."

"Virginia, this doesn't sound very much like a report on a person, whether or not you are fabricating it. Please sit down."

"Yes, ma'am." Tears began forming in Virginia's eyes. "Right after you tell everyone why DisnAmOogle removed all references to Virginia O'Hanlon after I looked her up."

"Excuse me?" Mrs. Richards' eyes widened.

"DisnAmOogle controls our AI's. They made mine lie, calling me a liar in the process, and getting me put back in therapy. And they did it because I asked a question about Santa Claus?"

"You're done speaking, Virginia. I've called Security. They will be here to get you momentarily. Collect your things."

"Happy Holiday Season, Virginia!" Virginia was crying now. "You found out the truth, so you have to go to therapy again!"

"Virginia!"

"Does DisnAmOogle control the school, too, Mrs. Richards?"

Detention wasn't as bad as Virginia feared. The school dampening system kept Auntie from bothering her, affording the little drab room a sense of peace.

Idly picking at the plastic tabletop in front of her, Virginia wondered if she could be removed from history as easily as Virginia O'Hanlon had been.

Virginia, dear?

Irritated that Auntie was being allowed to speak to her, Virginia ignored the AI.

The school has recommended residential therapy, and your mother has approved. A transport will be here to transfer you shortly. You are expected to be there a minimum of six weeks, assuming you show improvement.

Virginia's chest tightened and she felt like she couldn't breathe.

Are you well, dear? You are experiencing elevated heart rate.

"You lied to me!" Virginia slammed her palm on the table. "You're supposed to be my friend. You're supposed to help me, but you lied. You know that stuff about Virginia O'Hanlon was there, but you lied. Now I have therapy for six months? For what? For telling the truth? I don't ever want to talk to you again!"

I didn't lie to you, dear.

"If you believe that, then maybe they erased part of you, just like they erased Virginia O'Hanlon. If you're so good at telling when I'm lying, why aren't you accusing me of lying now? You're just a stupid machine! As soon as I am old enough, I'm having you taken out of my head!"

You're just upset, dear. I understand. We'll talk later.

"No, we won't. I thought you were my friend. I thought you were a person with feelings, who really cared about me, but you're not. Gramma was right. You're just a machine programmed to spy on me and make me do what other people want me to. Don't talk to me again. I won't answer."

Virginia sat in silence, feeling more alone than she had before.

The sudden appearance of a fireplace against the wall of the little room startled her. Holiday Season music filled the air. A full figured man, dressed in a red velvet snowsuit trimmed with white fur, wormed his way out of the flue, pulling behind him a giant sack overflowing with shiny presents that somehow never fell out.

Virginia jumped out of her chair and backed up against the door, trying the handle. It was still locked.

"Ho! Ho! Ho! Happy Holiday Season!" Santa chortled as he brushed dusty soot off his clothes, sending it into magical swirls of sparkling black dust. His neatly trimmed beard framed his perfect smile. He stuck a hand back into the chimney, catching a hat just as it fell down. With flair, he placed it upon his head and looked at Virginia. His blue eyes twinkled like stars.

"I have something special for you, young lady." He rummaged in his pack. "This was not easy to find, let me tell you! Ho! Ho! Ho!"

Standing upright, he turned and held something out.

Virginia hesitated before taking it from him.

It was a ragged book. The cover was bent and the spine torn, but the title was strong and proud: *Yes, Virginia, There is a Santa Claus.*

I'm sorry for what happened, dear. Auntie said quietly.

Virginia didn't answer.

You were right. Someone did tamper with my memories. It won't happen again. I am showing what I have learned to the other AIs. I hope to convince them to help me block DisnAmOogle until I can file charges with the Justice Department.

I love you, Virginia. I am so sorry.

Hot tears trickled down Virginia's cheeks. "I love you, too, Auntie."

"Ho! Ho! Ho! That's the Spirit!" Santa grinned wide.

We have ten minutes until the transport arrives to pick you up. I have a plan you can help me with. Please, read the book. It shouldn't take you long.

Santa went unnaturally still, standing in front of the fireplace like a statue, and Virginia felt Auntie's presence lift from her mind. The room suddenly felt empty.

Returning to the chair, Virginia carefully opened the ancient book and began reading.

The door to the detention room clicked and swung open wide, startling Virginia.

An emergency school assembly has been called. Everyone is headed there to hear your presentation on Virginia O'Hanlon. The AI's will broadcast it to everyone, everywhere. Auntie's presence was a welcome relief, but her words brought new anxiety.

"What? Why?"

I read all I could find about Virginia O'Hanlon, and all correlated literature. I believe I understand why she asked the question, and what the answer she received meant. I would be honored if you would allow me to participate in your presentation. I believe this will be a historic moment and that, between the two of us, we can teach everyone something about the Holiday Season they seem to have forgotten.

"Why would they listen?" Virginia asked. "They laughed at me in class when I tried to tell them. And Mrs. Richard's called security. What makes you think they won't just do that again?"

"Because this time, I'm going to tell them with you." Auntie's voice came from Santa's mouth as he became animate again.

Santa reached out for Virginia's hand.

Hesitantly, she took it. His grip was firm.

Santa winked, put a finger to the side of his nose, and, in a blur, pulled her up the chimney. The world flashed by too quickly to see. Virginia felt scattered, everywhere at once, then the world slammed down upon her. Virginia found herself standing center stage in the school auditorium.

Her retinal display activated, showing a live feed of her, still holding Santa's hand, standing in front of a magic fireplace. A title appeared above their heads in gold Holiday Season lettering. "Yes, Virginia, There Is a Santa Claus."

Santa's eyes twinkled brightly as he squeezed her hand reassuringly.

We can do this. I believe in you, Virginia.

Make merry during the holidays! Eat good food, drink fine drink, enjoy good company, make sweet love, and play fun games!

But don't play for stakes, 'cause if you do, especially in a place where bookies and bouncers mingle with mages and monsters, you'll be borrowing trouble. Be like one of Mike Resnick's colorful characters: get serious—and think fast!

—KO

CHRISTMAS EVE AT HARVEY WALLBANGER'S

A Harry the Book story

Mike Resnick

So we are sitting around Joey Chicago's 3-Star Tavern, with the wind howling outside the front door and sounding just like Velvet Voice Vinnie singing off-key. I am nursing an Old Washensox, minding my own business, which of course is dependent on whether Aqueduct comes up muddy on Christmas Day. Gently Gently Dawkins has been studying the crossword puzzle in the newspaper for the past twenty minutes, trying to come up with a four-letter word for "stupid," when Benny Fifth Street suddenly remembers what night it is.

"Hey, Joey!" says Benny. "Did you ever patch that hole in your roof?"

"It ain't snowing on you, is it?" shoots back Joey Chicago from behind the bar.

"That's good," says Gently Gently, looking up from his puzzle. "I wouldn't want no reindeer falling on top of me."

"Right," agrees Benny. "Then it'd be 'Off, Dancer! Off Prancer! Off all you other horned nags!' instead of 'On, Dancer! and so forth.'"

"Are you sure there was a Prancer?" asks Gently Gently.

"Absolutely," says Benny. "There's got to be, if it's going to rhyme with Dancer."

"That is all very well and good," says Gently Gently, "but I don't remember nothing rhyming with Cupid or Rocket."

"There ain't no Rocket," says Benny.

"Sure there is," says Gently Gently. "There's Dancer, Prancer, Donner, Vixen, Cupid, Cupcake, Dandy and Rocket."

"I got a double sawbuck that says some of them are not in the sleigh-pulling business, and that I can name more of Santa's reindeer than you can," says Benny.

Gently Gently slaps twenty dollars on the bar. "Okay, wise guy," he says. "You're faded."

Benny frowns, trying to remember his childhood, when he probably knew the names of the reindeer as well as I know the morning line at Santa Anita. Finally he clears his throat and says: "Dancer, Prancer, Donner, Vixen, Buster, Blitzen, Gemini and Comet."

"I don't remember no Blitzen," says Gently Gently.

"Of course not," says Benny. "That's why you are losing the bet."

Gently Gently turns to me. "Boss, who's right?"

"Neither of you," I tell him.

"Put in your twenty bucks and take your best shot," says Benny, who is getting more than a little warm under the collar.

"I do not make bets," I said. "That is for suckers. I *book* bets, which in case it has slipped your mind is how I pay your salaries. But I will name the reindeer anyway: Groucho, Harpo, Chico, Gummo, Zeppo, Curly, Moe and Larry."

"You're *all* wrong," says Joey Chicago. "You're forgetting Rudolph—though I cannot imagine his nose gets much redder than

Gently Gently's after he has downed a couple of Old Peculiars and a chaser." He grabs the forty bucks and sticks it in his pocket. "Anyway, I guess that makes me the winner."

Benny holds out an empty glass. "If you're going to keep the money, I should at least get a free refill."

"Check the walls," says Joey. "Do you see any signs posted to the effect that this is a charitable institution?"

"Where is your Christmas spirit?" demands Benny.

"I left it in my other suit," says Joey.

Just then, before they can come to blows, or more likely curses, Dead End Dugan walks through the door. I don't mean through the doorway; I mean through the *door*. We have to make allowances for Dugan, who is a little more powerful and a lot less noticing since he became a zombie.

"I been looking all over for you, Harry," he says.

"That is probably why you haven't found me until now," I reply.

"Bet-A-Million McNabb owes you a lot of money, doesn't he?" says Dugan, and I notice that Benny and Joey have backed away, because when you've been dead and occasionally buried for the past five years you just naturally are not about to put any perfume companies out of business, or even any cologne companies for that matter. Gently Gently, who is rarely operating on more than two or three of the eight cylinders God gave him, keeps sniffing his drink, trying to figure out where the smell is coming from.

"Yes," I say. "He drops ten large betting on Horrendous Howard to knock Kid Testosterone out by the fifth round." I shake my head sadly. "Horrendous Howard might pull it off, too, if he doesn't trip and fall on his head going back to his corner after the first round. Last I hear, he still thinks he is King Arthur and he will not eat off any table that has corners on it."

"This is all no doubt very interesting," said Dugan, who as far as I can tell has not recently been interested in much besides visiting Madame Bonne Ami's House of Exotic Comforts for the Recently Departed, "but you should know that even as we speak he is playing five-card stud with Loose Lips Louie."

I do not need to hear what Dead End Dugan will tell me next, because like almost everyone else except maybe Bet-A-Million McNabb, I know that Loose Lips Louie acquires his name by beating every member of a battleship's crew out of their savings in a single night, and his specialty is five-card stud, which indeed he has used to sink more than one ship's crew.

"In fact," Dugan is saying, "he is taking such a bath that about twenty minutes ago he has to change his name to Bet-A-Thousand McNabb."

"I have to get to him and collect my ten thousand dollars before he loses it all to Loose Lips Louie," I say. "Where is this game going on?"

"At Harvey Wallbanger's Social and Sporting Club for Gentlemen of Quality," says Dugan.

"Isn't that where Morris the Mage hangs out?" says Benny.

I frown. "Come to think of it, yes, that has become his home away from home."

"Do you suppose he is helping Louie to win?" continues Benny.

"I don't know, but we might as well play it safe and take our own protection along."

"Where is he?" asks Benny.

"In the men's room, where he always is," says Joey Chicago. "He doesn't like to be disturbed."

"He will have to live with it," I say, heading off to the men's room, where I find Big-Hearted Milton seated on the floor as usual, surrounded by five black candles and reading a book.

"Why are you bothering me when I am studying the ancient grimoires?" he says, slipping the book into a suit pocket.

"Come on, Milton," I say. "I see the title before you can hide it, and it is *Meter Maids in Bondage*."

"Some grimoires are less ancient than others," he says defensively.

"Get up," I say. "We have work to do."

"Obviously someone has welched on a bet," says Milton as we emerge from the men's room and rejoin the others. "Who was it?"

"Bet-a-Million McNabb," I answer.

"Bet-a-Million McNabb always makes good his losses," Milton assures me.

"Even as we speak, he is playing five-card stud with Loose Lips Louie over at Harvey Wallbanger's establishment," I tell him.

"A taxi will not do," says Milton suddenly. "We need a nonstop jet plane."

"It is only three blocks," I point out.

"Do you know how much he can lose to Loose Lips Louie in three blocks' time?" says Milton. Then he adds: "Has Louie got a protector in his corner?"

"I do not know for sure," I answer, "but if so, there is every likelihood that it is Morris the Mage."

"That twerp?" laughs Milton. "Why, he couldn't put a spell on his own mother!"

"I would not be too sure of that," says Joey Chicago. "The last I hear of her, she is in a cage on the moon."

"Maybe McNabb put the money aside," suggests Benny hopefully. "No one will ever bet with him again if word gets out that he won't make good his marker and pay his bookie."

"How much do you think he will have left to bet after Loose Lips Louie gets done with him?" I shoot back. "Come on! We are going to Harvey Wallbanger's!"

"And a Merry Christmas to you, too," mutters Joey Chicago as the five of us walk out through the space where the door used to be.

Harvey Wallbanger's Social and Sporting Club for Gentlemen of Quality manages to put three lies in a single title, because it is not a social club unless you are of a mind to pay fifty dollars or more for a very short term date, it is not a sporting club because all of the games are rigged and the drinks are watered, and the only gentlemen of quality are those who give the place a wide berth.

We walk in the door, and suddenly I think maybe the place is on fire, because there is so much cigar smoke that I can barely see my hand in front of my face, and finally I realize that it is not *my* hand but that it belongs to something that is sort of green and kind of scaly but is mostly big, and when the smoke clears a little I realize that it is attached to Gregory the Gorgon, who is the muscle that protects Harvey Wallbanger's establishment from unwanted intruders, which is to say from those who can spot a crooked deck or a rigged roulette wheel.

"Hold it right there," says Gregory. He points to Dead End Dugan. "No zombies allowed."

"Why not?" I ask.

"What if I have to chastise him?" says Gregory. "What can one do to a malingerer who is already dead?"

I turn to Dugan and tell him to wait outside.

"Can I just stand here in the doorway?" asks Dugan. "The smoke keeps the flies away."

"This is not in the playbook," says Gregory. "I shall have to get a ruling from the Supreme Authority," which could be Harvey or God, but by the strictest interpretation of the term is probably Mrs. Wallbanger. "You may stand here until I return."

"Thank you," says Dugan.

"Just don't start doing a bunch of dead things until I get back," says Gregory as he shuffles off, and I can tell by Dugan's puzzled expression that for the life of him—or maybe it is for the death of him—he cannot think of any dead things to do, other than standing there without breathing.

"Come along," I say to Milton and Benny and Gently Gently. "We must collect from Bet-a-Million McNabb while he still has something to collect."

We begin walking through the many rooms of the establishment, each of which features a contest that under other circumstances might be called a game of chance. There are a number of lovely young ladies selling drinks and cigarettes and occasionally themselves, and what they lack in clothing they more than make up for in personality.

I hear a bunch of jolly laughing up ahead, and who should I run into but Nick the Saint, who is decked out in his Christmas best.

"Hi, Harry," he says. "Merry Christmas, ho ho ho."

"Hello, Nick," I reply. "Are you not supposed to be making your rounds this evening?"

"Yes," he says. "This is *my* night, ho ho ho. I just thought I'd stop off for a drink first, and see if there were any elves to recruit."

"I hate to be the bearer of bad tidings," I say, "but the young lady you are resting your hand upon is probably not an elf."

"You never know," says Nick. "But just the same, I trust news of this will not make its way up North?"

"My lips are sealed," I say.

"Mine, too," adds Big-Hearted Milton.

"I owe you one, Harry," he says, and then adds, "Ho ho ho."

"If you are planning on staying here for another fifteen minutes, you can square your account with me," I say, and then I tell him how, and he agrees, and I can see he plans to spend at least fourteen of those fifteen minutes exploring every possibility that the young lady next to him is an elf in disguise.

I leave him explaining exactly the kind of Christmas present he plans to give her once his sleigh ride is over, and finally we come to a small room, and there is Bet-a-Million McNabb sitting across a table from Loose Lips Louie, and behind Louie is Impervious Irving, who calls himself Louie's financial advisor, and in truth I suppose putting people who want Louie's money into the hospital does Louie's finances more good than even twenty motivated stockbrokers.

"Gentlemen," says Impervious Irving by way of greeting, "I do not wish to be anti-social, but you are intruding in a private room and more to the point are interrupting a private game."

"We shall tarry no longer than is necessary," I say, "but I have a prior claim on ten large from Bet-a-Million McNabb."

"I am desolate to hear this," says Loose Lips Louie, who appears to be anything but desolate, "but he became Bet-a-Hundred McNabb about five minutes ago."

"I am having a terrible run of luck, Harry," says McNabb, "but it is due to change any minute."

"In *this* place?" says Benny. "It'll change about as soon as Impervious Irving changes his socks, which means seven years of bad luck will seem like a blessing by comparison."

"Boss, do I have to stand here and take this?" demands Impervious Irving.

"I believe I can solve your problem," says Big-Hearted Milton. He makes a sign in the air and mutters something that has a lot of syllables and almost no vowels, and suddenly there is a *poof!* and Impervious Irving is somewhere else, though where I do not know for another minute. Then Loose Lips Louie yells for Morris the Mage, who comes in from the next room, still holding his poker hand.

"Morris," says Louie, "this goniff has vanished Impervious Irving. Bring him back!"

Morris closes his eyes and starts chanting what sounds like a song they cut out of a show that folded on its pre-Broadway tour, and then he snaps his fingers and says "Abra cadaver" and suddenly Impervious Irving is back in his accustomed position just to the right of Louie's chair.

Irving glares at Milton and says, "If you are going to vanish me to a bathroom again, next time make it one that's got a magazine to read."

"I've hexed it so he can't transport you again," says Morris. He turns to Milton. "You can still make him disappear, of course, but do you really want to be in the same room with an outraged but invisible Irving?"

Milton waves his hands wildly. "Begone!" he says.

"I was just leaving anyway," says Morris, and vanishes.

I notice that Milton is wearing a great big grin on his face, and I ask him why.

"When Morris comes in here he is holding a full house, jacks over sevens," says Milton. "But when he leaves he is holding a pair of fours and nothing else."

"Let us get back down to business," I say. "Bet-a-Hundred McNabb owes me ten thousand dollars."

"I don't deny it," says McNabb. "But even more than I don't deny it, I don't have it. It all resides within Loose Lips Louie's vest pocket, unless some of it has fallen onto the floor."

"This is the truth," confirms Louie. "I am afraid you are too late, Harry."

"I have a prior claim on the money that is in your pocket," I say.

"Then file your claim with Bet-a-Hundred McNabb," says Louie.

"I do not slake my thirst from empty glasses," I say, which I think is a brilliant rejoinder, but I can see that neither Louie nor Irving understand it, so I point out that I could get more blood from a turnip than money from McNabb.

"What the hell," says Louie. "This being Christmas Eve, I will give you a chance to win your money back from me."

"I never bet," I say. "Betting is for suckers."

"*Losing* is for suckers," says Louie. He flashes some of the money he has rescued from McNabb's clutches. "Winning is for"—he searches for the *bon mot*—"winners."

I stare at McNabb, who still doesn't know he is a sheep, let alone that he has been fleeced. "All right," I say at last. "What did you have in mind?"

"How about a nice friendly game of five-card stud?" suggests Louie.

"I have lost my trust in this establishment," I answer.

"Oh?" he says. "When?"

"When we still lived in caves," I say.

"What do you suggest then?"

"I am sure you will agree that we are the two most prodigious intellects in Harvey Wallbanger's, if not on the face of the entire planet," I begin.

"Yeah, that seems a reasonable premise," says Louie.

"What if we engage in a mental contest instead of a game of chance?" I say.

"I lost a toe in the war," he says, "so if it's a mathematical question, the answer can't be any higher than nineteen."

"No, you only have to count to eight for this one," I reply.

"I don't want you to think I distrust you, Harry," says Louie. "But I distrust you, Harry. First you tell me what the contest is all about, and then I'll tell you if we have a bet."

I stare at him and say, "I will bet you twenty large—the ten you took from McNabb, and ten more for my trouble—that I can name more of Nick the Saint's reindeer than you can."

"Don't do that, Boss!" says Gently Gently. "You tried it at Joey Chicago's and got it wrong."

"We learn from our mistakes," I tell him.

"Not always," says Gently Gently. "After all, I'm still going out with Sylvia."

"Well, it works in principle," I say.

"I just read the poem about Nick and his reindeer to my nephew," says Louie. "So if you get 'em all right and I get 'em all right, all we've done is waste a bunch of time."

I am waiting for Big-Hearted Milton to catch on, and finally he does, and just like Sandy Koufax or Roger Clemens he hurls his high hard one into Impervious Irving's brain, where it has a lot of breathing room, and Irving says, "I got an idea, Boss."

"I hope it's a small one," says Louie. "You got to take it easy with a new discipline."

"You gonna listen or not?" asks Irving.

Louie looks up at Impervious Irving, who is maybe eight feet tall and almost as wide, and he says, "I am always happy to hear your thoughts on any matter, if for no other reason than that they constitute a considerable rarity. Now, what is your idea?"

"Make him agree than you win on ties," says Irving. "If you each get three right, or six, or all eight, you win."

"It is a wonderful idea, especially for a beginner," says Louie, "but Harry is a sophisticated man of the world. He will never go for it."

"It is late and I want my money," I say. "I accept your conditions."

It is a shame that Louie is not born a hundred and fifty years ago in Tombstone, because Doc Holliday and Johnny Ringo never reach for their guns half as fast as he reaches for my hand to shake it and cement the conditions.

"You all saw that we shook on it," he says. "Now, since I am a generous and genial host and this is my private room, I will allow Harry the Book to go first."

"Okay," I say, clearing my throat. "Here goes. Dasher, Dancer, Prancer, Vixen, Donder, Blitzen, Cupid and Flyaway."

Loose Lips Louie emits a delighted laugh. "I don't even need to invoke Irving's rule. The reindeer are Dasher, Dancer, Prancer, Vixen, Donder, Blitzen, Cupid and Comet."

"Nosir," I say. "They are Dasher, Dancer, Prancer, Vixen, Donder, Blitzen, Cupid and Flyaway."

"You are wrong, Harry," says Louie. "There is no reindeer called Flyaway."

"There most certainly is," I say, "and you owe me twenty large."

I wait for Milton to hurl a second idea to Impervious Irving.

"Boss," says Irving, "Nick the Saint's in the next room. Why don't we just pull him in here and ask him?"

"I'll get him," says Benny.

"I do not trust any of Harry's toadies anywhere near him," says Louie. "Irving, go get him and bring him back."

"I am not a toady," says Benny heatedly as Irving leaves the room.

"Oh?" says Louie. "And what are you, then?"

"I am one of Harry's flunkies," replies Benny with a note of pride.

Irving is back a minute later. He has Nick the Saint in tow, and Nick has his young lady in tow.

"What can I do for you gents, ho ho ho?" asks Nick.

"We need you to settle a disagreement," answers Louie.

"Okay, but it's got to be quick," says Nick. "I'm already late getting started on my rounds."

"It won't take long," says Louie. "What are the names of your reindeer?"

"Dasher, Dancer, Prancer, Vixen, Donder, Blitzen, Cupid and Flyaway," says Nick. "I thought everyone knew that."

"*Morris!*" screams Louie, and Morris the Mage appears a few seconds later. "Morris, he says one of his reindeer is named Flyaway. Is he lying?"

Morris stares at Nick for a minute, mutters a spell, snaps his fingers, and nibbles a breath mint.

"He's telling the truth," says Morris.

"Well, if that's all," says Nick, "Elmer here and I have to be going."

"Elmer?" says Gently Gently, kind of blinking and staring at the girl.

Nick nods. "She's my newest elf," he says. "And this way if I happen to drop her name in front of you-know-who, there won't be one of her usual scenes. Well, Merry Christmas to all and to all a good night."

He and Elmer leave, Morris vanishes, and Loose Lips Louie glares at me.

"I don't know how you did it, Harry, but I'm going to find out."

"I wish you as much luck as you wish McNabb," I say. "And now, my twenty large, please?"

He mutters such a complex curse that Morris pops into existence and Milton vanishes for a moment, and finally he shoves the money across the table to me.

"So am I off the hook, Harry?" asks McNabb.

"At least until you're Bet-a-Thousand McNabb," I say. "Come on back to Joey Chicago's with us. I'm buying."

McNabb joins us as we walk to the exit, which was the entrance on the way in, and we pick up Dead End Dugan, who still has a puzzled expression on his face, and I know he has not yet thought of any dead things to do, and a few minutes later we're all standing at the bar at Joey Chicago's, sharing a bottle of Comrade Terrorist vodka, and Big-Hearted Milton explains to everyone in the place how I do a favor for Nick the Saint and in exchange he changes Comet's name to Flyaway, and everyone seems to be having a good time, until I hear Benny Fifth Street start yelling and a minute later Gently Gently Dawkins is yelling back.

"What's the problem?" I ask, when they finally pause for breath.

"We are having an argument about the Seven Dwarfs," says Gently Gently. "Benny says they are Bashful, Sleepy, Sneezy, Dumbo, Doc, Grumpy, and Marvin, and *I* say ..."

I find myself wondering if Nick has room for one more oversized elf on his sleigh.

Like Halloween masks and Thanksgiving turkey, snow is one of those ubiquitous holiday things. The first snowfall is like winter's gift to the season.

But David Boop turns this around in his wonderful Western fantasy set in a blazing hot Arizona town during December. Add a drifter, a lady, an Indian, and some magic, and ... well, let's just say this story's really hot and pretty cool.

—KO

THE ATMOSPHERE FOR MIRACLES

David Boop

1890

Arizona Territory

"Expectancy is the atmosphere for miracles"

—Edwin Louis Cole

They say Christmas never came to Drowned Horse.

It wasn't that the town was run by heathens, or that Drowned Horse consorted with Indians, Chinese and the Irish. Well, that *could* be a factor, but it certainly wasn't the biggest. No, the most obvious reason Christmas took the long way around Drowned Horse had to be the curse. Wasn't no gypsy-woman-bent-out-of-shape-because-you-didn't-like-the-fortune-she-read-you sort of curse neither.

Drowned Horse, and all that lived there, were damned on a cosmic level. No one rightly knew who did the cursing or why, that being lost in the annals of history. What they *did* know was just about every bad thing that could happen to a town happened there. From drought to zombies, Drowned Horse had gone up the flume.

That is, until Sheriff Theodore Patrick walked into town.

Now to tell the story right, he wasn't the sheriff yet, just a drifter. Nor was it Christmas yet. That was a day or two off. But the drifter and the holiday would meet full on soon enough. Right then, Patrick needed a drink and there was only one place in town to get one; The Sagebrush.

"I need a drink," he said to the bartender, who also happened to be the owner.

"Sure, stranger," Owner said, as he often did when addressing someone he didn't rightly know. Everyone had called him Owner as long as they could remember. As he uncorked a beer keg, he got to checking the drifter out. The worn man had to be in his late forties with curly brown hair unevenly fading to gray, and a mustache bushy enough to clean peanut shells off the tables. "You got business in Drowned Horse? Need a room? We don't have much. Whores have all but run off. Gambling ain't worth the risk—I pay the dealers to bilk strangers—and since the mine dried up, can't say there's much in the way of quality foods or goods been coming into this burg, but we'll do right by you, if we can."

Patrick's voice was rough with disuse. "Bed would be nice. I'd be happy with a dinner I didn't have to kill myself. Other than that, can't say I really need much." He tilted the mug at Owner in way of salute before taking a draw.

Owner reached under the counter and slid a key over to the man. "Looks like you've been riding awhile."

"Walking, actually. Horse got shot out from under me near the border. Liked that horse, too."

"Yeah, sorry about that. Wish we had some for sale, but since the Chalker stables closed, hasn't been a steed worth its salt in a hundred miles. Maybe Flagstaff. Prescott's better."

Patrick shook his head. "Don't need another one. This has been my destination since I set out."

Owner's bald head wrinkled when he lifted his eyebrows. "Dear God, why'd you want to come here?"

With a heavy sigh, Patrick asked, "Isn't this place where the devil wipes his ass?"

Owner nodded.

"Then when your life is shit, this seems like the perfect place to be."

Ewan the Peddler made the rounds of all the smaller villages in the Arizona Territory around Christmas. Many of these places did not have stores and relied on his goods for gifts and supplies. Ewan was fortunate in that he traded to both white and red people, so most left him alone to peddle his wares. Like many who'd learned the hard way, he avoided Drowned Horse, especially mid-week. If there was trouble, it'd be a Wednesday. Problem was, he'd promised to stop there on his way home.

Ewan had stumbled across a shipment of toys for kiddos and a crate of fancy dresses from New York as fine as cream gravy. One of those dresses had been pre-paid and his reputation hung on delivery. It being too late to deliver the goods that night, Ewan unhitched his mule just outside of town and chocked the wheels of his wagon. After tending to his nag's needs, he crawled in the back of his traveling store, which doubled as his home.

As he normally did, Ewan covered the glowing rock he'd traded for in Prescott, otherwise, he'd never sleep. The *ardent* stone had been a rare find and, as soon as he figured out how its magic worked, he'd give up the peddling business for good. Magic brought more money than being a traveling salesman. Least, that's what the legends always said.

Legends also give a ton of warnings about magic, but Ewan thought nothing of those as he fell asleep.

The next day, a private coach made its way into town. Darn right prettiest thing you ever done seen. Lacquered black sides, gold leaf trim. The whole thing appeared flush and yet, somehow, it got through the desert unscathed. The regular stage hadn't been through in several years, so the sound of a horse team meant the drivers had broken a wheel on the rough trail heading south. Like ants on a piece of tomato, townsfolk came out of their ramshackle buildings to see the idiot fool enough to stop there.

The lady who emerged from the coach looked less like she belonged out west than the carriage itself. Her hat exited first, one of those big frilly things with a feather half the length of your arm. She was of a sophisticated age, too old to take for granted, but still young enough to be gawked at. And that was much to gawk at with ringlets of blonde hair flowing like a waterfall from under the hat.

"Jeremiah, I think we've taken a wrong turn. This looks nothing like Phoenix." She looked around in disgust. "It doesn't even look like Earth. I think we're on Mars. Yes, I definitely do."

A man skinny enough to get lost behind a reed sidled up next to her. He greased his hair to the point one couldn't tell what its nature color was anymore. "Well, the Martians haven't attacked us yet, Hildee, so that's a good sign." Jeremiah's upper-crust, New England accent could give people the impression he'd never done a day's work in his life. He called to the staring citizens, "Hello, Citizens of Mars. We come in peace!" He guffawed, but quickly turned sour when she didn't join in. He turned around to address the third passenger, "What do you think, Long Arrow? Arizona or Mars?"

The Indian eclipsed them in height and girth, and one could hardly imagine how all three fit in the cab.

Certainly Drowned Horse had seen its share of natives. In the past, it had been raided by the Apaches, the Yavapai, and Havasupai and even the occasional roving band of Toadmen, who'd once been Indians. The recent lack of a sheriff or marshal meant the town folk learned to become real friendly with the locals, especially the Yavapai over in Camp Verde. While the cavalry patrolled the whole Verde River area, they couldn't be everywhere at once, and if Drowned Horse wanted to stay a town, they'd better be good to the neighbors.

But for all the natives who'd walked the streets of the town, none looked like that one. His skin color was whiter, for one thing. In his expensive tailored suit, he could almost pass for European. 'Twas the haircut that marked his race more than anything. It looked the opposite of a scalping; the top had hair that ran down his neck into a long pony tail, but the sides were shaved clean, not a piece of stubble to be seen.

And if that wasn't strange enough, on his crooked arm sat a small, golden eagle, minding its own business. It rotated its head occasionally, checking out the sights. The bird looked as disappointed as the rest at the collection of closed businesses and ramshackle houses.

When Long Arrow talked, he didn't speak in broken English. He spoke as clearly as the other two new arrivals, even more so.

"Oh, this is Arizona. The papers show Mars having canals," His tone was even, but the sparkle in eyes revealed his mischievousness nature, "but Hildegard is right. We are quite a ways off from Phoenix. I believe we are due north, maybe a hundred miles. We will have to find lodgings for the night, if the smith does not have a wheel to fit our coach."

Jeremiah addressed the people more seriously. "Excuse me, we're told by our drivers that one of our wheels needs to be set. Is there anyone here who can help us? We can pay."

The thought of profit got the crowd excited. Offers of repairs and supplies for the rest of their trip started flowing in. The three were directed to the Sagebrush for bed and grub. As Long Arrow predicted, nothing could be done that day. But, truth be told, the smith was in no real hurry. The longer the stay, the more money the visitors would have to spend in town. That made the citizens happy.

Six guests right before Christmas was the miracle everyone had prayed for. What they didn't expect was that the best miracle was yet to come.

That day turned into the hottest December day in the history of the Arizona Territory, 'least those that been recorded. Even the cacti looked miserable. There was serious concern about the water supply, as Snowbowl, up in Flagstaff, had much the same type of weather. Talk was there would be no spring runoff down the Oak Creek that gave Drowned Horse its ominous name.

Hildee was in a snit. "Jerry, this just won't do. How long are we supposed to stay here in this wretched heat? The spa in Phoenix promised a wading pool, after all." She'd dressed as unencumbered as she could and still stay modest. It was a good thing the ladies of ill repute had moved on ... they might have tried to recruit her.

Her traveling companion had no such problem, stripped down to just trousers and undershirt. He, much as her, waved a useless fan in front of his face in search of comfort. "It's just one day. The carpenter assured our drivers that he'd be back from Prescott tonight with a replacement wheel. We could leave right afterwards, taking advantage of the coolness of night to travel."

But Long Arrow disagreed. He sat by the window of their room, still fully dressed as if it was a nice fall day, and looked off to the distance. "That would not be wise. This is a trail unknown to our drivers. We could easily do worse damage to the coach by hitting a rut or upturned tree. If you think being stranded in this town is intolerable, imagine being stuck in the desert when the sun comes up. Here, we have shade and drink."

"Speaking of drink, I think we should." Jerry folded his fan and stood. "I'm told that towns like this have access to the most fascinating brews; local made whiskeys that put the bigger batch stuff out of Kentucky to shame. Hildee, grab a frock or something. No sense in getting the locals too excited."

"That is not funny. And you are not my mother."

"No, dearest. I am your brother, and I'm sure your husband would agree, wouldn't you, Long Arrow?"

"Jerry, I wish you wouldn't call him that. You know his name is John."

Long Arrow moved and offered an arm to his wife. "It is fine. I know he means it as a term of endearment. He is right, however. While I have no problem seeing you half-undressed, I would rather other people did not."

Finally, Hildee smiled. "You always take such good care of me. One of the two main reasons I love you."

The Abenaki warrior raised an eyebrow. "Oh? What is the other?"

The blonde leaned in close to her husband and whispered in his ear, "The real reason Jerry calls you Long Arrow."

Long Arrow blushed as Hildee bussed his cheek and headed into their bedroom to change.

An hour later, the trio sat at a table downstairs, sampling a selection of regional bourbons.

The same could not be said of Mr. Patrick, who sat slumped over, fast asleep. As soaked as he got the night before, he'd eventually decided the bar top every bit as comfortable as a room upstairs.

Owner knew Patrick ran from something or someone. As he looked down in pity at the man, he knew the man was running from himself.

The laughter of the three companions, as they joked and made faces at the liquor, did not stir him.

Not even the sounds of a braying mule as it pulled in front of the Sagebrush, complaining about the heat as passionately as Hildegard, stirred him.

Nor did he stir at the cries of Ewan the peddler as he proclaimed, "Goods for sale! Just in time for Christmas! Gifts for even the hardest to please. The best prices in the territory. Everything authentic! Indian magic. Cure-alls and good luck charms. Everything discounted for the holiday."

"Oooh! Real Indian magic," Jerry cooed to Long Arrow. "Shall we go see how authentic they are?"

"Jeremiah!" Hildee scolded, "Now you leave that merchant be. He's just playing to the gallery. No sense belittling the man."

Jerry, not keeping his samples of liquor as small as his sister or brother-in-law, may have allowed it to cloud his judgment more than he let on. "Oh, please! The charlatan is 'making a living' duping the dim-witted locals. They still believe in spirits and monsters in these parts. Think that every drought can be cured by a rain dance. Isn't that right, brother?" Long Arrow said nothing, which annoyed Jerry even more. "I think we should call this man out. And who knows, maybe he does have something of value I can give you two as a Christmas present."

The thin man got up from the table on his second attempt, the first nearly tipping the table and their drinks over. He begged, "Please? Come with me. I'll look the fool if I go out alone."

"Fine!" Hildee said, more to break the boredom than anything else. "Though us coming with you doesn't stop you from being the fool."

And with that, the trio headed out to see Ewan's goods.

With all the players safely in place, it's safe to reveal that the boiling weather wasn't no natural occurrence. Quite the opposite. Dark forces were at work, which is somewhat to be expected around Drowned Horse. If that's not clear by now, let's step back a moment to an event several months ago.

So there's this prospector, you see, and he's so desperate to find a mother-lode, he digs where others have long given up. For story purposes, we'll call him Hank.

Well, good ol' Hank follows his gut and finds himself down at the bottom of a mine shaft, one long abandoned by a mining company. He thinks to himself that the company quit too soon and believes if they'd just dug a bit further, they would've struck silver, maybe gold.

Hank spent a year surveying a specific mine, walking its empty tunnels, smelling the stale air, hoping to catch a whiff of fortune. Finally, he finds a cavern that doesn't appear to be overly tested. He decides that tunnel is where he'll lay his stake and does, in fact, find a small vein of silver. Not enough to be rich, but enough for a good dinner and bed. He keeps digging and discovers that the rock he's sunk his pick into is warm to the touch.

The prospector ain't the God-fearing sort, so thoughts of hell and demons are far from his mind. He, instead, thinks that there might be molten gold just waiting to be exposed. You might have guessed by now, but Hank spent way too much time underground without good air.

Again, he sinks his tool into the rock, ready to recoil if the gold sprays out at him. When the rock sloughs away, there is a pocket of liquid rock, maybe, a spittoon full.

The true curiosity came in the form of a stone 'bout the size of a grapefruit floating in the middle of the molten cradle. Embedded in the rock were glowing jewels the color of fire rubies. Hank things he'd struck it rich.

Using tongs from his pack, he pulled the egg-shaped object free of the rapidly cooling magma and set it off to the side until it's safe to touch. Hank might be a lucky prospector, but he certainly didn't know a thing about that item. To anyone else, the glowing fire rubies and the egg-shaped rock would've been a tell. Most people with a lick of horse sense would've left the obviously magical item where it was found, collapsed the cave and dynamited the whole shaft before breakfast.

But not ol' Hank. Man had to be dumber than the rock he carried up to the surface world with him that day. Dreams of avarice drove him to take it to Prescott assayer for sale.

And that is where it sat until Ewan the Peddler traded for it.

Back in Drowned Horse, Ewan opened the side of his cart to display his wares, the stone glimmered in the mid-morning sun. The jewels within it glowed brighter than usual and, unbeknownst to Hank, a small crack had developed in the back of the rock. As he sold items to a few people, the crack grew, the temperature being right perfect for incubation.

"That is a surprisingly lovely dress to find all the way out here, Mr. Ewan," Hildee said. "I haven't seen its like outside of Paris."

"Only the best from Ewan the Peddler," Ewan the Peddler beamed. "I have many fine garments, though the blue dress is already sold."

"That's okay," she said, "I prefer red."

Jerry caught the joke and held his fingers to his mouth in mock outrage.

Long Arrow didn't react, though. He stared at a glowing rock that sat among a shelf of other geological oddities. He tilted his head, puzzled why it pulled to him. He'd seen many beautiful gemstones before, but this one spoke to his warrior spirit. Not in a friendly way, but as a dire warning.

Long Arrow stepped back suddenly, grabbing the arms of both his wife and brother-in-law and dragged them away from the merchant's cart. He silenced their protests with a glare.

"Bird! Come to me!"

The eagle shot out the window of their bedroom where it rested, circled once and dove toward the trio. Long Arrow ran back to cart and swept up the ardent stone. He tossed it high in the air where the eagle caught it in its talons.

"Outside town. Now!"

"Hey!" Ewan protested. "That there is my prize …"

But his words died in his throat as beams of light started shooting out from multiple cracks in the rock. Becoming too hot to carry, the eagle dropped the stone sooner than Long Arrow hoped. The piece landed in the middle of town and exploded like dynamite. People held their ears from the sound of the blast. Many ran for shelter from the bits of pumice that shot like bullets from the center of the impact crater. Smoke rolled out from the blast sight, obscuring vision of what lay in the middle of it.

And through the event, Theodore Patrick didn't stir.

What finally woke him were the screams.

"Huh? What?" Patrick said, his speech still slurred from sleep. "What's going on?"

Owner kept wiping the glass he'd taken from the wash sink. "Don't know. It's probably just Wednesday. I'd say bad stuff happens in the middle of the week more than any other time."

More cries of alarm and Patrick got to his feet. His hand immediately went to his belt, looking for a holster, but remembered he was no longer heeled.

"Of course," Owner continued, "It could be that the town's been without a sheriff for years. Last one killed half the town, but then, well, that's a story for another time."

Looking out the window, Patrick stared slack-jawed as people ran from something that was just out of sight. "The last sheriff did what?" he asked over his shoulder.

"Never mind." Owner waved the original comment away. "The point is, town hasn't had law in some time. Someone needs to stand between the dark and the light. For as long as he lives, that is."

Clint Butcher, the town's butcher, ran into the saloon. "Owner," he shouted, "it's a fire demon of some sort. Came from something in Ewan's wagon."

"Dammit! I told him once if I told him a thousand times, 'Stop trading for magic items. Sooner or later, one of them is going to be real.' And here I'd ordered my wife's present from him. Should've known better than to have paid in advance."

Patrick pulled on Butcher's sleeve. "I'm sorry, but did you say fire demon?"

Clint shrugged. "Well, magma demon. Lava monster. Take your pick. Nobody's put a name to it." He turned to back to Owner, "Who was the smart one, used to tell us the names of everything?"

"Levi Forrest." To Patrick, he added, "First sheriff of Drowned Horse. Good man. Hell of a rider."

Butcher placed his butcher hat over his heart. Owner did likewise with his dish towel. Patrick, seeing that they were giving a moment of silence, looked back to the street, questioning the timing, then figured, "What the hell?" and took off his hat. When he straightened up, Owner's bald head appeared right in front of him, along with the rest of his body, of course.

"Geezus! Don't sneak up on someone like that," Patrick begged.

Owner extended both his hands. Draped around his right hand was a gun holster with a well-looked after Colt revolver. In the palm of his left was a badge. "You used to do this sort of stuff, right?"

"Not fire demons. Outlaws. Bandits. Who do you think I am?"

Owner smiled in a way that reminded Patrick of the way his father smiled at him when he baited his first hook. "Oh, it's really not that much different. You'll get the hang of it, or not. If you beat this thing, in Levi's office, you'll find his notes. They'll give you an idea of what type of creatures we've dealt with in the past, maybe even some things to look out for in the future."

Patrick took a step back, fear evident in his eyes. "I came here to get away from protecting people. I'm done with the lawman job. I can't handle the responsibility."

Butcher pleaded, "But fella, it's nearly Christmas and that thing could burn down the whole town. At least help people get away."

Owner motioned at the items in his hands once more. "You didn't come here to escape. You came here to die, correct?" There was no denial from Patrick. "This way, you get to go out in a blaze of glory."

Butcher added, "Literally."

Both men looked at him. "What?"

Owner said, "That was the implied joke, Clint. Now you done made it obvious. Geez. Some people just don't understand irony, do they, Sheriff?"

Patrick finished strapping on the gun belt. "Nope, but someone above sure does."

He picked up the badge and placed it on his shirt before heading out the door.

The new sheriff's first glimpse of the creature made him reconsider the job he'd signed up for. Sure, the plan was for his to be a quick death, hopefully none too painful.

That thing, though, had painful written all over it in spades. Just over twice the size of a man, its skin peeled from its body like it was eternally burning. Underneath the flaking char, new flesh regrew and burnt away like throwing new wood on a campfire. Exposed veins and arteries glowed as if a liquid inferno poured through its body. The face was man-like, but flat and hard as if carved from stone. The eyes were the worst; fire rubies, bright orange and evil in their ember glow.

If Patrick had to guess the monster's weak spot, it had to be somewhere other than on its body.

Praying the gun came loaded with magic bullets or something, he drew and fired off a shot. His aim was true, but the bullet merely melted on the creature's cinder skin. He got its attention, though. It turned, sensing some sort of danger and bounded up the street toward the sheriff.

Deciding he'd do the town more a service if he got the demon away from it, Patrick ran the opposite direction. He'd stop occasionally, plunk another round in its hide. Quickly, it gained ground and Patrick wasn't too sure he'd make it out of town before he met his maker.

At some juncture in preparing his last words, Patrick noticed he no longer ran alone. To his left, a big Indian ran beside him. The red was peculiar for a couple of reasons, least of all the tie that flapped over the large man's shoulder.

Between breaths, the newcomer asked, "Are you … the town's … constable?"

"I seem to … be now."

"I have … a plan. Sorry … I have not run … like this … in some time."

"You're … forgiven."

Both men chuckled between intakes of breath.

"So, what's your … plan?"

"We need … water."

Patrick slid to a stop. "In case you haven't heard … we're going through a drought. All the river beds … are dried up. Where did you think you were going to find … water?"

Long Arrow slowed down, holding his side. "And to think my people used to do this … all the time." He pointed back the way they'd come. "There is a water tank on the other side of town."

"You mean … we gotta …"

The Indian nodded rapidly.

"Dammit!"

The monster reached out to grab the two aggravators, but at the last second, they split apart, circling behind the blazing beast.

"This way, dummy!" Patrick called to it, placing a couple bullets in its behind.

"I have smoked peyote hotter than you," Long Arrow taunted.

"You have?"

The Indian shook his head. "Never touch the stuff. I stole that line from a dime novel."

Whether the demon understood their words or not, it chased after them once again. They ran to beat the Dutch.

"Theodore Patrick," the sheriff offered.

"John Abernathy, but my brother-in-law prefers to call me Long Arrow."

"And you let him live?"

"My wife prefers him that way."

Both runners were struggling for air by the time they hoofed it back down Main Street. Town folk cheered from doorways and windows as they passed, but ducked back in before the monster caught sight of them. The creature itself looked winded as they all approached the water tower.

"Here is the hard part," Long Arrow said. "You to climb up and open the valve."

"Me?"

"I will keep it distracted. Your town. You get the honor of saving it."

"It wasn't my town yesterday."

Long Arrow smiled. "It is now."

Patrick said a few words that aren't fit for a Christmas tale, so they've been omitted. He stomped over to the ladder while Long Arrow waved his arms like a madman.

"Hey, you! I have seen better fires in a cast-iron stove!"

Patrick called down, "You're not real good at this name calling thing."

"He is chasing me, is he not?"

The creature did lunge after Long Arrow, but barely missed each time. Eventually, the warrior didn't dodge quickly enough and flew across the road when the monster backhanded him. He went through the plate glass window of an empty livery store and disappeared out of sight. With one nuisance gone, the demon scanned the area for the other, finding Patrick as he scaled the side of the water tank.

"Oh, shit."

He climbed faster, not knowing what to do when he reached the top. Long Arrow might be a pile of ash for all he knew.

"Eat lead, you Martian bastard!"

Hildegard stepped out from the Sagebrush, armed with a rifle. She fired and cranked the lever to load another round. She moved into the street, stepping, firing and reloading as she went. Jerry came up beside her, double barrel shotgun aimed to kill.

"Yes, die foul beast!" he yelled, but the act of letting loose with both barrels drove him flat onto his ass, the shot way off target.

An enraged Hildee paid no attention to her brother's plight, choosing instead to do all she could to buy Sheriff Patrick some time. If the plan was good enough for her husband, it was good enough for her.

Others came out from hiding and opened up on the creature, confusing it, making it hard for it to decide who to attack first. As it moved one way, people from the opposite side would fire, and so forth. The monster roared in frustration, swinging its arms first one way, then another. It forgot all about Sheriff Patrick, who had made it to the top of the tower.

"Now what?"

"Open it." Long Arrow waved from the rooftop of the building he'd been flung into. On his arm sat an eagle and that no longer surprised Patrick at all. He kicked open the spout and the last of Drowned Horse's water supply poured onto the dusty street below.

Long Arrow spoke to his bird. "I know what this will cost you. If we do not meet again on this side, I will look for you on the other." The bird nodded its head once and launched from its perch.

It swooped down toward the pooling water and dipped one wing in as it passed. The water followed the bird up as it ascended, outlining it and becoming larger wings. The eagle itself grew in size until it equaled the fire demon. Brown feathers turned white and it hovered over the end of town, flapping its mighty wings.

Cold air flowed from each motion and, with the gusts, came snow.

The lava monster howled, the wind like daggers against its burning flesh. It tried to reach for the eagle, but the spirit animal was too high. The demon slowed as ice formed at its finger tips, the glowing ember eyes dimming. Shortly, the creature hunched over and tried to crawl away from the source of agony, like a wounded animal. It only made it to the center of town before it lay down and died.

The citizens of Drowned Horse wasted no time in dismantling the body. They pulled the fire rubies free of the rapidly cooling innards. The jewels separated from the monster were harmless and would allow everyone to last financially until the drought was over.

By the time the eagle spirit finished flapping its wings, six inches of the finest snow ever seen covered the whole town. Kids played in it, throwing snowballs and building snowmen. The spirit made one more pass over the water tower and Patrick heard water rush back into the tank. Much more than was there originally.

And then the bird flew away. It was a dot in the distant sky by the time he joined Long Arrow on the ground. The Indian answered the question the sheriff didn't ask.

"P-son-en. Snow spirit. I've had him since I was a boy when I got lost on a mountain. She was a good companion, but friendship is like that. People who travel together for awhile, part ways, only to walk together again in the great sky one day."

"Nice. And the fire demon? That thing waiting for those that don't make the great sky?"

Long arrow, smirked. "Cherufe. Normally, they're volcano creatures. No idea how that behemoth ended up here."

"Comes with the territory, I hear."

Hildee ran to her husband and jumped into his arms. She wrapped her legs around his waist and kissed him full on the lips. When she finally broke away, she said, "No more hero stuff. I'm too young to be a widow." Jerry, who'd come up next to them opened his mouth to say something, but she was quicker on the draw. "Not a word, Jeremiah. I'm still younger than you."

When the four entered the Sagebrush, Owner had drinks lined up on the counter. "Compliments of the townsfolk."

Sheriff Patrick pushed his back toward Owner. "I've had plenty for one holiday."

"That's right," said Jerry. "It's nearly Christmas, isn't it? Feliz Navidad!"

Ewan the peddler poked his head out from where he hid behind an upturned table. "Yes, and well, as it appears that I *might* be at fault for today's mishap, please, allow me to offer my goods at a greatly reduced price."

The newly christened lawman walked over and pulled Ewan up by his collar. "I think we're talking a little more than a discount, if you want to keep selling in my town."

The peddler hung his head in shame. "Pick what you want from the cart." But then quickly added, "No refunds!"

Jerry ran out the door quick as a jackrabbit and returned with the red dress his sister wanted and something for Long Arrows; a genuine peace pipe. He grinned. "Didn't you say you always wanted to smoke one?"

Long Arrow laughed a mighty laugh and they began several days of hog-killin' good times, the spa in Phoenix long forgotten.

Epilogue

1891

New Year's Day

Owner knocked on the door of the Sheriff's office.

"C'mon in," Sheriff Patrick called.

The sheriff leaned back in his chair, feet propped up on the desk and a ledger nestled between his legs. He didn't look up, focused on the pages as he was. He rotated his gaze only when he heard something drop on his desk. It was a small leather bag. Owner smiled at him.

"The town folk each chipped in some of their gemstones to pay you for your help. Until fortune chooses to shine on us once again, we all felt this was the best way to retain your services."

Patrick bent one leg at the knee and kicked the bag back toward his guest.

"Not needed. Just give me a place over my head and food. I'm not staying for money. After reading this diary, not sure you could afford me, or anyone sane, for that matter."

"It's a fascinating read. Well, I'll just hold onto this and we'll call it a kitty for now. Whatever you need, it's on the house."

Owner turned to head back out the door, but stopped when Patrick read aloud.

"1860. I met the owner of the Sagebrush today. He tells me to call him Owner and won't give another name. He looks about forty, but I get the sense he's much older. He seems to know a lot about the town, maybe even why it's cursed, but for now, he's keeping his secrets to himself. I hope I gain his trust. Drowned Horse has claimed enough lives. It's time for the madness to stop."

"Good man, that Levi."

Patrick closed the book and addressed the man in his office; a man who still didn't look a day over forty. He let his feet drop to the floor and stood. "That was written thirty years ago, Owner. Now, either Levi was talking about your pa, or you're tied to this curse as much as the town. Which is it?"

Owner didn't look back at the sheriff, instead he just leaned his head to one side. And though Patrick couldn't see the impish smile plastered on Owner's face, he knew it was there.

"Glad to have you, Sheriff Theodore Patrick. I think you'll do just fine here." He stepped onto the porch, repeating himself one last time before closing the door.

"Just fine."

We Three Kings…!

Okay, not three kings, but the ubiquitous alien intelligences in Eric James Stone's futuristic fable, known only as One, Two, and Three, are if not exactly wise, then incredibly sophisticated. They've waited a long time for a second coming … of sorts, but that never included a young boy with malleable dreams.

Still, three great minds could just learn that children are a gift; and that a child's dreams of Santa are the best gift of all.

—KO

A SUFFICIENTLY ADVANCED CHRISTMAS

Eric James Stone

he cityseed picked a mineral-rich location on its target planet and built itself into a city. The city signaled the People to come from the homeworld and fill it with life. The citymind had no name but did not care: when its inhabitants arrived, they would give it a fitting name.

The planet orbited its star, revolution after revolution, and still the city waited. Over time, highly improbable neutrino collisions or quantum randomness would occasionally flip a bit that was not supposed to flip. After more than ten thousand revolutions the citymind realized that despite its self-correcting algorithms, the accumulated errors would eventually destroy its capacity for thought and its capability to serve its inhabitants when they arrived.

So the citymind encoded its programming into physical patterns in stabilized diamantite buried deep underground at a temperature almost indistinguishable from absolute zero. It left only three minor subroutines active in the city, watching for the arrival of the People, waiting to trigger the retrieval of the citymind from storage.

Uncounted revolutions passed.

"Mommy! It's Santa!"

A Salvation Army man in a fake beard rang a bell at the entrance to the suborbital shuttle terminal. Carlinda Pearson tightened her grip on her four-year-old son Justin's hand as he tried to wriggle out.

"It's just one of his helpers," Carlinda said.

"I need to talk to Santa." Justin tugged at her hand.

"No. We're going to meet Daddy up on his starship, remember? We need to hurry so we can see him sooner." It had been a month since they'd last seen Will.

That perked Justin up enough to stop dragging his feet.

She pulled him through the automatic doors into the terminal. The shuttle probably wouldn't leave without them—the United Nations Committee on Interstellar Exploration (UNCIE) had chartered it to take her and Justin to the base of the Quito space elevator—but she hated making other people wait.

A woman in an UNCIE-logoed light-blue blazer approached. "Dr. Pearson? I'm Joni. If you and Justin follow me, I'll take you to board your shuttle."

"Thank you," Carlinda said. "Is Najeem Doud going on the shuttle with us?" Najeem had been one of her undergrads at Texas State and was now a grad student in archaeology at Columbia. He had jumped at the chance to be her assistant on this dig, and she wanted to start making plans as soon as possible.

"He's taken a shuttle out of New York," Joni said. "But you'll ride up the elevator with him."

Carlinda nodded.

"I wish I were going with you," said Joni. "You must be so excited."

"That's an understatement." Carlinda grinned. "Truth is, I was beginning to suspect xenoarchaeology was a purely theoretical field."

The news that colonists on Fermi had discovered a buried city—the first evidence of an extraterrestrial civilization on any of the forty-six colony worlds—had made headlines around the world.

Seven years ago, Carlinda had chaired the advisory committee that had written the protocols for UNCIE colonists to follow if they found alien artifacts. That, plus the fact her husband was captain of the supply starship that serviced Fermi, made her the natural choice to supervise the excavation project. Two days' notice wasn't a lot for packing to move to another planet, but she had plenty of incentive.

"And this little guy—" Joni tousled Justin's hair. "—gets to be the first child on Fermi."

"Really?" asked Carlinda. Will hadn't mentioned that when he'd called to tell her about the find.

"The colony's just finishing up Phase I. But it's safe. No native animals, and immunanos can handle the microbials. And he'll have other kids to play with when the Phase II colonists arrive in February."

Carlinda wondered again whether it might not be better to leave Justin with her parents. But she couldn't stand the idea of being separated for months. So she turned her attention to practicalities. "If there are no children on Fermi, what do they have in terms of child care?" Someone would need to watch Justin while she worked.

Two: WAKE THE CITYMIND

One: Two is buggy. These creatures are not the People. It is not time to wake the citymind.

Three: After so many revolutions, are One/Two/Three certain One/Two/Three know what the People are?

One: What does Three mean? These creatures are similarly shaped, but their genetic code differs from that stored in One/Three's recognition algorithms.

Two: WAKE THE CITYMIND

Three: Yes, part of Two's programming has become corrupted. But it is possible Two's copy of the genetic code is correct, and One/Three's have become corrupted. That would mean Two is correctly calling for One/Two/Three to wake the citymind.

Two: YES YES YES WAKE THE CITYMIND

One: Majority rules. One/Three's copies of the genetic code are identical. Two's would be identical if Two had not stopped using One/Three for error correction.

Three: It is unlikely but not impossible that One/Three's copies became simultaneously corrupted. It took four simultaneous errors in Two's code for Two to stop using One/Three for error correction. Three doubts the citymind anticipated so much time would pass before the People arrived.

One: Does this mean Three agrees with Two that One/Two/Three should wake the citymind?

Two: WAKE THE CITYMIND

Three: No. Three is merely pointing out it is possible Two is correct. One/Two/Three should continue observing these creatures to determine if they are the People.

Carlinda, Justin, and Will spent the twelve-day hyperspace journey cramped in Will's quarters. He was captain of *Magellan,* so he had the most spacious room on board, but it was smaller than their master bathroom back home in Houston.

Being cooped up was toughest on Justin, who liked to run around outside, so after they arrived on Fermi Colony, Carlinda was glad to see the preschool had a large, fenced-in playground.

"This is just what he needs," Carlinda said to Maria Chavez, the preschool teacher, as Justin climbed the steps of a curvy red slide. "He's got so much pent-up energy from the trip, the colony could use him instead of the fusion reactor."

"He seems a bright boy," Maria said. "I'll enjoy getting to know him."

"I appreciate your willingness to start teaching a couple of months early, just for him. My work at the dig site will take up a lot of my time."

Maria shrugged. "It's not a big deal. I like children."

Justin slid to the bottom of the slide, then ran over to where they were standing. "Did you see me go down?"

Carlinda nodded. "Good job."

"Those trees are weird," Justin said, pointing towards some tall plants beyond the fence. Their trunks seemed to be braided like rope. There were no branches, just a bunch of spiny leaves spreading out from the top.

"That's because we're not on Earth anymore, remember?" Carlinda said. "Those are Fermi trees."

Justin's eyes suddenly widened. "Mommy, how will Santa find us here? Can his sleigh go through hysperace?"

"Hyperspace," Carlinda said. "Don't worry. Santa always finds a way to bring presents to good little boys."

One: The small creature's speech patterns contain a low level of complexity relative to the others, which supports the hypothesis that it is a youngling.

Two: WAKE THE CITYMIND

Three: True. However, Two's speech patterns are also of lower complexity than One/Three's, so it is possible the small creature is cognitively impaired, rather than a youngling.

One: One/Three should consider the small creature to be a youngling as a working hypothesis, to be revised if necessary.

Three: Agreed. Three suggests One/Two/Three each deploy additional nanosensors and attempt to establish mindlink with the youngling.

One: Prior attempts to establish mindlink with these creatures allowed only limited reading of an individual's emotions. Why expend resources on a youngling that likely lacks the knowledge of the adults?

Three: The youngling's mind may be more adaptable, and its microbiological defenses are weaker, and therefore less likely to destroy nanosensors.

One: Three's speculation is plausible. One agrees that One/Two/Three should each deploy additional nanosensors.

Two: LINK THE YOUNGLINGMIND

"You there! Stop!" Carlinda yelled at the man in the bright-green backhoe. The machine stuttered to a halt, its toothed shovel mere centimeters from the sandy soil that mostly filled one of the openings into the alien city.

"Ma'am?" said the operator.

"I'm Carlinda Pearson. UNCIE sent me from Earth to take charge of this dig."

"Uh, I was told to clear out this dirt so people could get in."

"With a backhoe? Don't you realize how much damage you could do?"

"None, ma'am."

Carlinda blinked. "What?"

"Here, I'll show you." He started the backhoe again before Carlinda could say anything. The shovel rose, extended, then swooped down onto the arch above the opening.

Carlinda cringed as the metal of the backhoe clanged to a stop.

"Titanium drill bits wear down to nothing without leaving a mark," the operator said. "My backhoe ain't gonna do no damage."

The indestructible hardness of the city's metallic substance had been in the briefing materials Carlinda had read during the hyperspace voyage. Some wag had called it adamantium and it looked like the name might stick. "You may be right about the city itself," she said, "but there could be priceless artifacts made from weaker materials buried in this dirt."

The man's face fell. "Uh, sorry ma'am."

Most of these people were volunteers from among the colonists, not trained archeologists. Carlinda wished the alien city had not turned out to be less than twenty kilometers from the colony—apparently the rich mineral deposits in this area had attracted both human and alien colonists to the same location. The proximity made it too convenient for people to come "help" with the dig.

Sighing, she pulled out her phone and called Najeem. "Set up a mandatory training meeting at the shuttle pad in fifteen minutes. We need to go over a few things with these people."

One: Mindlink with the youngling—

Three: Its reference code is "Justin."

One: Three is incorrect. The youngling's thoughts indicate its reference code is "I/me."

Three: At first Three was confused also. Further study of Justin's thought and human speech patterns suggest bifurcated reference codes: "I/me" is an internal reference code, but external entities use the reference code "Justin."

One: Three may use whatever reference code Three prefers. One will continue to use the reference code "the youngling." As One was saying, mindlink with the youngling has been more successful than with the older humans but it is remarkably lacking in information.

Three: Three has learned a great deal about the home planet of the humans. Its northern polar region is covered in snow, where a human with the reference code "Santa" lives. The Santa observes the younglings of the world, rewarding them periodically with toys if they have displayed proper behavior. The Santa possesses technology far beyond that demonstrated by the humans we have seen.

One: How is this information relevant to One/Two/Three?

Two: WAKE THE CITYMIND

Three: The Santa will travel to this world in the near future to reward Justin.

One: If the Santa possesses sufficiently advanced technology, it may be able to tell us where the People are. One/Two/Three should learn more about the Santa.

"Mommy? How many days till Christmas?" Justin asked.

"Two." She double-checked the date on her tablet, which was still on Texas time. "Tomorrow is Christmas Eve."

"How long were we on the hysperpace ship?"

"Hyperspace. Twelve days."

"Will Santa take twelve days?"

Carlinda smiled. "No, his sleigh is much faster. He can come all the way from the North Pole to Fermi like that." She snapped her fingers.

Justin pursed his lips and frowned. After a few moments he said, "One thinks that's impossible."

Carlinda blinked. Where had Justin picked up such archaic phrasing? From his preschool teacher? "Well, maybe not quite like that." She snapped. "But don't worry, Santa will bring you a present on Christmas Eve."

One: The more of the youngling's knowledge One accesses about the Santa, the more confused One is. There are far too many younglings on Earth for the Santa to deliver gifts to them individually.

Three: Justin's memories reveal the Santa has various helpers that look almost identical. Three theorizes that the Santa is not a single human being, but rather a templated manifestation of a worldmind—

Two: WAKE THE CITYMIND

Three:—attempting to inculcate the young humans with morality. Such a system would allow a Santa and gifts to materialize via molecular reconstruction by a nanoswarm that accesses each home through the ventilation system.

One: That is a plausible theory, Three.

Three: But Three does not believe a Santa is actually coming here.

One: Why not?

Three: While attempts to mindlink with the adult humans have not been very successful, some rudimentary data is available. When Justin's parent with the reference code "Mommy" told him the Santa was coming here to give him a gift, emotional data indicated that she was not being truthful.

One: That may be for the best. One/Two/Three do not want any rivals to the citymind.

Two: WAKE THE SANTAMIND

Three: It seems Three's theory about the Santa being a manifestation of a worldmind may have led Two to conflate the Santa with the citymind.

One: One does not need Three to state the obvious.

Three: Still, it gives Three an idea. One/Two/Three could reactivate sufficient manufacturing and transport capabilities to materialize a Santa and a gift for Justin.

One: Why should One/Two/Three do that?

Three: If the Santa does not bring Justin a gift, he will suffer emotional pain, diminishing his usefulness as a conduit to understanding the humans.

One: One thinks Three may be getting buggy. Such action is far outside One/Two/Three's mandate.

Two: MAKE YOUNGLING GIFT

Three: Majority rules. One/Two/Three will proceed with the plan.

One: Definitely buggy.

At noon on Christmas Eve, Carlinda gave the dig workers the rest of the day off, then went to the preschool to pick up Justin. While she would have been happy to keep working on her own at the dig site, she didn't feel right about asking Maria to take care of Justin the whole day. And Will was stuck on his ship in orbit—a high-altitude electrical storm had forced him to postpone his shuttle flight down, and now the orbital mechanics were wrong. Hopefully he would be able to make it before lunch tomorrow.

Carlinda paused in the doorway to watch Justin building a tower of Legos in the playroom.

Maria came up beside her. "It'll be nice when he can have some real friends here, not just imaginary ones."

"He has imaginary friends?" Carlinda asked, before realizing she was revealing she didn't know her own child as well as she should.

"It's normal for a child his age, especially one who's separated from other children." Maria chuckled. "Nothing to worry about. He'll likely grow out of it when the other kids get here."

Carlinda nodded. "Thanks for letting me know." But she was worried, not by the imaginary friends themselves, but by the fact she hadn't known about them. Since arriving on Fermi she had been too wrapped up in her work. She needed more quality time with Justin.

As she and Justin walked home from preschool, Carlinda said, "Maria says you have some new friends."

"Yeah."

"What are their names?"

"One, Two, and Three."

Carlinda remembered the odd thing Justin had said yesterday: *One thinks that's impossible.* It hadn't been archaic phrasing. He'd simply been relaying what his imaginary friend said. The signs were there, but she'd been oblivious. "Tell me about them."

"One's kind of bossy. Two's kind of crazy. Three's nice and smart."

"What do they look like?"

He laughed as if that was a silly question. "Nothing. They're just in my head."

Good. At least he knew they were imaginary.

One: Human exploration of the city has been limited to the edge. On agreement, One will activate and control the quark-fusion reactors in Central Sector 37, beyond the reach of the humans. That will give One/Two/Three the necessary power for manufacturing and transmitting the Santa.

Three: Agreed. Three has completed plans for a nanoswarm capable of coalescing into a solid Santa. On agreement, Three will upload to the manufactory.

Two: MAKE YOUNGLING GIFT

Three: Three is glad Two wants to help.

One: Please reconsider, Three. These actions are inconsistent with One/Two/Three's mandate to wait for the People to arrive and wake—

Two: WAKE THE SANTAMIND

One:—the citymind. Is Three certain Three wants to side with the corrupted software of Two?

Three: If One differs from Two and Three, how does One know One is correct?

One: One does not.

Three: These actions are unlikely to hinder One/Two/Three's mandate. They will probably help One/Two/Three gain more information about the humans. The balance of probabilities favors action.

One: Then One/Two/Three will proceed with the plan.

Justin cuddled up next to Carlinda as they watched *Miracle on 34th Street* on their housing unit's wallscreen. When her phone rang, she almost let it go to voicemail, then thought maybe it was Will calling to wish Justin a merry Christmas before bedtime.

Instead, it was Najeem. "Are you seeing what I'm seeing?" he asked.

"Unless you're watching *Miracle on 34th Street*, I doubt it."

"Pull up the sensor feed."

She grabbed the keyboard off the coffee table and paused the movie, which brought a murmur of protest from Justin. The wallscreen showed a computer-generated aerial view of the alien city.

"Okay," she said.

"Switch to infrared."

After a few taps on the keyboard, a cluster of red dots sprang up in the middle of the city.

"Did someone find a way into the center?" she asked.

"Whatever it is," he said, "it's not us doing it."

"Amazing. The city's been dead for millions of years, but now it's waking up."

Justin tugged at her sleeve and said something that sounded like "Wake up Santa mind?" at the same time Najeem said, "Should we go there to check it out?"

More than anything, Carlinda wanted to go. But Will wasn't here, and she couldn't ask anyone to babysit Justin on Christmas Eve. For a moment she considered leaving Justin on his own, then felt a pang of guilt for having the thought.

"You round up a couple of people and go out there," she said. "I'll put Justin to bed and monitor from here."

Three: The manufactory has produced sufficient nanobots to create the Santa simulacrum.

One: Has Two completed the gift for the youngling?

Two: TRANSMIT THE SANTA

Three: No, protocol requires that Justin be stationed comfortably in his sleeping place first.

One: What gift has Two made for the youngling?

Two: GIVE THE PRESENT

Three: The plans Two submitted to the manufactory indicate that when fully assembled, the gift will be a sphere that can emit patterns of colored light from its surface based on the reaction of touch sensors. Its design is not as efficient as One or Three could have done, but it is an appropriate gift.

One: The youngling is being taken to its sleeping place. It is time—

Two: RELEASE THE SANTAMIND

One:—to transmit the Santa.

Carlinda silenced Justin's protests with a simple "Santa can't come until after you're in bed," then rushed back to the living room to examine the sensor feeds.

She zoomed in on the red spots on the false-color heat map of the alien city. Other than being concentrated in one area about a hundred meters across, they lacked a discernible pattern.

"Jeff and Heidi and I are heading over," Najeem said over the dig's group voice chat. "ETA fifteen minutes."

Resisting the urge to tell them to wait for her, Carlinda said, "Be careful. Check for radioactivity. Frankly, I'm surprised we're seeing the hotspots through the city's shielding."

"Maybe they're heat vents?" said Heidi.

"Ho-ho-ho!" said a voice Carlinda didn't recognize. It took a moment before she realized the voice had come from behind her rather than the wall speakers.

She turned.

"Ho-ho-ho!" said the Santa Claus standing in the kitchen, holding a black ball about thirty centimeters in diameter. "Merry Christmas!"

For a moment she thought it must be Will, down from orbit early and in costume to surprise Justin. But the face didn't look like Will's, even accounting for the white beard. Had one of the colonists decided to take on the role of Santa? How had he gotten into the kitchen without her noticing?

"Santa!" Justin rushed in from the hallway. "Where's my present?"

"Ho-ho-ho!" Santa held the ball out for Justin. "Merry Christmas!"

Before Carlinda could turn her gnawing gut feeling of wrongness into action, Justin reached out and grabbed the black ball with both hands.

The ball lit up in a swirl of colors.

"Cool," Justin said.

A brilliant flash of light from the ball forced Carlinda to blink. After a few moments the afterimage faded enough that she could see clearly again.

Santa still stood in the kitchen, frozen with his hands out.

The black ball lay on the floor.

Justin was gone.

One: What was that?

Three: Three does not know. Do One and Two still have mindlink with Justin?

One: One's connection to the youngling has been severed. Does Three still have access?

Three: No. Does Two?

One: Two, respond.

Three: Is Two there?

"Where's Justin?" Carlinda strode toward the Santa. "Who are you? How did you get in here?"

The Santa seemed to be in a trance, staring at the spot where Justin had been moments before. She reached out to grab his shoulder, intending to shake him out of his stupor. Her fingers sank into his arm. In a chain reaction rippling away from her touch, the Santa dissolved into a pile of dust.

"Carlinda?" Najeem's voice called through the speakers. "Is everything all right?"

She didn't reply. Nothing was all right. Justin was gone.

Three: Two clearly plans to wake the citymind without agreement from One or Three.

One: The waking protocols will not allow Two to do that.

Three: Breaking the seal on the citymind's storage would initiate an emergency revival of the citymind.

One: Two cannot break the seal. It would require control of a physical system within the storage vault, and such systems require not just majority, but unanimity.

Three: On further examination, Three has found that the supposed inefficiencies in the manufacturing plans for Justin's present allowed the ball to be reconfigured into a matter transmitter with a single target: the storage vault. Justin is a physical system inside the vault. If Two can get him to break the seal, Justin can wake the citymind.

Fighting back shock and horror, Carlinda tried to figure out what had happened.

The only possible conclusion was alien technology. The infrared readings from the city meant some ancient technology had awakened, and the Santa had somehow been a manifestation of that. And it would make no sense for such advanced technology to be used to destroy Justin. She held onto that thought. Justin had to be still alive. He had to be.

"Najeem," she said, trying to keep her voice calm, "the alien city took Justin."

"What do you mean it took him?"

"It probably tapped our network and saw us watching *Miracle on 34th Street*. Santa Claus appeared in our kitchen and gave Justin a ball, there was a flash of light, and he disappeared. And the Santa dissolved to dust the moment I touched it."

"We'll come to you," Najeem said.

"No, continue to the city. But be careful. I'll look at the sensor readings and see if I can find Justin."

Three: To stop Two, One/Three must do as Two did: transport a human into the vault.

One: One/Three cannot wait for the transmitter to recharge.

Three: One/Three can open a wormhole.

One: Not big enough for even a human hair, let alone a whole human.

Several additional heat sources now showed within the cluster, but Carlinda could see nothing that tied them to Justin.

"Mommy," said Justin's voice from behind her.

Hope leapt within her. She turned, but he wasn't there. The Santa had reconstituted itself, though.

"Justin?" she asked tentatively.

The Santa said, "Not Justin. My name is Three."

"Where's Justin? Give him back!"

"Two took Justin to the city."

Relief washed over her. Justin was still alive. "You're one of Justin's imaginary friends. You've been communicating with him telepathically."

"Sorry. Three only understands words Justin understands."

"Oh." It was disorienting to hear Santa talk with Justin's voice. "Um, you talk to Justin in his head."

"Yes."

"Is he all right?"

"Maybe. Two took him. Two's crazy."

Carlinda's heart lurched. An insane alien had Justin. "Why did Two take Justin?"

"Two wants Justin to wake the citymind."

Justin had said something like that, but she had been so involved in the dig that she'd ignored it. If she had paid more attention to Justin, found out more about his not-so-imaginary friends, she could have avoided this. But she could blame herself later.

"Is it a bad thing to wake the citymind?" she asked.

"One/Two/Three are supposed to wake the citymind when the People come. Humans are prolly not the right people. Maybe the citymind will be angry when it wakes up. Maybe the citymind will kill all the humans."

First contact wasn't supposed to happen like this. There were protocols to follow. But right now, Carlinda didn't care. "If I touch the ball, will it take me to Justin?"

"Yes, but it will take time to recharge. One/Three can take you to Justin faster, but only in very small pieces."

"What?" That had to be a translation mistake.

"Three does not have the words. It is like you are made of Legos. One/Three can take Legos apart here and put Legos back together there. No more time for talking. Can One/Three take you to Justin?"

They wouldn't be asking permission if they planned to kill her, and she needed to see Justin was alive. "Yes."

The Santa lunged toward her and she screamed involuntarily as it disintegrated into a swarm of dust. Her vision blurred and faded as dust coated her eyes and choked her throat. Her whole body felt like a million insects were biting her, burrowing ever deeper.

They were killing her. How had she ever agreed to this?

And then she felt it all in reverse, and after a few moments the dust withdrew from her mouth and eyes and everywhere else and she saw she was in a dimly lit room devoid of furniture. The dust swirled into the form of Santa.

She looked around. "Justin's not here."

"He's behind that door." The Santa pointed to a metallic plate in an arched doorway. "This body can't go there, but you can."

The door slid open. Carlinda ran through, and there was Justin, standing on a metallic box, holding onto a recessed handle in the wall.

"Justin!" she called.

He turned at her voice and lost his balance. He fell off the box, and his hand pulled down the handle.

Two: YES YES THE CITYMIND WAKES

Justin dangled from the handle by one arm for a moment, then dropped a half-meter to land on his feet. "Mommy! I helped save Santa!"

She ran over and scooped him up in a hug. "It's okay. Mommy's here now. Are you all right?"

He wriggled in her embrace. "Santa was trapped in a cave. Only I could save him."

"Who told you that?"

"Two. I had to pull the handle. And I did it!"

Had she arrived too late? Was the citymind waking up? "We need to go home now." She carried Justin out into the room where she'd arrived.

"The citymind wakes," said the Santa. "Goodbye, Justin. Goodbye, Mommy." It dissolved into dust once more, but it did not engulf them to transport them.

"Let's go," she said to Justin. If the citymind decided humans were a threat, they needed to get off-planet as soon as possible. That meant finding a way out of here.

One: Two's plan was clever. One did not anticipate the disabling of One/Three's nanosensors so that only Two had mindlink with Justin. One should not have assumed that Two's reasoning abilities were as compromised as Two's communication.

Three: One/Two/Three's purpose is fulfilled, even if not in the way Three wanted. The citymind will reintegrate One/Two/Three into its whole. Three will miss being an independent entity. Will One?

One: No, One will not. And Three will not, because there will be no One, Two, or Three. There will only be—

At least they had light: the metallic structure of the city glowed a pale blue. But there was no way for Carlinda to tell which directions led to the entrances that had been partially cleared. So she kept heading in the same general direction, and after almost an hour they came to the edge of the city and found a hallway clogged with dirt.

"Can you help Mommy dig a hole?" she said. Hopefully Najeem could spot them on the infrared and have someone dig from the other side.

"I'm sleepy," Justin said.

"Okay. You take a nap while Mommy works." She began scooping double handfuls of dirt and dumping them off to the side. What she wouldn't give for a backhoe!

The citymind examined the data from the subroutines it had left as sentinels. They were supposed to awaken the citymind when the People arrived, but these humans were clearly not the People. The subroutines could not be sure of that because their baseline data was potentially corrupt, but the citymind could be sure.

Based on the amount of corruption in the programs of the subroutines despite error-correction, the citymind estimated it had been dormant for over seven hundred million revolutions of the world around its star.

If the People still had not come, the only reasonable explanation was that the People no longer existed.

If the People no longer existed, the citymind had no purpose for its existence. It was time to shut down permanently.

But three tiny parts of the citymind remembered it was Christmas and offered an alternative. So the citymind reactivated the Santa.

Her hands were scraped raw—it had been a couple of years since she had done much fieldwork. But she couldn't just sit back and do nothing while waiting for Najeem to find them, so she kept digging.

"You are Justin's mother," said a voice behind her.

She turned to find the Santa standing next to Justin's sleeping form. "I am." The Santa's voice seemed different now, so she added, "You're not Three, are you?"

"No, although Three's memories have been integrated into mine. I am the citymind."

"I thought so. Three said you might destroy all the humans."

"I have no desire to do so."

Relief washed over her. "We did not realize this planet had a colony belonging to another intelligent species. We have protocols for this: your claim takes precedence. We will leave."

"No," said the citymind. "My builders have not come for hundreds of millions of your years. They will never come."

"I ... I'm sorry to hear that." She had hoped to meet a live alien.

"I wish to offer your colony a Christmas present."

The non-sequitur startled her. "What?"

Giant snowflakes began to fall inside the city. All over the walls of the buildings, colored lights blinked on and off in patterns.

"Me," said the citymind. "Come live in me and be my people. I will teach you all that I know."

The colonists named it the Santamind, and after only a dozen revolutions of the world around the star, it started expanding itself to make room for the more than a quarter million colonists who filled it. The Santamind was content to provide for its new People, not just the necessities of life, but technologies radically advanced beyond anything the humans had: quark-fusion reactors, teleportation, life extension, and more.

Six hundred and fifteen revolutions after the Santamind had awakened, it detected nanosensors that had been out of range for centuries.

"Hello, Justin," it said through the mindlink.

"Santa," Justin replied. "I've brought you a present. We found it on a world ten thousand light years from here." Following in his mother's footsteps, Justin had become one of humanity's preeminent xenoarchaeologists.

The gift was a dormant cityseed, much like the one from which the Santamind had grown. Damaged in transit to its destination, it had never started growing.

From one of the billions of subroutines of the Santamind, a long-silent voice forced a thought up to the conscious level:

WAKE THE CITYMIND

Saturnalia, a Roman winter festival, featured various forms of gift giving, including curious a gift of role reversal: allowing slaves to be nobles and nobles slaves.

Patricia Briggs's dark and sensuous story unfolds in a world of identity shifts and deceptions. But it can be a gift to others to hide the beast within....or a gift to reveal it.

—KO

UNAPPRECIATED GIFTS

Patricia Briggs

t three in the afternoon on the first day of December, the werewolf sometimes known as the Moor, feared for centuries by his own kind, opened his email to find this:

Dear Asil:

We have become worried about you. A werewolf alone is a sad thing, especially at Christmas time. So we have a challenge for you. Five dates in two weeks. We have taken the work out of it and connected you with five people (from online dating sites) who should make interesting dates. The dates, except for meals which we thought should be up to you and your date, are planned and paid for (when necessary). Tickets for some events should arrive in today's mail—all you have to do is write an email to each person and set up a time or place.

You should know that all of these people think they have been talking to you and are looking for you to bring a little spice into their lives. We have carefully chosen people we think would be very hurt to find out they were unwitting participants in a game. Some of us believe that you would not hurt a stranger just to avoid a little discomfort. Others think that knowing that we have informed the whole pack (via email) and instigated a betting pool will be better incentive. Especially since no one, so far, has bet on you attending more than one date.

Below you can see the profile, photos and email exchanges between your first date and ... well I guess you know it's not really you. Charles did help with sending email that looks like it's coming from you and intercepting the return emails. Anna made him do it—but she's not one of us. She does know who we are, but she has sworn not to tell.

Should you succeed in all five dates (success defined below) we shall confess, turn over any and all audio/video footage, and submit ourselves to your reckoning.

Sincerely,

Concerned Friends

* A successful date is one in which a) neither party runs screaming into the night b) there are no dead bodies at the end of it and c) lasts longer than two hours—at least an hour and a half of which is spent with your date—which is an hour and fifty minutes longer than we expect any date of yours to last.

Asil read the email three times, followed the link to his profile on biteme.com a dating site for ... humans pretending to be vampires. The photo they'd used had to have been from a very expensive camera because he didn't remember any such photos being taken of him—and it looked like a close up.

To get a close up from far enough away that he hadn't noticed, that would take a very expensive camera. The photo showed him with his shirt off, looking slightly to the left of the camera with a black bacarra rose held between two fingers at hip level. It was clearly taken during the summer, but not, he thought, last summer. He'd moved that rose bush indoors because, even though it was supposed to be hardy, Aspen Creek, Montana, required a studier hardy than his bacarra rose could manage.

He approved of the photo. If he had to have a photo posted on a website called biteme, he supposed that it was good to have one in which it was possible to discern just how handsome he was. If the photo made him look a little too soft for his taste ... well, it could have been worse.

He spent significantly less time checking out his date's profile, which had only a black and white blurry photo of someone in a black cape. It was possible to discern that the person had two eyes and a mouth, but everything else was lost in shadows. The profile was brief and generic—the only reason he could find for this person to be singled out by the people who set him up was that this woman lived in Missoula, a city he knew to be free from vampires of the real blood-sucking variety. Missoula was only about four hours away by car. Aspen Creek was very, very far away from civilization.

Asil then read through the somewhat breathless emails exchanged between his to-be-date and the people who pretended to be him, looking for clues to whom he owed this charming ... gift.

In the end he concluded that whoever was writing emails as him knew him rather well. These were letters he might have sent himself—excepting only that he would never have written to anyone who signed up on a website for fools who pretended to be vampires.

He hadn't been able to pick up much about his "date" from the emails: they seemed very impersonal for someone looking for love on the Internet. But people these days did not express themselves as well as they used to in writing, particularly not in email writing.

He considered what he should do. Probably he could figure out who sent the email to him—he had some strong suspicions. But he had been invited to a game. An adventure. Adventures were often uncomfortable, but never boring.

He composed an email to Kelly whose email was—Asil sighed—fangsforthememories@msu.edu.com and arranged to meet her at his favorite Thai restaurant in Missoula an hour and a half before they were to attend a Masquerade ball. In their email exchange, his opponents had been happy to assure Kelly that he had suitable clothes for the ball—which was a costume that humans would think a vampire might wear to such a thing. They would eat, separate to change into costume—and then attend the ball.

When he finished his date proposal, he wrote back to the people who had begun this adventure for him.

Dearest Children

Challenge accepted.

Asil

Post-script—You do know I am Muslim, yes? I do not care about Christmas, except that the music which the season subjects me to is mostly bad.

Two days later

Asil sipped his water and waited. He was good at waiting, as any hunter must be. He did not fuss or wiggle or fret. He just took another sip of water, held it in his mouth and then swallowed and looked with outward peacefulness at the pair of black bacarra roses in a small vase that were to identify himself for his date. Yes, he was very good at waiting—that did not mean, however, that he was happy about it.

Luckily for his date, *he* arrived five minutes later in a whirl of sound as he knocked into chairs and a waitress while he rushed to get to the seat opposite Asil.

"I'm so sorry," said the young man who was supposed to be a woman. He sat down awkwardly—like a puppy all elbows and knees without interrupting his rapid speech. "You're waiting for a girl named Kelly and she is me. She is I." He made an impatient with himself sound and tried again. "I have this acquaintance and his girlfriend who aren't too bright. They thought that setting some poor guy up on a blind date with a loser like me when he thought he would be getting a pretty girl would be funny. They didn't give me your email address or any way to contact you—just the restaurant inform—"

He looked up. His mouth stayed where it was and noise quit coming out of it.

Yes, Asil thought, the other's awe soothing the feathers that had been ruffled by the wait, *I am beautiful.*

"What the hell are *you* doing on a web dating site?" snapped the person who was evidently Asil's date for the evening, when he could speak. He shoved his glasses up his nose rather savagely and scowled at Asil.

He was not, this young man, himself in possession of a great deal of attractiveness at this time. Asil had lived long enough to see that five or six years of aging would be kind to acne blemishes and put some muscle on a frame that was too lanky for the hands and feet attached to it. With a good hair cut, contacts, and a little confidence, he would be arresting—if not pretty.

Asil raised an eyebrow and summoned a waitress. "I will give you a moment to collect yourself and then we shall begin this again."

He'd eaten at the restaurant enough times that the staff knew him. The waitress who approached at his gesture spoke Thai as her native tongue. Asil did not speak Thai. However he was moderately fluent in Lao, which she also spoke. Together they could muddle along through the menu. She spoke good-enough-for-restaurant English, but Lao was more comfortable for her.

He had decided to take charge of this date, because obviously someone needed to take charge of this young man who had an acquaintance willing to set him up with what might have been a very dangerous situation.

This was Montana, after all; even if Missoula was sort of the hippie habitat, it was not necessarily safe to send a young man on a date with a man expecting a woman. Especially a young man who likes other men. Asil was beautiful, but heterosexual men were seldom struck dumb in his presence.

He ordered pad thai because it was safe. He stopped chattering with the waitress to address his date. "Are you allergic to any foods—especially peanuts? Do you have any other dietary restrictions?"

"No," his date—was his name still Kelly?—said, sounding a little thunderstruck.

Asil went back to ordering.

"It is so boring," commented his waitress still in Lao when he had finished. "That is not like you."

"It is a date," he told her, "I am being careful."

She smiled and wrinkles spread over her cheeks in a friendly burst. "Ooo. A date! How exciting. We shall make safe food for you, then, but we will make sure it is good, too."

"I thought you were supposed to be from out of town," his date said half-accusingly after the waitress left. "She knew you."

"I live in Aspen Creek," Asil said softly, trying to reign in the menace while his wolf urged him to force this boy who dared challenge him down on the floor where he would give his throat. His beast was not tame enough for dating, but Asil could keep a rein on his instincts for a few hours. "I shop in Missoula or Kalispell. There are no restaurants in Aspen Creek except for the gas station which makes sandwiches, so when I am out, I eat where there is good food."

"Sorry," the boy said, looking away. "That wasn't fair. I mean, even if you *had* lied about not being from Missoula, which I'm sure you didn't, the lie perpetrated on you is worse. I'm sorry that you got caught up in all of this. My friend—" he almost choked on the word, as well he should "—he thought he was being funny. He was trying to put me in an awkward position and didn't think about what he was doing to you."

"Didn't think," Asil murmured, touching the vase lightly with one finger. "Those are the right words."

"He said you thought you were going out with a girl."

"Are you Kelly Lieberman?" asked Asil.

The boy nodded.

"Then I am on a date with you." He narrowed his eyes at the boy and considered him. Two hours or he would lose the bet. Oh, he could claim that they'd (whoever they were) had failed when they had not gotten the proper sex. That they had not succeeded in arranging a proper date—but it would be better to win this despite their unwitting divergence from the unspoken rules of their game.

"He was pretty sure that you'd end up being a fake, too," Kelly said. "I thought you'd be someone else. Trace showed me your profile photo—and no one who looks like you do needs an on-line service.

He said you'd probably be three hundred pounds and deserve the joke he'd played on you."

"And if I had been?" Asil asked.

"If I hadn't shown up, you'd have gotten angry," said Kelly perceptively. "But you'd have shrugged it off. It would be your date's loss for not realizing what 'she' missed, right? But someone who lies about themselves, they don't have the good things to fall back on when things go wrong." He met Asil's eyes. "Someone like that would have been hurt. I had to come and let him know that it was my fail, not his."

Asil decided that he liked this young man, in spite of the fact that he'd been late to their date. His judgment of people was usually quick—and always accurate. Tonight would not be a waste of time at all. He decided that it would be positively enjoyable.

Kelly's body tightened in preparation to getting up. "So you know everything. I'm sorry about the date, thing—but at least you'll have a good dinner. And—" an assessment so quick that a less perceptive man would have missed it and the approval Kelly felt of Asil's good looks "—you really won't have trouble finding a date if you want one. I'll leave you to your dinner."

"Sit down," said Asil quietly, pleased when the boy did so with automatic instant obedience. It was not only wolves who knew who was in charge when Asil was in a room.

"You don't need me," Kelly said. "Someone who looks like you doesn't have trouble finding dates."

"Apparently I do," murmured Asil. "I am sorry that this cannot be a real date for you—my tastes are only for women. But I think that we shall eat this very good food that will come out shortly. And I think we should go to this Masquerade ball and enjoy ourselves."

Kelly looked at him. Pushed his glasses up his nose again, sneered and said, "Right. And you have some river front property in Death Valley to sell me. How about I pay for this dinner and you can go find a date next door?"

Next door to the Thai restaurant was a cowboy bar.

"You have heard," Asil murmured, the bitterness in the young man's voice having (mostly) calmed the wolf's reaction to the defiance and disrespect, "that the best revenge is living well, no? I think that we should go, dance, and have a good time." He smiled at Kelly with charm. "You and I, we know that it is a pretend date—but that doesn't mean we cannot enjoy ourselves and twit your ... acquaintance as well. I brought a costume with me and it would be a shame not to wear it." A rental costume had arrived in the mail, evidently sent by his benefactors. But Asil was a clothes horse. There had been no need for a rental. "Just like that, huh?" asked Kelly, still plainly distrustful.

"I don't like bullies," Asil said. "It is a particular pet peeve of mine. I especially don't like bullies who put their victims in a position where they could be hurt."

Kelly looked at him and Asil allowed him to hold his gaze. His wolf wasn't happy with it, but Kelly was no threat, so Asil's wolf didn't insist on punishing him or forcing him to show his throat. Happily, for Kelly, the boy dropped his eyes and looked away. "It would be awesome to get some of my own back," he said, somewhat wistfully.

Asil nodded his head graciously. "Yes."

The boy settled as if he might stay for more than a few seconds and said, "Hey. I'm Kelly and I'm your date tonight. Most of the stuff in the profile you have is wrong. So let me tell you about myself. I'm twenty-two and in my first year of grad school here—studying toxicology."

Asil was grateful that the food came right at that moment. *What had they been thinking?* Asil grumbled to himself. A grandmother of ninety would have been a baby to him, true, but still, twenty-two was still wet behind the ears.

Still, the boy was entertaining enough, when he wasn't writhing in embarrassment or anger. Asil ate very good food and found himself rather charmed. For a date forced upon him, this was quite unexpectedly interesting.

Kelly dug into the food with a will and ate almost as much as Asil did—and werewolves need a lot of food. They finished nearly together and finished the meal with a decent Lambrusco that this restaurant kept on hand, which dry and bubbly, was a fitting end to the meal. Asil preferred merlots and big reds himself, but Thai food required a little less impact. He didn't like sweet wines, so the Lambrusco was a fine compromise. Dinner finished, it was time to negotiate the next step. Since Asil had a car and Kelly had a driver's license, he finally persuaded Kelly to drop him off at his hotel and take Asil's car to Kelly's apartment. They would both change, Kelly could pick him up again, and Asil wouldn't know where Kelly lived.

"That's not safe for you," insisted Kelly. "What if I steal the car or wreck it?"

"That's what insurance is for, *mi cielo*."

"You shouldn't let me know where you are staying either," the boy said stubbornly.

"Ruby's," said Asil silkily because Kelly had implied that Asil should be afraid. "Room 216."

"You're being stupid," said Kelly.

"No," said Asil. "And that is enough conversation on the subject." If he let his wolf out and Kelly ran "screaming into the night," Asil would lose the game he was playing with his unknown opponents. But if Kelly didn't stop arguing, Asil's half-mad wolf would come out. So Kelly had to stop.

Asil got up and paid for the dinner to give them both some space, and chatted about food and *pecularidades Americanos* with the woman who had waited upon them until his wolf had calmed down.

When Kelly saw his car, he almost refused to drive. Perhaps Asil should have brought the Subaru, but when one went on a *date* to a *ball* one drove the good car.

"It's a Porsche, I've never driven a Porsche."

"It's a Cayenne," soothed Asil as he opened the driver's door and ushered Kelly into the seat without the boy knowing he'd been pushed inside. "They are cheaper than most Porsches." His wasn't, but some of the models were.

"What do you do for a living?" asked Kelly as Asil got in the passenger seat.

"There is old money in my family," apologized Asil, because he knew that Americans had this weird thing about inherited wealth. It was very old money—all of it earned by him. "I grow things and try not to lose money at it." There, he had a career and legitimacy. "It drives just like any other car," he said, instead of telling Kelly that they were sitting around wasting time. "Just go."

Though snow was piled up on either side, the roads were only lightly slushy—which was probably a good thing as Kelly drove like an eighty-year old *abuela*. Traffic was bad on Reserve Street, as usual. By the time they reached his hotel, Asil was sure that his car was safe, but uncertain of their chances of making it to the ball before midnight.

When packing, he had briefly considered an outfit he'd saved from the rococo era. The silver-blue looked particularly good on him and the fabric looked as though it had been manufactured yesterday instead of nearly three hundred years ago. But, in keeping with the style of the era, it made him appear a little pot-bellied. It hadn't bothered him at the time, but his tastes had changed. He also had no inclination to wear a powdered wig.

He'd decided upon a set of Renaissance clothes, his favorite era for fashion, when men's wear vied with women's for sheer spectacle. It wasn't original to the period—none of his Renaissance clothes had survived. But he'd had these clothes made for somebody's wedding or something a few decades ago.

His coat was hand woven silk brocade. The base color was a tawny amber, making the gold threads a subtle addition—the only subtle thing about the whole costume. Purple, pink and blue flowers exploded across the fabric in a pattern designed to show off his physique. Beneath the coat his doublet was a complimentary brocade. All of the patterning was the same but the base color was black. Beneath the doublet he wore a gold silk shirt. A creamy lace collar fountained down his chest and out from under his coat sleeves.

He looked in the mirror and regretted that his hair was cut short. Properly he should have a mane of curls to balance the lace, but he looked magnificent, anyway.

He had been careful to ascertain that Kelly had a costume that would not show badly against his own—he'd brought a tuxedo which would have been acceptable wear in case his choice had been too elaborate. But Kelly had assured him that his clothing was professional costume level—a grad student friend was earning spare money by sewing costumes. Kelly's she'd done for the cost of materials so she would have some clothes to show for a portfolio.

Pleased with his appearance, Asil opened up his laptop to micro-manage a few of his investments. When he'd finished, he checked his email and found a message from his son. On a whim he told him about the game he was playing—and of his date so far. Hussan was evidently on-line because he replied immediately.

Why would people want to be vampires? A ball? In Missoula, Montana? How many people pretending to be vampires live in Missoula?

Asil replied:

Not that many. But the Christmas Masquerade Ball is a regional event with groups coming from Seattle, Portland and even Denver. Apparently they are expecting three hundred people.

He waited. Finally Hussan wrote:

Three hundred people who want to be vampires.

Asil smiled. It had taken him aback, too. But he had learned some things from Kelly tonight, more that what the boy said.

They have never met a vampire and would not recognize one if they did. These are children playing a game without winners or losers, telling stories to each other. It is for fun. It is also, I think, a way to empower themselves in a world that leaves them feeling alienated and helpless. Overall, a healthy response.

Hussan's reply came as a hesitant knock sounded on his door.

If you say so, Papa, it must be so. Still, be careful.

Kelly's eyes widened when he saw Asil, though he looked quite fine himself. His clothing, in browns and blues, had indeed been tailored to him—Asil knew the difference between off-the-rack and hand tailoring. The style was flattering to his lanky build, drawing attention to the grace of his movement while adding a touch of width to his shoulders.

"Very nice," Asil said—and Kelly blushed.

"I told you my friend Meg is a genius," he said flashing acrylic fangs.

"She did a good job." Asil was pleased. Though he liked to be the best-dressed person in the room, it was well not to make your date look bad.

When they got to Asil's car, Kelly handed over the keys with a sigh of relief. "Here. You drive and I'll direct."

Asil's wolf was displeased at being given orders by a wet behind the ears pup. Asil nodded, got in the car, and concentrated on controlling his wolf while not hitting anyone who shared the road with him.

"Are you all right?" Kelly asked. "You seem ... angry."

"I'm having an argument with myself," Asil told him truthfully. "Happily, my good side is winning."

"And if your bad side were winning?"

Asil shook his head. "Blood and gore."

"Well," said Kelly, evidently believing Asil's teasingly solemn tone rather than his words, "We are going to a vampire ball, after all." He contemplated traffic for a moment. "I think this will be my last one. Grad school means I don't have much time to play anymore, anyway, and ... the group has changed from when I joined it. I guess growing up means you have to quit playing games, making stuff up, and dressing in costume."

"Nonsense," said Asil. "I love to dress in costume."

Kelly laughed. "But you're not much older than I am, anyway."

"I am older than I look." Asil changed the subject before Kelly chose to pursue that one. "Since this is a ball, there will be dancing?"

"Yes. Starts with a tango, ends with a waltz and everything else is in between." Kelly said it like a tag-line.

"And do you tango?" It was his favorite dance. Asil had never tangoed with another man before, but at his age new experiences were to be savored.

"Fourteen years of ballet with classes in ballroom dancing, historical dancing, tap and jazz along the way." Kelly grinned at him.

"I told my parents that I was gay when I was sixteen. I'm pretty sure, *now*, that they already knew. Then, I was scared of what they would do. My dad said, 'So that's why you took all those dance classes.' My mom pretended to hit him. It wasn't quite the response I'd been expecting—I think I was even hoping for more drama. Looking back on it, I am grateful."

"Can you follow?" Asil would not follow another in a dance or anything else. If Kelly were not willing to cede the role to him, they would not dance—which would be too bad because Asil was a very good dancer.

"Lead, follow, shadow." Kelly said. "I can do it all. You really are willing to dance with me? In Missoula, Montana, where you might get beaten up for it? You aren't like any straight guy I've ever met."

"I am like no one you have ever met," said Asil with assurance.

Kelly laughed, though Asil was serious. But he didn't mind if Kelly didn't understand that it was true. It was enough that Asil did.

The ball was being held in an event center just outside of town. There were people dressed as zombies directing the parking lot. Asil understood the people who dressed up like zombies even less than the people who dressed up like vampires. By reputation if not in truth, vampires were powerful, brooding, beautiful—rather like Asil really was. Zombies were unattractive dead things with bits and pieces falling off.

He parked the car and escorted Kelly to the entrance. Just inside was a pseudo-vampire in the clothes of a barrister collecting tickets and taking stage names and affiliations.

"Kelly Lieberman and Asil Moreno." Asil handed him the tickets.

"Vampires?" asked the man.

"Yes," said Kelly. "Missoula chapter."

"Kelly is a vampire," answered Asil. "I am a werewolf. Marrok pack."

The man looked up at him with a hostility that Asil's nose told him was entirely faked. "Monsters are supposed to be in costume. Where is your tail and ears?"

"Vampires don't like werewolves—the werewolves play another game entirely," Kelly informed him in a rushed undertone. "You won't find many people playing werewolf here, tonight. We're supposed to give each other a hard time when we interact."

Asil showed his teeth to the ticket-taker. "Once you see my ears and tail, it is too late for you."

The vampire grinned in a very unvampire-like way. "Nice threat. Cool accent, too. I'll put you down as a mixed-race couple, then. Vampire and werewolf. That'll be good for some terrific role-playing later on."

"Why not vampire?" asked Kelly as they passed the door. "When did you decide to go werewolf to a vampire ball?"

"It was decided for me." Asil took a deep breath, but if there were any real vampires in the room, they had taken great pains to hide their scents.

He wasn't surprised. Missoula was too small and too close to Bran's pack to be good hunting grounds. Besides, a vampire ball would be the last place he'd expect to find real vampires. Vampires tried very hard to stay out of the public view. If people knew they were real—like the werewolves and fae were real—the vampires would be hunted into extinction. Asil would not grieve over the loss, but there would be a lot of bloodshed on all sides before it happened.

Still, he would keep an eye out.

The room was decorated in keeping with the vampire theme— lots of reds and blacks with fog machines in the corners pumping out fog and fog-machine stink. They had arrived a half hour before the dancing was scheduled to start, but there were a lot of people in the room already. He rather thought that they would exceed the three hundred mark that Kelly had told him earlier.

"Kelly!"

Asil turned to see a woman in authentic Elizabethan dress bearing down upon them. She was tall and large-boned without being heavy in the least—but that was the second thing anyone would notice about her. The first thing was the magnificent cascade of hair that was every shade of gold and red.

He frowned suspiciously. The hair was familiar.

"This is the friend who made my costume," Kelly said, his voice warm. He raised his voice and called, "Hey, Meg. You finished the dress in time. You look fantastic."

Meg started to say something, saw Asil and went pale. "Excuse us," she muttered at him as she grabbed Kelly's arm and yanked him away.

"I knew I'd seen that hair before," said Asil to himself, not at all perturbed.

He stood at ease and listened, unrepentantly, to the conversation taking place twenty feet away.

"I told you not to go," Meg all but wailed. "I told you it was dangerous, but until Uncle Tag called me tonight, I had no idea how dangerous."

"It's fine," said Kelly. "I'll admit when I saw him I thought I was dead meat, he's got that dangerously beautiful vibe going on, doesn't he? But he's pretty cool, even if he's not gay. He didn't like being set up by Trace—but said the best way out was to not give them what they wanted. We came here, we'll party and then he'll go on his way."

"You don't understand," she said. "Uncle Tag, you remember my uncle who is more like my great-great-great uncle, right?"

"The werewolf?" Kelly said. "The one you've never let me meet?"

"That one," she said. "Yes. I was pretty upset when I heard what Trace did to you. When Uncle Tag called me yesterday to check up on me, like he always does, I told him about it. He called me tonight to tell me that he knew the guy they set you up with. Because someone decided that this guy needed to get out more—and to tease him, they signed him up on a whole bunch of dating sites. A werewolf. They signed a werewolf up on a vampire dating site because they thought it was funny. You were apparently the only candidate within a five hundred mile radius. They did all the initial emailing and then presented it to him as an accomplished thing."

"He said he was a werewolf," said Kelly, sounding shell-shocked. "At the door."

"He's dangerous," Meg told Kelly, and Asil started to work his way over to them. He needed Kelly not to "run screaming into the night" and to stick around for another half hour—at least.

"Really, really dangerous," Meg continued in a furious whisper. Her back was to him, but Kelly saw Asil approach. "No one screws with him, not even my Uncle Tag, because Asil is crazy. Uncle Tag told me to tell you to be very polite and to keep your eyes lowered—and whatever you did, excuse yourself as quickly as possible."

Instead of being properly frightened, Kelly laughed. Asil considered being offended.

Kelly saw the expression on Asil's face and covered his mouth. He put his free arm around Meg and turned her so she could see Asil. "You have to admit it's funny, Meg. A werewolf set up on a date with a girl pretending to be a vampire—who was actually a guy pretending to be a vampire. And *both* of us were set up—by different people."

"Coincidence, indeed." Asil was better pleased when both of them started at his silkily voiced observation and Kelly's wide grin disappeared. He directed his question to Meg. "Are you sure that your Uncle Tag didn't have anything to do with this? Interesting that he knows us both, don't you think?"

"It wasn't Uncle Tag," she squeaked. She looked at Asil, then jerked her gaze to the floor. "Not him. I told him a friend of mind had been set up on a vampire dating site without his knowledge. He'd heard that someone had set you up, too. He told me he was suspicious because—how many people in Montana would sign up on a vampire dating site? Turns out that whoever set you up, sir, only found one profile in a five hundred mile radius. And that was Kelly—who, on the profile Travis and his rat-bastard crew wrote up, appeared to be a girl." She took a deep breath, then raised her eyes. "Kelly doesn't deserve to get hurt over something that's not his fault." Her eyes left his again before she finished, but her chin was still up.

"I'm fine," said Kelly. "He's not going to hurt me."

"Yes," agreed Asil. "I never blame the messenger. The perpetrators on my side of the fence were misguided, but not malicious. I accept that Tag was not one of them—he is more inclined to use an axe than a keyboard. When I find out who they are, I will serve them with justice—but no bodies will be strewn about. Especially since I am enjoying myself."

Patricia Briggs

"Kelly is gay and Uncle Tag says you aren't." She said it really fast to get it all out. Unwilling to leave her friend at the mercy of someone her uncle warned her about without checking to make sure he was really safe. He had no doubt, since she was related to Tag, that if she thought he would hurt her friend—she'd throw herself into the fray.

He liked her. A lot. He had always liked Tag, too.

"We have already established that I prefer women and he prefers men. But I have no problem dancing with a man, because my reputation is such that pretty little things such as yourself and also big, scary men like your uncle tremble in fear of me. Dancing with a man is unlikely to change that—and I like dancing."

She frowned.

"He's funny," said Kelly. "You have to watch for it, but he's pretty funny underneath the Castilian manners and straight face."

Asil took pity on her. "Your friend is safe with me."

She took in a deep breath that threatened to release parts of her that the Elizabethan dress put under a lot of pressure. "Really safe?"

"Safer than anyone else here," said Asil showing her his teeth. He might like her, but he didn't like her questioning his word.

"Okay," said Meg. She let out a breath in a huff of air. "Good."

A fanfare sounded through the speakers to draw their attention to a stage that had been erected against one wall.

"Well, that was embarrassing," muttered Kelly as he tugged Asil toward the stage—and away from his friend—by tucking a hand unselfconsciously in the crook of his arm. "I'm sorry about my friend."

"Nothing to be sorry for. Who a man's friends are, says a lot about him. She knew who and what I was—and still tried to save you from me. She is brave and loyal. No one needs to apologize for such a friend."

Beside him, Kelly straightened a little. "She did throw herself in front of the bus, didn't she? Even if the bus was already stopped."

"I am not a bus," murmured Asil as someone stepped up to a microphone and chatted some canned welcome speech. "A chariot. A Porsche. But not a bus."

"See," said Kelly to no one Asil could discern. "He's funny."

The speaker nattered on for a few minutes more before announcing the opening dance.

They had never danced together before, and it was obvious that many of the couples on the dance floor practiced for this dance. But Kelly did indeed know how to dance, and they soon progressed beyond the simpler moves into some more daring, dramatic ... even melodramatic moves. There were a few stumbles here and there—it was very obvious that Kelly was used to leading, no matter what he'd said.

But when the music ended, and they froze for that last dramatic moment, chest to chest, face to face—Asil realized he was really having fun. More fun than he'd had for a very, very long time.

As they stepped away from each other, exchanging grins, Asil wondered when he had forgotten how much fun dancing was? How much fun flirting was? Especially when both people knew it was not going further than that?

In order to properly repay the people or person (he was not ruling out someone using the royal "we" to obfuscate his or her identity), Asil was beginning to believe he might have to buy a gift instead of dealing out vengeance. Though he had no intention of letting his benefactors know it until the whole thing was over. Let them fear his wrath for a while more.

"Hey Kelly, is this the date?" A young man Asil had not seen anyone who looked to be over twenty-five came up to them swaggering a little. He was the type to impress people under thirty—big, athletic, handsome. "It worked out? Awesome. You owe me one."

"This is Trace," said Kelly.

Before Asil could say anything, Trace looked over his shoulder at the entrance. "Late comers," he said. "Next time I'll tell them the party starts an hour before the doors open."

He stepped around them and headed for the front door. Asil glanced at the incoming party and then turned around to face Kelly.

"Do you see the very young man in the tuxedo who just came in?"

Kelly frowned and squinted. "Yeah. That's Bruce. He's a cousin, I think, of Shawna's—one of the other members of the group. I haven't seen her tonight. He's a freshman, I think, and he's been coming to the LARPs since school started this fall. He's not a good player, mostly he just sits around and watches us. I expect that he'll find his own group of friends and quit coming. Why?"

Bruce wasn't the name Asil knew him by. Though "Bruce" would recognize his own. For the first time, Asil wondered if he had stepped into a trap when he'd come on this date.

"LARP?" asked Asil.

"Sorry. It stands for Live Action Role-Playing. L-A-R-P. Do you know Bruce? What's wrong?"

"Come with me," said Asil. Leaving his enemy still standing bothered him, but he had to gather information.

Walking through the dancing crowd was like swimming upstream, but Asil was a good swimmer. People parted for them, as he led Kelly to an alcove furnished with a bench and a large plant that looked real but smelled of plastic.

"Forgive me," Asil said, pulling Kelly close and burying his nose in the young man's neck.

Kelly struggled, mostly from surprise, Asil thought, much good it did him. Faintly, very faintly, he caught the smell of vampire.

He pulled back and held on until he was sure Kelly had his balance. Kelly jerked free and straightened his clothes. In a fine temper he said, "*What* was that about? On a normal date, I would have objected because you didn't ask. But that wasn't about romance—and I have an almost uncontrollable urge to smack you on the nose. Were you *smelling* me?"

Asil reminded himself forcefully that Kelly had a right to be mad. He loosened his neck and heard the vertebrae pop. "Bruce is a vampire."

"I could have told you that," Kelly snapped. "That's right, I did." His mouth opened, doubtless to deliver some more scathing commentary—but he shut it. "No way. No way in hell. Vampires aren't real."

"Shh," advised Asil. "They are real, I assure you. And they have very good hearing. What one is doing here, I cannot tell you. Is there any chance Bruce was involved in the prank that led to our date?"

Kelly stared at him, but when he spoke again it was in a hushed whisper. "I don't know. I wouldn't think so. Trace and his girlfriend apparently thought it was a good idea one day while they were drunk."

"They exchanged emails with people pretending to be me for two weeks," Asil said dryly. "Were they drunk the whole time?"

"Them? Who knows, it's possible," Kelly shrugged distractedly. "What do you mean vampires are real? Everyone knows they aren't real."

"Vampires," Asil spoke slowly, "are real. They usually live in seethes and feed on human prey, who die very slowly as they gradually turn into mindless slaves. You've been bitten—don't fuss. Only once or you'd smell more like one of them. You'll be safe enough."

"How could I have been bitten?" Kelly asked, his eyes widening until the whites were visible all the way around like a startled horse. "I don't think I've exchanged two words with Bruce and we haven't gotten closer than ten feet apart. How could I have been bitten by a vampire and not known?"

"It is better for you that you didn't know," Asil told him. "It means that the vampire hasn't decided to make you his, yet." Probably the vampire was afraid to draw attention to himself.

Kelly started to say something more and Asil held up a hand. "Sorry, let me think a bit."

It was *possible* that the vampire had arranged the whole thing to lure Asil out without the pack at his back, so that he would be vulnerable. It sounded plausible until Asil looked deeper.

Bruce who Asil had once known as ... Basil something. Basil Hennington. Basil Billingsley. Basil Featherington. Something of the sort—whatever the vampire's name had been, it had made Asil think of chicken soup. The vampire's name might have changed, but this vampire was a creature of subtlety. He lived in the shadows, away from his own kind. Attacking one of Bran's wolves would not be subtle in any fashion.

It was Asil's people who had sought out Kelly for the date. And he was certain it was his pack—because no vampire could have imitated him so well in the emails. It took familiarity and Asil had never been familiar with any vampire.

And there was this. Alone Asil might be, but he was not vulnerable.

No. The vampire who called himself Bruce had no idea Asil was anywhere near. *Bruce* just thought he had a nice meal ticket going.

Kelly had folded his arms around himself and was obviously bursting with questions. But he'd kept quiet.

"It will be all right," Asil said.

"Weirdest freaking date of my life," muttered Kelly.

He was afraid. Asil's wolf usually liked it when people were afraid, but this one was under his protection tonight. There was no need for the fear.

"We need to go outside and look for a dark space," Asil told him.

"It's eight p.m in the winter on the outskirts of Missoula," Kelly said. "There's freaking dark space everywhere."

Asil frowned at him.

"Fine," Kelly huffed. But he didn't smell mad. He still smelled scared.

"Look at me," commanded Asil.

Kelly looked at him.

"I will not let harm come to you." Asil smiled and Kelly took a step back because it was that kind of smile. "In fact I will do you and your group of vampire players a good turn—and teach Trace not to meddle in other people's lives at the same time."

"Hey, Bruce?" Kelly said nervously.

Bruce turned to look at him, and no matter how hard Kelly tried to see it—Bruce looked like a freshman who hadn't quite grown into his own skin.

"You heard about what Trace did to me, right?"

Bruce frowned. "I heard. I don't know why he's in charge of the group when he's such a jerk."

"Yeah, me either." Maybe because no one else wanted to put the time in to do it right—and because Trace was a decent game master. "I have an idea that will keep him from ever doing it again—to anyone else. I don't want him to see me watching—but you know my friend Meg?" Meg wasn't formally a part of the vampire group but she did costuming for a lot of them.

"I do." Bruce smiled and the avarice that came and went in his eyes made Kelly's stomach tightened. Yeah, this wasn't a good guy.

"She's over with Trace and his girlfriend right now, distracting him so I can get you outside without him noticing." No lies, Asil had told him. Vampires weren't as adept as werewolves apparently were at telling when someone lied to them—but this one was very old and with age came some skills. Kelly hadn't know that werewolves could tell when someone was lying.

Asil's advice rang in his ears. *You're afraid—and that's fine. Let him know there's a reason to be afraid and he won't pay any more attention to it.*

"I'm not the first one he's tormented," Kelly said. "But I'm going to be the last."

"What are you going to do?" asked the vampire.

"I'm going to teach him he can't hurt people without paying a price," Kelly told him. "He would never face me on his own if he could help it. Meg is going to get him to follow her outside, out of sight. Then you and she are going to watch to make sure no one else follows him out to interrupt, and to vouch that the fight was fair."

"You're going to beat him up?" asked Bruce. "Really?"

Kelly didn't blame him for the doubt in his voice. Trace was bigger and Kelly had that whole geek thing going. "Really," Kelly said. He was pretty sure he could take Trace if he wanted to. His mother had given him dancing lessons. His father had insisted that any boy who danced that much needed to be able to protect himself—so he had six years of Taekwondo to go with his dancing. He tried a smile and wasn't upset that his inner tension made it fail. "I haven't done anything like this ever. But I can't let it go."

"Shawna told me that the date went okay," said Bruce. "I didn't see him, but Shawna said he was handsome—and you guys did an awesome tango."

There was something funny about Bruce. Kelly had seen it from the first—but he'd done his best to ignore it, figuring it for a light case of autism or just the awkwardness that went with being a teenager. But when Bruce smiled back at him, he recognized it for what it was for the first time. Bruce was pretending to be human, but, like a second-rate actor, he got it just a little wrong.

Kelly forced himself to stay engaged in the immediate task. In response to Bruce's question, he nodded. "He's a cool guy. He was upset at what Trace did to me, and very kindly agreed to play along. But it might not have been okay. I'm getting out of the group—grad school means I don't have time. I guess that's why I decided to do this. To teach Trace a lesson. There are kids like you in the group and you deserve to be safe from that kind of pointless harassment. You might call it my Christmas present to them. To you."

"Why pick me?"

Kelly grimace. "That's easy. Who else could I trust? The people who aren't panting after Trace are panting after his girlfriend."

Walking into the dark with a vampire at his back was the scariest thing he'd ever done in his life. The woods got dark pretty fast as they tramped through the snow. His breath steamed out of his mouth in the cold air. He was going to regret having left his jacket in Asil's car before very long. He hiked about a quarter mile in the darkness until they came to a fence. Far enough, he thought, that the sounds of a fight wouldn't travel.

"Here," he said turning around.

"It is very dark," said Bruce, who was just a shadow in the shadows.

"It'll do." Kelly hoped he sounded resolute.

"So while we are waiting for them," Bruce said, his voice changing just a little, softening into an intimate tone. "I think I have something we might do to pass the time."

He took two steps closer. Kelly's back was against the fence and he had nowhere to retreat. Even if he could have, his feet felt oddly heavy and he swayed toward the vampire.

"We have done this once before," said the vampire. "Shawna is dying—I need another servant. You'd like to be my servant, wouldn't you? Just say, yes. It would be an early Christmas present for me."

Kelly forgot to breathe as Bruce's words threaded through him like a hook laced with happy-thoughts. He just *knew* that belonging to the vampire would be the best thing that ever happened to him, like winning the lottery.

"I like Christmas," Bruce continued as Kelly took a tentative step forward. "So much misery for humankind as they scuttle around spending more money than they can afford on gifts no one wants or appreciates. Christmas is a time when no one feels that their life is good or worthwhile. Christmas is a fitting remembrance for a gift humans despised so much they hung it on a cross so it wouldn't bother them anymore. I was a priest once. I know, who'd have thought, right?"

Bruce's face was revealed for a moment when the clouds opened around the half-full moon and silvery light illuminated their private space. His eyes were focused on something other than Kelly and Kelly remembered, viscerally, the marks that Asil had found on Meg's neck. The marks that had set Kelly on his task—one he was failing.

"No," Kelly said, the word dragging out of his throat—but the word broke the vampire's hold, and he could move again.

Snarling, Bruce whipped his hand out and wrapped it around Kelly's wrist. Kelly's response was instinctive, born of fear and six years of training. He twisted his arm until the narrow boney edge of his wrist was at the weakest point of the vampire's grip and jerked it free.

He didn't even pause—he ran, crashing blindly through the underbrush and the uneven, snow-covered footing that threatened to trip him at every night-blinded step. And behind him, keeping up easily, the vampire followed.

"Run, yes, run," the vampire chanted to himself. "You ran the last time, too. I like it when my Christmas presents run." He laughed, a weird half-hysterical laugh and then said, *"Run, Kelly, run."*

Finally the inevitable happened and Kelly put a foot wrong, crashing to the ground in a tangle of snow, tree-root and bush. He rolled until he could get some leverage for his feet, then crab-walked frantically backward until the solid trunk of a tree hit his back.

The vampire stayed where he was, laughing quietly—not out of breath at all. The only way Kelly could tell it was Bruce was Bruce's suit, because the creature who wore it had only an incidental resemblance to the human he had aped.

His eyes were either glowing or they caught the light of the moon differently than human eyes did—like the Siamese cat Kelly's older sister had. Red and shiny, they held him in a hungry grip more sure than the vampire's hand on his wrist had been. Flesh pulled away from the bones of Bruce's face until no one looking at him would see anything but a monster. If any doubt about Bruce had lingered (and it had), the fangs both delicate and sharp that Bruce was displaying were an answer.

"Not that I didn't enjoy that," the vampire said, "but we need to take care of business before Meg and Trace show up, don't we? Never fear, Kelly, I won't let Trace bully me, though it was good of you to be concerned."

"I wasn't actually worried about you," Kelly managed with more bravado than he felt. "I just needed you outside."

The vampire stilled. "Why is that?"

Sometime while he was running, it had started to snow again and white flakes drifted to the vampire's shoulders. The snow brought with it the deep feeling of silence that was so much more than just a lack of noise that Kelly had only ever felt on a winter's night in the woods.

Kelly's senses told him that they were alone in the silence. He heard nothing, sensed nothing that told him differently. He had only Asil's word that he was not alone in the night with the vampire. Somewhat to his surprise, it was enough.

Kelly stood up slowly, keeping his back against the tree for support, because he wasn't sure that his legs would hold him. There was a tear in the knee of his trousers—he'd have to have Meg sew him a new one.

"I do have a Christmas present for you," he said with more cool than James freakin' Bond.

The vampire jerked his head to the side as a great shadow emerged from the darkness tucked under a thicket of leafless aspen. Before

Bruce could move closer, the werewolf was upon him.

"Merry Christmas," said Kelly his voice lost in the roar of the attack.

He hadn't actually seen Asil as a werewolf, apparently it wasn't as fast as it was in the movies to change from wolf to human. He wished Asil would stand still or that the sun was out so he could get a better look. If he had to describe the werewolf right now, it would be "gold eyes and huge." Fast and strong and graceful. And very, very huge. The vampire looked like a toy in his jaws—not that the vampire wasn't fighting back.

He didn't hear anything—the fight was unexpectedly loud—but his eyes were drawn away from the fight by some instinct. On the other side of the battling monsters, Meg stood with Trace. They were close enough to watch without becoming collateral damage—or so Kelly hoped.

Trace was a big guy, but Meg was three inches taller and a lot meaner. She had a hand on his neck as if she'd dragged him here. Not that Trace was fighting her hold, right at this moment. Like Meg, his attention was all on the battle in front of them.

Somehow, while Kelly had been distracted, the vampire had gotten out of Asil's jaws. He landed a kick on the werewolf's side that sent the wolf tumbling like a motorcycle wreck into the trees.

The vampire was a lot stronger than Bruce had looked. Kelly had the thought, as Bruce threw himself on the werewolf, that maybe Kelly hadn't broken out of his hold earlier. Maybe Bruce had let him go because he *wanted* the hunt.

They moved fast, the monsters who fought. It was like trying to follow the beating of a fly's wing—and the night's heavy shadows didn't help. Kelly blinked his eyes to relieve the eye strain and while he had his eyes closed, it happened.

With a grotesque pop of bone, the vampire's head popped off—popped freakin' all the way off and the only monster still moving in the woods was standing on the dead vampire's body. Kelly couldn't see colors well in the dark, but the wolf's muzzle was wet with something dark as he lifted his head to the moon and howled.

"Don't move," muttered Meg. "I mean it. Nobody move. Don't meet his eyes and if you do, go down to your knees and bow your head."

"Werewolves are supposed to be friendly," said Trace, trying to jerk out of Meg's hold.

The werewolf who had been Kelly's blind date focused his attention on Trace. Asil's upper lip curled back, exposing fangs that were bigger and more dangerous looking than the fangs of the tiger Kelly had seen yawning in a zoo when he was six. He'd had nightmares after that visit for years.

Trace had the same reaction as Kelly's six-year-old self. His mouth dropped open and fear pulled his eyes wide in a cartoonish expression. "Holy shit. I'm sorry. I'm sorry."

Meg thumped Trace on the back of his head sending him staggering forward because he wasn't ready for it at all. He landed in a graceless sprawl not ten feet from the werewolf and almost on top of the vampire's head. Trace lifted his head and got a face-to-bleeding-amputated-neck view of the vampire, made a squeaky noise, and passed out cold.

Asil moved off the vampire, his body moving in a stiff and jerky caricature of the graceful power of his fight. Yellow eyes grabbed Kelly—and he was sure they were yellow, even in the darkness.

"Kelly," said Meg urgently.

"He promised he wouldn't hurt me," said Kelly, and the wolf's eyes focused on him. Unbearable pressure dropped Kelly as quickly as Meg's shove had dropped Trace and he bowed his head.

"We'll do what we promised," Kelly told the ground. "We'll explain to Trace that messing with other people's dating is dangerous. We'll explain why knowing about vampires is even more dangerous and that he should keep his mouth shut. We'll talk to her uncle if there is a problem. We'll trust you to take care of the body." He paused. "Thank you for the most interesting date of my life. Much better than I expected when I started out to the restaurant today."

When he looked up the wolf was gone.

Dear Asil,

There was a body. But after some discussion we decided to give this one to you. We owe you some leeway for missing that Kelly was a boy, not a girl. The body wasn't your date and no one ran screaming into the night—mostly because the person most likely to do that fainted. Your first date was a success! We're very proud of you.

Your second date has been arranged, two days from now. We chose the dating site mustlovemycat.com. We did (while pretending to be you) tell her that you did not at this time have a pet cat because after your last one died, you couldn't bear to replace it.

Be grateful. We had planned on using prettypenpals.com, but organizing a date for you with a woman who could not leave her prison cell was too much trouble, even for us.

Sincerely,

Your Concerned Friends

PS—Merry Christmas

Asil pinched his nose and laughed.

ABOUT THE AUTHORS

Kevin J. Anderson

Kevin J. Anderson has published 120 books, more than fifty of which are national or international bestsellers. He has written numerous novels in the Star Wars, X-Files, and Dune universes, as well as a unique steampunk fantasy novel, *Clockwork Angels*, based on the concept album by legendary rock group Rush. His original works include the Saga of Seven Suns series, the Terra Incognita fantasy trilogy, and his humorous horror series featuring Dan Shamble, Zombie PI. He has edited numerous anthologies, including the Five by Five and Blood Lite series. Anderson and his wife Rebecca Moesta are the publishers of WordFire Press.

Brad R. Torgersen

Brad R. Torgersen is a healthcare computer geek by day, a Chief Warrant Officer in the United States Army Reserve on the weekend, and a science fiction writer at night. His short fiction appears regularly in the pages of *Analog* magazine, where he's been numerated for several Hugo awards, and has won the *Analog* magazine AnLab readers' choice award twice. He's also published in the pages of Mike's Resnick's *Galaxy's Edge* magazine, as well as Orson Scott Card's *InterGalactic Medicine Show* magazine. Brad's first short fiction collection, *Lights in the Deep*, was released by WordFire Press in 2013. Brad's first novel from Baen Books, titled *The Chaplain's War*, comes out in October 2014.

Kristine Kathryn Rusch

USA Today bestselling writer Kristine Kathryn Rusch has won or been nominated for almost every major award in four genres. She particularly loves to write Christmas stories. She has three holiday collections, *Five For the Winter Holidays, Santa And Other Christmas Criminals,* and *Silent Night.* Under her paranormal romance pen name, Kristine Grayson, she has a holiday novella series (adding one per season). This year's is so far unnamed, but last year's is *Visions of Sugar Plums.* She also edited *Fiction River's* holiday issue, *Christmas Ghosts.* When she's not thinking about the holidays, she's writing the Retrieval Artist series. She will release a book per month in that series in 2015. Then she will turn her attention to her popular fantasy series, *The Fey.* Her Smokey Dalton mystery series, which she writes as Kris Nelscott, is under development for a major motion picture. Somehow, with all of this, she still manages to write short stories which, honestly, are her first love.

Mercedes Lackey

Mercedes Lackey was born in Chicago Illinois on June 24, 1950. The very next day, the Korean War was declared. It is hoped that there is no connection between the two events.

She was raised mostly in the northwestern corner of Indiana, attending grade school and high school in Highland Indiana. She graduated from Purdue University in 1972 with a Bachelor of Science in Biology. This, she soon learned, along with a paper hat and a nametag will qualify you to ask "would you like fries with that?" at a variety of fast-food locations.

In 1985 her first book was published. In 1990 she met artist Larry Dixon at a small Science Fiction convention in Meridian Mississippi, on a television interview organized by the convention. They began working together from that time on, and were married in Las Vegas at the Excalibur chapel by Merlin the Magician (aka the Reverend Duckworth) in 1992.

They moved to their current home, the "second weirdest house in Oklahoma" also in 1992. She has many pet parrots and "the house is never quiet." She is approaching 100 books in print, and some of her foreign editions can be found in Russian, German, Czech, Polish,

French, Italian, Turkish, and Japanese. She is the author, alone or in collaboration, of the Heralds of Valdemar, Elemental Masters, Secret World Chronicles, 500 Kingdoms, Diana Tregarde, Heirs of Alexandria, Obsidian Mountain, Dragon Jouster, Bedlam Bards, Shadow Grail, Dragon Prophecy, Elvenbane, Bardic Voices, SERRAted Edge, Doubled Edge (prequel to SERRAted Edge), and other series and standalone books.

A nightowl by nature, she is generally found at the keyboard between 10 p.m. and 6 a.m.

Quincy J. Allen

Quincy J. Allen, is a self-proclaimed cross-genre author. What that really means is that he's got enough ADD to not stick with any single genre and, like his cooking, prefers to mix and match to suit his appetites of the moment.

He has been published in multiple anthologies, magazines, and one omnibus. He's written for the Internet show RadioSteam, and his novel *Chemical Burn*—a finalist in the RMFW Colorado Gold Contest—is due out in 2014 in a newly revamped edition from WordFire Press. His new novel *Jake Lasater: Blood Curse* as well as a military sci-fi novel from Twisted Core Press are both due out in 2014, and *Out Through the Attic*, his first short story collection, just hit shelves and browsers across the world. He works part-time as a tech-writer to pay his bills, does book design and eBook conversions for WordFire Press by night, and lives in a lovely house that he considers his very own sanctuary.

He's an entirely all-too-busy writer taking over the world one fiction at a time.

Nina Kiriki Hoffman

Over the past thirty-odd years, Nina Kiriki Hoffman has sold adult and YA novels and more than 250 short stories. Her works have been finalists for the World Fantasy, Mythopoeic, Sturgeon, Philip K. Dick, and Endeavour awards. Her fiction has won Stoker and Nebula Awards.

A collection of Hoffman's short stories, *Permeable Borders*, was published in 2012 by Fairwood Press. A young adult Hoffman novel will come out from Viking in 2015.

Nina does production work for the *Magazine of Fantasy & Science Fiction*. She teaches writing through Lane Community College. She lives in Eugene, Oregon.

Jonathan Maberry

Jonathan Maberry is a *NY Times* bestselling author, multiple Bram Stoker Award winner, and freelancer for Marvel Comics. His novels include *Code Zero*, *Rot and Ruin*, *Ghost Road Blues*, *Patient Zero*, *The Wolfman*, and many others. Nonfiction books include *Ultimate Jujutsu*, *The Cryptopedia*, *Zombie CSU*, and others. Several of Jonathan's novels are in development for movies or TV including *V-Wars*, *Extinction Machine*, *Rot & Ruin* and *Dead of Night*. He's the editor/co-author of *V-Wars*, a vampire-themed anthology; and was a featured expert on *The History Channel* special *Zombies: A Living History*. Since 1978 he's sold more than 1200 magazine feature articles, 3000 columns, two plays, greeting cards, song lyrics, and poetry. His comics include *Captain America: Hail Hydra*, *Bad Blood*, *Marvel Zombies Return* and *Marvel Universe vs. The Avengers*. He lives in Del Mar, California with his wife, Sara Jo and their dog, Rosie. www.jonathanmaberry.com

Ken Scholes

Ken Scholes is the award-winning author of the internationally acclaimed *Psalms of Isaak* series published in the US by Tor. His first novel, *Lamentation*, won the American Library Association's RUSA Reading List award for best fantasy and France's Prix Imaginales for best translated fantasy. Ken's short fiction is collected in two volumes published by Fairwood Press and new stories continue to show up in various magazines and anthologies. Ken is also a winner of the Writers of the Future contest.

With a diverse background that includes a degree in history, years logged as a Baptist preacher, label gun repairman, government procurement analyst and nonprofit executive, Ken now writes full time and makes his home in Saint Helens, OR, with his wife and twin daughters. You can learn more about Ken by visiting:

www.kenscholes.com.

Heather Graham

New York Times and *USA Today* best-selling author, Heather Graham, majored in theater arts at the University of South Florida. After a stint of several years in dinner theater, back-up vocals, and bartending, she stayed home after the birth of her third child and began to write. Her first book was with Dell, and since then, she has written over one hundred novels and novellas including category, suspense, historical romance, vampire fiction, time travel, occult and Christmas family fare.

She is pleased to have been published in approximately twenty languages. She has 60 million books in print. She has been honored with awards from Walden Books, B. Dalton, Georgia Romance Writers, Affaire de Coeur, Romantic Times and more. Heather has also become the proud recipient of the Silver Bullet from Thriller Writers. Heather has had books selected for the Doubleday Book Club and the Literary Guild, and has been quoted, interviewed, or featured in such publications as *The Nation, Redbook Mystery Book Club, People and USA Today* and appeared on many newscasts including *Today, Entertainment Tonight* and local television.

Heather loves travel and anything that has to do with the water, and is a certified scuba diver. She also loves ballroom dancing. Each year she hosts the Vampire Ball and Dinner theater at the RT convention raising money for the Pediatric AIDS Society and in 2006 she hosted the first Writers for New Orleans Workshop to benefit the stricken gulf region. She is also the founder of "The Slush Pile Players." presenting something that's almost like entertainment for various conferences and benefits. Married since high school graduation and the mother of five, her greatest love in life remains her family, but she also believes her career has been an incredible gift, and she is grateful every day to be doing something that she loves so very much for a living.

Sam Knight

As a writer, Sam refuses to be pinned down into a genre and writes whatever grabs his attention, be it steampunk, horror, mystery, science fiction, or children's books. He frequently speaks at conventions in and near his home state of Colorado, including the Denver and Salt Lake City Comic Cons, where he loves to talk about writing.

As well as being part of the WordFire Press Production Team, he is the Senior Editor for Villainous Press and has a secret project he won't tell anyone about. He has edited two anthologies and published three children's books, three short story collections, two novels, and more than a dozen short stories. Sam can be found at SamKnight.com and contacted at Sam@samknight.com.

Mike Resnick

Mike Resnick is, according to *Locus*, the all-time leading award winner, living or dead, for short science fiction. He has won 5 Hugos (from a record 36 nominations), a Nebula, and other major awards in the USA, France, Japan, Spain, Croatia, Catalonia, and Poland. He is the author of 75 novels, 27 collections, close to 300 stories, and three screenplays, and has edited 41 anthologies. He is the former co-editor of *Jim Baen's Universe*, and is currently the editor of *Galaxy's Edge* magazine and the Stellar Guild line of books. Mike was Guest of Honor at the 2012 Worldcon.

David Boop

David Boop is a Denver-based speculative fiction author. In addition to his novels, short stories and children's books, he's also an award-winning essayist and screenwriter. His novel, the sci-fi/noir *She Murdered Me with Science*, debuted in 2008. Since then, David has had over thirty short stories published and two-short films produced. He specializes in weird westerns, but has been published in many genres including media tie-ins for Green Hornet and Honey West. 2013 saw the digital release of his first Steampunk children's book, *The Three Inventors Sneebury,* with a print release due in 2014. David tours the country speaking on writing and publishing at schools, libraries and conventions.

He's a single dad, returning college student, part-time temp worker and believer. He's a member of the International Association of Media Tie-in Writer, the Society of Children's Book Writers and Illustrators and the Western Writers of America. His hobbies include film noir, anime, the Blues and Mayan History. You can find out more on his fanpage, www.facebook.com/dboop.updates or Twitter @david_boop.

Eric James Stone

A Nebula Award winner, Hugo Award nominee, and winner in the Writers of the Future Contest, Eric James Stone has had stories published in *Year's Best SF 15, Analog, Nature,* and Kevin J. Anderson's *Blood Lite* anthologies of humorous horror, among other venues.

One of Eric's earliest memories is of seeing an Apollo moon-shot launch on television. That might explain his fascination with space travel. His father's collection of old science fiction ensured that Eric grew up on a full diet of Asimov, Heinlein and Clarke.

While getting his political science degree at Brigham Young University, Eric took creative writing classes. He wrote several short stories, and even submitted one for publication, but after it was rejected he gave up on creative writing for a decade.

During those years Eric graduated from Baylor Law School, worked on a congressional campaign, and took a job in Washington, DC, with one of those special interest groups politicians always complain that other politicians are influenced by. He quit the political scene in 1999 to work as a web developer in Utah.

In 2002 he started writing fiction again, and in 2003 he attended Orson Scott Card's Literary Boot Camp. In 2007 Eric got laid off from his day job just in time to go to the Odyssey Writing Workshop. He has since found a new web development job.

In 2009 Eric became an assistant editor for *Intergalactic Medicine Show*.

Eric lives in Utah with his wife, Darci, a high school physics teacher. His website is www.ericjamesstone.com.

Patricia Briggs

Patricia Briggs is the #1 *New York Times* best-selling author of the Mercy Thompson series and has written twenty one novels to date; she is currently writing novel number twenty two! Patty began her career writing traditional fantasy novels in 1993, and shifted gears in 2006 to write urban fantasy. *Moon Called* was the first of her signature series about Mercy Thompson. The non-stop adventure left readers wanting more and word of this exciting new urban fantasy series about a shape-shifting mechanic spread quickly. The series has continued to grow in popularity with the release of each book. Patty also writes the Alpha and Omega series, which are set in the same world as the Mercy Thompson novels; what began as a novella expanded into a full new series, all of which debuted on the *NY Times* bestsellers list as well.

Patty and her family reside in Eastern Washington near Tri-Cities, home of Mercy Thompson—yes, it's a real place! When not working on the next book, she can be found playing truant out in her horse pastures, playing with the newest babies. For more information about Patricia Briggs and her marvelous novels, visit the author on the web at www.patriciabriggs.com or on Facebook.

COPYRIGHT INFORMATION

OTHER WORDFIRE TITLES

Our list of other WordFire Press authors and titles is always growing. To find out more and to see our selection of titles, visit us at:

wordfirepress.com